Her husband's death is just the beginning of her marital woes.

Rachel's humiliation over the discovery of her late husband's affairs turns to fear when one of his mistresses sends her a poisoned bouquet. But finding the source of the killer flowers is only one step on her path to solving the mystery her husband left behind.

Deputy Dan Weston is with Rachel when the bouquet arrives, and he's at her side as she deals with so many of the secrets that come to light after her husband's death. Dan has carried a torch for Rachel since puberty and he's not going to let her dead husband's vindictive girlfriends come between them now. But that means finding out who is sending snakes and poisoned posies before one kills Rachel.

Books by Shea McMaster

Rachel Dahlrumple
Her Foreign Affair

Published by Kensington Publishing Corporation

Rachel Dahlrumple

Shea McMaster

LYRICAL PRESS
Kensington Publishing Corp.
www.kensingtonbooks.com

Lyrical Press books are published by
Kensington Publishing Corp. 119 West 40th Street New York, NY 10018

All Kensington titles, imprints, and distributed lines are available at special
quantity discounts for bulk purchases for sales promotion, premiums, fund-
raising, and educational or institutional use.

Special book excerpts or customized printings can also be created to fit
specific needs. For details, write or phone the office of the Kensington
Special Sales Manager:
Kensington Publishing Corp.
119 West 40th Street
New York, NY 10018
Attn. Special Sales Department. Phone: 1-800-221-2647.

Kensington and the K logo Reg. U.S. Pat. & TM Off.
Lyrical Press and the L logo are trademarks of Kensington Publishing Corp.

First Electronic Edition: November 2011
eISBN-13: 978-1-61650-3291
eISBN-10: 1-61650-329-7

First Print Edition: November 2011
ISBN-13: 978-1-61650-895-1
ISBN-10: 1-61650-895-7

Printed in the United States of America

To strong women everywhere, who survive with grace and dignity.

Acknowledgements

With Special Acknowledgement to On a Clear Day You Can See Forever
Vincent Minnelli 1970
Starring Barbra Streisand and Yves Montand
Distributed by Paramount Pictures

Additionally, I can't thank KM enough. First of all, she gave me
The Sisters of the Agave reference. I look forward to the official
incorporation. Count me in as a charter member. In other books
she's provided advice, humor, and even her house, both literally and
figuratively. Many's the time she gave me a bed, supplied wine, food,
and took me shopping.

Blog partner J. Morgan and Beta Reader Extraordinaire, Carlee,
provided the fuel and encouragement for this, my true first venture into
writing First Person. I wasn't sure I could do it justice. You kept me
pumped up and excited.

Last, but not least, my editor. Piper, we've been in this writing thing
a long time, meeting as mere babes in the woods. You keep me on the
straight and narrow. Many thanks!

Foreword

The town of Bonchamps, CA is fictitious. It's set, roughly, in the middle of farm land in Kings County, California, in the San Joaquin Valley. Some of the towns and landmarks mentioned are real, but their involvement is part of my made up town and if I got any details right, it's due more to accident and the experience of growing up in Livermore, CA in the sixties and seventies.

Chapter 1

"I'm not coming home."

My husband's declaration dropped my stomach right down to my toes. Despite the oven-intense heat of the day, cold chills raced down my spine.

"Burt?"

"At least not tonight."

My poor ticker, which had stalled, started beating again at double time.

Dizzy from the brief panic, I closed my eyes and tilted my head against the headrest. In my heart, I knew one of these days he wouldn't add the last qualifier. I feared that day almost as much as I dreaded him coming home.

When my cellphone had started ringing a few moments earlier, I'd been engaged in backing my husband's pickup into the ancient barn-like structure we called the garage. Somehow, half blinded from the sun reflecting off the pool, I'd gotten the truck into the bay without hitting anything, found my phone, and caught the call one ring before voice mail picked up.

"I tried the house. Where are you?"

So much for, *Hello, sweetheart, I miss you and can hardly wait to be home.* But after nearly twenty years of togetherness with Burton Earl Bruckmeister, I really didn't expect anything else. The romance in my life pretty much lived only between the pages of the books I read. Leaving the windows down, I killed the engine and silence descended for the space of a breath.

"Just pulled in. Had to stop for the ice and drinks, remember? Fourth of July party tomorrow? At our house? Ring a bell? What do you mean you won't be home tonight?"

"Of course I remember." Ah, I'd managed to irritate him. His tone hit the exact edge that cut into me, not that I'd ever tell him how deep. Even on the phone, I'd learned to control my flinches, showing just enough for him to be satisfied I heard and obeyed.

As hot as it was outside, over ninety last I'd heard, I had a little irritation going as well. The AC in his truck refused to work and he'd taken my car, the one with the working AC, for his week-long business trip. I'd let it go because I needed the truck for our order of drinks for the party--a checklist item I'd taken care of, at the expense of adding to my irritation. The liquor store had been unusually busy, involving a forty-five minute wait for the clerk to load the supplies into the truck.

"You got everything?"

"All eight of the coolers are stuffed with ice, beer and soda, and in the truck. How long until you're home?" Last time I'd tried to get the coolers out by myself, a hundred-quart ice chest had dropped me on my backside and landed on my ankle, putting me in a cast. That had happened six years before, and he never let me forget how stupid I'd been. "I can't do this alone. You promised to be home no later than seven tonight."

We'd been married seventeen years--had just celebrated our anniversary, also my thirty-ninth birthday, a few weeks prior. Nothing special. Dinner with my father and the neighbors followed by lukewarm, obligation sex. Some amethyst jewelry made by a local artist Burt patronized and a sack of iris bulbs to add to the flower beds because he couldn't find anything more exotic. Seventeen years just didn't trip the old romance meter anymore, I'd thought. Then again, flowers were better than furniture, or his taste in lingerie. He got a painting I'd found at a local gallery.

"It can't be helped, Rachel, so stop whining. You know how important these conferences are for networking. A couple of the guys from L.A. County asked me to fill out their golf party in the morning. One of their usual players can't make it."

"So? Why do you have to be their fourth?"

Burt heaved a sigh I could almost feel through the phone. "Rachel, they've had this time reserved for a year. You can't just waltz in and out of this course. They've booked four, and one of their usual party went to jail last week, so they got caught short."

"Jail!" What kind of people were these? "What did he go to jail for?"

"What does it matter? I didn't call you for a third degree. This is business. You like the nice cushy lifestyle you live because I provide the bulk of our income, don't you? Well, this is part of the game." I couldn't fight the flinch his angry bite produced. "Dammit, Rachel, we've been married long enough I shouldn't have to explain myself. I'm not coming home. Deal with it."

Not ready to let go protesting the inconvenience of his absence, I pushed a little more. "So if you back out now, can you make it home by eight?" I tried to remember exactly where he'd gone this week. With the advent of cellphones, location had become unimportant, especially if he drove to the seminars or conferences. We lived more or less between L.A. and San Francisco, so most of the large conference centers were within a three- to four-hour drive and rarely rated a plane ticket.

"You know I love you, but sometimes you try my patience." He drew in a deep breath and put some control back in his voice. Although I thrilled to the first half of his sentence, the second half killed it. I also wondered who might be listening. Background noise provided no clue. One of those golf-playing bigwigs? "No, Rachel. I'm not backing out. I figure we'll finish up around noon and then I'll drive straight on from there. If I don't stop for lunch, I might make it by two, more likely three."

Three? The party started around four, or when people drifted back from the rodeo and the other Independence Day events in town. If I left the coolers in the truck, the ice would be completely melted by then. Outside may have been ninety, but the garage had to be closer to a hundred and twenty. Not for the first time, I considered putting air conditioning in the building. Of course, it was impractical as the garage was nothing more than the old carriage house at the back of the lot and had barely been updated with overhead doors and some basic earthquake reinforcing. Hay still littered the loft and gaps between the boards were big enough for birds to fly through.

"What am I supposed to do? I can't leave the coolers in the truck that long."

"Call John. Or one of the others. I've helped their wives often enough, one of them should be more than happy to help you. Just don't call Miguel. He flirts too much."

Right. The very notion was laughable. Burt, who flirted with everything in skirts, worried about thirty-year-old Miguel flirting with me? Our resident EMT who lived at the far end of the street, Miguel was so in love with his wife and brand new daughter, he talked of nothing else. As for Burt, Marge Olsen told anyone who'd listen how he'd groped her ass the year before. And he continued to insist he'd been drunk enough he'd thought it was me in the dark. Considering it had been years since Burt had groped any body part of mine in public or private, and Marge's bra and ass were several sizes larger than mine, I didn't buy his line.

From where I sat I could see the entire length of our street. The flash of sun glinting off silver flake paint on a low muscle car caught my attention. Only one car like that ever prowled our street. It belonged to Deputy Dan Weston, younger brother of my next door neighbor, John Weston.

My eighth grade year, John and Dan had moved in next door with their parents after their dad was assigned to the Lemoore Naval Air Station to the north of our little town on the west side of California's San Joaquin Valley. After growing up and several years of seeing the world courtesy of Uncle Sam, John took a transfer to Lemoore himself, bought the house from his parents, and had moved home with his young family only a few years past. Dan followed a couple years later, after a wound put him on the Navy's retirement list. He'd spend the past twelve months meandering about the county in a deputy's uniform without a hint of the career-ending injury.

I considered John and his wife, Cyndi, close friends, but Dan, well, he and I had never gotten along well. When he showed up, I stayed away. If we bumped into each other, we'd nod and move on as quickly as possible. Stuck in the same room, we looked the other way and found someone else to talk to. Things had always been awkward between us and showed no sign of improving.

Ask the Westons to help? Not without including the man slowly rolling up their driveway in the sleek, sixty-three Corvette. I couldn't help wondering what it would feel like to drive the beast. All that muscle at my control...

"Rachel? Stop daydreaming and listen to me."

"I'm here, I'm here. Was just looking around to see who's home. John's brother just drove up." I ran one hand over my hair, smoothing back any strands that'd escaped from the chignon I wore for work. My skin was damp, but the dry air took care of the worst sweat, evaporating it almost as soon as it formed. Maybe I didn't have visible sweat stains down my back or under my arms.

"For God's sake don't ask him. I don't like the way he looks at you."

That did it. I laughed. More of a snort, the bane of my existence, but still a laugh. "He never looks at me, much less speaks to me. No one does, Burt. Getting jealous in your old age?" His forty-ninth birthday wasn't far off. Just a few weeks.

"I care about my wife and make note of those hitting on her."

Not that I'd seen signs of either situation, but what the hell, I decided to go for broke. "Then come home and *you* hit on me. You might be surprised at the response." I gave it my best throaty purr.

"Stop clinging. It's not like you to be needy. I'll call when I'm on my way. Call the admiral. One of his boys should be around to help." Another one of our neighbors on the street, the admiral had recently retired from command at the nearby base and had grandsons hanging about for the summer.

"Yes, Burt." Too hot and too tired to fight, I sighed as any hope of support, understanding, or attention from him drained away. "Whatever you say, Burt." It was as close as I ever came to truly voicing any discontent. He knew how unhappy I'd become, but what Burt said amounted to Burt's law and, as the number one resident of Burtland, if I didn't obey, well, let's just say he knew how to make my life miserable.

"Stop pouting. If I were still in the Navy, you wouldn't have me home most weeks out of the year."

"If you were still in the Navy, we wouldn't have volunteered to host the party this year."

"Deal with it, Rachel. You're more than capable. I'll be there tomorrow."

And with that, he disconnected. So much for, *I love you*, or, *have sweet dreams of me tonight*, or, even, *goodbye*.

Deflated, discouraged, and irritated by the usual mid-summer heat added onto a normal Friday night weariness, I dragged myself from the truck, hauling a pizza and a salad from the local joint, along with my purse, from the cab.

If I'd known I'd be eating alone for the fifth night that week, I would have skipped the food stop altogether and made a salad from the fresh items growing on the other side of the house. Though I'd inherited the garden, I'd modified the landscaping of our large lot so flower gardens lined the circular front drive, and a vegetable garden grew on the west side of the house. More flower beds dotted the back yard, brightening the large lawn wrapped around a long lap pool and spa. The garage, set back on the east side, bumped up against the lot-line shared with the Weston's driveway.

Juggling my dinner and grumpy mood, I stepped from the garage and heard a throat clear from the other side of the low hedge that marked the division of properties. Unable to avoid him without being supremely bitchy-rude, I turned and smiled at my childhood nemesis. "Hi, Dan."

"Rachel." He nodded, and late day sunlight glinted off the golden streaks in his brown hair. Why did men get the beautiful hair? Even from a half dozen feet away I could see dark lashes shading what I knew were hazel eyes. Mostly green with bits of amber. Eyes that looked me over from head to toe, and I found myself wanting to hunch over, as if I could hide from the unaccustomed appraisal. I distracted myself by looking at his new mustache. The hairs themselves were short, but the growth pattern extended down each side of his mouth. Fu manchu? Briefly I wondered what that kind of mustache, well, any mustache really, would feel like. Burt had never grown one.

"Need help?" Once more he nodded, but in the direction of the pizza box and the bag hanging from my arm, and his gaze returned to my face. Was I relieved or disappointed? Oh God, had he seen me checking him out? Honestly, I couldn't remember the last time I'd caught a man checking me out, maybe like I was attractive or something. It was enough to set off a nervous reaction.

"With this? No…" Oh hell. "But I do need help with the coolers. Think you and John can get them out of the truck and put them out under the trees?" At his raised brow, I rushed on. "Burt won't make it home until tomorrow, I just got off the phone with him, and I can't lift the coolers by myself, and if I leave them in the truck they'll just melt four times as fast and nothing will be cold tomorrow, and I won't have time to run out and get more ice or I'll miss the parade, and there's still so much I have to do tomorrow that I really can't let it melt…" And I was babbling. I knew it and let my words fade away.

Dan had half-turned toward the house, where Cyndi most likely spied from the kitchen window. She could see not only into my house, but the back porch and a part of the yard as well. He waved and the shadow of a hand waved back.

That taken care of, he turned and strode through the break in the hedge. "Why don't you put your dinner in the house, then come out and show us where you want them? Sure you want them out back and not up on the porch?"

"The porch would be fine, but then I'll have to move them again, and I can't move them by myself. I mean, I have in the past, but then…" I closed my eyes. I never spoke this much and certainly not this fast or with this much inane detail. Rachel the Cool, the Calm, the Organized. In control, Mistress of the Library, nothing ever shook me up. Well, except my husband ditching me the night before a major event. Man, that really sucked, as my younger patrons would say. Well, not the little ones, but the teens…and maybe a few of their younger siblings who'd picked up their language.

"I heard about your broken ankle when one of these fell on you."

He had? Like a blinded owl, I blinked at him. "Uh, yes. A full one. I was trying to get it out of the back of the truck."

"Well, we won't risk it again. Since the porch is on the north side, let's put the coolers there, and tomorrow I'll help move them wherever you need them, all right?"

"What's happening?" John asked as he approached. "When's Burt getting home?"

"He's not." When John cocked a brow, exactly as his brother had done moments ago, I rushed back into babbling. "*Tonight.* He's not coming home *tonight*, but he'll be home tomorrow afternoon. He's been held up by, um, business."

"Ah," John said, but turned an inscrutable look toward the garage. "Whatcha need, Rachel?"

Dan shoved his brother toward the open door. "The coolers need to move."

I hurried to the house and managed to deactivate the alarm about the time they carried the first cooler up the porch steps. I dumped the pizza, salad and my purse on the kitchen island, then rushed back out to...I didn't know, but the thought of helping had crossed my mind. It quickly became clear they didn't need my help, especially since I was still dressed for work in a skirt and heels, albeit very low ones. In eight quick trips, they had the coolers tucked into the shadiest part of the porch, where hopefully they'd remain cold until tomorrow afternoon when the neighbors would arrive with more bags of ice. Since we were hosts, the drinks were on us, and Burt liked his beer icy on hot days.

Thankfully we didn't have to worry too much about designated drivers because almost everyone walked, one nice part about a neighborhood party. However, we would have a few guests from town, such as my dad and pastor, who'd drive. All in all, we expected close to a hundred people. About half of those would be under twenty. And yes, our yard was big enough to accommodate them comfortably, if a bit on the cozy side.

When they finished, John invited me to join them for dinner. "You've been alone all week, I'm sure you're ready for some company. We'd love to have you."

Ignoring the sideways glance he sent toward his brother, I batted away John's hand with a laugh when he tried to grab my elbow. "Thanks, but I still have a lot to do tonight. Really." Backing away, I put distance between myself and the Weston brothers before I caved to temptation. "Thank you. I really appreciate the help, I do, but I can't. Not tonight. Burt's home next week, maybe we can do it then."

John and Dan exchanged a look, one I wasn't sure I wanted to interpret. "Sure. You and Cyndi work it out. We'll see you at the parade, right?"

"Wouldn't miss it for the world." Actually, without Burt, I'd already decided not to go. Who went to a parade by themselves? Where was the fun in that? Besides, without Burt I had half again as much work to do getting ready for the barbeque.

Chapter 2

Kicking around our big, empty house, I spent a disgruntled evening hauling crates of party supplies, tables and folding chairs out of storage. Dining alone had involved shoving the pizza in the fridge, and picking at a quarter portion of the Greek salad. However, one more night without Burt snoring in my ear held a certain attraction.

For background noise I'd turned on the TV, and to my surprise the opening credits of *On a Clear Day You Can See Forever* popped onto the screen. Reliving a moment of my youth, I tried out Barbra-slash-Daisy-slash-Melinda's most definitive line to see how it worked with my name.

"My name is Rachel. Rachel Winifred Dahlrumple Bruckmeister."

Somehow it didn't sound the same as when Barbra-slash-Melinda said it. Disgusted with the false hope that saying it aloud would make it somehow more magical, I went about my tasks.

The movie had become so deeply rooted in my past, practically from the moment of my birth, which took place on the evening the movie opened, Wednesday, June 17, 1970.

No, I'm not clairvoyant like the character Daisy Gamble. If only. Would have saved me a whole lot of trouble. No, it will take a little more explaining.

As the story goes, my parents went to see the film mainly as a distraction for my mom in the uncomfortable end stages of her pregnancy, but also to escape the summer heat, if only for a few hours. Why they chose this movie over another had to do with dishy Frenchman Yves Montand who played the male lead, a psychiatrist. Well, dishy in a 1970s European style. In the film he was still hot by any day's standards in that older-man appealing way. At least I always thought so. Mom did too, which was why my father indulged his hugely pregnant wife.

In the movie, Barbra Streisand, regressed through hypnosis by Yves, announced, "My name is Melinda. Melinda Winifred Waine Tentrees."

Complete with upper crust British accent instead of the Brooklyn whine of her other character identity, Daisy Gamble. At this point, the character played by Yves sat up and took notice.

Somehow my name doesn't carry quite the same impact.

In any case, my middle name, Winifred, came from that movie. My mother loved the film, and swore destiny played a hand as she went into labor at the theater. They dashed from cinema to hospital and five minutes before midnight, I made my debut.

Because of this, Mom wanted to name me after the characters in the film, but my father ruled out the entire name she put together. Eventually they settled on Rachel after his grandmother and Winifred as a compromise. Had I been consulted, I would have voted for Melinda.

I was raised listening to bits of the songs, in particular, "...*who would not be stunned to see you prove, There's more to us than surgeons can remove?*" and hearing Mom prattle on about names and destinies. Sadly, I'd never lived up to anyone's expectations or great hopes for my life, yet, each time I watched the movie, I searched for the divine inside me, the spark of life that brought a character like Daisy to life so brilliantly.

Alas, like every other time I'd seen the film, I didn't find my spark of divine inspiration, but went about my chores and sang along with the songs as I'd been doing from the time VCRs were invented and the movie became available on tape. Because of Mom, I knew the movie inside out and backward. In fact, it had been some years since I'd seen it because it always reminded me of her and made me miss her even more.

By the time I finished for the night, I had precious little energy left and spent only a few moments on the dark porch, listening to the hot San Joaquin Valley night. Right alongside the crickets, the hum of air conditioning units filled the night air. I debated taking a swim, but even the thought took too much effort.

Entirely too ready for bed, I was upstairs and in the middle of my nightly regimen of allergy medications--those with hay fever have always found summer in the valley brutal--when I heard an odd noise from the front of the house.

Raccoons, coyotes, or even one of the neighbor's dogs commonly wandered by to sniff around. Because of the coyote possibility, I decided to take a look. The last thing I needed was them getting into the coolers. I considered the possibility of kids from the street getting into the beer, but not seriously. The parents in our little neighborhood would make the punishment more excruciating than the hangover they might have the next day, and the kids knew it.

Besides, it never hurt to double check the security, a habit drilled into me by Burt from our days of living near San Jose, and one he'd not let slip one bit since moving to my tiny hometown. In our first years, he'd reminded me nightly, especially when he was away, until I had the habit deeply ingrained in my bones.

Not particularly happy to deal with strange noises on my own--that's what husbands were for--I pulled a robe on over the t-shirt I slept in when Burt traveled. He preferred something a bit more revealing, or nothing at all, when he was home. I found it bemusing since he hadn't turned to me in true love in months, possibly a few years. Not counting the lukewarm sex on our anniversaries. That hadn't been lovemaking in the slightest.

I debated grabbing my smaller handgun, but the double barrel shotgun made a better choice. I kept the cartridges filled with rock salt, which would hurt enough but not cause serious injury. *Thank you, James Bond.* The shotgun had the advantage of being more visible and could be used as a club if a dose or two of salt didn't deter the pest. I pulled it from under the bed and padded down the hardwood stairs on bare feet.

Being afraid wasn't an option because I just couldn't work up the emotion. Small town life bred it out of a person. I knew these people as well as I knew myself. I'd grown up in the house built by an ancestor less than a generation after the Civil War. Most of my neighbors had moved onto our street when the original homes were built in the late 1970s, after my parents subdivided the land. In the small, tight-knit community of twenty-one homes, we always looked out for each other because that's what neighbors do. Still, caution was all to the good, thus the security system had been installed shortly after we'd moved into the house.

I peered out a sidelight, flipped on the porch light and detected no sudden movements or creepy sounds. Reasonably confident I'd find nothing more than the hot night, I deactivated the house alarm and opened the front door. Nothing unusual beyond the screened security door greeted me.

Well, except for a long white box sitting at the edge of the porch. An item so out of the ordinary, I didn't know if I should be intrigued or alarmed.

First of all, Burt never sent cut flowers. His gifts tended toward jewelry I'd rarely wear, and live plants I knew he'd picked out from an anniversary gift guide. Not a bad trait in a husband, really. Better than his taste in lingerie.

Second of all, the florist never delivered after six o'clock in the evening, any day of the week. Certainly not at ten o'clock, when the sidewalks all around us were already rolled up for the night. And if she had, she would have rung the doorbell and not run off. As I said, small town.

Sometimes the younger kids who came into my library brought me a handful of daisies, or those "really pretty yellow flowers" also known as wild mustard. Because of my allergies, I'd let the mustard wilt and tell the kids the plant was too delicate for a vase and was best left in the fields. I liked the daisies and kept a vase especially for them. But kids only brought me flowers at work. Never at home.

Trapped by indecision, I heard a car start up next door, to the east. My left. Ah, right. Deputy Dan. I recognized the growl of the sports car. It occurred to me that the last month or two he'd been a regular weekend visitor, unless he had patrol duty, and then he'd still swing by. Things slow on the dating scene? Surprising. If I'd gone for dinner, I would have caught the news from someone about his dating habits. Not that his habits mattered to me, but it did seem odd, him not having a date on Friday night.

Seeing as how he was the law, and had to drive past my house, that tipped the scales. I leaned the shotgun against the wall and swung open the screen door.

Sure enough, Dan's Corvette backed down the drive and into the circle where our street ended. My house stood like a grand old queen, dead center, at the back of the curve, a hundred years older than the other homes on the street. As I watched from the corner of my eye, in part because his headlights blinded me and in part because I didn't want to openly acknowledge his presence--very mature, right?--he hesitated before shifting the car into first gear while I approached the box. A box designed to hold a dozen red roses.

If they were roses from my husband...well, he'd better be behind a bush ready to jump out and make up for being a selfish prick the last couple of years. One heartfelt apology, one meaningful session of making love, and I'd probably forgive him anything. After all, while our life might not be perfect, I couldn't imagine life without him. All that time together had to stand for something.

Rumbling with a sexy, throaty purr only a high powered car could produce and mean it, the 'Vette crept forward, coming even with the path from the street as I crouched and realized just how short my sleeping outfit was, coupled with the fact I wore no panties. I could only pray darkness and the hem of my robe hid that detail. Despite my potential for exposure of the embarrassing kind, curiosity got the best of me and I lifted the lid of the box. Tissue mostly hid what seemed to be an arrangement of greenery with a few blooms inside, and I could see a card tucked into the leaves under the tissue.

As rumbly as his car, the deputy's voice reached me without being too loud. "Everything okay, Mrs. Bruckmeister?"

Oh, I'd become Mrs. Bruckmeister, had I? I'd been Rachel earlier. Okay, fine. I could play it that way.

Mildly surprised he'd actually spoken to me--for the second time in one day, no less--I looked up to see him leaning toward the open passenger window. When the hell had he grown so damn cute? I'd really tried not to notice over the past year, but since my husband wasn't looking at me anymore, well, my eyes had done some wandering, and my mind some wondering.

Even more so when I'd been blown off one time too many. Hours later, it still stung. If I had an affair, or gave the impression of having one, would Burt spend more time at home? I dropped that thought in a heartbeat. I just wanted Burt around when I needed him, like for party preparation. I didn't want him underfoot *all* the time. Having him hanging around tended to interfere with my reading.

"I think so... But I'm not sure. Did you see anyone drive by? Someone dropped off this box." Though my face heated at a few words of attention from the deputy, I still didn't know what to think about the flower box.

Not Burt, then who? A secret admirer--my first, unless the admirer were under ten and they tended to be not so secret--or a prank? And in either case, why? Why there, why then? I couldn't help but wonder at the coincidence of Dan and the box showing up at the same time. Had Dan put it there, then waited for me to come out and find it? And there I crouched in a ratty t-shirt barely covered by a thin, very short, pink kimono sort of robe. One good breeze and he'd know about the missing panties.

Must've been the magic words. Dan threw the car in reverse, and backed it up to the start of the circular drive. Before I could say *Deputy Dawg*, or worry about my state of dress--or lack thereof--he'd parked on the drive in front of the house.

"You opened it?" He strode toward my porch. Well, if he had put the box there, his reaction didn't feel right. Shouldn't he have been more flirtatious instead of angry?

"Well, yeah. How else am I supposed to figure out what it is?" I dropped the lid and reached for the tissue. "Some sort of floral arrangement." A light breeze blew one half of the tissue back and revealed a bunch of greenery, the stems artistically bound with a white satin ribbon. I lifted the small envelope from where it nestled in the leaves. My name was printed in block letters on top. "And it's for me."

Odd, the handwriting looked nothing like Burt's or anyone else's I knew. As the librarian, I saw a lot of different handwriting styles on a daily basis. The sample I held was completely unrecognizable.

I remained crouched on the porch, so when he stood on the step below, he towered over me. "Recognize the handwriting?"

"Suspicious much?" The breeze kicked past and blew a strand of hair into my eyes. I was about to push it back when Dan bent and gripped my wrist.

"Stop. That's poison oak and, if I'm not mistaken, ragweed."

I must have looked pretty dopey staring up at him. A gust of hot breeze carried a swirl of dust and pollen to my face as I reacted to the warmth and strength of his hand wrapped around my wrist. Before I could think of something to say, much less move, I sneezed. Truly elegant and attractive.

"That box is one mass of toxins. Aren't you super allergic to hay fever stuff?"

Stunned, I let him pull me up. He knew that about me? Then again, in our little town, who didn't?

I looked up at him but didn't see anything beyond professional concern. Even one step down, he stood taller than eye level with me. I still had the envelope in my hand. "Yes. I live on allergy meds all spring and summer." And weekly shots. All of which I'd left sitting on the bathroom counter upstairs. I might have been able to ditch them all if we'd moved to the coast, but every year Burt reminded me we couldn't afford living there. Another sneeze rocked me and my eyes began to water. Applied in a timely manner, the meds made it possible for me to live a somewhat normal life, including time in my allergy-friendly garden where I'd planted low pollen plants as defined by the Asthma and Allergy Foundation of America. Unfortunately, I was about an hour past my usual time, so I sneezed on Dan's fine white t-shirt again.

He didn't flinch, but he did stare at me for a few seconds.

"Sorry." I reached to wipe away the miniscule spots, but he stopped me.

"Let's get you inside. Don't touch anything, hear me?"

"Yeah, yeah. I've dealt with poison oak before. How'd you recognize it in the dark? My porch light isn't very bright."

"I have good night vision."

I could only wonder what that meant as he dragged me past the screen door he held open. I liked to skinny dip in the pool out back from time to time, but only very late on the darkest nights. Had he been able to see me from his brother's kitchen window? I'd almost done it tonight. Heat raced across my face.

"Where do you keep your first aid kit? I assume you have something to treat this."

I lost my train of thought with my next sneeze, which echoed in the foyer as we passed through. "What?"

"Your first aid kit. Where is it?"

"The cabinet by the back door." After a few bouts with stubbed toes on the pool apron and bug bites from working in the yard, I'd found it easier to have the kit on hand for fast grabbing.

Dan stopped by the sink and turned on the water so I didn't have to touch the faucet. He had me drop the envelope into a plastic baggie, and after pumping soap into my hands he began searching the contents of the first aid box.

"Calamine? It doesn't do diddly, Rumple. Not on poison oak."

Rumple? Good heavens. I half snorted, half sneezed. "There's a name I haven't heard in twenty years."

Once I'd cleaned my wedding rings, I pulled the set off and dropped it into the little dish on the window sill. I'd never liked wearing rings when doing dirty work in the kitchen and often left them there overnight. Burt objected every time he saw me do it, calling me irresponsible with how I treated the two-carat diamond on the engagement ring. I figured I saved the ring set some wear and tear. Especially on the days I forgot to wear the set altogether. The first time he'd caught me at work without... Well, I'd learned to be very careful when he was in town.

Dan stiffened, shot me an irritated glance, and kept digging. "Mint oil? Menthol? Camphor? Lanacaine? Do you have anything along those lines?"

"Aloe with Lanacaine? Witch hazel, rubbing alcohol..."

His hand plunged into the box. "Antihistamine cream and hydrocortisone. Those'll work." Appropriate tubes captured and officially subdued, he turned and observed my scrubbing efforts.

Unusually fast, the sting had started to set in. Thank God for his exceptional night vision. I would have carried the box into the house and set it on the counter before recognizing the toxic plants. The oil from the poison oak would have been everywhere, not to mention the evil pollen of the ragweed.

"Who'd you piss off?" Dan handed me a paper towel. "Pat, don't rub."

"Aye, aye, Deputy." Off duty, he wore jeans, a no longer quite so pristine white t-shirt, and three day stubble. Yowzer. Even though I'd been married for seventeen years, I had no immunity to all that raw manliness standing six inches away from me for the second time that day. Young manliness. Two years younger than I. Twelve years younger than my husband. I patted my hands and face dry, did my best to delicately blow my running nose, and tossed the paper towels into the trash.

"Funny." He squeezed out the antihistamine cream first. "Rub that in and we'll follow with the hydrocortisone. Got a pair of chopsticks or tweezers?"

"What?" Out of the blue, the question struck me as bizarre.

"I want to read the card inside the envelope," he said slowly with exaggerated patience and a touch of sarcasm. In truth, I'd been thinking about him to hide my real turmoil. My mind, still reeling from the fact someone would send me such a rotten arrangement, had trouble catching up to him.

"Tweezers equals no touchy." He wiggled the fingers of one hand.

"Funny." I repeated his one word sarcastic answer before sneezing, that time into the sink. "Top drawer, grab one of the wooden pairs of Japanese chopsticks. They have the pointier end." I took the fresh paper towel he handed me, and oh-so-demurely wiped my running eyes and drippy nose.

"You're a real comedian, library lady. Exactly what do you wear under your proper suit of straight skirt and prim white blouse, with your hair up in a bun?"

He gave me a look that raked me from head to toe and back again. Shocked at the appraisal as much as the comment, I stared back. I could have sworn he had X-Ray vision because he looked at me as if my clothes weren't there at all, as if he knew what I didn't have on underneath. If I hadn't had goo all over my hands, I would have pulled my robe tighter. Instead, my entire body flushed and I squeezed my thighs together, internally swearing I'd never set foot outside my bedroom without panties ever again. Or had I really had the opposite thought, as in I'd never wear panties again? Damn, I needed a remedy to counteract what the man did to my brain.

"I've seen you in your natural habitat. You just need to raise the hem on your skirts four inches, change out the flats for stilettos, undo a couple more buttons and you'll have all the teen boys hanging out. County literacy will soar."

His comments were so outrageous, if I hadn't known him for twenty--mumble--years, I'd have reported him to the Sheriff. Instead, my mouth dropped open partly in shock that he'd said so many words in a row to me. On the other hand I'd watched cop shows and recognized his attempt to distract me while he extracted the card enough to read it, but I was outraged all the same. To hide my hot face, I bent to the task of rubbing the soothing creams into my hands.

Seriously, he hadn't tried walking, bending, crouching, and climbing step-stools all day in a thong. Even worse, a garter belt and stockings. Men! I'd like to see him do it. I'd stick to my comfy Lycra. Besides being comfortable, it gave a little tummy control, too. As for heels, he needed to get real.

But I did vow, silently, to think about the shorter skirts.

"I'll ask again, Mrs. Bruckmeister, are you aware of any enemies?"

I looked up from my lotion rubbing and took in his expression. Blank. All teasing gone. Cop mode.

"I'm a simple person, Deputy Weston, you know that. Steady and calm. Boring. I don't offend anyone, and no one gives me trouble. Unless you're talking about Jose Delgado, who is three weeks late with the last book he checked out."

"I don't think Jose wrote this note." He looked at it again, and his eyebrows drew together. With a deepening scowl, he turned it so I could read it through the clear plastic.

The handwriting on the card matched the envelope. Black, block letters, innocuous enough, aside from the message. Ah, yes, the kicker.

Let him go. We want to be together. Start divorce proceedings. Or better yet, end your pitiful life. Your choice. For now.

I could only imagine my expression at that moment. Dan's gaze was glued to my face, which first felt hot, then cold. My head swam and my breathing wheezed in and out, as ragged as my stuttering heartbeat.

That bastard. The low down, scheming, rotten, lying, slimy, vile, despicable...

"Care to revise your statement?"

A few quick blinks brought the deputy back into focus, though I could feel the airways in my lungs constricting.

"I know who's going to die, and isn't going to be me," I whispered. "Chinese water torture is too good for him. Splinter those bamboo chopsticks and the minute he gets home, they're going under his fingernails. After that, his balls." I'd learned a few things from my father's stories of 'Nam. And of course, reading about the war. After all, I was a librarian. A curious one. I'd read nearly every book on our well stocked shelves. Except the really dry science and technical books, which I left to the geeks. And I meant that in the nicest way. I liked geeks. Briefly, I considered doing a search on torture techniques when I returned to work Monday morning. If I could hold off that long.

The tanned face so near mine blanched as he flinched. "Easy going, ma'am."

Right. I wasn't known for saying such things. I wasn't known for saying much.

"Well?" I demanded, possibly a tad harshly, but I'd earned the right. My fragile world had just vaporized before my eyes and it was far too soon to see what might be left. If anything. The only future visible looked like a rapidly expanding black hole.

Someone wanted me dead. But who? My husband? His girlfriend? God, that hurt. I hated cheaters. I hated what they did to families, especially the children. Even though I had no children, divorce loomed in front of me like a huge gaping maw. I wanted to wail, gnash my teeth, and obliterate something, anything. Of course, I was Rachel the Mouse, so I did my best to hide the violent urges building inside. Rachel the Meek never, ever, let loose with her most primitive emotions. She hid them deep, keeping a calm, submissive, accepting face turned toward the world at large.

Then again, my harsh tone might have been part of that breathing trouble I so very much wanted to control. "What would you do?"

For the first time I could remember in our long, long history, Dan looked directly, and very deeply, into my eyes. The sympathy, sincerity, and concern on his face hit me before the actual words did. Already overwhelmed from too many emotions boiling in my heart and head, I had no defense or response for his reply, or the way he ever so lightly caressed my cheek with the back of his fingers. When had he gotten so close?

"Well, Rachel, since I'm not the kind of idiotic ass your husband is, I wouldn't be stupid enough to screw around on the most amazing woman anywhere. Were I the lucky one to have you, I wouldn't leave you alone long enough for you to ever feel abandoned."

Aside from the asthma and allergy thing, I was a healthy woman. I'd never, ever, once fainted in my life. But the shocks to my system that night hit too hard. A poisonous gift, a nasty note, knowledge I didn't want of my husband's cheating ways, and a gorgeous, younger man, telling me he considered me amazing and not plain, boring, and mousy… The zing I felt in my tummy from his touch did me in.

Black waves engulfing me, limbs losing strength, I slowly collapsed and Dan caught me at the last moment of consciousness. Like any nineteenth-century heiress worth her crumpets and tea, I fainted right into his arms.

Chapter 3

July 4, 2009, started out pretty much like any other Saturday morning.

Aside from the events of the previous night, that was. I certainly did my best to ignore them, not that it did any good. In order to continue, a brief explanation should suffice.

After fainting, I came to on the living room chaise with our EMT neighbor, Miguel, backed up by Dan and Cyndi, bent over me. A blanket covered my lower half. Too embarrassed to ask how much Dan had seen, I ignored him and concentrated on breathing per Miguel's instructions. Cyndi, God love her, fussed about, pouring coffee and water. Trust her to turn my malaise into a tea party.

Miguel kept a bottle of oxygen and an Epi-pen on hand for the very rare times an attack overtook anyone in the neighborhood. As he usually looked at me when mentioning it, I'd pooh-poohed the implication for about three years. Only now his smug smile assured me he considered his forward thinking had finally proven my protests moot. Dan dashed upstairs to get my meds and it took an hour before they were all confident enough of my stability for me to kick them out.

From their silence on the issue of Burt, I suspected Dan hadn't said a word--or they chose to ignore it. I did notice the flower box had been carefully bagged. He took it and the note for analyzing, after ordering me to lock and alarm the house, then go to bed. For a moment he sounded an awful lot like Burt and I wanted to stick my tongue out at him. Probably because, unlike Burt, he looked just the teeniest bit worried about me, I nodded instead.

So, Saturday morning, desperate to not think about the night before--seriously, fainting with no underwear on under a very short night shirt? I knew I'd never be able to look the deputy in the eye again as long as I lived--I rose after only two hours sleep, showered, dressed all the way, took care of my morning med doses and went downstairs for breakfast that might as well have been sawdust for all I noticed. While I drank my coffee on the back porch and did a visual inspection of the backyard--the coolers remained untouched--John brought over his secret weapon, his six-year-old steel magnolia, Mindy. Knowing I couldn't hold out against the sweetest little girl ever born, they coerced me into meeting them in town for the parade. Over the years, John had learned to shamefully use his adorable child against me, and I'd yet to find a way to counterstrike. Okay, so she was my child of the heart and I would have stolen her from them in a heartbeat, and he very smugly knew it.

Because their car barely held the family of five, I had a choice; a five-mile drive and hassle with parking, or walk a few hundred yards across the seasonally low river and risk wet feet. In my present mood, a mixture of mystification, humiliation, denial and simmering anger, I did my best to focus on my surroundings rather than my anguish. In truth, I should have stayed home because I just couldn't find it in me to put on my normal happy face. I'd completely fried my mind trying to figure out who'd sent the weeds. Since she--whoever she was--had made the delivery, did it mean Burt really was at a convention? And playing golf? The fact he hadn't answered his cellphone in no way reassured me. Never mind he almost never answered his cell when I called, but he usually called back within an hour. Hadn't happened yet.

I slung a tiny purse with keys, phone and cash over my shoulder, made a barely dignified slide down the river bank, and picked my way from sand bar to sand bar across the extremely low waterway that separated our neighborhood from town. I loved my Crocs and had made it a point to wear them specifically for crossing the river. They dried fast, and standing around in a wet pair of shoes and socks all day didn't appeal. Besides, they were cute and matched my outfit. A tough combo to beat.

The walk gave me a chance to study our small town from an angle I rarely got the chance to savor. Typical of the stereotype, we weren't much more than a wide spot around a county highway about twenty miles off I-5 running down California's San Joaquin Valley. A farming community settled in the last half of the nineteenth century, most of its homes had started out Victorian, and then morphed with twentieth century modification.

The moment I scrambled up the far bank and crossed the sports fields where the fireworks would be set off later, I met people streaming from the houses, and heading toward downtown. Beneath the large trees, mostly oaks and sycamores, standing in the wide yards, natural shade covered the broad streets. The trees didn't cool much as the ambient temperature soared, but I appreciated their protection from the direct sun. I strolled down the middle of the street--the sidewalks were all full--and exchanged greetings while looking away from curious stares. Burt's absence was noted but generally ignored in the way that small town gossip always made the rounds but stopped short of the object, which saved me from a lot of *poor dear* comments. Looks, I could deal with. Pity? I could do without. I slowed my steps and let the people flow past, giving my attention to the little ones who knew me from the library.

At one point I had three of the little critters hanging off me, not normally something I considered a problem. Right then I couldn't pretend they were mine. Instead, the hole inside felt bigger than ever. I'd always wanted kids, but they'd never happened. I extracted myself from the hugs and sent them off with their parents.

"Miss Rachel!" A masculine voice overrode the chatter going on around me and I considered ignoring it, but then he repeated my name much closer. I turned and saw a blast from the past flagging me down.

Jim Santos. Now there was a memory. As he strode my way, looking much the same wearing worn denim and a dark tan cowboy hat, I flew back in time to a few stolen afternoons hidden under the drooping branches of a weeping willow. *My God, did everything have to be thrown at me at once?* That was all the time I had to think before he caught me up in a hug.

"Wow, stranger," I said. Completely lame, but I honestly had no small talk in me.

"Is that all the greeting I get, *querida*?" He lifted me just enough to spin me around and kiss my cheek, forcing me to cling to him. "Has it been so long you no longer think of me with kindness?"

"It's been more than twenty years, you oaf. Put me down." I slapped at his shoulder and noted how much he'd changed since that Homecoming week so very long ago. Twenty-four years, but the memory still had the power to make me blush. He was broader and stronger, yet still lean in the hips. And hard. Oh boy, was he hard all over as he held me close. I prodded his muscled-in-iron-shoulder with a finger and almost broke the nail. "What are you doing here, and where's your family?"

He set me down and brushed a strand of hair from my cheek. "Mom and Dad went on ahead an hour ago. Mom won't be happy if someone takes her spot."

Jim had always been a touchy-feely one, and since we'd shared a certain--ahem--rite of passage, just the two of us in a well hidden spot beneath a tree, well, I guessed he felt a certain right to touch me. I didn't see it that way. I was married, and as such I'd put old boyfriends and lovers behind me. I stepped away, imagining the gossip from the many witnesses around us getting back to Burt. I secretly bet he'd find a way to turn it around on me and make it look like I'd been the cheater.

Funny how gossip about Burt had never reached me. The reminder of his alleged betrayal hit me afresh, flipping my stomach over once more, and I turned toward town.

"Ah yes, in front of the diner. No local would dare take her spot, or let a tourist move in, for that matter." Mrs. Santos had her territory, and that was that.

Jim kept pace with me and when his hand brushed mine, I shoved both hands in the pockets of my sundress.

"You're alone, Rachel. Why is that? Where's your big handsome husband?"

Whether it was the question or the tone--had it really been a sneer?--I didn't know, but the probing turned up the heat on my anger a notch.

"Out of town on business. Due home in a few hours," I answered shortly, ignoring the sideways glance he gave me.

"Why did you come from the river? Ever revisit our spot?"

What was he trying to do? Did he know about the delivery last night? Had he made it for someone else?

Whatever the reason, he'd stepped on my last nerve. "Jim, if you want to talk to me, catch up, or hang out, drop the subject of our past. I'm a married woman and last I heard you were married. Twice. Where're your wife and kids?"

"Okay, okay." Jim backed off and shoved his hands into the pockets of his jeans. "My second divorce was final last week. No kids from either marriage, except a couple step-kids I'm helping put through college. Mom heard a rumor of you getting a divorce, so I was just testing the waters. I'm home for the holiday and Monday I'll be back at work."

The word *divorce* in conjunction with my name knocked the breath from me and stopped my forward motion completely. "Wh-what did you say?"

Jim managed to stop with me. "I'm just in town--"

I turned on him and stabbed a finger into the middle of his chest. "No, the part about *me* getting a divorce. Where did you hear *that*?"

Jim shrugged uncomfortably and adjusted his cowboy hat. "Mom heard it somewhere in town last week. In case it's true, you should know she approves. Thinks you should take him to the cleaners."

I must have blanched and appeared ready to keel over because Jim caught me by the shoulders and backed me up to the strong trunk of a tree. "Easy, Rachel."

Control. The word floated into my head as I forced myself to take long, slow, deep breaths. After a minute, I felt stronger, but my heart still raced. I'd barely decided I needed a divorce lawyer, yet the town already knew about it? How blatant had Burt been and how had I not noticed? Damn him! Damn him for ruining the holiday, for making me an object of vicious gossip, and damn him for, well, everything! When I got my hands on the son of a bitch, he'd know the depth of my fury. We might end up canceling the party because Burt would be too busy salvaging his belongings. Or his life. I hadn't decided which just yet. It was a toss-up at that moment.

"Rachel?" Jim's voice brought me back to my surroundings and I noticed people regarding us with curiosity as they passed. His hands held me securely, which was probably a good thing as my legs trembled on the edge of collapse.

"I'm okay," I said, knowing it to be a lie as I shrugged away his hands. He stepped back. "I didn't mean to upset you."

I looked up and found him looking contrite. Another handsome man. More handsome than he'd been as a youth. I remembered the power of those dark, almost black eyes, but the feeling remained that, a memory.

"I don't know where the rumors came from, but there's no divorce in motion." Yet. Come the following Monday morning that would change, unless Burt came home with some very convincing proof. Then again, I didn't think he could. My heart dropped again, and I resisted the urge to pull off my wedding set and fling it down the nearest storm drain. The hand wearing it curled into a fist. I might need it to pay for the lawyer. Then again, the diamond would make a nice mark on Burt's face when I punched him.

"Okay. Let's forget I passed on stupid gossip. I don't want you mad at me. Friends?" He held out a hand.

I cautiously took it and gave it a shake.

Jim used our clasped hands to gently tug me away from the tree. "Sure you want to go to the parade?" He asked it softly, as if concerned I might fall apart. Granted, he was right to be worried. I was damn close to a breakdown right then.

"Yeah." The words felt wooden and flat, but I forced myself to speak, hoping a feeling of normalcy would return. "The Westons will be looking for me if I don't show up soon. They made me promise."

"Who?"

"You remember John Weston? He lived next door to me. Between us in age."

"Oh, right. The super jock." Jim nodded.

"He bought the house next door from his parents. I'm meeting him, his wife, and three kids."

"Let me walk you into town."

I could have refused. Probably should have, but his presence felt vaguely familiar and somewhat comforting. With him beside me, I realized I hadn't liked walking alone. On the other hand, wouldn't Jim's presence instead of Burt's draw more comments than me walking by myself? Hard to tell right then. I shrugged away from the tree and resumed the trek toward Main Street, where the parade would start in twenty minutes. If I weren't there by then, John would come looking for me. And Mindy had informed me everything would be ruined. So I was stuck.

We walked in silence for a block before I found some small talk inside me. "What do you do these days?"

"Construction."

I glanced sideways at him again. I'd bet he still wielded a hammer. His already-darker Hispanic skin tone was more so from the sun, and I could make out the bulge of well-toned biceps beneath his worn chambray shirt with the sleeves rolled up.

The crowd began to thicken with the Elks, VFW, American Legion, Boy and Girl Scouts, and various other civic-minded groups lining up for the parade, so we had to move to the crowded sidewalk. From there we greeted members of each of these groups that kept the town busy with enough dances, pancake breakfasts, and ice cream socials to keep everyone up on the latest gossip and the teens out of too much trouble.

When Jim's arm brushed against mine again, it seemed more natural, a result of being crowded together, not him trying to octopus me.

"Miss Rachel!" "Miss Rachel!"

The cries of my age ten and under fans increased as we drew closer to downtown, where most of our buildings radiated the pride of renovated historic gems. The sense of permanence soothed my heart, and I could finally breathe enough to feel the satisfaction of connecting with my deep roots. Although the throng held more tourists than townies, I felt a sense of belonging. I should, my mother's family had helped build the tiny rustic haven.

Close enough to the Big Sur Coastal region south of Monterey and Carmel, Bonchamps had always attracted tourists and visitors who meandered down our shady streets to shop. The town stayed old-fashioned on purpose because we, the townspeople, wanted it that way.

Of course, we couldn't remain entirely nineteenth century. Tucked in side-by-side with the old standbys, Jim and I strolled past shops with artists of every kind. Athough the Main Street beauty salon and barber shop were institutions, we also passed an art shop, an herbs and spices tea merchant, a colorful kite shop, two independent book stores, a few antique stores, a deli, and all manner of specialty boutiques.

We also had the choice of organic goodies at a fancy café, but I usually stopped at Barb's for my clandestine donut fixes. I waved to her through the window when we paused at her corner.

As the crowd had grown denser, Jim had taken my hand to lead me through the thicker concentrations of people on the sidewalks. I let myself *forget* to pull my hand from his, and got lost in a deep sense of community. These were my people. Their families had been here for well over a hundred years. Like my family, and me, they weren't going anywhere. When I remembered the hand I held didn't belong to my husband, I dropped it, but not before Barb noticed and raised a brow. Feeling a little sick to my stomach, I waved away the coffee she held up to tempt me inside.

Patriotic to the center of our red, white, and blue little hearts, tradition demanded we go all out to celebrate national holidays. Independence Day was no exception and probably our biggest draw of the year. Bunting draped the entire length of the parade route down Main Street. Vendors trailing streamers and balloons, selling everything from silly hats to lemonade and cotton candy, worked the crowd. The crowds swelled around me, surely sending seizures of rapture into the hearts of merchants and tax collectors alike. We moved on, and I stopped long enough to buy a big cloud of pink cotton candy. I had no intention of eating it, but the kids would all love a sticky handful.

Jim noticed I'd dropped behind, and he came back for me.

"You don't have to guard me, you know," I mildly complained.

"Don't like me anymore?" He pinched a bit of my cotton candy with an exaggerated wink and a waggle of the eyebrows.

"Jim…" I sighed in exasperation.

"Okay, I get the hint. You're not interested in fooling around." He pinched another bit of fluff and stuffed it in my mouth.

The sugar dissolved on my tongue. "No kidding."

"Let me hang with you today, Rachel. I like to see a pretty woman smile at me, and you seem a little down. Let's cheer each other up for old time's sake?"

Yeah, I could already smell the grass and leaves in the secluded hollow under the weeping willow. I knew just what kind of old time's sake cheer he wanted.

"I'm not much in the mood for cheer and I'm meeting friends," I reminded him. "Besides, your parents are expecting you." I pointed to where his mother waved at us.

"Where are you meeting the Westons?" He waved back and his mother settled into her folding chair, content in her spot.

"They're a little farther down the street, so you'd better skip over to your parents and let me continue on to my party."

"Afraid folks might misinterpret two friends hanging out at the parade?"

"Exactly." Especially since no one in town had ever known about our, uh, friendship. Unless he'd said something. I never had. In fact, we'd already drawn far too much attention. Raised eyebrows popped up all around us.

Jim gave me a long look that felt entirely too intimate, too knowing, and it sparked a bit of wondering in me. What would have happened if he'd stayed around Bonchamps instead of moving off to Monterey and beyond? Did I feel any attraction for him? Compared to the fireworks Dan had set off last night, Jim just didn't reach me in the same way, but he didn't leave me cold, either.

"Look, the parade is starting soon. I need to move on. Come to the party tonight. It's at my house this year." He knew what party I meant. "We can probably find time to talk then. Bring a suit, we always play water polo." No, we probably wouldn't find time to talk, but he'd get to see me acting like a proper wife with a proper husband and having fun. Dammit, I would have fun, I swore. I expected it to be very fun tossing Burt out on his ear right after I made him clean up from the party.

"I'd love to. Thank you." Jim captured my hand and kissed the back of it. He could be very charming when he made the effort. That much I did remember.

"See you later." I waved to his parents and pressed into the crowd, a little relieved to shake him. The strain of keeping up a conversation, and the upset of his revelation made me desperate to be alone for just a few minutes before I faced the Westons.

As I walked, I forced myself to see the people around me.

I usually loved watching everyone enjoying themselves. The little ones especially, with their sticky faces and eyes round with awe. If I looked hard enough, maybe I'd find a touch of magic, since I had so little to enjoy in my life at the moment.

Out of Jim's sight and alone in a sea of mostly strangers, I paused and leaned against a refitted iron lamppost, the metal radiating summer heat through the fabric of my cotton dress. It felt far more solid than I did as people jostled by, seeking the perfect vantage point from which to watch the parade. I'd never before attended the parade by myself, and didn't like it at all. I may not have been deliriously happy with Burt, but his place was with me, as he had been for nearly half my life. In a way, it felt as if I were missing a limb. A diseased one that required immediate amputation for sure, but the sense of loss was the same. As much as I hated him and what he'd done to me, to us, would I always miss him once I cut him away?

Across the street was one of two buildings, shops with apartments overhead, Burt and I owned. The owner of the jewelry store, a forty-something single mom who went by the name Ohm--derived from her initials, I'd been told--made jewelry and sold holistic doodads. She stood at her window staring out at the crowd, looking about as disgruntled as I'd ever seen her. Her son, a sweet twelve-year-old who visited the library almost weekly, caught my eye when he waved. I waved back before continuing my appraisal of the crowds.

The other building we owned, in addition to two small houses, was several blocks farther along the street, and housed a store specializing in organic, handspun and dyed wool, made by a co-op of sheep ranchers from the valley. If I'd been a knitter, I would have shopped there frequently. However, my talents had never been along those lines. Nor did I spend much time in the jewelry store. Burt brought home enough of her work, I didn't need to shop there, too.

As I scanned the filling street, I noted other business owners and managers keeping an eye on the crowds and kids. Sonja Neumeyer, the hotel manager, had her hands full pouring iced tea on the porch of the hotel, even with her kids helping. She was one of three single moms I knew to be friends with the jewelry maker. They pretty much stuck together. Any one of them might have caught Burt's eye at one time or another.

A tall figure, uniformed in the forest shades of tan and green of the sheriff's department--complete with flat brimmed hat--strolled in my direction and cut off my dark speculations. I shrugged off my wounded pride long enough to enjoy the sight of Dan subtly controlling the crowd. He certainly drew more than his fair share of fascinated female stares. Though there seemed to be a few thousand people between us, our gazes caught. After a head-to-toe appraisal that paused somewhere around my middle and left my heart beating double time, he pointed up the street.

Sure it was the heat of the day making me breathless, I nodded, then shoved off my anchoring lamppost to join my neighbors one block up. Surely he couldn't have been wondering about my underwear. Could he?

Because I had to work at keeping my turmoil from showing, I missed a good portion of the parade. I waved when the Westons waved. I waved to anyone who called out my name, and my face ached from keeping a smile pasted on it. John and Cyndi both found excuses to pat me on the shoulder from time to time and the kids took turns passing me bits of candy tossed from the floats. Mindy took charge of my lap as my special angel while ten-year-old Aggie and eight-year-old J.J. scrambled for the treats. Let them think I was upset over Burt's absence. Sooner or later they'd learn the true reason, but not here, not now. They didn't say anything, so I didn't confess.

As Dan worked crowd control, we got glimpses of him from time to time. I had trouble meeting his eyes the few times he caught me looking, but my gaze kept straying his direction enough that I made my excuses and hurried home as soon as the clean-up clowns started down the street, sweeping up behind the horses. I had other concerns to deal with, and drooling over the deputy wasn't one of them. It was just the one that kept jumping to the top of my *Most Urgent* list.

Chapter 4

The walk home took far less time than my walk into town, as I once more focused on my philandering husband. People tried to stop me, but I merely smiled, possibly somewhat grimly, and kept moving. By the time I reached the river, I didn't care if I got wet and plowed my way through the meandering streams twisting around the sandbars. I even stomped through a few pools, which got my skirt wet and cooled my legs.

Per his phone call the previous night, Burt expected to be home a good hour or two before the beginning of our annual neighborhood party. When the neighbor scheduled to host had to beg off, we'd volunteered, which worked out well, as--until my surprise gift--we had reason to celebrate more than just the holiday. That's what the neighborhood still thought. Our split would shock them all, unless any of our *friends* knew something about the nighttime delivery, or knew more about Burt's cheating.

Hell, it was my life, and I was shocked. And angry. And incredibly hurt. The wound was so deep, I knew for certain I'd never recover from it. It was so cavernous, I could barely breathe around it.

But about our celebration…amazingly enough, we had one. A reason to celebrate, that is. A promotion for Burt. A big one. And his oh-so-convenient excuse for being away the past week. Newly promoted to the position of County CIO--that would be Chief Information Officer--he'd told me the twice-a-year seminar on Business Ethics was mandatory and he was required to attend the first possible session.

Did I have STUPID *and* GULLIBLE tattooed on my forehead?

All right, all right, after the previous night's little gift, I supposed I did, but honestly, what if it was merely a prank? I didn't exactly have proof of his cheating. Plenty of suspicion, but no proof. His phone call could have been on the up and up. Stranger things had happened, which explained why they'd fenced off Area 51.

On the other hand, why schedule a week-long seminar the week before a major holiday? Obviously Burton Earl Bruckmeister considered me too brainless to understand. Of course Burt had to accept the golf invitation, too. Never mind he hadn't played in five years and his clubs sat in the garage covered with cobwebs. I didn't even want to address the issue of what other kinds of putts he might be making. The very thought of him, doing that, with someone else…

As soon as I got the back door open, I ran to the bathroom and threw up the sugary junk the Weston children had forced on me during the parade. I wanted to convince myself it was due to the sugar. Unfortunately, I could eat almost as much candy as them without burping.

What really made me sick? I hadn't questioned him. I'd taken Burt's words on faith. In the light of day, and after the ominous delivery, I began to think differently. Once I'd brushed my teeth and held a little water down, I contemplated all the ways I'd been monumentally idiotic while I filled the bathroom with rolls of toilet paper and fresh hand towels. Then I paced, stewing and steaming, waiting for him to haul his philandering ass home so I could have the pleasure of kicking it out the door.

After the party, of course.

The party. With a groan I slammed into the kitchen, hauled pitchers from the cabinets, and started making iced tea and lemonade while trying to envision how to go about kicking him out. I didn't want to have to spend the evening explaining why Burt and his clothes were out in the flower beds, much less cause damage to my daisies and iris. Some things one just doesn't do in a small town. However, after the delicious deputy had seen to reviving me from my asthma attack-slash-faint, I'd spent the first half of the night hauling clothes out of the closet, then spent the other half putting them back--why should I have to pack for Burt?--all the while plotting evil ways to tell him I'd drag his two timing--Three? Four-timing?--sleazy butt through court.

It would be hard to pinpoint any one emotion I felt, but all raged in competition with the heat of the day. The week leading up to the party I'd been so happy about his promotion, but when celebrating, my reasons, though no less joyous than his, were completely different. It would mean more traveling for him. Training, staying at the leading edge of technology. Long hours on the road. Weeks off at seminars and conventions. Glorious time for me to be alone and for the first time, truly enjoy a vacation my way. At home. Yeah, I had been all for his promotion. The raise was pretty nice, too, but the real reward for me was the time my husband would be away. Bliss.

After the nighttime delivery, bliss would mean the house completely to myself, decorated my way, without his lies and the rules he imposed. And the lovely alimony checks I'd squeeze out of his miserly grasp. See if he had funds for tomcatting around when I got through with him.

In my angry energetic mode, I attacked the last of the party preparations on my list with a vengeance until I had to stop. Hot and sweaty, I finally headed back to the kitchen and the relative coolness of my house. Relative, because eighty-five inside seemed cool in contrast to the ninety-seven outside under the century old trees enclosing three sides of the back yard. Normally, I'd have left on the air conditioning, but in just a few hours the screen doors would be swinging open and slamming shut. The breakable knickknacks were already locked in our library, as they wouldn't mix well with the young ones who always waited until the last possible moment before racing into the house to use the restroom. So, in the interest of sanity, no AC for the day.

As was common for me, I found solace in the kitchen. Barefoot and chugging down a glass of iced tea poured from a jug in the fridge, I stood near the big box fan. I loved the way the air flowed up under my dress, small runnels of air zooming up the line of my spine and between my breasts before shooting up to whisk away the sheen of sweat coating my neck. Besides cooling me, it also soothed me in an odd way. It felt silly, wicked and naughty, especially on those days when I wore nothing under my dress, which after last night, wasn't today. And I wouldn't wear the dress much longer. Soon I'd change into a swimsuit and tie a sarong around my hips. Add a large hat and dark glasses, and I envisioned myself sauntering around the yard doing my best femme fatale impression. If it earned me a single grope, I'd call it a success.

Three o'clock had just passed and I expected Burt at any minute. For the moment, everything on my list had a check mark. As the neighbors arrived, the brawny men folk would gladly heft that ice chest, light those coals, or carry a load of whatever, wherever it needed to go. Families would arrive with their contributions, folding chairs, kids and toys, make themselves at home, and the festivities would ramp up until it came time to line up the blankets and chairs along the river and watch the fireworks. As smoke drifted away from the final barrage, leaving behind the smell of sulfur and a ringing in our ears, the exodus would begin, leaving behind bare tables, full trash barrels and a trail of damp footprints through the house.

As far as the party went, my furious energy had powered me through every task, mine and Burt's, and all I needed were the guests. Bags of charcoal waited to fill the Texas-sized grill. The tables had their plastic covers weighted down in case a breeze decided to come by. Underneath, people would stash their coolers filled with mountains of ice to keep the potluck salads cool. I'd even run an extension cord for the ice cream makers and Judy Marshall's monstrous electric roaster filled with meatballs and covered with several jars of grape jelly. Believe it or not, it made a fabulous sauce for meatballs, Little Smokies, and Vienna sausages. Seriously. Good stuff.

While I usually anticipated the city fireworks display, I directed more thought to the fireworks to come later. I debated asking Deputy Weston to be on hand to help me throw the big ass out. But first, the party.

Long ago generations had termed the party as BYOSOB. Officially it stood for Bring Your Own Salad Or Beef. Or Beer. Or Beverage. Or as the women privately defined it: Bring Your Own Son Of a Bitch. Legend had it my great-great-grandmother and her contemporaries had come up with that version. The old family tree boasted several truly feisty women. How the kick-ass gene had bypassed me remained a mystery.

Yeah, I had an SOB for one more night. If he made it through the party alive. The more I thought about it, the madder I got. To distract myself again, I focused on the blown-up photo of the very first Fourth of July barbeque hanging on the backside of the free-standing fireplace that divided the front room from the kitchen. The tradition went back more than a century and was always interesting to think about.

In my mind, I visualized the original map of the valley. I found it a great way to travel. I could almost go all the way back to when the first white settlers arrived. As the gold fever petered out, farmers chose one side of the county--the flat side--and ranchers the other--the foothills of the coastal mountain range. Our house, on one of the original ranches, was more or less built in the center of our section, so it'd been the gathering spot for a hundred years, give or take twenty. Rising and falling with the country as a whole, we'd had a few years when celebrations were thin, such as during a world war or two.

Since my great-great-great grandfather, Joseph Reginald Martin, was a rancher who married a farmer's daughter, our land tended to be regarded as neutral ground. He'd built the house near the river, providing us with a prime location. It was here the tradition had begun. The ranchers brought the beef, the farmers brought the side dishes, and my beloved ancestor, one of the town's founding fathers, provided the meeting spot.

The photo before me depicted the Centennial celebration. The trees towering over my back yard were mere saplings then. Shade had been

provided by wide-brimmed hats and parasols. Snow and large chunks of
ice had been specially hauled down from the Sierras the winter before
to provide cooling for the hand-squeezed lemonade. In the sepia toned
photo, children and adults looked stiff and hot, but by all accounts, and
old Joe's journals, a rousing time was had by all.

The history of my mother's family, many of whom stared out from
photos scattered around the house, belonged to the valley nearly as much
as to me. My grandfather--that would be William Robert Martin--third
generation military man, came home from World War Two, took a look
around and saw a need of housing for returning vets, but he hadn't liked
the new style of tract housing.

Being an officer, he'd been a bit removed from the plight of regular folk,
so he chose a parcel of land on the northeastern corner of our spread, on
the far side of the tiny town nearby, and started building. Modest homes to
be sure, but not the miniature boxes being thrown up in squished-together
rows as had been popular in other parts of the country. Full quarter-acre
lots with room for large gardens and children. The semi rural lifestyle
filled with peace and quiet appealed to many of those suffering what we
now call Post Traumatic Stress Syndrome. Minor officers with young
families snatched up the one hundred lots, and the building business
boomed for a few years, expanding Bonchamps from a few hundred to a
few thousand souls.

Not long after my birth, my parents took a leaf out of the old man's
book, but looked closer to home. One acre lots, twenty of them, ten on
each side of the long straight drive leading up to the ancestral home,
backed by a wide swath of open land referred to as the green belt, ringed
by eucalyptus trees. No backyard neighbors to worry about. Plenty of
room for kids and pets in the clean air. Luxury homes for senior officers
close to retirement from the Naval Air Station up in Lemoore, successful
artists looking for a bit of country solitude, and a few minor celebrities
and movers and shakers from Hollywood who couldn't afford Malibu.

Home, as I knew it, was a spot where I'd lived most of my life. The
house, a Victorian built by my three times great grandfather, added onto
by his son, and remodeled a few times, became too large for Dad and
filled with too many memories of Mom after breast cancer took her in
the late nineties. At Dad's offer of mortgage-free living, Burt and I sold
our Las Gatos house and moved home from Silicon Valley just before the
big telecommunications market crash. The one that started falling before
9-11 and almost completely collapsed after. I started out part-time at the
library while Burt took a civilian position at the NAS, which eventually

turned into work for the county. We took our turn at renovating the old girl, bringing her back to life with elbow grease, authentic details and thoroughly modern appliances. All designed to look antique, of course, but packed with the latest in efficiency and comfort.

Taking in the details, I slowly turned. My ancestors would have been pleased with the renovations. We'd carefully opened up most of the first floor and extended it out ten feet with a conservatory entirely enclosed by UV protected glass walls on the east side, giving my next door neighbor, Cyndi, a clear view of my kitchen, living room, and dining room. For privacy, blinds could be dropped and drapes closed. Although I tried, I couldn't remember the last time we'd closed the drapes. It had been years since we'd made love on the dining room table, or the sofa. The very thought opened a hole in the pit of my stomach, which nearly doubled me over in pain. I did not want to throw up my iced tea.

The openness of the first floor also let me see the car driving up the road. It wasn't unusual to see a County Sheriff's Department vehicle in the neighborhood, but this one mildly surprised me.

Though there were a dozen plus deputies, I knew it had to be Dan Weston. I didn't expect the Sheriff to arrive for another two hours and only Dan ever patrolled our exclusive little neighborhood. He couldn't have possibly found any identifying marks on the box so soon, such as fingerprints, which were unlikely as our suspect had probably worn gloves to avoid contact with the highly irritating oil of the poison oak.

Assuming he'd mosey on by like a hundred other times, I watched with only a smidgen of idle curiosity. Okay, maybe more than a smidgen. My heart leapt. Just a little. Funny how when I thought of Burt my heart sank, but when I thought of Dan it leapt. Possibly a message there? Maybe he had super detecting skills I knew nothing about... No, I knew enough to recognize wishful thinking on my part. In real life, forensic mysteries weren't solved overnight. I knew that.

However, I convinced myself that most of my mind was centered on trying to guess exactly when Burt would make it home and how I would confront him. Or not. Today or tomorrow? I hated fighting before a party because it meant we sniped at each other in front of guests. And of course, I always paid. One way or another.

Tomorrow, I decided. Tomorrow I'd confront him and start tossing his clothes out the window. Worked for me.

I also managed to convince myself I had time for a nap, having had no more than two hours of sleep the night before, and I dismissed the presence of the official vehicle. I assumed the sound of tires crunching over gravel came from Dan turning into his brother's drive. However, the sound of footsteps on my porch did catch my attention.

Still enjoying the wind from the fan, I looked over my shoulder to see the deputy of my thoughts peering through a window. He did something of a double take at air blowing up my dress. At least the dress hung below my knees. No chance of him getting a peek up my skirt. I waved him in and reluctantly turned away from the fan, my heart sinking before kicking into double time. Could my heart take all the extra activity? Starting, stopping, speeding up…it made me dizzy.

The door swung open and Deputy Weston, spit shined and polished in his perfectly pressed uniform, stepped inside. He held his flat-brimmed hat tucked under his arm. Even after working the parade, he didn't look hot and wilted. Had he gone home to change?

Before then, I'd never seen him looking so crisply official. It certainly emphasized the devil-may-care good looks that continually had him beating off women with his nightstick. Yes, he had the baton hanging from his fully loaded utility belt, along with his gun and a dozen other tools of his trade. Proper and by the book, he had at least one pair of handcuffs on that belt. Did he ever use those handcuffs for non-official purposes? For a heartbeat, I envisioned him handcuffing me to the banister and having his wicked way with me. Just how big was his nightstick? The one behind those pressed uniform twills.

Mentally rolling my eyes, I let the thought vaporize. Like he would ever really unbend enough to have a personal conversation with me, contrary to the bantering of the night before. That had been business, and the chit-chat had served to make me talk. But then he went and did things like taking a good long look at me. Which he didn't do then.

Because of his younger age, I'd never considered Dan might find me appealing, and any mild attraction I might have felt for him stood no chance against our mutual avoidance, which had been in place as long as we'd known each other. I'd managed to convince myself his *amazing woman* comment was a part of my dreams while in a dead faint.

In fact, other than Burt, I couldn't remember any man ever looking at me *that* way because of my looks. Maybe Jim counted, but usually those looks had come because of the property I would one day inherit, never for me.

I looked okay. No warts, clear enough skin of a berries and cream shade, which I generally protected with hats and sunscreen, but managed always to get a sprinkling of freckles across my nose every summer. Straight hair of a mousy tone hung to my shoulders. No perm, curling iron or rollers had ever made a difference. It had no gloss, it didn't throw off sparks of red in the sunlight, it hung blah-ly from my head, neither thick nor thin. A few inches shy of medium height, I had a medium build including average breasts and slightly more than average hips. Pear shaped. Burt liked to say I had hips just right for fucking. Good handholds. Mr. Romance? Not.

"Dan." I greeted him cautiously. The way he stood, stiff and blank faced, started to set off little alarms in the back of my head. More like a little bell a lady once used to summon servants to the dining table.

"Mrs. Bruckmeister." His eyes shifted to a spot just past my head, indicating a level of discomfort higher than usual. Probably because I'd swooned into his arms the night before. Once more, I wondered how much of me he'd seen and my cheeks burned.

A flash of pink to the left caught my eye and I turned to see Cyndi hurry down her drive far enough to take the path through the hedges. Probably wanted to see why Dan hadn't stopped at her house.

"Would you like some ice tea? Ice water?" Always a good hostess, no matter the circumstances.

"No. Thank you. Ma'am." He swallowed heavily, then reached back to open the door for Cyndi, who'd just run up the four wide steps to the porch.

"Thanks," Dan muttered to Cyndi.

Was I supposed to hear that? He'd called her to come over?

"Dan," she gasped. Not stopping at the door, she came right over to me, wearing a look of tragedy on her doll-like face. My heart clenched hard enough for my blood to feel icy. What was going on? Had Dan told her about the weeds and the note? Those bells chiming in my head became a bit more strident. More like the bell at the drycleaners, the one on the counter to let them know break time was over and they needed to come up to the register and take care of business.

"Ma'am..." Dan started, his voice strangely flat.

"For God's sake, Dan," I said. Exasperation made my voice sharper than I'd intended and he flinched. "You've known me more than half your life, can't you use my name?"

His eyes widened. Clear hazel eyes, a little more green than brown, rimmed by dark brown lashes, their tips bleached by the summer sun, just like the ends of his slightly long golden brown hair. Disgusted with myself for noticing his looks instead of questioning the visit, I waved toward the grouping of seats near the front windows.

Cyndi took my hand, pulled me over to the sofa, practically pushed me down, and sat beside me. She didn't even take the time to smooth her dress to keep it from wrinkling where she sat on it. The perfect southern blonde, Cyndi never just plopped down on a seat. The bells in my head grew louder, more like the bell choir at church, only not quite so pretty.

Reverting back to her best Pensacola drawl, Cyndi cooed, "Oh, honey…"

"What?" I demanded. Already on edge waiting for the cheating scum of my life, this sympathy didn't help.

Dan remained on his feet, but he came to the end of the sofa, forcing me to look up. I hated that. Burt did it to emphasize his power over me and I fought the temptation to jump up onto the sofa so I could tower over a man for a change.

Because Cyndi held me in place, I snapped at him. "Don't just hover there, driving me crazy. If you have something to say, just spit it out."

Dan inhaled and cleared his throat. "Rachel… Your husband…Burt is…dead."

"Oh." Staring at Dan, I blinked. I sensed more than heard Cyndi speaking, as her hands clutched mine. I couldn't hear over the bells of Notre Dame roaring in my ears, as if I stood in the belfry with a dozen different bells of all sizes swinging chaotically. No tune, just great ponderous, vibrating booms and spastic little tinkles filling in the spaces. I almost put my hands over my ears to block out the sound, only nothing could ever be loud enough to drown out just one thought.

Burt's dead.

Burt. Dead.

Damn. I didn't get to kick his ass out. I'd've killed him for that if I could.
Wait. He was already dead.

Dead.

Okay.

I inhaled deeply as I searched for something to say. "Well then, there are plans to adjust…"

Cyndi's hands tightened around mine and, somehow, the cold glass dripping condensation left my other hand. Clammy, cold sweat ran down my back and the stars gathering before my eyes claimed my attention. Lovely glittering black and gold confetti type sparklies. A strong hand grabbed the back of my neck, and forced me forward until my head stopped between my knees.

"Breathe." Soft and strong at the same time, the voice in my ear overrode the bells. Masculine. Not Burt. Kinder. Warmer. Certainly a strange thing to notice, but I breathed because the voice wanted me to. I breathed and listened to the voice even though my skirt partially blocked my air. It said everything would be okay. I had friends to help me.

Shaking off the hands holding me down, my vision cleared and I sat up. "Of course they'll help. Everyone does each year. But we'll need to draft someone else to supervise the beer." The only thoughts I could seize had to do with what other jobs Burt had. Generally he did as little as possible by drifting from group to group, giving the impression of being in charge and doing everything, while actually doing nothing. "Dan, you could take over the beer station. You'd keep people from indulging too much." I slapped my hands on my thighs and prepared to stand. With Burt not coming, I had more work to do.

Dan wrapped a hand around my wrist, keeping me on the sofa. "Rachel." I looked at him. "Well, if he isn't going to be here…"

"Rachel, did you hear me? Don't you want to know…?"

His hat rested on my coffee table, his thigh, his body, tight against my left side, fingers entwined with mine. He smelled good. A bit like leather and country air. The warm hand against my back must be his. A smaller, gentler, more feminine presence hugged me on the right. Cyndi grabbed my hand again and the two of them gently restrained me, like bookends, holding me in place. How different they were. One small and cotton candy soft, the other solid, strong and smelling so darn good.

"How?" The question automatically left my lips. Not that I really much cared other than to be pissed he'd taken away my opportunity to practice some truly evil revenge, but as Dan had pointed out, a touch of curiosity would be expected. Maybe he'd been expecting something more, but I couldn't manage more. Maybe later.

"The coroner says heart attack, but he wants to do an autopsy to be sure."

"If he wants to…I suppose…sure." If it was a heart attack, then why the fuss?

"Do you know where he was last night?"

"A conference of some sort." I frowned at Dan. Hadn't we discussed this? Oh right, maybe this was for Cyndi's benefit. She didn't know about the weeds. Did she? "Some mandatory ethics thing to do with his new job. I can't remember where the conference was. L.A.? Somewhere down there, I think. Only crazy L.A. people would schedule such a thing the week before a holiday. He called last night to say he'd be home this afternoon in time for the party. I expected him about now…"

"Oh, honey." Cyndi sobbed from my side. Why? I wasn't crying, so it didn't seem as if she should.

I stared into Dan's hazel eyes, crinkled with concern. Given enough time, I could have counted his eyelashes. Maybe. He had thick ones, whereas I needed three coats of mascara to make mine visible, much less thick.

The sound of tires on gravel made me look beyond him to the drive. Two men climbed out of another sheriff's department cruiser.

Dan glanced in the same direction and waved to the two men passing in front of the windows. They mounted the steps and entered the house without knocking. Sheriff Mark Johnson and Mayor Carl Arguello. Who next? The fire marshal? The entire town council?

Dan tensed, as if to stand, but my hand gripping his stopped him. His gaze returned to mine, questioning. I tightened my hold, silently begging him to not leave me. The way he held me shifted, grew more intimate, more supportive. Less the news bearer, more the protector. I didn't think to question it. A warm and solid presence, I didn't want to let go of him. Cyndi was the one falling apart, but I couldn't comfort her. Not at the moment. Maybe later.

"Rachel," the mayor said.

"Carl." I interrupted whatever he was gearing up to say and extended my greeting with a nod to include Mark. "Thank you for coming. Dan just--just told me. We were getting into the details."

Mark's eyes narrowed on Dan for a moment and I felt him shrug as I pulled his hand into my lap. The two newcomers sat on the sofa across from us, perched on the edge. Mark wore his uniform, in contrast to Carl already dressed for the party, complete with baggy swim trunks, clashing Hawaiian shirt and sandals. Side by side, they made an almost laughable picture.

"Rachel, Pastor McHugh is coming," Carl said. Another of the crowd from preschool onward, we'd known each other forever. From one of the immigrant families on the far side of town, Carl'd done well, rising to the top of the city political heap. Smart and as honest as a politician could be, I trusted his sincerity. "What can we do? Anything. Just say the word and we'll do it."

Weariness washed over me and I closed my eyes. Honestly? I just wanted them to go away. Somehow I didn't think they would.

Chapter 5

A very important truth hit me, something I'd taken for granted, much the same as most people do.

When disaster strikes, you find out who your true friends are.

I opened my eyes enough to see Mark and Carl exchange a look much like the one Dan and John had exchanged the previous night. Par for the course. Most of the time they thought I was either crazy or too dense to understand the look. I was smarter than people tended to give me credit for, but I forgave them because although they didn't understand me much, they tolerated my oddities--if curling up with a good book instead of hunting for snakes and spiders was considered odd, which it had been back then--when I displayed them, as I'd tolerated, or rather ignored, theirs. Snakes and spiders--ugh. For the most part, people, and by people I mean grownups rather than my littlest customers, never noticed me any more than they noticed last month's bestsellers on the library shelves. But no matter what they thought of my quirks, we'd stood together more than once through the years.

Dan's hand skimmed up my back and under my hair, until his large, warm hand gripped my nape. Thinking he might be preparing to push my head down between my knees again, I leaned back into his hold. It was an intimate touch, far more than the situation required; however, the contact felt right and I didn't move away. Neither did he.

"Rachel," Carl tried again, this time leaning forward, elbows on his knees, looking deadly earnest with gray hair at his temples blending into black. When had that happened? "Burt's body is being brought back from the casino by ambulance. It's going to the morgue at the Naval hospital. Since he's a veteran and all."

"Always a good place for a body, I suppose." Something glittery shimmered before my eyes. I blinked to clear them. "Unless you want to send it straight to Ever Faith Mortuary."

"Rachel, you need to know…to understand…" Pity filled his eyes and I leaned into Dan a little more. Cyndi shoved a tissue wad into my hand, then used another to dab at her eyes.

"I understand," I said. "He's not coming. I get it. That's fine. The party can still go on. It's not like he does much to help out." I looked to Cyndi. "You'll tell John? I'll need help cleaning up the yard tomorrow. Maybe he can organize a few of the neighbors to help." I almost blurted out the fact that I'd be tossing Burt's clothes along with the party trash, but both Cyndi and Dan squeezed my hands like they were juicing lemons.

"Oh, honey." Cyndi sniffled, her big blue eyes looking more so as they filled with fresh tears that leaked over the edges, streaking what little mascara remained right down her cheeks. "Don't you worry about that."

"I'm not worried." I shook her hand enough to get her to relax her grip and turned back to the men watching me from across the coffee table.

Another vehicle pulled up in the half circular drive and parked carefully in front of Dan's cruiser. Everyone in the living room turned to see who it was. Pastor McHugh and Dr. Sorrenson climbed out of the doctor's shiny black sedan. Wow, all the heavy hitters were turning out. Behind them, a county paramedic unit pulled up, blocking the rest of the wide drive. Had they brought Burt here by mistake?

Mark stood and opened the door to the newcomers. Dr. Sorrenson held up his hand and no one climbed out of the ambulance. Was this a new service? Emergency people anticipating a potential emergency? Did they expect one here? Okay, so I'd had ambulances called for me a couple times due to asthma, but those had been completely different situations during especially heavy pollen years. Certainly not in the last six years, unless people insisted on counting the call to Miguel the previous night. Why now? Because of that minor incident?

Down the street, neighbors left their houses, coming out to stand on their lawns, their faces turned in the direction of my house. For a moment I imagined myself out there with them, people drifting together one and two at a time. *What's happening?* they'd ask each other. *I don't know. The sirens weren't blaring…*

A pair of my visitors moved the coffee table back and Pastor crouched at my feet, his frail-looking, elderly hand resting on my knee. He'd been my pastor my entire life; from baptism to confirmation, first communion and marriage, he'd been there for the milestones of my life. A new associate pastor had been brought in to help him ease off a bit and begin edging toward retirement. Not that we'd seen any difference.

"Rachel?" His voice carried more strength than one would imagine. Going on seventy-five if he was a day, he moved with more grace and vigor than men half his age. I'd always imagined I could see a clean, pure white aura shimmering around him, pulsing with heavenly energy. That aura seemed sharper, yet warmer right then. Someone carried in a chair from the dining room for him, but he waved it away. "Rachel, child, tell me what you're thinking."

"No one has volunteered to take over Burt's spot at the beer table for the party tonight. If we could get that matter settled…" I wanted to rub the building ache in my temples, but my bookends still imprisoned my hands.

"Don't worry, lass. The party will be taken care of. Would you like us to cancel it?"

"No, don't do that. What would I do with all the…stuff? No need to cancel the party." I could just see cases of drinks and stacks of paper and plasticware filling the garage for months.

"Fine, fine." He patted my knee. "We'll turn it into a grand wake, shall we?"

"A wake?"

Dan's hand tightened gently on my neck, giving silent approval. It felt good.

"Yes, lass. A wake to celebrate Burt's life. A chance for people to process."

"Oh. I guess that makes sense."

"Now, Rachel, about Burt. Do you want to go to the morgue and identify the body?"

The question hit me as odd. "If you know it's him, then he's been indentified, right?"

I looked over the pastor's shoulder toward the Sheriff. "Mark? He's been identified, right?"

"Yes, Rachel." Mark looked away with a small cough. "I answered the call with my deputies. It was him."

Relief flooded me. Between my grandparents and my mother, I'd seen enough dead bodies to last me a lifetime. "Oh, well, then that's all right." It occurred to me Dan had been trying to tell me something earlier. "Where did you find him?"

Throats cleared and Pastor made room for the doctor in front of me. Dr. Sorrenson's hand gripped my chin and tilted my face up so he could see my eyes. "Rachel," he said in his calm, soft way. "How are you feeling? Lightheaded at all?" His other hand wrapped around my right wrist, strong fingers searching for my pulse. "Your eyes are a bit dilated, your face a tad pale even for you. Are you up to hearing the details? How's your breathing? Is that a touch of wheezing I detect?"

No wheezing, so I shrugged off his questions. "I suppose I'll have to hear it sooner or later. Might as well get it over."

"Brace yourself, honey," Cyndi whispered from my side and I felt a prick of annoyance. All these people knew?

I managed to turn my face toward Dan. Had we been alone, I could have leaned forward an inch and touched my lips to his. "Just tell me."

Emotion I couldn't define filled his eyes and he swallowed before soldiering on with the rest of the news. "He was at the Tachi casino, in the hotel, with a woman. He died while…"

I closed my eyes. I didn't need to hear the rest. With all the evidence in front of me, I could no longer hide from the truth. So many people thought I had the perfect life. A handsome, popular husband, a big house, land, and a good job. I'd even once had the one vital thing that had faded away. Love. Well, love and trust.

For months I'd made him wear condoms the few times we'd had sex, claiming I couldn't orgasm without the stimulation of a certain ribbed brand. Instead of fixing our problems, I'd brought home the highly specialized condoms and insisted they were necessary to my pleasure. Necessary to keeping me disease free was more like it, if I'd never been brave enough to acknowledge my suspicions.

A doormat. That's what most people thought of me. A mousy personality to go with my mousy-colored, lifeless hair. Submissive and compliant to any strong figure. Where did the trait come from? My mother certainly wasn't submissive to my father. She'd run the show, with a very few notable exceptions. My name for one. And my grandmothers, well, there'd never been a more domineering pair of females ever created. Not that my father or grandfathers were weak men. Absolutely not. They were strong men, well matched with strong women, providing absolutely no answer whatsoever for my personality, or lack thereof.

"Rachel, you can change your mind about the wake." Dan got through to me as the doctor's fingers tightened on my wrist, shifting as if he'd lost contact with my pulse.

"Do we…" Oh Lord. We lived in a small town. And he'd died less than twenty miles away from home. As I'd begun to suspect, presumably everyone already knew about Burt's philandering. How many had seen him at the casino flaunting his mistress? As recently as that day I'd seen people flush guiltily and stop their conversations as I approached on the street. I'd seen the smug looks from certain females of my acquaintance. Was I the last one in town to open my eyes?

"Doc, I think she's going into shock," Dan said calmly.

"Who?" I managed to whisper past my tightening chest. It came out on a wheeze.

Someone held my forgotten glass of iced tea in front of my face.

"Take this, Rachel, it's for your asthma," Dr. Sorrenson insisted, with a pill held to my mouth. He dropped it in and pressed the iced tea glass against my lips. The pill felt like an antihistamine I took on a regular basis. I swallowed.

"It doesn't matter," Cyndi spoke up.

"It matters. Who?" I repeated, and sipped more before tea ran down my front.

"No one from Bonchamps," Mark answered. "A woman from San Jose, according to her license."

Oh. Worse, in a way. Someone Burt had probably known from the years we'd lived in Silicon Valley while he worked for a semiconductor company. Had their affair been going on that long? Ten years or more? Was this the reason we'd never had children? If so, Burt had been the world's biggest fool. Children would have kept me busy. More than one doctor had assured me the problem didn't lie with me and could find no reason for me to not conceive, yet it had never happened. Tests had proven Burt capable, but somehow the two ingredients had never mixed properly. At one point, I'd privately wondered if he'd had a vasectomy on the sly and used someone else's samples for testing, but that line of reasoning had never made sense. Then John had moved home with the wife he'd found while stationed in Florida and their babies became mine, Cyndi my sister, and the pain of no children of my own slowly atrophied into a numb spot in my heart.

"Who?" I demanded.

Mark pulled a small notebook from his shirt pocket and flipped through several pages. All for show, I was sure. The man had a mind like a steel trap and could remember every time I'd ever dunked his skinny butt in the city pool. "According to her license, her name is Julianna Worthington. Age thirty-two, with an address in Los Gatos. Know her?"

"No." Not really. Maybe I'd heard the name before as someone Burt did business with. As in, *"You remember Julianna from the Christmas party at Worthington and Smythe Semiconductor. Old man Worthington's daughter. He's put her in my old position and is grooming her to take over when he retires. He asked me to give her a hand. Good business networking is all it is."* The Speech. From about a year before. Or was it the prior month? I'd heard The Speech several times, of course the names and circumstances changed from time to time, but the basic lines were standard Burt.

On the other hand, a touch of relief swept me. It wasn't one of the handful of single women in town such as Cecile the florist, Sonja from the hotel, C.C. Gibbs who'd cared for Mom, or heaven forbid, our tenant Ohm, with the new age jewelry shop.

I saw the people gathered around me exchanging furtive glances. Had they expected me to react differently? When had plain old Rachel ever fallen apart? They'd never seen me crumple and cry. Not when my grandparents died one after the other, and not when my mother finally succumbed to cancer. My father had cried buckets at my mother's funeral, but not me. I'd wrapped my arm him and changed out the tissues he soaked, but I didn't advertise my misery or produce gallons of tears.

I'd had a deal with Cyndi and her children. I was the calm one in the center of the storm. I supplied the bandages, ointment, kisses and hugs chased by the cookies and lemonade she provided to soothe any remaining hurts. She was bon-bons, I was boo-boos. And they expected me to change in the face of Burt's ignominious death?

"Tell me the rest." As long as we were on a roll, they might as well tell me everything now, like a surgical strike.

"Rachel, I don't think..." Dr. Sorrenson began but I shook my head.

"No, there's more, and I'm sure I don't want to know, but it seems the rest of you do know. I can't stand the pity looks, so tell me."

Yes, guilt did flush several faces.

"They were...in the act," Dan said gently. "He died...on top of her." He cleared his throat. "This morning. Just before noon."

Catching one last quickie before heading home to the ball and chain? Had there ever been an ethics seminar? Certainly hadn't been a golf game on a big name course.

"Is that how they were found?" Burt was--had been--a big man. Six feet, three inches, and inching closer to two hundred fifty pounds every year, despite working out and my attempts to provide a healthy diet. I knew exactly how heavy he was. Had he collapsed on me, I would have been trapped. And I didn't qualify as a tiny thing of fluff. If I had the picture of the right woman in my head, lil ol' Julianna qualified as pretty tiny. Amazing, really, that he hadn't crushed her to death. But maybe I was wrong. Maybe Julianna was the tall, athletic brunette. No, she would have been able to push Burt off and perform CPR. Must have been the tiny redhead.

"Yes." Dan's calm response solidified the images in my head.

Shamefully, a giggle escaped me. My heart barely beat, an icy block settled in my chest, and I felt dizzy and sick, but a sense of the ridiculous touched me. "Was she…is she…" I couldn't even ask, not quite knowing how to phrase the question.

"She was trapped for about twenty minutes," Mark said. "It took her that long to, uh, loosen the knots…" He cleared his throat and looked away. "She's traumatized."

Shaking Cyndi's hand loose, I could finally use mine to speak for me and held it up to stop any further words of description. Loosen knots? He'd had her tied up? Well, chalk that one up in the *TMI* column. I didn't care about Julianna whatsherface's frame of mind. Served her right. Call me bitchy, but she'd been the one sneaking around with a married man pushing fifty. A man well past his prime, though still fairly handsome. Frankly, his age and size were the reasons I'd begun to insist on the top position. The thought of him having a heart attack in the midst of orgasm had occurred to me more than once--a la the beginning of *Private Benjamin*--and Burt, being somewhat lazy, hadn't argued. Said he liked the view. I hadn't cared about that. Besides, I could only get a decent orgasm on top.

"So, you're telling me an untold number of emergency personnel, hotel employees, and the entire town council, know the details?"

Several heads nodded solemnly.

"Is it too much to hope everyone will keep their mouths shut about the circumstances?"

Doubt filled the silence. Small town, county grapevine syndrome. The details would eventually spread and the pitying looks would follow me throughout town. Nothing new there.

"For tonight, please, keep it as quiet as possible…" My small spurt of defiance left me and weariness filled the hole left behind. Dr. Sorrenson pressed the iced tea glass to my lips again and I drank deeply, more to please him than from any great thirst.

Finished, I pushed the glass away and leaned against Dan. Why? I'd already come to rely on his strong, solid presence, which fit me comfortably in a way I'd never imagined. I'd known him, known these people around me, more than half, if not my entire, life. Until that day, I'd never once imagined turning to Dan. We'd never been friends. Distant acquaintances, but not friends, casual or close.

"Rachel, do you have pictures? Scrapbooks?" Pastor McHugh would think of something like that. I privately thought of him as an expert in the matter of death. His guidance had been invaluable with all those other deaths in my life.

Sniffling, Cyndi answered for me as I began to cough. "I know where they are. I'll get together a remembrance book. People can write in it tonight."

A hand patted mine as my coughing eased for a moment and my head began to float off my shoulders. Good thing Dan's hand held it in place.

"Your inhaler, Rachel." Good old Doc held it to my mouth and I obediently inhaled. Almost immediately my chest began to ease, taking away the feeling of constriction in my lungs.

"Don't worry, lass. We'll do up a right and proper wake tonight."

I nodded once before my eyes closed and blackness enfolded me.

Chapter 6

I woke with a start to a dark room. Sparkling light came from the windows, illuminating the room around me enough to see I lay on my own bed. Gold, red, green and blue light filled the room, complete with the sound of small explosions. Disoriented and confused, in part due to the heavy fog weighing down my head, I struggled to figure out how I'd gotten there.

Before I could fully comprehend the fact my doctor had probably sedated me while providing medicines for my asthma, a shadow stirred from a chair in the corner.

"S'okay, Chi-chi."

Dad. No one else called me that. A holdover from the Halloween Mom had dressed me as Carmen Miranda. A measure of peace settled over me, calming the panic that had woken me with my heart pounding.

"The fireworks. You've been asleep for hours." His weight settled on the side of the bed somewhere near my waist. The familiar coolness of his hand brushed away strands of hair stuck to my sweaty face.

I'd been groggy from allergy potions before, but something felt different. "Doc slipped me something."

"He did. In addition to a powerful antihistamine, he slipped you a mild tranquilizer. I ripped him a new one for it."

"Thanks. I'll do a follow up."

Dad's hand stopped at my cheek and I turned into it.

"I'm sorry, Chi-chi."

What he had to be sorry about I couldn't fathom. For Burt's cheating ways? For not knowing sooner? For not being there when the town fathers ganged up on me?

Then again, maybe he was sorry for not stopping Doc from drugging me.

Oh, how I hated to be drugged. So much so, I took as little medication as possible, dumping my allergy concoctions the moment the pollen count dropped, and rarely drank more than one glass of wine at a time. Over a long evening, a very long evening, I might drink two with an hour or more between. Burt had once slipped me a pot-laced brownie and I'd been sick for two days. I'd hated it and threatened him with dismemberment if he ever did that to me again. He'd already reached that conclusion on his own; seemed I was as dull stoned as sober. He'd been hoping for hot, unrestrained sex and I'd fallen asleep on him. It had reinforced my belief in Karma.

"Not your fault." Coming awake, I took in more details, such as I still wore my sundress, and lay on top of the covers with a light coverlet over me. No wonder sweat coated me. The weather had been so hot lately I'd been sleeping practically nude and uncovered. With a small fan aimed directly at me, and the AC on. "Dad..." My sluggish brain still couldn't make the words form correctly in my mouth.

"I arrived in time to see you pass out. Dan carried you up here and Cyndi made sure you were laid out comfortably while I called Burt's parents. John's doing the host thing, with lots of back-up. We've been taking turns looking in on you."

"Thanks, but I'm okay. Really." Especially since Dad had already made the phone call I'd just realized I hadn't made. I'd have to talk to the Bruckmeisters soon, but first contact was taken care of.

Dad fell quiet and we listened to the fireworks going off across the river.

"Do you want to watch the last of the fireworks? There's a good view from here."

I'd sometimes wondered, but as we were always at the neighborhood party, I'd never had the chance to find out. What would it be like to make love while watching the fireworks display? Not likely something I'd ever find out.

Dad offered a hand and I accepted his help to sit up, then stand. The comfort of his arm around my shoulders provided support. We pulled open the French doors to get a better view of the bright colors lighting up the night sky.

Two floors down, in the backyard, what looked like a few hundred people sprawled in chairs, sat on the grass around the pool--a handful even lounged in the spa at the end far of the pool--captivated by the show. The water reflected the fireworks beautifully. Faces stared in rapt wonder as fiery streamers shot into the sky before forming graceful falling arches that died before hitting the ground.

Only one person seemed to notice the opening of the doors. He stood in shadow beneath one of the trees, John, Cyndi and their kids nearby, but otherwise alone. Someone had dimmed the lanterns around the edge of the yard and his face hid in the shadows, but Dan Weston looked my way.

Was he concerned? Worried? Or wondering why my husband had cheated on me? Or could he possibly even somewhat commiserate with Burt and fully understand why? Maybe he spared a thought to wonder why someone as confident, strong, handsome and virile as Burt had chosen someone like me. That was probably it. Or what about his comment last night? Had I hallucinated it? Dreamed it up? I nodded, ever so slightly, to convey the message I was A-OK. Awake and somewhat functioning.

Sulfur smoke stung my nose and I pinched it to stop the sneeze building inside.

Dan might've been the only one to notice me then, but if I sneezed that would've changed. After all, I'd been cursed with my father's sneeze when I'd have rather had my mother's. Her sneezes had been small and delicate. Something like a kitten's. Lady-like. The kind of sneeze where everyone smiled, obviously thinking, *How cute!* as they hauled out their pristine handkerchiefs. Instead, I followed in my father's footsteps. When we sneezed, the world knew it. As a child, it had gotten me tagged during more than one round of hide-and-seek on hot summer nights. The damn allergies had plagued me most of my life.

Come to think of it, Dan had tagged me more than a few times. There were nights when I'd swear he'd been stalking me. The first couple years, he'd been small enough I'd easily escaped him. Somewhere about tenth grade, the hide-and-seek games had tapered off in favor of going to the movies, roller skating and finding hidden bowers along the riverbank.

However, there was one hot night when someone brought up the idea of reviving the old neighborhood game. Rolling our eyes, we'd gone along with it to teach the younger kids on the street. The elementary kids I babysat had squirmed with joy at being included.

Dan got elected as the first *It*. As he counted off against the trunk of the old oak in their front yard, I grabbed the hands of two giggling kindergarteners and hurried them off to my third favorite hiding spot behind the lilac bush at the edge of the porch. Perfect place for watching *It* search the circle at the end of the street, since we'd decided to stick to a five-house boundary. Once he turned away to search on the far side of the circle, the spot made for an easy scamper to home base, by running behind the house and coming up from the east. Those gigglers gave away our position and while they ran for base, I ran the other direction, hoping to draw him away from them. That part worked well enough, but over the school year Dan had grown taller than me, his legs longer. Where before

I'd been able to outrun him, I found myself losing ground, fast. I aimed for a loop behind the house, hoping to shake him in the shadows, but he'd been on my heels from the start.

I might have made it, but Dad had laid out a new planting bed with large rocks that afternoon. My hurdling technique was rusty at best since I'd opted out of track that spring--something to do with the discomfort of running with breasts--and my toe caught the large stone marking the corner of the bed. Arms flailing, I flew like an injured goose and landed face-first on the grass. Yes, I was grateful for that small mercy, but not for the grass stains on my new jeans.

Dan landed on me, sending me face first into the grass again. In getting up, his hand grazed the side of my breast, his lips my neck. In pure outrage, I used my arms and tried to do a push-up to get him off me faster. Somehow in him pushing off and me pushing up, we rolled until he lay on his back with me on top of him, also on my back. That wasn't so bad, but where he'd grabbed onto me, well, horny teenage dreams were filled with such gropes. He held my then peach-sized, newly budded breasts, firmly cupped in his hands. And Dan was no longer a scrawny geeky kid.

Mortification!

In scrambling away from him, I didn't stop to consider being gentle. Not having brothers, I didn't quite understand how close I came to gelding him. Instinct told me to get as far away from him as possible. He wasn't quite a freshman, for God's sake! John's tag-along little brother. How dare he feel me up! Too furious for words, I left him writhing on the back lawn. Someone came looking for us, and from my room I heard shouts that brought the neighborhood running. Dan was able to stand a few minutes later and limped from the backyard. Come to think of it, that was probably the last time we'd ever looked at one another until the previous night. I hadn't thought of the incident in years. One of many uncomfortable memories my mind shied away from.

But right then, serenaded by fireworks, we looked. I caught a glimpse of light reflecting off what looked like a glass bottle tipped to his mouth. Most likely soda, since he still wore his uniform.

"You've got many good friends down there," Dad said between explosions. "There are also quite a few people here to gawk and gossip."

The words broke the tentative link I had with Dan and I let my gaze roam. I couldn't make out individuals easily, but clearly a good portion of the town had flocked to my backyard, swelling the usual number of partiers by four or five times. "News spreads fast, eh?"

"Nowhere faster than a small town. It's been an eventful couple of weeks and people are all stirred up with curiosity, with the local drama every bit as juicy as anything in the news."

I couldn't help but flinch at the truth of his words. On the national celebrity level, Ed McMahon, the Publisher's Clearing House pitchman, had died only a week earlier. A few days later, Farrah Fawcett and Michael Jackson had died the same day. One due to a long battle with cancer, the other a heart attack. Or drugs. The coroner's investigation had only begun. I was actually more bummed about the death of Billy Mays, the man who'd convinced me to buy OxyClean. It had been a hell of a summer already.

"You aren't the only one to have a husband die in the company of a mistress today," Dad continued.

The word mistress made me cringe, but the tidbit of news piqued my curiosity. "What?"

A small, half smile twisted his lips but it didn't look happy. "Some football player in Tennessee got himself shot last night. Looks like he was murdered by his twenty-year-old girlfriend, who then shot herself, but the police aren't confirming it yet. They're just guessing. A girlfriend his wife knew nothing about. People have been glued to their iPhones following the updates."

Pain like I hadn't been able to feel for myself stabbed straight into my heart. The poor woman. The wife, I mean. Why did I feel so badly for her, and yet couldn't seem to feel much for myself? My head dropped sideways to Dad's shoulder. "So they're comparing my situation with hers?" That hurt worse than Burt's death.

"Not when I'm in earshot, but yeah. The double sensation has the rumor mills running at full-tilt. The irony of our small town drama eerily paralleling that of a big sports figure seems to make them feel important somehow."

Small town people with their small lives. I knew it well, being one of them. "So much for keeping it quiet." I sighed.

"Wasn't ever going to be a chance of secrecy, Rachel."

True, but I had hoped.

"I know it's soon to be asking. I mean, with you passing out, it's only been in your consciousness about thirty minutes, but there are decisions to be made. For one, you'll need money and the bank might have your accounts locked up come Monday. Don't worry about it. I'll cover your expenses until the money is freed up. Shouldn't take more than the death certificate for your joint accounts."

"Dad, you don't have to…" I had some money set aside no one knew about, but I was grateful he'd offered. I had no idea about the extent of our bank account. Accounts? Burt had handled the money. I had a check card, an American Express, and he'd handed me cash every two weeks. We bought only gas with the AMEX, and I'd never been allowed to use the check card without first discussing it with Burt. If I'd needed more than the usual allowance of cash, he demanded receipts to prove where the money had gone before he gave me more. That experience had been humbling enough the first, and only, time. I'd never risked it again.

"Not up for discussion. I can afford it and it should be a slam dunk. One month, maybe two. I won't notice it." My burst of profound relief died with his next words. "Item two, the funeral."

God, the funeral. Like the money, it was a point I didn't want to deal with. "Let Pastor arrange it. Pull a couple photos from the albums, or I have a stack on my desk. I don't care. Plain and simple. Enough to drop him in the plot."

Somewhat grimly Dad chuckled. "I'll see if there are instructions in his will."

"Fine." I'd read his will, a hundred years ago when we'd had a pair done up. With no children, I couldn't foresee any complications. He'd been my heir, I his. A few bequests to our colleges, some charities, but we didn't have enough to make elaborate plans, as far as I could remember.

The fireworks paused and the crowd took a breath as the last sparkle flickered out. Time for the grand finale. Our fireworks crew did the same every year. Sometimes the pause was a few heartbeats. One year it had been five whole minutes. Rumor had it a connection had broken because the newest kid on the crew tripped over the wires. I looked down at the yard again, right where Dan had been a few minutes earlier. I could see a booted foot, enough to note it pointed toward the house and not the river.

It's probably cliche to say the grand finale began with an explosion of booms and crackling pops and screaming whistles. But that's just what I'd always loved about a Fourth of July fireworks display. Though the crowd didn't know what colors or shapes would burst before their eyes, everyone knew it would be dazzling and spectacular and loud.

Everyone in my yard held their breaths anticipating the glorious all-out end to the half-hour long show.

Boom! Boom! Boom! The rockets left their stands, screaming into the air.

Someone had a radio on and turned up the music. *The 1812 Overture,* of course. Tradition. And it hit me in the gut as it had every single year without fail as the yard lit up. Some of the vets, from Korea to Iraq and

Afghanistan, flinched a little. Dad, a Vietnam vet, was no less affected, but he stood stoically. Had he not had his arm around me, he might have actually stood at full attention, possibly saluting.

Still staring at the spot under the tree, I saw Dan once more. He leaned against it, one foot bracing him against the ground, one knee bent with foot placed on the trunk. He was a vet, one of the first to go into Iraq at the start of the war on terrorism, only out of the service a year because of some mysterious leg wound, but his attention wasn't on the grand finale.

By our gazes alone, we were drawn together like the old Hollywood trick of using changing depth focus, making distances seem to grow closer. I'd always thought it a hokey manipulation. Until that moment. I mean, if Bonchamps were stuck in the early part of the last century, then why shouldn't it be possible for me to fall into a waking dream? As the fireworks exploded over our world, it seemed Dan only had eyes for me, and I for him. Unless I was mistaken and Dan actually stared at my father? The snort meant to be a laugh left my nose before I could stop it. No way on this earth could Dan have heard it, but he broke into a grin.

I just knew God would strike me down. One breath would send one of those sparks to my roof, catch the shingles on fire, and I'd burn to ashes on my way to Hell for daring to snort during the Grand Finale of the Fourth of July Fireworks.

My husband of seventeen years, a former member of the military, patriot to the center of his soul, had broken one of the most sacred of vows. For it, he'd died, caught in the act, with his pants down and his ass in the air. God had seen fit to take care of him. Well, then maybe, if I were actually lucky enough, God would strike me down and end my dull, miserable life right there, right then.

But, no, God had finished with striking down sinners for the day, and He'd gotten a couple really big ones, because instead of being smote by a stray thunderbolt, I found myself smirking back at a man I didn't even like. Yet, because of his kindness to me the day before and earlier in the afternoon, I felt inexplicably bonded to him.

Maybe I was a tad overwrought, hysterical, possibly even shocky, but I found the situation hilarious and I laughed. And continued to laugh until I snorted, then cried, and Dad pulled me into my room, shutting the doors behind us.

The icy dam I'd been shoring up since the previous night broke, and I let loose the wails that had been building up for more than days, more than weeks, more than months. I shrieked and screamed out my anguish until arms younger and stronger than my father's pulled me against a stronger and more muscular chest. Not that my dad was frail. He wasn't. For a man midway into his sixties, he stayed in pretty good shape and a lot of women eyed him speculatively. But there were stronger, younger men around, one of whom had me in his arms. Instead of calming, despite feeling even safer, I added small punches with my clenched fists to the wails and shrieks ripping from my very soul. The arms held me tight enough I couldn't work up much force, not enough to make him flinch at all, but the release of energy worked. For me.

The oddest part was I didn't cry out Burt's name. Not at all.

I cried for that poor woman across the country. My curses were directed at her husband. At all cheating men. I screamed at the Luv Gov of South Carolina, the cheating slime who'd slunk off to South America to visit his mistress. I snarled at men who ignored the fact their wives had sacrificed careers, figures, great hair, clothes and the ability to wear fabulous shoes to keep the lives of their men smooth and comfortable, organized and on track, their children on the honor roll and out of jail. If men didn't want to be the center of their family's universe, what did they want? Had we not evolved enough to have power over, and focus, the instinct to promote the species? Were we not strong enough to control our hormones instead of letting them control us?

A rough voice whispered in my ear, assuring me not all men were creeps. Not all men allowed testosterone to rule their heads or hearts. I didn't believe it. Yes, yes, I had a great example of just such a man in my father. My grandfathers. But many of the men, and dare I say a few women, who passed through the doors of the library weren't very discreet about the games they played behind their spouses' backs. We saw it in the news every day. Example, the governor and the football hero. Hero, my ass. Men worthy of looking up to didn't keep mistresses when they had a wife and kids at home.

I'd never considered athletes heroes, anyway. True champions are those men and women who keep our country safe and protect the rights of others across the globe. Heroes are the people who defend and protect abused children. Heroes are the people who look after the senior citizens and make sure they have heat, lights, food, clothing and companionship.

I was no hero, but I sure knew plenty of them. One of them held me right then, keeping me safe from myself.

The arms tightened, almost squeezing what was left of my rage from me. I clung to that body, dripping tears, sweat and more than a little snot on the uniform shirt with all kinds of stuff poking me. I'd never imagined how hard all those badges and patches were. Not to mention all the stuff on the utility belt. The flashlights and whatnots encased in hard black leather were enough to bruise my stomach. God's truth.

But me, being me, couldn't keep my tantrum up for long. Like a bee sting, something poked my arm. Worse than the stiff badges sewn and pinned on the deputy sheriff's uniform.

Only one thought cleared my mind before dark closed in again. The damn doctor had dosed me again.

Chapter 7

Waking to sunlight pouring through the wispy excuse for curtains in my room struck me as a surreal experience. My eyelids weighed a thousand pounds apiece and refused to stay open longer than the flutter of a hummingbird's wing. The brass band from the prior day's parade practiced inside my head. Old Walter on the bass drum had a particularly enthusiastic beat going. As for the gnomes who'd sneaked a bag of cotton inside my mouth...well, they had just better plan on hiding for the rest of their natural lives. And since they were in cahoots with my needle happy doctor, they'd better warn him to take cover as well. I was pissed and I was coming after all of them.

As soon as I could figure out how to lift a finger.

A feat not as easy as it sounded. Apparently someone had glued me to the bed, like the time in high school when our choir had made All-State. Only it wasn't people who'd been Super Glued. Oh no, the boys in the choir had done worse. They'd glued down the lamps, the phones, the receivers on the phones, the ash trays, you name it. Whatever was loose in the motel rooms became *not* loose with the application of Super Glue. Oh yeah, the parents were thrilled about that little round of high spirits. So thrilled we scraped gum off desks and bleachers for a month.

Another attempt to lift a single eyelid failed.

I heard movement, footsteps crossing from beside my bed to the door.

"She's waking up." Cyndi's whisper sounded about as quiet as a jet engine when she spoke to someone apparently in the hall. The next time she spoke, I could tell she'd turned back my direction. "There, she just grimaced."

Yes, yes I had. She certainly didn't need to shout it out. Particularly since there seemed to be a rush of footfalls, people coming upstairs would be my guess. Didn't seem to be much wrong with my ears, though my eyes still didn't want to open.

I just wanted to know one thing: what had that malpracticing bag of bones given me? I was so going to sue his ass into bankruptcy court. I'd own his house, his practice, and then I'd really make him pay.

The bed dipped at my hip, making me roll slightly into whoever was intent on magnifying my misery.

"Rachel?" Speak of the devil, the old wind bag quack himself.

"Lawyer," I croaked. I wasn't entirely sure that's what they heard, but that's what I'd meant to say.

"Here's some water." A straw poked my lips until I opened them enough for it to slip inside. Sweet, sweet water, cool and wet, trickled down my throat. If there were drugs in this, I'd really sue.

"Lawyer," I repeated.

"Lawyer? You want your lawyer? Why?" Dr. Sorrenson asked, clearly confused. Who did he expect me to ask for?

"Gonna...sue...you." My lips reached for the straw again, but he'd pulled it back and water dribbled on my chin and down my neck.

"Sue? Me?"

I almost laughed at the outraged tone.

"Drug...me...again..." Finally, I worked up some moisture. "Drug me...again...and I'll sue. Mal--mal-prac-tice." Ha! Couldn't keep me from speaking.

Warm chuckles filled the room. Not just the doctor and Cyndi. My left eye finally fluttered open and I had the impression of several people hovering at the foot of my bed. Who did they think I was? Queen Elizabeth? The first one. Like in the movies where her rooms were constantly filled with courtiers. Certainly they didn't mistake me for Henry VIII. His chambers had also been filled with the politically upwardly mobile and the fawning hangers-on. Then again, I might have had a bit of double vision going on.

"I agree with her." Bless my father. He may have sounded amused, but I heard the steely tone underneath. "She doesn't like being sedated, and I don't think it's healthy for her."

"For the most part, I agree," Dr. Sorrenson said. "But her...condition last night was too precarious." Had he meant to say hysteria?

"It was healthy," Dan said flatly. "She needed to let it out."

Go Dad. Go Dan. Their support gave me the strength to open my eye for a full two seconds. Enough to aim my hand at the doctor's tie and grab it. Once in my hand, I held tight, or as tight as a newborn could. I felt that weak and uncoordinated. It was enough to get them to stop talking about me.

"No more," I said as firmly as I could.

Doc Sorrenson had no trouble removing his tie from my pathetic grip. "I promise, no more sedation as long as you don't try to hit people. Hit all the pillows you want, but give Dan another black eye and I'll put you under. Fair warning."

I'd given Dan a black eye? Both eyes opened and searched for the darling deputy. Too intense, the light forced me to close my eyes again before I found him.

"Too bright," I said.

"If you had some decent drapes or blinds we'd be able to accommodate you," the deputy said with a touch of wryness in his voice.

"Humph." Malignant growth. "Water."

The straw once more poked between my chapped lips and I gave a good strong pull. That was why I never drank to excess. I hated the hangover. Sedation hangovers seemed to be just as bad. How long would it take the junk to clear my system? I whimpered when the straw was pulled away, but felt relief at the same time. I was coming out of the effect.

"Rachel?" Dad's voice came from close by my right ear. He must've been standing near my head and the fact I could track directionally encouraged me more.

"Dad."

"Can we get you anything?"

"Some privacy?" As I woke up, so did other parts of my body. I needed the bathroom.

Doctor Sorrenson's hand curled around my wrist. "Pulse is getting stronger. Think you can walk?"

"Unless you paralyzed me or I have a cast on my leg I didn't have before, I think I can walk." I eased my eyes open again, taking it in slower increments this time. The doctor had a small smile on his face. Cyndi hovered behind his shoulder looking anxious. Usual for her when things weren't perfectly humming along perfectly. Her words, not mine.

The deputy hid from me. Granted I had limited line of sight at the moment, but I considered it just plain bad manners on his part. I wanted to see the black eye.

"All right then, we'll just clear the room and give you some privacy, unless you'd like Cyndi to stay and help?"

I glared at the doctor. Cyndi help? I loved her like a sister, really. I also knew her shortcomings when it came to medical type assistance. Not her forte.

"Someone will be right outside. Holler if you need help."

The room quickly emptied of extra people and I heaved a sigh of relief. At last I could kick off the sheets. I felt smothered. The breeze from the covers flying across the bed felt glorious on my sweaty skin.

My almost bare, sweaty skin. I gasped. I was practically naked!

"Rachel? You all right?" The door muffled the anxious voice of my father.

"I'm fine!" I squeaked. Squeaked? Me? All right, I hadn't expected to wake up *en dishabille*, wearing a barely-there chemise type of short gown. So barely-there, it was all but transparent and made up of less than a yard of thin-as-air fabric. One Burt had given me. And that was all I wore. Not another stitch. Naked. As in no panties. Who'd pulled off my panties? The dress and bra I could see, and at least they'd slipped something over my head, but no panties?

Embarrassment sent a heated flush from my toes to the roots of my hair and zinged out to every digit I had. That got the blood pumping and helped me sit up. I only swayed once. One direction. Not to be confused with back and forth. I used the sway to swing myself onto my feet, which then worked well enough to shuffle me off to the bathroom. I didn't trust any of them, so I shut the door. That was all the time I had for contemplating my future before my body insisted if I didn't sit...

The urgency passed, and I began to look around a bit. On the back of the door, my robe. Good. Right next to it, Burt's robe. Not good. I swore to burn that sucker by the end of the day. Or cut it into rags. No, burning seemed better. God only knew what...ugh. Burn barrel, I decided. Definitely. Hindsight said I should have done it Friday night. Just like I should have dumped his clothes rather than put them back.

The shower revived me immensely. Almost as good as a cup of coffee. I set the water to lukewarm and stood under the spray, letting it beat against my skin, wakening my blood even more.

Roughly forty-five minutes after I'd entered the bathroom, I was ready to leave it. Still wet, my hair was combed into its natural born straight style, center part, no bangs. No makeup would ever hide the ravages on my face, so I didn't bother. Usually I never left the house without at least a swipe of the mascara brush and a layer of lip gloss.

I tightened the belt on my robe and pulled the door open. My room was blessedly empty. The debate about whether to put on something other than my robe ended quickly. I had people in my house. Sunlight sparkling on the surface of the pool tempted me for a moment. A nice long swim would be just the ticket...but again, I had people and I had just taken a shower. Pool chlorine on freshly shaved legs tended to sting. Yes, I'd shaved my legs. Not normal for a woman who'd just lost her husband? Sunday was one of my days to shave and changing my routine right then didn't seem like a wise thing. So yes, I'd shaved and applied a liberal portion of lotion to battle razor burn and alligator skin. Knocking on forty's door was no time to give up good habits.

Since I didn't expect to go out that day, I dressed in a simple sundress of well-worn, soft denim. Nothing fancy. Sleeveless, v-neck, calf length, big pockets. A good hang-around-the-house dress, perfect to cover a swimsuit. Bare feet. Most of my shoes lived downstairs in the front closet and I kept some sandals for gardening on the back porch. I'd never been big on wearing shoes in the house.

From downstairs I could hear those people waiting for me, chattering like subdued magpies. Coffee and bacon aromas reminded me I hadn't gotten dinner the night before and with one o'clock in the afternoon approaching, I needed food.

I felt so hungry I wanted to gnaw on the first bit of meat walking past. Right then, as I reached the bottom of the stairs, Deputy Dan appeared. How had I ever missed the fact he'd grown into a supremely beautiful man?

For a very brief moment I wondered if he'd been the one to undress and tuck me into bed, maybe he'd slipped off my panties, and a wave of shyness swept over me until he turned and I saw his eye.

"Ohmigod!" I reached for his face and very gently touched only my fingertips to his cheek, staying clear of the bruising. His left eye had definitely blackened. "I did that?" For the moment my stomach took the back seat. To my knowledge, I'd never hit another human being, much less inflicted such violent bruising--okay, so maybe I'd already hurt Dan once, but it had been unintentional. I'd rather stab myself than cause such an injury. Well, unless it was to beat the crap out of Burt. I could lower my principles for that cause. But to assault Dan? Would this man always suffer each time he came near me? My cheeks burned and my ego shrank to the size of a dust mote. I was not worthy of the care he seemed bent on giving me.

A grim smile twisted his lips. "Let's just say you didn't help it."

"I'm so sorry!" As I already touched him, it was only natural to comb back his hair with my fingers. An odd look crossed his face, but I got one stray curl to lay down where it belonged. My hand stopped at his nape, fingers still buried in his thick locks. To keep a precise, military look, he really needed a cut, but I couldn't find it in myself to suggest it. He still wore his deputy uniform, but wrinkled and tear stained, it looked decidedly worse for the wear. "Have you been here the entire time?"

He didn't smell worse. A fresh soap scent clung to his skin despite the golden brown stubble darkening his jaw. A slow flush deepened the color of his tan. Interesting. The hide-and-seek memory came back to me, and I put a new interpretation on the long ago scuffle. As a grown woman, I wondered how a replay would play out. Double use of the word play intentional. Suddenly I wanted to play. And not that old time version of hide-and-seek. I could think of an entirely new version I wanted to test out and once again I wondered if he'd been the one to strip me down. Probably not, but a girl could dream, couldn't she?

It's possible that, had there been such a competition, I should have been crowned the worst wife in the world. I'd just had my anniversary and roughly twenty-four hours after my husband's death, I'd begun flirting with a man I'd rudely rejected close to thirty years earlier. I could see it then, I had not only rejected him, I'd stomped on him, literally, if unintentionally. The very fact he didn't flinch away from me in the hall spoke volumes for the maturity he'd gained.

I really hated admitting it to myself, but other than our anniversary weekend away, my husband hadn't touched me intimately more than once a month in a long time. I was starved for simple human contact and the little I'd had from this man the day before had been like a single drop of water in a parched mouth. In touching him, a low electric buzz tingled up my arm and warmed the frozen core I'd been living with for some time. Despite the awful swelling and bruising on the left side of his face, his eyes were clear and looked back at me with an expression I couldn't put a name to. Intellectually I couldn't, but my body had its own interpretation.

I wanted to go back to the night of hide-and-seek and have a do-over. Instead of struggling to get away, I would let myself get caught. Instead of flying over a rock and sliding to a stop on my face, I'd find a corner in deep shadows and let him lower me to the ground. Or back me up against a tree. Would the groping of my breasts be an accident then? Or what about Friday night? If I hadn't fainted, might we have made it past the awkwardness and found something else?

Heat gathered in my center, leaving my head short of blood and feeling light as air. Or maybe low blood sugar accounted for the sensation. Or remains of the sedative. Whatever. Dizziness assaulted me and I clutched at Dan. Already darkening, his eyes narrowed on my face and his hands encircled my waist. For the first time in my life, in the grip of his big hands, my waist felt tiny. A feeling to make a girl swoon, as if I needed more of a reason.

Chapter 8

Dan's voice stayed low. "Rache? You'd better get something solid in your system."

Where we stood, we were hidden from those in the kitchen. If I knew those people, and I felt I did, Dad and Cyndi were cooking. Dad liked to putter in the kitchen and Cyndi couldn't stand to be left out. At the moment, she had a running monologue going answered by occasional grunts. No one paid us the slightest bit of attention. An invitation to join me upstairs was on the tip of my tongue when Cyndi let out a shriek.

"Oooh, that bitch. I'm going to rip her lips off the next time I see her. We can *not* let Rachel see this."

"What'd you find, lass?" Pastor's mellow tone did nothing to slow Cyndi's tirade.

"Look what she wrote! I'd throw out the page, but enough other people, kind people, signed it I don't want to, but how do I deal with this?" she wailed.

"Easy, lass, let me take a look…"

Dan leaned forward to murmur in my ear. "She's been going through the memory book from last night. People left random comments and memories about Burt."

I'd heard her mention it yesterday afternoon, but it hadn't really stuck. Given a choice, I wouldn't have made a book available. I didn't want to know what people thought of Burt. I knew what I thought of him, enough said. Their thoughts would be false and give me no comfort whatsoever.

"Hmm, I see what you mean." Pastor's voice carried a frown.

"I mean, really, why would someone write that? '*Your husband will be greatly missed by the women of Bonchamps.*' Oh, what am I saying? Valley slut number one, Sabrina Wakefield. I suppose she could have written something worse!"

"Well now, can't you just cover it up?" Dr. Sorrenson weighed in on the issue.

"Oooh, might work. Print off one of the photos we took last night…" Cyndi had a mission. Good, it would keep her busy.

I could always bury the book with him. Or burn it. Why waste good money on a plot? Better to scatter his ashes to the winds and let him serve as fertilizer. Hey, land for caskets cost an arm and leg when the farmers wanted to plant every square inch of flat ground. However, as much as I wanted him to burn, we tended to not do cremations. In fact, his plot and mine had already been purchased and waited, alongside the rest of my family in the Bonchamps cemetery. Could I kick his cheating corpse out? I made a mental note to ask Pastor.

Dan's hands tightened on my waist. "Would you rather I bring something upstairs to you? You don't have to face anyone today if you don't want to."

As much as the offer appealed to me on sooo many levels, I shook my head. Avoiding the inevitable would only draw out the agony.

"All right. Let's get you some food."

"Coffee," I said.

"Coffee, too."

Dan turned without letting me go and tucked me up under his arm. Just to make sure I didn't collapse on my way across the room, not because it felt so wonderful. Which it did. To me, anyway. He'd probably do the same for any shaky woman he came across.

The minute the others spotted my presence, the memory book slammed shut and the Sunday Chronicle landed on top of it. From San Francisco. We'd always been far too small for our own daily paper.

"Anything interesting in the news today?" I asked.

"Michael Jackson's memorial is scheduled for Tuesday and the McNair death has been ruled a murder," Dad said.

"Lucky for them. Who is McNair again?"

"Former quarterback of the Titans."

"Ah, the ones with the really adorable head coach." The only reason I ever watched football? To gawk at the gorgeous men, of course. Joe Montana will forever rule as my first football crush. Hey, Niners all the way. But Jeff Fisher of the Titans, what a cutie pie. And no one before or since has been as adorable as Peyton Manning. McNair, I barely remembered. Good QB, but otherwise he'd never hit my radar. Not the way Jerry Rice, Brett Favre, or Shannon Sharpe had. There were a few class acts. "And he was murdered by his little floozy?"

"They aren't saying yet, but a gun was found under her body and they aren't looking at any other suspects."

"The wife is always a good suspect." Thank God Burt had died elsewhere. I shuddered. Dan noticed and rested a hand on the back of my neck as he had the day before. Amazing how the touch calmed me right down.

"Not in Burt's case." Dan used his quiet voice, oddly loud in the sudden silence of the kitchen. "Coroner says his initial findings indicate a heart attack."

"Guess those clogged arteries were good for something after all." My attempt at black humor fell flat. "Otherwise I would be the PMS." I looked around the room and noted all the blank faces. "PMS, guys, among other things, also stands for Potential or Prime Murder Suspect. Or my personal favorite, Pass My Shotgun. Then there's Popcorn Movie and Soda. Pre-Marital Sex. Pissy Mood Syndrome. Processor Memory Switch. Power Management System--that would involve chocolate and ice for hot flashes."

"Performance Management Solutions," Dad joined in. He got it.

"Purchase More Shoes," Cyndi added. "Pedi, Mani, Style."

Dan grinned. "Pedestal Mounted Stinger." Ah yes, the military connection.

"Pack My Suitcase," I quipped as faces relaxed into relieved smiles.

"Pepperoni Mushroom Sausage." Dad laughed. "My favorite pizza for those…times."

"Pac Man Syndrome." Dan again. He'd loved the game as a kid. Rumor had it he owned a restored game console.

"Pistachio Mint Strawberry ice cream," the quack said.

"Punish Men Severely." I glared at my doctor, who held up his hands.

"I promise, no more sneak attacks with the syringe."

"Good. Do it one more time and you're looking at a malpractice suit." I delivered the warning with narrowed eyes. "And don't any of you ask me how I feel or what I'm thinking. To settle the questions now, I'm fine except for being ravenously hungry, and I'm not thinking of anything whatsoever beyond food and coffee."

A mug, already filled, slid across the kitchen island. Dan poured a healthy dollop of cream into my cup and made sure it connected with my hand.

How did he know my coffee preference? Except for the occasional mocha indulgence from the café downtown, I liked my coffee strong and blond, sometimes referred to as heavy on the moo.

"All right, Rachel Winifred, breakfast first." Dad slid a loaded plate after the coffee and Dan nudged me onto a long legged stool. Like a soft blanket, comfort surrounded me in the kitchen, truly the heart of my home.

When planning the renovations, I'd taken into consideration a lesson I'd learned years before. People always gathered in the kitchen, no matter how formal the dinner party. With that in mind, we put most of the money into remodeling the kitchen. Thankfully, the first floor had unusually high ceilings--twelve feet, which worked beautifully for our purposes of creating the feeling of a great room.

Since I never sat on the guest side of the granite topped center island, I had a unique view of the unofficial hub. Normally I stood on the business side, cooking up a storm while friends gathered on the stools. Sometimes I'd put them to work chopping vegetables or stirring dips and dressings. Most often I'd serve up little plates and they'd sit, eating and sipping wine while I finished the cooking. Eventually we'd drift to the long dining table off to the side. Or we'd stand around and eat over the island.

That morning I was the guest, sitting and eating while Dad and Cyndi took care of the cooking, which Cyndi'd managed to do between reading pages of the memory book before I'd come down stairs. Cyndi might not have functioned well in a crisis, but she could cook. In fact, we'd done parties together often enough she knew my kitchen as well as her own. I'd earned my share of compliments, but Cyndi could take a simple frittata and turn it into a piece of art. I bowed in the face of her superior culinary genius. Bandages versus baking--a fair trade.

The plate before me held pancakes, scrambled eggs, and bacon. There was also a platter of sliced fruit, possibly left over from the day before, though with the mob I'd seen in the yard, I couldn't imagine there'd been a crumb left behind, much less a plate of fruit. After a sip of coffee-- heaven!--I pointed my fork at the book hiding under the newspaper. "So how many people showed up last night? Roughly." My first bite of eggs tasted like ambrosia. A broken off piece of bacon swiftly followed.

"Since our usual crowd runs about ninety, give or take a few," Dad said, "we're estimating close to four hundred. A few came and stayed only fifteen to twenty minutes. Once they'd heard you weren't coming down, they wrote a note, then eased off. The roads were jammed to the point some folks came by way of the river."

Mouth full, I grunted. I'd bet they'd left, disappointed to not see my reaction. Either that or they'd stayed to take advantage of the party in progress and gossip. I had a feeling the visitors would be starting soon and was surprised they weren't pounding on the door already. As soon as the thought occurred to me, I swiveled on my stool and peered around Dan toward the street. And swallowed to clear my mouth. Did I see a road block?

"The department decided you didn't need people pestering you today." Dad confirmed my thought. "Dan suggested it."

The man of the hour merely shrugged. "We figured you didn't need the doorbell ringing every two minutes and your neighbors were troubled enough last night with the traffic."

"My God." The thought hadn't even occurred to me, and yet, as I thought about the wall-to-wall carpet of people in my yard last night, I could only imagine that in all likelihood, anyone who'd had time off must have been called in. The Fourth was a time when the Sheriff's Department had to be on high alert, along with the Fire Department, the nearby Naval Air Station and the National Guard. "Remind the Sheriff to send me a bill for any overtime not in the budget," I said. We weren't a large county, and heaven knew the budget was tight.

Turning back to my piled-high plate, I caught Dad's nod of approval. "I've already talked to Mark. Whatever extra time is put in up until the funeral, he'll let us know and donations will be gratefully accepted."

The word funeral made my stomach clench hard enough that the sip of coffee and the few mouthfuls of food I eaten threatened to make a reappearance. In an effort to get a grip, literally, I let my silverware drop to the granite with a clatter, and grabbed the edge of the counter. I stared at my father, not seeing him. I saw nothing but the haze closing in around me. *Please don't let me be sick, please*, I begged.

"Breathe," the friendly voice said in my ear. Was that my new mantra? *Breathe*. Right. I breathed.

I inhaled and slowly exhaled. My vision cleared after a few rounds and I blinked the nausea away. In a replay of the previous afternoon, I found a cold glass at my lips. This time I clamped my mouth shut until I realized Dan held the glass.

"Nothing but pure filtered well water, Rache," he assured me. His lips twitched as if holding back a smile, but his eyes were concerned.

Maybe this was why the bereaved sought the nothingness of sedation. Everyone around me had begun to wear odd looks, as if they expected me to fly apart with no warning. Maybe they were right. I'd never been the type to fall apart, or I hadn't thought so until the previous night. Thankfully Dan didn't let go, even when I wrapped my hand around the glass and, by coincidence, his hand.

"It's okay. You don't have to do anything today if you don't want to," he repeated himself from earlier.

Thankfully his hand was there to guide mine as I trembled, unsteady as a toddler learning to drink from an open cup. Would Dad change his opinion on sedation if I asked him for a plastic cup? Or one of my covered coffee cups? The steadying force of Dan's hand as we lowered the glass back to the counter hid my quaking from the others, though they all watched me like hawks. Dr. Sorrenson particularly.

"She'll be fine, folks," Dan said. "You watching her like a specimen in a petri dish isn't helping. Our Rachel is strong and steady, just give her time to get balanced again."

That broke up the concentrated observation.

Our Rachel? When had he claimed me?

"All right, so we hunker down for today. Do a little swimming, sunning, grill a few burgers and just unwind." My dad. All practicality. Calm in the face of any storm. Then again, compared to his tours of duty in Nam, this was peanuts. Gotta love military men.

With a moment to just sit and contemplate, the kitchen filled with the sounds of cutlery on stoneware as people took seconds or thirds of breakfast, it occurred to me I hadn't seen the children or John, or anyone else. Normally by now the neighborhood would be buzzing with the sounds of yard work and children scampering from one end of the street to the other. Instead, it was quiet enough to hear the birds chirping.

"Where're my babies?" I asked Cyndi, and picked up my coffee again.

Dan moved the water glass out of the way, then reached for a piece of my bacon. On principle alone I grabbed his hand to keep him from snatching it away. He had the nerve to laugh at me. As if he'd planned it all along, he lifted the bacon to my mouth. He was feeding me! I didn't know whether to slap him or kiss him for it. The boy had audacity, for certain. Would have served him right if I'd bitten his finger, but I stopped just short of it. There was that bit about the black eye I didn't have the complete answer to.

The delicate sound of Cyndi clearing her throat reminded me there were other people in the room and I wasn't acting like a newly widowed woman, but rather more like a merry widow, which might be appropriate in a few years, but was highly inappropriate right then. I bit off the bacon and let him have the rest. If he wanted it. I wasn't quite sure how he felt about girl cooties these days, or more to the point, my girl cooties. Until Friday night, he hadn't been within touching distance in years.

"We didn't think you wanted to be woken up by the little hellions," Cyndi said. Damn if her blue eyes weren't twinkling with amusement.

Apparently the daring deputy had no problem with my cooties. He ate the other half of the bacon strip and reached for my fork.

I tried to grab my fork back, but he merely scooped up more eggs and brought them to my lips. Fine, he didn't trust me to feed myself. "I'm awake now. There's no reason for John to be exiled to the house with the darlings." I took the offered bite.

Anyone peering into the room, and listening closely, would have heard various variations of choked laughter about then. No one but me called them darlings. As I mentioned before, they were evenly spaced at twenty-three months apart, their birth months lined up with precision. John hadn't had much luck planning the day of their births, but he'd done well with the year and month part.

Aggie, the eldest at age ten, was a cotton candy platinum blonde like her mother. Right down to the huge round blue eyes. They'd named the poor thing Agatha. Who named a child Agatha anymore? Apparently it had been Cyndi's grandmother's favorite niece's name. Or maybe it was her favorite cat's name. Aggie was born the April following their traditional June wedding.

Born in March, just shy of two years later, John William Weston, Jr.--J.J. rather than Johnny or Junior--appeared right on his pre-ordained birthday. Patience paid off, John once told me, his manly chest puffed out with pride.

John's whole demeanor came off as very manly. Like his younger brother, he had beautiful golden brown hair that wanted to curl as it grew out, but his eyes were a true, pure sage green. Not as interesting as Dan's amber-streaked green, but still handsome enough. I'd always adored John like a slightly older brother. A year ahead of me, he'd been there for all the embarrassing moments of my teenage angst. Most embarrassing of all, he snapped the strap of my first bra the first hour I wore it. He paid for it.

J.J. fell to earth, a nut right off the tree. At age eight, he already showed certain signs of his father's personality. The little girls all adored him, and he'd made it a habit to cuddle up to his curvaceous teen babysitters, who adored him, too.

Last, and by no means the least, the absolute darling and apple of everyone's eye was Mindy. A February baby, she'd obediently chosen Valentine's Day. At six she had all the poise and confidence of a true southern belle. Where she'd learned to bat those eyelashes...I swore it was genetic. Something like that couldn't be learned. I patiently awaited the day she discovered the pageant world and had warned John, on more than one occasion, he'd better have a tidy sum set aside for the event. If he was lucky, it might be two more years. Unless I had a sleep over the night of the Miss America Pageant…yeah, the thought had occurred to me more than once.

Mindy inherited John's green eyes, only a shade deeper, his thick hair and a feminine version of his roman nose. Blonde, like her mother and sister, only on her the color resembled pure gold in the sunlight. Otherwise, she was molded after her mother, from the shape of those beautiful eyes to the dainty ankles. According to pictures, her slender figure was identical to her mother's at the same age, so genetics said she'd grow up with similar hourglass curves. Her daddy and uncle practiced at the shooting range on a regular basis.

These were my babies since I had none of my own, though I had been thinking about adopting a dog. A dog would keep me company at night, especially with Burt gone, and the children would help me take care of the pet.

The one thing I really regretted about missing the party the night before was hanging with the kids. I loved helping them make ice cream and sneak cookies while their parents weren't looking. We always jumped in the pool and played water polo with the rest of the kids--including the big ones who were supposed to be parents. Mindy was still small enough she played referee from the side. The players listened. Early the previous summer, she'd picked up the rules from watching and her sense of justice demanded everyone play fair. Just the week before, she'd sidelined her father for dunking me. The kid should have been born mine. Now that I'd remembered hide-and-seek, I wanted to revive the old game here soon. Before the boys got old enough to start getting sneaky ideas.

"I want my babies. Poor John, I bet he's ready for some lunch by now," I said.

"Fine, I'll tell him to bring them over…" Cyndi started to turn for the phone, which chose that moment to ring.

Just to be a smart ass I said, "If it's the press, I have no comment."

Dan's hand tightened on my shoulder. A moment later, he let go to take the handset Cyndi held out to him.

"Weston."

He sounded so official, but who would call him here?

"Fine, let them through, but next time call my cellphone like I told you earlier," he said and hung up. "Florist has a few dozen arrangements wilting in their van."

"Flowers?" As far as I knew, flowers were sent to the site of the funeral. Who sent flowers the day after the death? Dan and I exchanged a glance and he subtly shook his head. No news on the weeds, or no more had showed up. I was relieved and frustrated.

"Yes ma'am. Seems the people of Bonchamps and the surrounding area wish to convey their regards and support to you."

"What am I supposed to do with them?" I didn't want a bunch of flowers cluttering up my house. It smacked of pity to me. Not to mention an increase in allergens I didn't need.

Dad spoke up. "Why don't you take the cards, make a note about the arrangements, then send the flowers on to either the cemetery to be distributed among the graves, or even to the hospital? That way you can acknowledge the thought and share the wealth."

"Bless you, Daddy." Relief washed through me. I normally might have thought of that kind of thing, but the ability was beyond me at the moment.

"I'll do it, honey." Cyndi came around the island to give me a hug. "Don't you stir a muscle, I just need a pen. Call next door and tell them to come on over."

"I'll do it." Dan already had his cellphone dialing. I could get used to this treatment.

"Rachel, if I might suggest...?"

I turned to look at Pastor McHugh.

"You have a digital camera, right?"

I nodded. Cyndi, darn her little fluffy soul, had gotten me into scrapbooking, only I liked to do it digitally while she stuck to film.

"Why don't you get a photo of each arrangement? Someday you might want to do a collage..." Bushy white eyebrows raised, he let me consider the idea.

"I can't imagine... But I suppose. At least then I could say I'd seen each one."

"There's a good lass."

Me and Lassie, we were obedient, all right.

Chapter 9

To say I found the volume of flowers baffling, was like saying the Statue of Liberty was tall. Sort of an understatement. Many of the bouquets made sense. The mayor, the sheriff, the church ladies, the base commander, and a few of my older neighbors. Those I'd almost expected, and they'd probably be followed with some sort of hot dish offering, or the church ladies would organize a week of meals and have dinner delivered at five o'clock on the dot each night to get me through the week. I'd done my share of providing bereavement meals and flowers, I knew how it worked.

What baffled me the most were the other two dozen, or so, arrangements. The florist, Cecile, told me that was all she could fit in the van. Her seventeen-year-old son, Phil, unloaded each vase so we could harvest the cards, take notes and photos, then put them back in the van. Thankfully, Cyndi and Dan put their heads together with Phil, organized the kids to help, and took care of that part.

Dad asked Cecile to do the same with the others at the shop and forward the cards to us. Someone managed to give her a thumb drive to copy the photos onto. I also made arrangements for her to handle set up and distribution of flowers sent to the church for the funeral, whenever that would be. The moment I had access to some money, she'd get a huge tip. When I hugged her, she responded warmly, if a bit sheepishly at first. How many flowers had she sent to Burt's girlfriends? Had he tried to explain them away as business expenses? For that matter, had she slept with Burt?

While I was thinking about a tip, Dad acted on the thought with his wallet out, and forked over several twenties for her efforts.

Even then, when she drove away, three arrangements sat on the porch. I looked at Cyndi, who merely shrugged and directed Dan, John, and Aggie to carry them in. Cards in hand, she marched inside without another word.

Apparently some arrangements were too precious to forward. I have to admit they lent a cheery lift to the strained atmosphere, though they were a bit of a mixed bag.

One arrangement was an obviously costly, huge bouquet. Gladioli, delphinium, roses, and all sorts of exotic blooms made for a tall, gorgeous red white and blue addition to the dining table. When questioned, Cyndi simply said, "The county." Okay, the board had gone all out. Burt had been one of them.

The second arrangement, an old mayonnaise jar stuffed with Shasta daisies, touched me deeply. My library guild ladies apparently had talked the florist into delivering them. Had they been turned away by the roadblock? The flowers had to have come from Mrs. Scarborough's garden. She was ninety if she was a day and had been the librarian when I was in grade school. I'd spent a lot of time with her, roaming the stacks of the air conditioned library over summer breaks. Those flowers meant far more to me than the arrangement from city hall.

The third was a large basket, with a big pink bow on the side, stuffed with flowering sweetheart rose bushes. Blush pink, to match the bow. As far as roses went, I approved. The care instructions card said there were four potted bushes in the basket. When I read the card, *All my best thoughts and wishes for you, Dan,* my knees weakened. Heat washed my cheeks, and a peek his direction confirmed he watched and loved my blush. Heaven help me, the man was definitely flirting with me, and I shamelessly flirted right back! Good thing my guardians had chosen to keep me in seclusion for the day, or the rumors would have taken an even more interesting twist. I could only imagine what they had to say after the previous night. It was petty of me, but I hoped they were still glued to the internet news about Michael Jackson and the unfolding McNair story. Murder-suicide was so much more interesting than a plain old cheatin' heart attack. Right?

"All right, listen up everybody." I clapped my hands and Mindy ran to me. Too big to leap into my arms--and believe me, I missed that--she settled for wrapping her arms around my waist, and I held her close, a bit desperately, to be completely honest. "We're going swimming this afternoon." Silence reigned for a moment. "I know, I know, not a dignified way to mourn, but if it will make everyone happy, I'll wear a black suit."

The reactions were mixed. Dad looked thoughtful, Pastor raised a brow, Doc looked worried then resigned, John kept his face blank, and Dan tried to. Depending upon how much spying he'd done without me noticing, it was entirely possible he'd seen, or heard about, my black bikini. I was tempted to wear it, but as I said, we had mixed company and I'd already chosen my suit for the day. Then again, there was still the unresolved panty question between us.

"Anyone under forty-five who isn't in the pool in fifteen minutes gets an extra dunking. If anyone needs a suit, there are spares in the cabana. I hope?"

Cabana was a loose term for the small tent-like structure we put up each summer, a steel frame structure, which supported a pointed white nylon roof. I'd made sides for it out of striped canvas in seashore colors with a divider curtain down the middle. A couple of baskets held a mish mash of suits bought each year at the clearance sales. I generally had at least one of each size for each gender from toddler to 5X and there were hooks inside for clothes. Boys on one side, girls on the other.

John gave me a quick hug before following his squealing children out to the pool. They'd come in bathing suits, their normal summer wear except for church, and I could already hear the splashes and shouts as they cannon-balled into the water.

Doctor Sorrenson decided to take his leave. Fine by me. Once he was gone, he couldn't jab me with a sneaky needle. I was still groggy enough to resent his method of calming me. What next, Valium in my coffee?

Dad took Pastor out to the cabana. Cyndi looked from me to Dan, who showed no sign of coming or going just yet. Using my eyes, I gave her the signal to scram. I wanted to talk to the deputy.

The screen door slapped behind Cyndi and silence fell in the house. I had a lot to say, yet, words deserted me. Still, there was always…

"Thank you."

Dan shoved his hands in his pockets. "For what?" How a grown man who'd seen action in a warzone could look so much like a teen was beyond me. He didn't quite blush, but he looked like he wanted to.

"For the roses. They're very pretty. I know just where I want to put them so they'll bloom most of the year."

"Good."

Again, I wondered where my competent, confident deputy had gone. Were we back in junior high at the first dance? He stood in the entry where a short stack of folded clothes sat on a bench that dated back to the building of the house.

"I see John brought you something clean. Does this mean you're off duty?" It was like trying to get the shyest kindergartener to tell me the title of his favorite book. In many ways, grown men resembled their younger counterparts.

"Uh, yeah. Off duty."

"I'd like you to stay and swim. Unless you have other plans I'm interrupting…" Absolutely a leading question. I didn't know the status of his love life. At one point he'd been dating Cecile, the lovely florist, but I hadn't seen evidence of a continuance in a few months. "You must be sick of this place by now."

"No, no plans. Yeah, I'd like to stay. I haven't had much time for the kids lately."

Not exactly what I wanted to hear, but I couldn't dislike a man who liked his nieces and nephew. I'd seen him playing with them before, even babysitting so John and Cyndi could get away for a weekend. A few times we'd even competed for the honor of keeping the kids. John and Cyndi had it made in the babysitting department. He was a good uncle and would probably make a good dad, if he married soon. At thirty-seven he was kind of pushing the limit. Then again, at thirty-nine, my expiration date was pretty much upon me. Another reason to curse Burt.

I'd always wanted kids and without any of my own I'd adopted almost any kid who came within arm's reach. I'd added a lot of adopted kids over the years, and had helped increase literacy in the county. There were even a few young twenty-somethings who came by the library for the latest bestsellers and stayed to talk about the last one they'd read.

"Well then. Good. You can put the clothes upstairs and use the shower after swimming…if you want." I didn't want to presume too much. "As I said, there are suits out in the cabana. I'm sure you'll find something that fits." Yeah, I knew he would. If I had to guess, I'd say he was a thirty-six. About six-one, he'd probably have a thirty-four inch inseam. I had to make myself look away. Then again, there had been all those people out back… "Unless I got cleaned out last night. And since I don't want a dunking, I'd better get out there."

"You'll get dunked anyway," he predicted.

"True enough. Um, about your weapon…" I nodded at his waist. "Do you need to lock that up?"

"That would be best."

"I have a safe. In the office. Unless you like having quicker access…?"

A smile matched the amusement in his eyes. "I don't think we're in danger here."

"I don't either." Who'd want to harm me? Actually, it was a good thing Burt was already dead. Had the heart attack not killed him, I'd be tempted.

To get to the office, or rather my library, I had to walk past Dan. Close enough to feel the heat radiating from him and smell him again. Still fresh, with a hint of clean sweat. It had been awfully hot outside with the floral delivery.

Relief swept me as I discovered the door had remained locked from the previous night. Plain good sense with strangers in the house, and there had been an unprecedented number on the property. I still hadn't looked in the powder room to catalog the damage. Had there been enough toilet paper? How filthy were the hand towels? The floor? The sink? Too much to worry about right then. The main reason I'd been planning to build a fully plumbed cabana. As one of the oldest houses in the valley, people were curious about it. I didn't mind small groups looking around, but the night before had been a mob.

Come to think of it, how messy was the yard? How many people had helped themselves to suits and towels from the cabana? I didn't want to think about it.

Next to the library door stood a tall vase with silk flowers. Around the neck of the vase I'd tied a ribbon, upon which hung a grouping of half a dozen old keys. One fit the lock on the door.

"Pretty lame security there, Rumple."

Ah, there it was again. The name he and John had thought so clever so long ago. "Uh-huh. Watch this, Deputy Dawg."

"Haven't heard that one before," he said, heavy on the sarcasm.

"You're so smart, lawman, see if you can open this door." I handed him the key ring. "Do it quietly so you don't wake the neighborhood."

"This room is alarmed?"

"Why don't you try it and see?"

"You're setting me up, aren't you?"

"Oh, like you never set me up?"

He flicked through the keys and finally settled on the middle one, a skeleton key that dated back to the nineteenth century. "My father would have tanned my hide for setting up pranks on a girl."

"Good thing he never caught you at it, isn't it?"

Dan returned my smirk. "Prove it."

"Ha! No wonder you went into law enforcement. I bet you're one of those cops who knows how to plant drugs and alcohol on a pull-over, aren't you?"

"Every cop knows how to do that. I'd just never resort to it. With the idiots around here, it would be taking advantage of the mentally challenged. Unsporting." The key slid into the keyhole below the doorknob and turned, rolling the tumblers around. "Got that part. What's the secret to not setting off the alarm?"

"Hmmm, should I tell you?" I wondered aloud. "I mean, if she can't trust the law, who can a girl trust?"

"The government trusts me, which should be good enough for you." A simple statement, and yet, so loaded, especially when he looked down at me, his eyes with a definite bedroom cast to them.

"Yeah, like they trusted Burt, and we now see how trustworthy he was." We both flinched.

A high security rating didn't mean the person holding it was morally pure, just that the government knew all his dirty secrets so he couldn't be bribed by a hostile entity. Joe Schmoe down the street could be a murderer or pedophile of the worst sort, but if he knew how to program the space station, he'd get top security clearance. As long as he and his friends told the government all about his nasty habits. To my everlasting mortification, I'd had to tell the stranger conducting the security interviews my husband liked to spank me.

Oh that was so bad of me. Obviously my brain was rumpled. "All right, since you're trusting me with your weapon, I'll trust you with my security system. Inside, to your left, is a keypad. You have fifteen seconds to deactivate it."

"Okay, but I need the code."

Did I stop to question why I told Dan this? My dad knew the code, but not the reason behind it. Burt had known the number, of course, and the security company in town knew it. God looked after little children and fools, and since I was obviously a fool--cheating husband? Yeah, I'd turned a blind eye so I was the fool--I went with my gut. But I also needed a little fun, and Dan was turning out to be an entertaining conversationalist.

"Think about it, what would be the most obvious four-digit code?"

"Your birthday. Zero-six-one-seven."

Surprise thrilled me. "You remember?"

"I remember a lot of things." His eyes glanced down at my breasts and held for a long moment before returning to my face. I could almost feel his hands holding me. Wanted to feel them holding me. "But your birthday is too obvious."

Not quite sure how I did it, I found my normal voice, not the lust filled one. "True. It's also my wedding anniversary. Again, too obvious."

"So what else is important to you? I know you like historical facts. The Centennial bash? Zero-seven-seven-six?"

"Not bad, Deputy, not bad at all, but also too obvious. Actually, you'll never guess, so I'll give you a clue. The date I lost my virginity."

That made him choke. "You remember the date?"

"Don't you?"

"I remember who, I remember where, and I remember it was August, but I don't remember the exact day."

Men. I heaved a sigh and he shrugged. How typical.

"September eighteenth," I said. "Nineteen eighty-five."

I wasn't sure if I should be flattered his jaw dropped nearly to his chest.

"You were just fifteen!"

I nodded. Yeah, a most memorable date in my personal history. "Jim Santos had come back for Homecoming the weekend before. I'd bumped into him at the dance."

Face thunderous, Dan nodded. "I remember watching you dance with him."

"You were there? You remember?"

"You forget, I skipped a year. I remember a lot of things. So the code is zero-nine-one-eight?"

"Yeah, and don't forget to add an extra one on the end. Nine will send a silent alarm, indicating a hostage situation."

"And do you know how many people, and by people I mean criminals, know that trick?" He shook his head. "That little stunt will get you killed." Without an ounce of hesitation, he had the alarm deactivated in about three seconds. "I'm now in the inner sanctum. So, September eighteenth, eh? What happened?"

I shut the door behind us and turned the lock. Chances of us being interrupted were too high with the number of people out back. I was breaking my own rule by showing him at all, much less with other people around. If we took too long, someone would come looking for us and I didn't want to be surprised with the hidden safe open. One of the hidden safes. There were two more in the room, hidden in the oh-so-usual spots. I ignored Dan's questioning expression and started across the room, dodging antique furniture.

"The room that time forgot," the smart ass behind me commented. Dan, not my ass, though I secretly acknowledged myself as a kindred spirit. I just kept my thoughts to myself. Most of the time. Tended to surprise the hell out of people when I slipped up and vocalized one of those thoughts.

Didn't mean he didn't have a point. The one room I'd kept as original as possible. Dim due to UV blocking shades and climate controlled for the books, we'd had it alarmed as a separate zone because we kept our most valuable of valuables here.

"It was the week after homecoming. Jim had taken a few days off to come home. We met up after school and he took me riding on his motorcycle. Nothing as exciting as a Harley, but exciting enough for naïve little me." I hadn't ridden on a motorcycle since, and considered it a shame. I really wanted a ride on a Harley, but Burt had finished with his motorcycle days long before we met.

Dan's eyes widened a bit--he had a Harley--then narrowed. "Please, don't tell me he raped you."

"Oh no, no. Nothing like that."

The relief on his face was mixed with something else I didn't want to define, and short lived. "Technically, by your age, it was statutory. I should arrest his ass for that."

"Too bad the statute has run out. Besides, I wasn't complaining." He could ponder that thought for as long as he wanted.

I moved to the mantel over the fireplace on the far wall. The entire surround was thick and elaborate, hand carved oak, beautifully preserved from a hundred-odd years of weekly applications of lemon oil. "Only two people know about the safe I'm about to show you. Me and the guy who installed it." I looked over my shoulder and found Dan closing in on me. "Dad doesn't know about it and neither did Burt. Once Mom knew she was dying, she showed me this cabinet."

"Then maybe you shouldn't show me."

"I want to. Burt's death has shown me that the end can come without warning. I want one other person to know about this." I didn't question my motives any deeper as to why I'd picked Dan as the lucky soul.

"It should be your dad," Dan insisted and put his hand over mine where it rested on the carved wood. "The secret should stay in the family."

Dan had no way to know the pain those words caused. "What family?" I whispered. "I'm the last. I have no children to pass this house on to."

And my husband had left me with no hope of ever having any.

Chapter 10

Dan's hand tightened on mine and for a moment I thought he might hold me or kiss me. It was there in his eyes, but it sat side-by-side with the distance we'd always had between us. Yet, the wall had started crumbling. Had it begun Friday night?

The wall wasn't down yet. I drew in a deep breath to steady my shot nerves. A phrase I never ever thought I'd use in reference to myself--shot nerves. I'd definitely unraveled the night before and hadn't quite put myself back together. "The secret is a hidden lever." With his hand over mine, I moved my thumb under the edge of the ornate molding. "It slides along here, and the door pops open below, like so."

I stepped back and Dan bent to take a closer look. "I'd never have found it."

"It's a bit worn, so it's harder to find unless you know exactly where to look." Latch released, I reached for the three-foot tall column on the left side of the fireplace. On hinges I kept oiled, it silently swung open.

"Very ingenious," Dan said. "Natural seam lines hide the fact the whole thing opens."

"Exactly. And since I'm a bit more paranoid than my ancestors, I had a fireproof safe custom built to fit in the spot."

Not wide or incredibly deep to begin with, the fireproof walls further reduced the useable space, but it was large enough to store folded documents, several stacks of paper money, some gold, and a couple handguns. I spun the dial. "Same as the door, but reversed, starting with the year in two digits, so 85-19-18-09." The door swung open easily. "I'm afraid there isn't room for your utility belt, but there is room for the gun."

"I see you have one already." After my nod of permission, he reached inside and pulled it out. The grin on his face warmed my insides up quite nicely. "Dan Wesson? Did you choose that brand on purpose?"

I wished, though I was looking at smaller handguns of the same brand. Something I could stick in a purse if I had to. My father liked to say, *it's not paranoia to be prepared for any emergency.* Civil war could break out at any time. Or a drug war. "Dad bought it. About the time I started showing signs of puberty."

Dan checked the chamber, the safety, then sighted it, aiming at a painting on the wall. Slightly disheveled, jaw stubbled from not getting a shave, and blackened eye, he looked a bit like a desperado with the gun held out. Put a beat-up Stetson on his head...the stuff of romantic westerns.

"Didn't scare Jim Santos off." With a grunt of approval, he lowered the weapon and took time to look over the workmanship.

"Actually, it did. Dad was a little late by then, but he didn't know it. Jim came to pick me up Friday night and Dad had it out on the coffee table, along with a few other guns. Made quite a show of cleaning them. Probably didn't hurt he had a couple hunting knives out as well."

That got a laugh. "A time honored cliché."

Yeah, the neighborhood men folk had made it a tradition to take the boys out and teach them to shoot. I'd pushed my way into a few of those sessions and could claim a fair level of competence.

Dan carefully placed my gun back in its holder. With a snap, he released the cover on his holster and extracted his service piece. Showing extreme comfort and confidence in handling his weapon, he showed me the chamber was empty and the safety set. "Is that why you chose that date for the combos?"

"Sort of a reminder to be careful who I let into my panties." Was I playing with fire or what? The look he gave me just about singed me.

"A message, Rumple?"

"I...I...I don't know what made me say..." I found myself backing away, my face as hot as a five alarm fire.

"Easy, Rachel," Dan said soothingly. "I'm not going to jump you. I have more manners than to seduce a newly widowed woman, no matter how hot she is."

As if my hand could somehow push my heart back down into my chest, it flew to my throat. Unable to look away, my gaze locked with his.

"Make no mistake." He continued, not moving an inch from where he stood--he didn't have to with the intensity of his gaze. "I do find you disturbingly attractive, despite how you've tried to hide yourself. I remember the young girl with more guts than good sense. I don't know what life has done to you, or that bastard of a husband, but right now I'm seeing more good sense than guts."

The accusation, if that's what it was, made me gasp and flinch. My brain sort of fizzled out. There'd been a big point in what he'd just said and I wasn't equipped to deal with it beyond acknowledging he'd most definitely just staked some sort of claim on me. For what purpose, well, my mind refused to acknowledge it. Men didn't come on to me, so I couldn't be entirely sure that had just happened.

"And if you think that was a compliment, think again," he said. "But you have a good excuse for having a lack of both guts and common sense right now. I like to think you're smart enough to know you can trust me with anything. I'd just about had a small panic attack thinking of you telling the first guy to come along about this hidey hole." He closed the safe, spun the dial and hid it all away again by gently closing the secret door. "I like seeing the stack of cash you have stashed away. Were those all hundreds?"

"Mostly, but there are some fifties and a bunch of twenties."

"About ten thousand?"

"More or less. Mom always said a woman should have some ready cash on hand for emergencies." I purposely, continuously, forced myself to forget it was there, while making monthly additions to the stacks. Over the years it had added up.

"Like having accounts locked up in probate?"

"Or having a sudden need to leave the country." I loved that Sandra Bullock line from the movie *While You Were Sleeping*. I'd taken a lesson from her. "My passport is in there, too."

"The security precautions you have here are good and I advise you to remain extra vigilant. Lock your doors at night. Keep the windows locked as well and set the whole house alarm when you go to bed."

Certainly an odd turn of conversation. What was he talking about? "Are you trying to frighten me on top of everything else? Why?"

In that moment, he looked very tired. Had he slept at all last night? From the creased and wrinkled state of his uniform, I'd already guessed he hadn't gone home, but had he slept here or next door?

"I didn't want to say anything." He dropped his head back and stared at the ceiling. "I shouldn't have hinted at it, but…" His head tilted back down and he pinned me hard with cold eyes. "You're smart, but you tend to not see things right under your nose. You live in an imaginary world where hate doesn't exist. It's wonderful to see such innocence, but the reality of this world will get you killed if you keep on like that."

What? I stumbled against the arm of a settee and perched my butt on it, lest my legs collapse and send me to the floor. "Well then Deputy Dan, why don't you just spit it out? You think someone wants to harm me?"

From his shirt pocket he pulled a plastic baggie with a small card inside. Like from a flower arrangement. Just like the one from Friday night. "This was attached to another bunch of ragweed and poison oak. Like the first one, I think there was another, more irritating substance on the leaves."

"Omigod," I whispered. Once was bizarre, twice was alarming.

"In light of the message, I'm ready to conclude someone *really* doesn't like you and wants to make you suffer. Cecile's kid had no idea it was in the van. He's the one who handled it and he's the one most likely being treated for skin irritation right now. And considering the arrangement from the other night had some sort of extra irritant sprayed on the leaves, I'm sure he's probably more than a bit uncomfortable if these were the same."

"So that explains the fast reaction," I mused. Great. "What does the card say this time?" Despite the evidence, and I did trust Dan to recognize the irritating plants when he saw them, I couldn't comprehend the mindset of the attacker. Had I done something to harm someone? Not intentionally, that was certain. Did Burt's lover think I'd killed him? To spite her? But I hadn't even seen him since Monday morning!

Dan held the bag up for me to read the card inside. The handwriting was the same, and still not one I recognized, but maybe the cops could match it up somehow. Clearly printed in black ink with a bold hand, the message was quite, quite simple.

He didn't deserve to be saddled with you. I wish it had been you who'd died.

This made absolutely no sense at all to me. Yes, someone hated the fact I still lived, but who and why? Had she coveted more than my husband? My house? My inheritance? Or rather, my potential inheritance. Dad and I had been discussing a plan to donate the land to the county for a preserve, or something philanthropic, and the house to the city as a historical landmark, or give it to John and Cyndi to turn into a fancy B&B. It was that, or seek out artificial insemination or adoption just to give me an heir. With or without Burt's approval. Once, I'd briefly toyed with the idea of having an affair, but I'd thrown that idea out as being reprehensible. Go figure.

Speechless, I merely shook my head.

"You don't know who would send this? You don't recognize the handwriting?"

"No."

"It was a long shot," he said as if reassuring me I hadn't failed some test. Apparently he'd moved into cop mode on me. "I'd hoped something might have come to you since the other night. Tell me, did you have anything going on the side, as revenge?"

Now that was laughable and I didn't attempt to hold back. "Me? Have a toy boy on the side? Are you nuts?" That was the funniest thing I'd heard in a very long time. While I howled, I snorted, Dan frowned at me.

"It's not so farfetched an idea."

The irritation in his voice calmed me down, but giggles still bubbled up inside. "Sure it is. The last male to look at me with any kind of lust was Tommy Sanchez when I promised him he was next on the list for *Harry Potter*."

Dan raised a brow.

"He's nine and reading the books in order. Book five has a long reservation list with the fourth and fifth grade crowd."

"Well you're wrong about the male population of the county not noticing you." He carefully touched the bruise around his eye.

That stopped the giggles. "Did you get the shiner defending my honor?"

He smiled grimly. "Maybe. In fact, I'll warn you now, Jim Santos is back in town. He came by last night and was making noises about how..." Dan cleared his throat, "how much he admires...uh...you."

Of course he'd been there, I'd invited him myself. But to get in a tussle with Dan? It didn't make sense. "He swung at you?"

"Actually, it was an accident." Here he looked aside. "J.J. overheard the comment and was going after Jim. I managed to stop J.J. with my face."

Holding back the smile was very difficult. I had to lower my eyes so he didn't see my laughter. "I'll have to find a way to reward my smaller hero. You too."

"Do it by being smart about locking up, all right? Lay low, make your lawyer come here, and handle the other arrangements by phone. Control the situation rather than let it control you."

Boy, he sure knew how to kill a flirty mood. "Hiding out smacks of being controlled," I pointed out.

"In this case you have the excuse of mourning. At least let us provide the impression you're deeply anguished." He held up a hand at my protest. "You *will* be deeply anguished if you have to face the gossip in town."

He had a point. I nodded my reluctant agreement.

I heard the back screen door slam. "We're about to be invaded. We should join the swimmers."

Dan tucked the bagged card into his breast pocket and unbuckled his utility belt. "Might as well leave this here. You'll continue to alarm this room, right?" He moved to within six inches of me and practically wrapped an arm around my waist as he dropped the belt with a thud onto the settee behind me. This brought on a brief fantasy of him undressing right there. *Search me, deputy. Please.* He was close enough to do it, and once more I wondered about what he'd seen Friday night, and whether he was my panty-remover of the night before. I wanted to ask, but chickened out.

"Um, yeah, we can do that. I usually don't during the day, when I'm home, as I'm in and out of here a lot." I waved to the table behind the desk, where stacks of scrapbooking sat waiting for my attention. I also liked to read there in the evenings. "I only alarm it when there are large parties going on. I hide the breakables in here." My lips ran off without me, babbling on like an idiot. Anyone could see the mentioned articles on top of the massive desk. One of my ancestors had loved to spend the winters doing woodworking. Hence the mantel, the desk, several tables, and the hand carved bookcases which lined the two interior walls. Lots of oak and walnut in these parts. Every now and again, Dad pulled out the old tools and made repairs as needed. He'd been invaluable in helping with the restoration and remodeling.

Speaking of babbling...

Dan started casually unbuttoning his shirt and I wanted to put my tongue to another use altogether. "If you don't get moving, I'll beat you to the pool. And for that, I get to dunk you."

And that would be a bad thing...how? Right. Widow. Mourning. Stop flirting. Well, except for...

"Not a problem, deputy." I reached for the buttons on my dress and grinned at the widening and darkening of his eyes. Working the buttons slowly, I eased past him and started backing toward the door. He followed, the hunter after his quarry. "But somehow, unless you're wearing trunks under that uniform," and if he were, they were bikinis, not baggies, "I think you're going to be the rotten egg."

"Oh?"

When the door met my back, I reached behind me and twisted the knob. Since I held the front of my dress closed, he couldn't see anything, hard as he tried. He pulled his shirt from his pants and shrugged it off. Oh my... God had surely broken the mold after making this one. Golden brown hair dusted a torso that could have been the model for David. Not pumped up and over built, he was perfectly formed. Firm pecs, rippled abs, strong arms. They'd have to be strong to have carried me up the stairs. Shoulders of a quarterback, rather than a lineman. And tan. Scrumptious enough I wanted to bite.

That lovely thought was interrupted by Aggie shouting our names.

I opened the door and turned toward the kitchen, where she stood looking around for us. "Here, Aggie. We're just on our way out. Uncle Dan needed to put away his tools."

"You're not in your suit yet?" Her gaze bounced from me to her uncle behind me.

"Uncle Dan is a bit behind the game," I said and let my dress fall off my shoulders, "but I'm ready." The soft denim fell to the floor. Let him get a good look at the low-low back of my black suit. The front didn't cover much more, but it was a one-piece and it covered my ass. Just barely because of the high cut legs, but enough to be decent around the children.

"Race you to the pool!" I zipped past her. Before I hit the grass beyond the patio, she flew past me. The screen door slapped a second time and I knew Dan followed. But he still needed a suit. I laughed as I ran. I hadn't felt so young in years.

I was inches from the edge of the pool when I was grabbed from behind. That dirty dog! He snatched me up into his arms and leaped. I just had time to wrap my arms around his neck before the cool water closed over our heads.

Chapter 11

I had more than a little fun that afternoon.

It was neither appropriate, nor respectful of my late spouse's memory. In all honesty, he wasn't a completely horrid man. After all, my parents and most of the town had liked him. I had fallen in love with him for a reason, it was just a little hard to remember at times.

Grief does strange things to a person. It brings out so many emotions in varying degrees, and it's incredibly difficult to sort them out. This, my father likes to say, is why people really need to allow themselves two years to fully mourn. He also thinks divorce is the same. In essence, divorce is the death of a marriage and should be processed in the same manner. With time and reflection.

So I'll digress a bit and reflect.

To be totally honest, my marriage had decayed like a patient with a slow growing, terminal cancer. It had begun dying in tiny stages, so small I hadn't seen the irreparable damage for what it was. An argument here, a hurt feeling there, a tiny dig of revenge which didn't feel nearly as good as one would hope.

When we met, I was in my final semester of college, and Burt the final months of his last hitch with the Navy, a nice cushy officer position near San Francisco. Upon retirement, his communications, IT, and electronics expertise with the military moved us into the Silicon Valley arena. Burt was so handsome and charming, I couldn't believe my luck. I knew I was plain, especially when I stood next to him or the trophy wives of his colleagues, but I also knew he loved me, and I basked in that love. Life was very good, as long as I didn't look at it too closely.

Seventeen years. How arrogant we'd become as the landmark years passed. At seven years we congratulated ourselves for continuing to live in a relatively blissful state. I was still young, only twenty-nine at that point. We enjoyed long vacations we wouldn't have been able to arrange or afford with small children, we told ourselves. We rarely ate hotdogs and mac 'n' cheese, and then by choice and only gourmet versions. We entertained often and spent weekends in wine country or in the mountains. Burt skied and I greeted him at the end of the day with hot buttered rum and hotter loving in front of the fireplace. I had my beloved books to keep me company, but I was always there to welcome him home. It was the good life and our friends envied us.

Year eight seemed pretty good too, but Burt was approaching forty. He didn't look it, being quite fit, and his light hair didn't show the beginning touches of gray unless one really looked. If we were going to have kids and still have stamina to keep up with them, we needed to start trying. We had a lot of fun with the trying. At first. By the end of the year, I remained optimistic and we went into year nine of our marriage seeking medical advice. The quest to get pregnant became our focus. Or rather, my focus.

Hindsight being twenty-twenty, that was when the little tears in our marriage began to happen more and more, with less healing patching them up. Year ten brought a grand celebration tainted by fermenting resentments. Loving became a mechanical process designed solely to bring about pregnancy. Other stresses took a toll as Burt made the transition into upper management in a highly competitive field on the verge of collapse.

With the dawn of the new millennium, the telecommunications markets took a big hit and many companies heard the bells tolling soon after 9-11. A year later, with layoffs imminent, we moved home.

My home, not Burt's. He claimed San Diego as his home port, but like many military men, he'd moved around a lot and as a result didn't feel a strong tie to one place. The proceeds from selling our home were enough to allow Burt to take on a vastly lower paying job doing IT work for Lemoore NAS to the north of us. I started part-time at the library and with our savings we slowly worked on renovations. Instead of investing in the unstable markets, we invested in the house and a few properties around the county. Of the two of us, Burt claimed the role of money genius, so I left it all in his hands. Every now and again I'd ask for an update and when the markets started improving, he made cautious investments. As far as I knew, we were doing just fine. Holding steady, even making small gains.

Since our savings were finite, I didn't argue when he put me on a tight budget. I economized and started a vegetable garden. Cyndi taught me to can. That was how I started stashing cash. A twenty here, a five there, handfuls of ones and jars of coins, all carefully hoarded, well under Burt's radar. I knew if I showed him my cleverness, he'd reduce my budget and then how would I save up for special Christmas presents?

Incredibly naïve? Most certainly. I grew convinced a woman has an obligation to look at the statements and bills. Neither partner should have total control of the finances. Husband and wife should pay bills and make investment decisions together. Know where the money is! Or isn't, as the case may be.

So that Sunday afternoon, the day after my husband's death, I purposely put my troubles on the back burner and jumped into the fun with both feet. Or rather, let myself be hauled in by the delectable deputy, who'd jumped into the pool with his uniform pants still on. He'd managed to kick off his shoes, but he'd soaked everything else, including his wallet, the contents of which he laid out on a table to dry in the sun. The man carried a nice bundle of cash and the only pictures were of his brother's family.

The lovely day faded into a lovely evening with grilled burgers and fresh vegetables picked from the garden. We ate, drank and laughed. We played and lounged and generally reassured ourselves it was good to be alive.

I also got a sneak peek at the delicious backside of one certain deputy who didn't pull the cabana curtain closed all the way. Sigh. Too bad he hadn't turned around. Cyndi caught me peeking, so I made an effort at ignoring him, as much as he'd let me. My resolve didn't last long. Amazing how often I could surreptitiously touch someone--and be touched back-- while playing water polo. All that contact with wet flesh...

Mind you, we had the children around, as well as my father and pastor. Sort of put a damper on the whole flirting thing. Especially when the day drew to a close and said parent informed the deputy we'd be okay for the night and to thank the sheriff for the continued presence of the force. They'd just ramped it down from a full roadblock to officers taking turns rotating past our neighborhood. Obviously Dad planned to stay. He kept an eye on the proprieties, since I didn't have the sense to do it myself.

Monday morning, the sun rose without a care in the world, never noticing the busy little ants we were crawling across the surface of the earth. The world kept spinning, no matter how much I wanted it to stop. A curse, and a blessing. Burt's father liked to say, *a hundred years from now no one will care.* True enough, but right there, right then, oh yeah, I cared.

I woke with the sun after a night of restless dreams. No drugs had pulled me down too deep to dream. I was almost sorry for that.

In the first round of dreams Burt had been on his knees, begging forgiveness at first, then towering over me, taunting me with his girlfriend in our bed. Dan rushed in at some point and challenged him to a duel with Bowie knives that melted into stalks of ragweed, which left my eyes watering and swollen. I couldn't swallow, couldn't breathe, and I felt my heartbeat slowing, my steps faltering as I tried to reach Dan and pull him away. I woke at that point, gasping for air, my heart pounding.

I'd pulled a pillow down on top of myself. After a peek out the window and a sip of water, assured the world remained stable on its course, I crawled back in bed and drifted into sleep again. A new dream started. Dan, making love to me while Burt stood over us, laughing and giving Dan pointers.

"She likes pain," he said while I cried out my protest. I liked a *little* erotic pain, but not pain for pain's sake. Burt had been blurring that line the past year, making me more and more reluctant to have sex with him. Thankfully, in my dream, Dan didn't listen, but rather, tortured me sensually in his own way, his talented tongue and fingers taking me to the edge but never letting me climax. I woke for the second time sweaty and groaning in frustration.

The emptiness of the big bed felt emptier somehow. I may have been used to Burt being gone a week at a time, but he'd come home for weekends. Like a circadian rhythm, my body acknowledged an absence of so long and then he was supposed to be back. Disconnected though we'd become, I did miss him. I also didn't miss him. Or rather, I wanted him back so I could vent my hurt and rage upon him. Just long enough to kick him to the curb and throw his belongings after him.

Well, I couldn't kick him to the curb, but I could purge his deceitful presence from the master suite. Starting with the bathroom.

I rolled out of bed, wearing a lightweight summer sleeping outfit of shorts and a top. Wasn't going to catch me waking up mostly naked with a room full of people again.

No sooner had my feet hit the floor than Dad tapped on my door. I was beginning to wonder if all parents develop a finely tuned sense that instantly alerts them to the waking of their offspring. Is it an instinct the species is born with, or does it grow alongside the embryo? And once in place, does it ever go away?

"Rache? You awake?"

"Yeah, Dad," I called out. "Just heading for the shower."

"All right. Breakfast in thirty minutes."

"Make it forty-five and you have a deal."

His chuckle came through the door. "All right, Miss Smarty Pants. Forty-five."

Not one to pass up breakfast, or any meal made by someone else, I headed for the bathroom thinking it wouldn't take more than a few minutes to clear Burt's presence from the room. First thing to go, his bathrobe. I spread it on the bed thinking I could toss his toiletries and assorted odds and ends on top, bundle it all up, and deliver it in one neat package to the trash can.

The basic toiletries were easy enough. He'd had a good portion with him in his shaving kit, but back-ups filled the vanity. Spare razor, shaving cream, manly shower gel and the netted scrubber he liked best were easy to toss. Toothbrush, aftershave and spare deodorants. Things got much more interesting when I dug deeper into the drawers on his side of the vanity. I had mine, he had his, and we avoided each other's like the plague. When I bought supplies for him, I left them on the countertop so he could put them away. I figured I'd know what was in the drawers as if I'd put them away myself.

What's that saying about assuming? Right.

The top drawer was normal enough. Spare toothbrushes, toothpaste, a bottle of aspirin and the leftover pain pills from his hernia operation two years before. Spare razor blades, styptic pencil and miniature rolls of floss from the dentist. A comb, brush and tube of hair gel. Dust. How the heck did drawers get dusty? No matter. I dumped the old narcotics in the toilet and flushed. The rest of the drawer I emptied onto the robe.

The next drawer proved more interesting and contained items I knew I hadn't purchased hiding behind the ones I had. Rogaine. Really? I'd never seen him use it. There were also empty, or nearly empty, bottles of prescriptions I'd never picked up for him. Viagra and Cialis. A few which looked more serious and had confusing pharmacological names, and the dates were recent. All within the last three to six months. Not prescribed by Dr. Sorrenson. Filled in San Jose. I set those aside, fully intending to use the *Physicians' Desk Reference* to look up the ones I didn't recognize. If that didn't clear things up, I would ask my own doctor or go see the prescribing doctor. Surely, as his widow, they'd release the records to me, wouldn't they?

There were also herbal supplements and vitamins. Saw palmetto, said to enhance male functions. And…the all natural male enhancement product from TV? Tiger Balm for sore muscles and Bag Balm for softer skin. My, my, my, Burt had been feeling his age, hadn't he?

The bottom drawer was the most telling. Nair. For what? I didn't use it. A box of condoms, not the brand I insisted on, several bottles of cologne I'd never bought. He'd always been a Paco Rabanne man and had refused any others I'd brought home. Fine with me, the Paco had been my favorite on him. So what was with the others?

I forgot all about the cologne when I found a bottle of lubricant. Sex lubricant. Next to it a strange looking gellie...thing. I looked closer and eventually figured out it was some sort of masturbation device. I didn't know the names for such things! But investigation and semi-educated guessing indicated it went with the lubricant. Again, neither item I'd ever seen before. Just where the hell had he been spending the money he said we didn't have to spare?

At the back of the drawer were a few boxes of disposable mineral oil enemas. He'd used one on me once and I'd complained enough he'd never tried it again. How many did he have, and did he use them? I didn't recall seeing them in the trash, but that didn't mean anything. If he'd wanted to hide their use from me, it was easy enough to do. Obviously, considering the unfamiliar items in his drawers.

Shaking my head at the mystery, I emptied the other two drawers onto the growing pile. Under the sink, I didn't see anything out of the ordinary. Toilet paper and extra bottles of shampoo and conditioner. Female products he'd never touch. Cleaning supplies. Nothing special. There was even a box of hair color.

That made me pause and reach to the back. His drawers too full, I supposed, he'd put a box of Sandy Blond men's hair dye behind my traveling makeup bag. The one that hadn't moved from its spot in two years. Burt had been covering his gray? How could I not notice something like that?

Supplements, prescriptions, sex aids and hair color.

Completely gobsmacked, I sat right down on the floor and stared at the box in my hand. He'd always scoffed when I'd wanted to try a different shade. Nothing exotic or wildly different from my natural color, just something to shine it up a bit, make it a little more noticeable. Nicer. He'd always laughed and said I was perfect just the way I was.

If that were the case, then why had he stepped out on me?

What would I find next? Height enhancers? Tiger striped bikini briefs under the whitey tighties? Angry, confused, and hurting, I scrambled to my feet and hurried into the bedroom, where I tossed the box on top of the pile.

Forty-five minutes later, Dad knocked on the door. In answer to my call to come in, he found me sitting on the edge of the bed, still in my pajamas, slumped over, hands hanging limply from my lap. Behind me, the bed was piled three feet high with all Burt's belongings from our bedroom suite. Clothes on one side, thrown into a heap, taking up a little more than half the bed. I refused to fold them. On the other side were things I'd never seen, things I'd never expected to see. Half of which I could guess the uses of, but had never been given the chance to consider exploring.

Sick and shattered, energy drained away, leaving me not much more than a quivering mass of goo. The evidence I'd uncovered led me to believe not only had Burt had affairs--note the plural--but he'd brought them home. To our bed. *My* bed. How had I never once noticed? And it hadn't been simple sex. No. They'd played games here. Dark games. Games involving leather, feathers, restraints and strap-ons.

There were movies and the camera they'd been filmed with, carefully aimed so faces couldn't be identified, though hair color and style led me to believe I recognized a few of his...playmates. I'd found those in shoe boxes stacked on the shelf in his closet where I couldn't see without a stool. I'd pulled over a chair to stand on. There were lotions, potions, vibrators and dildos I'd never seen. Once I'd found those, I pulled mine from my bedside drawer and added them to the pile. How could I be sure they'd been used only by me? Not that I had many, but still...ick. What really killed me was adding my Hitachi wand to the pile. How long would it be before I could bring myself to replace it?

"Rachel?" Dad asked slowly, his gaze zipping past me to the two piles and back again. "Honey? What is all this?"

One hand brushed the tears from my cheeks while the other waved at first the clothes and then the...other. "Exhibit A: Burt's normal life. Exhibit B...The side no one but his floozies knew about."

Dad's lips tightened, pressed together, and his eyes grew stormy. "Is the bathroom cleaned out?"

I nodded.

"Good. Take some clothes in with you and go have a nice long bath. Real long. I'll take care of this."

I could only stare up at him, more tears slowly rolling down my face. I felt like I was five again and Linda Sue Jackson had told me no one in kindergarten liked me because I was bossy and didn't know anything. Daddy had come into my room that night determined to find out why I wouldn't come down for dinner. Teacher had called home to say I hadn't been the same after recess. I wouldn't talk to Mama and I wouldn't play with the friends who came knocking. I didn't even want to play with my dog, a German Shepherd named Gretel who'd been my companion since I was born. When she wouldn't stop licking me, I'd banished her from my room. Confused, she'd curled up outside the door and whined.

It was then Daddy told me how he'd always been small for his age, a constant target for bullies. His father had told him what he was about to tell me. Bullies were really cowards who were jealous of the people they picked on. If Linda Sue Jackson said no one liked me, then the opposite was really true because it meant no one liked her.

But I didn't think he was right. Linda Sue had all the girls on her side of the playground, and most of the boys too. Wise and knowing, Daddy had told me to keep my eyes open. Just be myself, smile at everyone, including Linda Sue. Just smile and be nice. When Linda Sue started being mean, I was to walk away. I could go play near the playground monitor if I wanted to, but the main thing was to just smile, be nice, and walk away. In a few weeks, he promised, I'd see things from a different perspective.

And he'd been right. After a few weeks, hardly anyone played with Linda Sue anymore. They didn't all play with me, but some would and our groups would mingle, reform, mingle again, and soon enough we were all friends. Except Linda Sue. And then I had the opportunity to tell her what my Daddy had told me. It took her a little time to come around, but eventually she dropped her bully attitude and we became great friends through most of grade school, until her dad got transferred and they moved away.

Years later, Daddy once more faced a dejected, rejected me, in my bedroom. Only this time it wasn't the playground bully being mean. It was my husband, the man who'd sworn to love and cherish me, who'd promised me fidelity forever, who'd leveled a devastating blow.

Dad took my hand and dragged me to my feet and into his arms. "I'm so sorry."

That was the second time he'd apologized. "Why are you sorry? I chose him."

The breath he drew in was shaky, but his arms around me weren't. "I saw things deteriorating. I don't know how many times I started to take him aside and have a man-to-man chat. I wanted to so badly, and yet, I'd resented other people interfering with your mother and me. People who loved us and meant well, yet didn't understand our relationship. I was determined to not butt in. But I blew it, baby. I let you down. I was supposed to be there, on your side, making sure he took good care of you. I failed you. And for that, I'm sorry."

The lump in my throat grew big enough to choke a horse. "It's not your fault." I clung to him as he clung to me and I felt moisture soaking into my hair, just as my tears soaked his shirt. "I love you, Daddy, and now it's just the two of us. We're going to get through this. I'll get through this, with your help."

God as my witness, he shook and swallowed convulsively, trying to hold back his sobs. I was tired of holding it in, but too drained to rage as I had night before last. We stood supporting each other, for a long, long time. I could feel the lonely ache in his heart, the hole left by Mom's death. I was all the family he had, and he was mine. We'd made it before, we'd do it again. We had the land. We had each other.

We were drying our faces when the doorbell rang.

"I'll go," he said. "You take your bath. Once I get rid of the intruder, I'll bring back some garbage bags and carry this mess out of here, okay?"

Sniffling away the last of my tears, I nodded. Good thing Daddy had strong shoulders, because I was going to do some leaning.

Chapter 12

When I emerged from the bathroom where I'd allowed myself a good long cry in the shower, I was surprised to see Dan tying a knot in a large plastic garbage bag. The doorbell must have been him. I could hear footsteps thumping down the stairs.

"This is the last bag," Dan said, his gaze taking me in from the wet hair I still combed, the simple chambray dress I wore, to my bare feet, before coming back to my tear swollen eyes. That one look did more to dispel the lingering distaste from my morning's discoveries than anything else I could think of. Even with the darkening purple around his eye. Hopefully it would start fading soon. "Unless you want us to bag up the bedding as well?"

In the shower, I'd been wondering about that myself. I'd loved my set of sheets, quilt and matching hangings on the old four poster bed we'd had modified to work with a king sized mattress. Perfectly coordinated, decorated in navy blue and white. The navy was a concession for Burt, who'd protested at the lavender I really coveted, but I'd made it work very much to my satisfaction. However, if I was going to clean house...

"All the way down to the box spring. I hate to think of what was done on that mattress when I wasn't home." I reached for the hangings, simple panels of polyester netting, and yanked. Silk. I'd replace the canopy swags with silk. In shades of lavender, sage and rose. My haven, my way.

"I take it we're going shopping today?" The smile on Dan's face was a bit grim, but it held a touch of approval as well.

"We?" I noticed he wore jeans and a tan polo shirt rather than his uniform. "I thought you were on duty today?"

"I am, but my duty is to hang out with you and see if your weed sender tries again. We sent the two arrangements and their cards to the state crime lab. Might be some time before we get results back, so we're going to try this the old fashioned way." His grin widened when I frowned at him. "Catch them in the act. Red handed." As if tossing a pillow, Dan heaved the trash bag into the hallway.

"Ah, I see, a return to traditional methods."

"It sucks to be a small force sometimes, but then again…" That smile didn't bode well for my stalker "…there's nothing quite like wrapping your hands around the suspect and slapping some cuffs on 'em."

In light of my discovery, and distaste, of the toys, it was odd that I could see Dan cuffing me to this bed and…interrogating me. A shiver of pure lust made me want to shake myself like old Gretel. A dog. Right. Maybe I'd visit the animal shelter today.

Clearing my throat, I turned my attention back to the bed and resumed stripping it. "Sounds like local forces get to have all the fun."

"Nah, we spend a lot of our time dreaming up some big bust just to amuse ourselves, right before we congratulate ourselves for having a peaceful jurisdiction."

"Is that when you pull into Barb's Donut Hole?" I hadn't intended the double entendre, however, an interesting picture formed in the naughty recesses of my mind.

"Wouldn't want to miss the Deputy's Special, now would we?" And his comment didn't help.

Maybe it was the sex store I'd tossed out of my room, but my mind took to wandering down roads only read about in books I kept hidden in my bedside table. Oh, we had them at the library too, I'd never approved of censorship or book burning, but I kept them tucked away beside the psychology section under Human Sexuality. The reference librarian's desk had a direct view of the section so the under-eighteens didn't stand a chance at sneaking peeks or checking them out.

Curiosity tweaked, I eyed Dan and his cocky grin. What had I been missing? Deputy's Special? Or was that, Deputies Special? Special Deputy? "Is there such a thing?"

"Sure there is."

And what was that wicked twinkle in his eye about? It only fueled my fantasies at the moment. Burt hadn't looked that good in a pair of jeans in ten years. Then again, Dan was twelve years younger than Burt. Two years younger than me. If I jumped him, would that make me a cougar?

I pushed *that* thought away and forced my mind back to the repartee. "What is it, this deputy's special?"

"I can't divulge the details and it's not on the menu. You'd have to pass the initiation first."

"Initiation?"

"Sure, all deputies new to the department have to go through it."

We had the mattress completely bare. The man was seriously good at the banter-to-distract thing. I'd have to remember this sneaky side of him.

"Your dad and I can get the mattress downstairs. You want all this stuff donated, or taken to the dump?"

Something else I'd deeply considered under the shower. Oh God, I'd have to replace the hand-held shower unit! The desire to drag Burt out of his coffin and strangle him grew to be almost overwhelming.

"Burn the bedding…and the *accessories*." What else should they be called? "Donate the clothes. Do you think the homeless shelter could use them?"

"Don't worry about it, we'll find something. John's out front with a truck. We'll see everything gets where it needs to go."

"And when do I hear about the initiation?"

"You're not even close to being ready to hear about it." There, the twinkle came back and my world felt balanced again. Weird, considering I carried a bag holding the remains of my marital bedding. Pillows, drapes, sheets and even the quilt I'd loved. Thankfully it wasn't an heirloom or I'd have been especially pissed.

At the bottom of the stairs, I discovered more helpers. In fact, Mindy had a grip on a bag making odd noises as she dragged it across the floor. It certainly didn't contain clothing or bedding.

"Mindy!" I dropped the bag I had and rushed after her. I pictured the bag snagging on a nail or rock and tearing open to reveal things she shouldn't be exposed to.

John looked up from where he heaved bags into the truck. "What? Leave her alone, she's doing a good job."

"John Weston," I growled and pulled the bag from her hands. "Sorry sweetie." I spared her a quick smile and turned on her father. "John Weston, you should be ashamed of yourself putting this precious angel to work hauling such nasty stuff."

All male innocence, he spread his arms and shrugged. "What?"

I thrust the bag into his stomach and held it there until he wrapped his hands around it. "You would be extremely sorry if this bag ripped open while your little baby girl hauled it out to the truck."

He frowned at me as if I'd gone insane and opened the bag. "Holy Mother!" It was almost entertaining how his face drained of color. Hard to do under his tan, but he managed to look ghostly gray. I think he would have loved to burn the bag right there. Or take it home and thoroughly check it out. Instead, he closed it with the tightest knot I'd ever seen on a trash bag.

Hands on my hips, I couldn't resist scolding him. Some men were just too cute for words and John could be one of them. "If you're going to put her to work, you have her pick dandelions. You do not have her dragging Burt's trash out of my house."

Aggie popped up from the back of the truck. "What's that, Daddy?"

The last time John's face turned that red, he'd been caught with his hand up Becky Dorn's skirt at the Sadie Hawkins dance. "Never mind, sweetheart. Get the last bag settled and we'll just run this stuff right on into town. Got the donations separated from the trash? Rachel, are those last bags for the dump?"

Considering the bedding hadn't been washed, I nodded.

"Alrighty then. J.J., you're with me. Aggie, you and your sister do whatever Rachel needs you to do. Hear me?"

"Yes, Daddy." She vaulted the side of the truck bed and landed like an Olympic gymnast, disappointment tingeing her voice. John had the presence of mind to tuck the bag he held behind the seat in the cab. Given half a chance, Aggie would have poked her nose into it. Even J.J. eyed it with curiosity.

"Better make the dump your first stop." I gave the comment my driest tone and got a glare in return.

Dan and Dad came up behind me with the mattress. John pulled me out of their way, leaned close and dropped the volume of his voice. "No shit, Sherlock. I want the details later. You can't put a bag of stuff like that in my hands with no details."

"I don't know where all it came from and I don't know who it got used on, but it wasn't me."

John gave me a hard hug. "Don't worry, it's gone." He jumped in the truck and drove away.

Mindy didn't allow me time to watch the intimate garbage of my life fade away. She tugged at my hand, reminding me I needed a dose of little girl hugs. Despite her size, I lifted her into my arms, grunting like a baboon. She'd grown so much and I felt my age when lifting her, but I needed the scent of candy-soft baby girl. Just enough of it clung to her still to be comforting. Like all my adopted babies, time refused to leave her alone.

"Don't be sad, Rachel. We're here to give you all the hugs you want."

Thank you, Lord, for providing me with an earthbound angel.

Her sweetness got me back into the house, where I spent the rest of the day making and taking phone calls. The lawyer called to say he'd come by with the wills late that afternoon--Burt's for obvious reasons and mine to discuss updates. The bank confirmed I needed to get them a copy of the death certificate and I'd be set. The credit card companies agreed to put holds on his cards and they also wanted copies of the death certificate. The morgue wanted to know which funeral home would get the body. The funeral home wanted to know how I wanted to proceed, the date and location of the funeral, and which casket I preferred. I promised to stop by the next day to choose, since Dad wouldn't let me order a plain pine box. The church said they could accommodate a funeral on Thursday or Friday. I chose Thursday, and had to call the mortuary back. Thankfully they could also accommodate me. And last for the day, but by no means the last official I'd have to deal with, the county recorder's office--how long did it take to get multiple certified copies of the death certificate? They seemed to think I could pick them up on Wednesday.

Somewhere in there, I'd managed a phone call to Burt's parents, but more important to my frame of mind, the nearest furniture store. I knew exactly what mattress I wanted. John and Cyndi did the pickup run for me with a stop to grab a set of plain sheets and a few pillows. At least I'd have a place to sleep, since Dad had moved into the guest room. Sweet thing that she was, Aggie washed everything for me and made the bed. Santa would have a new iPod for her at Christmas.

Mindy, my little darling, worked by my side and sorted out pictures of Burt while I worked the phone. She didn't understand Burt's disgrace and we, the adults, did our best to pretend we missed him. I let her pick her favorite pictures of him from the scrapbooks and photo albums and found it interesting she mainly picked ones where he was with me or John's kids. She had a picture in her mind of her Uncle Burt and that was what the world was going to see. J.J. found a poster board and made color copies of the pictures. Together, he and Mindy assembled a collage for the funeral. For the big one to set beside the casket, Mindy chose the last photo of Burt in his dress whites, and we gave it to Pastor to use it for the program and the obituary going into the more popular newspapers in the area.

For the most part, it seemed like an exercise of going through the motions, because the people I spoke with were far more knowledgeable on the subject of death than I. Dan listened in, and Dad provided support, assistance, food and iced tea as needed. He remembered the drill from previous deaths. His parents. Mom's parents. Mom. The list was becoming unbearably long. Sadly, it always grew, never diminished.

My lawyer arrived at Miller Time. A man who reminded me of the old country lawyer stereotype, David Levitz had been our family lawyer as long as I could remember. Soft leather briefcase tucked under his arm, he also carried a casserole sent by his wife, wrapped in thick dishtowels and still hot from the oven. One wouldn't get this kind of service in a big city.

Cyndi sent in a pitcher of iced tea--no beer left after the party, I'd been extremely sad to hear--with a plate of cookies. Dad settled down in one armchair near the fireplace while David took the other. That left me an ancient settee. Reluctantly, I sent Dan and the kids from the library. Nothing had been comfortable about the day; I didn't expect going over the wills to be easy, but neither did I anticipate any surprises. But when David asked Dan to shut the door, one of those pesky little alarm bells tinkled in the back of my head.

I was so not liking bells those days.

"I'm sorry for your loss, Rachel," David started off gently.

"I'm sorry for the truths uncovered by it."

"Makes things more difficult than they already are," he murmured and pulled a moderately thick folder from his satchel. "However, for your sake, timing was good."

The first niggle of dread hit and I carefully set down my glass. "Go on."

Wrinkled by a lifetime of California sun, David looked older than his early sixties. He'd inherited my family's legal affairs from his father. He knew us. And his deep brown eyes looked sadder than I'd ever seen. "I'm waiting for more information, but late last week I was contacted by a lawyer from San Jose inquiring about certain details concerning the Martin family lands."

Ice hit my veins and from the corner of my eye I saw Dad tense up.

"What? Why didn't you call me immediately?" I demanded. Had Burt started writing a new will? Had anything been signed?

"I got the message late on Thursday and was in court on Friday. I called him this morning, but he was out of the office and I haven't heard back yet. I wanted to have all the facts. I'm also hoping, in light of Burt's death on Saturday, that nothing was signed and the will I have is still in force."

If these shocks kept up, I'd have to check into restful mental facility. Shady Acres or Sisters of the Agave. The mythical ones who distilled tequila, grew limes and avocados, and had a deal with a corn chip maker. I'd heard their Friday night mandatory quality control sessions were one of the better perks of membership.

I wasn't sure I was up to all these surprises. For a moment, I thought about McNair's wife and how she was dealing with similar shocks. Maybe we could form a support group for widows done wrong.

"That said, there's another possible complication."

"There's more?"

David gave me a worried look.

"I'm not going to faint. Just spit it all out."

Taking refuge in looking at the papers in his hands, he pursed his lips, drew in a deep breath, and let it out. "It's entirely possible Burt may have a child by another woman. A child whose mother might try to place a claim on the estate."

Chapter 13

How many hits could I take and still get up off the floor? God and Burt, weren't done with me. Fine. Well, I wasn't down for the count. Yet.

"Who? When? Where?"

David quite possibly had a good idea my frame of mind bordered on fragile and pissed. Forty-plus years of dealing with the law had probably exposed him to just about every human emotion possible. He just wasn't used to seeing it in me. Mousy-doormat-never-complains-low-maintenance-Rachel was dying fast, and spitting-mad-out-for-bear-Rachel was taking her place even faster. Devastated-distraught-ready-to-beat-someone-or-something-Rachel had the complete attention of the two men sitting in the library. Pretty much like the version of me who'd been sedated twice on Saturday. David had obviously heard about the sedations because he glanced at Dad, silently asking if I was going to suddenly become the Tasmanian Devil. The cartoon one.

"The information came from the lawyer representing the woman who called in his heart attack. She claims she's pregnant and swears the child is his. Of course we'll require DNA verification," he said quickly, answering the demand forming on my lips. "However, as the child is unborn, her attempt is a long shot at best."

"How soon before a DNA test can take place?"

"By Amniocentesis, after the fourteenth week of pregnancy, so we're looking at three to four months before testing, at the earliest. Results take about a week, according to the limited research I did this afternoon. She could drag it out much longer."

"And what will that do to probate?"

"Depends on how aggressive she gets. Could draw it out." David paused, watching my face, which from his expression was probably as pasty white as dumplings. "Rachel, I'll make it my top priority to secure the documents from the San Jose lawyer. I've also passed on the message about DNA verification. It could be she's angling for an out of court settlement, thinking you'll want to keep everything as quiet as possible."

"Blackmail? She thinks blackmail will work?" I could hear my voice rising in pitch, yet could do nothing about it. I had a vise closing around my throat.

David nodded. Did that mean he understood I wouldn't settle without a fight? "Do you suspect any others might come forward?"

"Others?" I squeaked. Considering I hadn't expected what I'd heard so far, how could I possibly guess about that? For all I knew, he had one or more families scattered about. "What am I supposed to do about the money in our accounts? His life insurance? Damn, I forgot to call them today." I dropped my head into my hands and leaned forward, elbows digging into my thighs. "I don't even know what bills are due. I have no idea how much money is involved."

Dad's welcome presence settled beside me. How much I needed him. For a moment, I wanted Dan there. What the hell? In just a few days I'd come to depend on him as if he were my husband. Fortunately I recognized my skewed perceptions, but I couldn't twist them back to normal again. I wasn't sure I wanted to.

"We'll figure it out after the funeral, Rache."

"The funeral," I echoed. "What does his will say about the funeral?"

Papers rustled and silence fell for a few heartbeats. "He leaves the arrangements up to you. Burial in the pre-purchased plot in the Bonchamps cemetery."

"Can I move him outside of the family section?"

"Um…" Dad hedged. "Let's discuss it a little later. We'll need to talk to the cemetery."

"I'll buy a new plot if I have to. I don't want him near me in the hereafter. I don't think old Joe would like having him in amongst the Martins." That would be Joseph Reginald Martin, the one who'd built this house nearly a century and a half ago. Burt wasn't his kind of kinfolk. I was sure of it.

"We'll talk," Dad promised. "Anything else, David?"

"That's all for now. If you need money, Rachel…"

I shook my head and suspected Dad did as well. "I'll manage." It wasn't as if I were destitute. I worked full-time these days as the head librarian. My salary wasn't stellar, but it was respectable and I didn't have a mortgage. As far as I knew, we had no great debts. A payment on my car, but I could sell his truck to pay off the loan. Or most of the loan. Where was my car, anyway? His wallet? Luggage from his trip? Too many things to think about. I wanted to go up and crawl into my bed.

"I'm sorry, Rachel," David said quietly. "You don't deserve this pain. I'll be in touch with any new developments."

From some hidden well deep inside, I found the ability to raise my head and extend my hand. "It's not your fault."

"I'll do the best I can to see this through quickly for you."

"Thank you."

Warm and kind, he squeezed my hand. "I'll see myself out."

Alone. I needed to be alone. "Dad," I whispered. "Go on. I just want to lie down for a bit. Right here."

He hesitated for many reasons, two or three of which popped to the top of my head. But he didn't argue. After making sure I had a pillow for my head and a light afghan over me, he slipped from the room, but left the door open an inch. In case I called out, or so he could peek in on me, or probably both. Another one of those lingering habits of parenthood?

Curled up to fit on the settee, I did my best not to think. At times, that might be possible, but this wasn't one of those times. My head ached and I didn't know if I'd ever breathe normally again. Visions of my life scrolled past my eyes and I sent out silent cries to my wise ancestors. Grandfathers and grandmothers who certainly had some wisdom to share. Did not at least one of their spirits reside in the very bones of the house? There'd never been a hint of a ghost, but I would have welcomed one if only they could find a way to communicate with me.

The depths of Burt's betrayal--make that betrayals, plural--were inconceivable. I didn't think I was such a horrible person that he had to go to such lengths. Had he been planning to leave me? Why didn't he just come out and say it? How hard would it have been, if he was no longer in love, to say, "I'm leaving. I want a divorce"? I wouldn't have fought him. Possibly questioned, but I would have agreed. If he'd known anything about me, he would have known that. I'd never fought Burt, not even on the big things. What he'd wanted, he'd gotten. It had never mattered how I'd felt about anything. So, why all the hidden maneuverings?

But above all, if I was so unlovable, why had he married me in the first place? He had pursued me. Why? For the house and land? There were other women with bigger legacies, better connections, out there. What had made me so attractive to him?

There were, of course, no ready answers. Eventually my eyes blinked one last time and I drifted into a fitful doze.

I woke to darkness and the feeling of someone watching me. The presence was calm and comforting rather than hostile. A warm hand rested on my cheek, then smoothed the hair away from my face. Nice.

"Time to wake up, Rumple. You have to eat."

Dan. He sat on the floor, face mostly level with mine. Light from the hall illuminated the back of his head, leaving his face in shadow but his voice, his scent, how his presence made me tingle, easily identified him.

"You're still here?" I didn't push his hand away, rather I turned into it. Fresh soap, a mild vanilla mint I recognized from the hand-milled bar in the powder room. Recently washed hands. Nice. A man who washed his hands before touching me.

"Not leaving."

"More poisoned posies?"

With one finger he brushed my temple. "Nothing to worry about," he said softly.

Damn. Another nasty flower delivery. What did the sender want? I'd read plenty of mystery novels and true crime, but not one story line popped up to help me figure this out. My brain felt short circuited. Numb. Fried.

Sleep. If I could just sleep it all away, maybe in a week it would be all better.

"I'm not hungry." More like I didn't want to move. Now or in the near future. In fact, I couldn't imagine ever feeling happy again. Unless he kept touching me.

"Not an option. I expect at least ten healthy bites. Then we'll go for a short walk. Just down the block and back."

"Did you know he colored his hair?" Why the hell that popped out of my mouth, I had no clue, but there it was.

"Figured it out when I saw the box." Didn't faze Dan a bit. Did he encounter this type of randomness in the people he protected and served?

"He never would let me color my hair. Every time I talked about it, he laughed it off. Said I didn't need to. Said I was pretty enough without it."

"Well, he was right about that. Can't fault the man for having the good sense to marry you. He lost big points later on, though. His taste in women went right on down the hill after you. But once you've had the best..."

Okay, so I wasn't drugged at the moment. Maybe he *had* called me the most amazing woman in the world the other night. Although stunned, I still didn't buy it. If I was so damned amazing, then why weren't men chasing me down the streets? Why didn't construction workers whistle at me? Why had no one ever tried to grope me in the dark at a cocktail party?

"I've heard," Dan said softly, "some women say a new cut or color gives them a lift. Doesn't change who they are inside, but it perks them up a little. If you want to change your hair, go for it, but do it for you. Not for anyone else. Hell, I'll even drive you to the salon if you want."

Peering at his face through the dark didn't reveal much. All I had to go on was the gentleness of his hand stroking my face and hair, the soothing rumble of his voice.

"So you think I should do it?" Did this mean he really did want to see me change?

"Rachel." His head dropped forward as he groaned in a very hopeless male way, the one I knew said he didn't understand anything about the inner workings of my brain. The exasperation he expressed, I recognized as purely male. "Don't do this. No head games with me. It's simple. Do it or don't. Won't change how I, or anyone who matters, feel about you."

Sigh. Men. No help at all. But now he'd brought it up, how did he feel about me? Pathetic, me thinking like a teenager instead of a middle-aged woman. "You serious about taking me? Because I don't want to do it here in town. Gossip. I also need a dress for the funeral."

"We'll make a day of it. Where do you want to go? Hanford? Visalia? Carmel? San Luis Obisbo?"

"You'd go all that distance for me?"

"Wouldn't do it for Cyndi, might for Aggie, definitely for Mindy."

I laughed, just a small snort of laughter.

"Aggie wouldn't appreciate it quite like Mindy," he explained quickly. He was right; Aggie'd just as soon go to Hanford and get it over with as quickly as possible. She'd do lunch readily enough as long as greasy burgers edged out white linen.

"Do the girls need dresses for the…Thursday?"

"I have no clue." He sighed. "What have I just agreed to?" Yeah, he groaned, but he didn't really mean it.

"Carmel," I decided. It was a little over three hours drive, but he'd offered. "I want to spend some time at the beach. I want sea air. And if all else fails, if I can't find anything in Carmel…" The eyebrow lifted again and I couldn't stop the smile. "There's always the Gilroy outlet mall."

Maybe he regretted the offer, but he smiled while shaking his head. "Great. If we're going to make a day of it, then we need some dinner and to talk to our *compadres*." With natural born athletic grace, he unfolded from the floor and pulled me up with him. "They're starving and don't want to wait dinner any longer, so up you go."

I could feel the tension between us, like an elastic string trying to pull us together. I wanted so badly to lean into him, to feel his arms around me, his lips on mine. If anyone had asked me to place a bet on it that minute, I would have bet everything I owned, would ever own, that he felt the same. But we both held back. Even when he cupped my face with both hands.

"Rachel," he whispered. "I want..." Abruptly he released me and stepped back with a snort of disgust.

"Dan." I reached for him and he took my hand, but stayed two steps away.

"No, Rachel. Not now." But he had a gleam in his eyes. He very much wanted to do...something. Right then.

I wanted it too. "But--"

"No." He cut me off. "Your husband isn't even in his grave yet. You need to work through the stages of grief. You're not ready."

"Oh, I'm ready." That much I knew.

"No, you're not." He said it with such conviction I stared at him. "I'll explain later. But I know you're not."

"Fine. Question for you, then."

He nodded.

"Is Burt's body still at the morgue? Does the coroner still have it?"

If he were startled by the change of subject, he didn't let it show. "Why?"

"I want a complete...exam. Autopsy? I want to know what was in his bloodstream and I want to know if he was fertile."

That did get a raised brow. "Why?"

"I want to know if he had a vasectomy or was he able to impregnate a woman."

A quick blink was his only outward reaction. "Okay."

"Can they determine that after death?"

Dan shrugged. "There'd be some scarring from a surgery. I suppose they could determine that much."

"Good. Do you have a way to contact the coroner directly?"

He nodded readily enough, but the question was there.

"The mistress is claiming she's pregnant. I want to know as soon as possible if she's lying. I don't want to wait until the baby is born."

Sympathy filled his eyes. "Would you like me to call?"

"Will you get in trouble? Is the investigation closed?"

"Pat and I go way back. Doesn't hurt to ask, now, does it?" And then he smiled.

That smile was really growing on me.

"If you don't ask, the answer is already no," he said.

"I also want to know what medications, or drugs were in his system."

"Anything specific?"

"There are some bottles upstairs."

"We'll drop them off on our way out of town. Does that work?"

I nodded and he squeezed my hand lightly.

"Good. Get out to the dining table before your dad comes looking. He's been giving me the eye today."

"What? He doesn't trust you?" I knew Dad trusted him to keep me safe, but I didn't think Dad was blind to the growing feelings between Dan and me. He'd proved it last night when he kicked Dan out. He'd probably do it again.

"Oh yeah," Dan chuckled, "he trusts me to try and steal you away. Which I'm going to try to do tomorrow. We'll probably end up with lots of company."

"Too bad." I sighed. "I've always wanted to ride in a 'Vette."

Gleaming in the dark, the look in his eyes thrilled me right down to my core. "Let me make this phone call first, then I'll see what I can do."

Chapter 14

I should have considered myself lucky part of my wish came true. Not much about the whole situation felt lucky to me at that point.

Friday at noon, dressed in all our black finery, some more fine than others, we climbed into my father's Cadillac SUV and headed for the church. The catering company had orders to not let anyone in until we called to say we were on our way, and I reminded them the library was alarmed and if tripped, I'd get a call on my cellphone. Which would be a bad thing in the middle of my husband's funeral.

The funeral *had* been scheduled for Thursday.

However, things had a way of changing and plans got adjusted.

Ten after noon, we arrived at the church. Dan drove and Dad played escort. I would have preferred it the other way around, but Dad wouldn't have accepted any other arrangement. He'd been watching all week and clearly knew of the growing feelings between me and the dashing deputy. And Dan did look very dashing in a dark navy suit. Not his uniform, though he certainly was entitled to wear Navy dress, but he refused to accord Burt the least consideration as a retired member of our country's forces. I didn't blame him a bit.

Pastor met us at the door and led us around the sanctuary to the anteroom off to the side of the altar.

Waiting--the service would begin at one--we mostly sat and I drew in the peace of the church. We'd been over all the details, so there was little to say. The hearse from the mortuary would arrive a few minutes before one. Pastor had given the pall bearers their instructions, so they'd be on hand at the front of the church. In fact, we were so well practiced and choreographed I didn't have to worry about one detail. Not even a handkerchief, as Dad and Dan each had half a dozen stuffed in their pockets. I had nothing to do but think about what had passed and what would come to pass.

Monday night as Dan had led me to dinner, I was certain I knew how the week would work out.

Wrong.

Dad had more news for us.

On Saturday, Burt's effects had been brought home by the sheriff. In all the upset, the items had been stashed in the front closet and forgotten. While I'd napped that evening, Dad had opened up the suitcase and briefcase and sorted out their contents.

The contents of the briefcase had been illuminating, to say the least. In addition to a safe deposit box key I'd never seen, we found unsigned, but definitely in progress, a new will. A draft with mark-ups and notations for his lawyer. Also, paperwork for Burt's life insurance--fortunately also unsigned and not filed--designating a new beneficiary. Whatsherface. That Julianna person. No wonder she had her lawyer on me. This was the policy from his job with the county and worth three times his annual salary. Not taking his recent raise into account, it was still worth in excess of three hundred grand. Bet she was crying over that. She'd been expecting Burt to divorce me and marry her. Because of the baby she said she carried?

That led to more lawyer conferences on Tuesday. And phone calls to the nearest banks trying to locate the mysterious box. And insurance company, pastor, and mortuary conferences. Thankfully the funeral director made arrangements with the Navy to do whatever needed to be done in accordance with the wishes of Burt's parents. They expected a funeral with full military honors, so who was I to buck their final request for their eldest son?

Schedule changes came about because Pastor said many people had inquired about a viewing. As if they had a choice in this? However, despite Burt's lying and cheating on me, he had been a beloved resident of Bonchamps and the county. Like McNair, despite all the investigation uncovered, people didn't want to acknowledge the disrespect he'd shown his family.

During our marriage, Burt had charmed our community and they wanted to remember him for his past good deeds and not the rotten heart within him. So the schedule changed. It also worked better for the Navy representatives.

The shopping I did on Tuesday involved caskets and funeral items instead of couture. Also, since our local paper only came out weekly, notices had to be printed up and posted all over town. The printing place put a rush on it and on Wednesday Cyndi took the kids into the local towns and asked store owners to post the notice in their windows.

The viewing, which I'd planned to skip, slid into a Thursday evening time slot. That meant embalming and makeup. Open casket. My least favorite type of funeral. Burt's uniform had to be found. Thankfully, Dad had thought ahead and had rescued it from the Good Will pile and stashed it in the guest room closet. The details came raining down until I had only Thursday afternoon for shopping, which ruled out Carmel. A quick look online narrowed my search down to Ann Taylor. That meant Fresno. Yes, Fresno. Not the first place I generally thought of when it came to high-end shopping. Go figure. They had a mega mall with nice stores and all the amenities anyone could ever want in a one-stop shopping experience.

Cyndi found a salon and made me an appointment for the full treatment. Hair, facial, nails, pedicure. I drew the line at body waxing. We compromised on my eyebrows.

By Thursday evening, I was dressed in one of two Ann Taylor little black dresses, modest heeled pumps, spray tanned bare legs--nylons in that heat? No way!--wearing a black hat with a modest brim, the whole of which was draped with a square yard of black organza veiling that disguised my new do. I refused gloves--I didn't want to hide my newly manicured deep red nails, to Dad's horror--but accepted a lightweight shawl to cover my bare arms. Yes, both dresses were sleeveless and above the knee. The fact they might be mistaken for cocktail dresses didn't bother me. After all, where had my husband been when he'd died? Uh huh. If my feet could have stood the four-inch Blahnik's I'd seen on sale, I would have worn them, but Dan reminded me funerals meant a lot of standing and walking across grass. I really wanted those shoes, not the least because Dan really liked them too, if the way he'd stared at my legs had been any indication.

Why two dresses? Two events, both were on sale, and I hadn't been able to choose between them. Dan, bless his soul, had stuck to his word to take me shopping. We'd even gone in the 'Vette, though we had the rest of the Westons following us in their SUV. Oh darn.

Friday I was very thankful I'd bought both dresses, as the one I'd worn the previous night had been spilled on, both coffee and punch. Wrinkled beyond redemption, I'd tossed it in the trash the moment I'd removed it. How decadent to toss away a sixty-dollar dress after only wearing it once! At least it had been on sale.

The adventure to the mall on Thursday had been the best part of the week. While football fans snaked their way through a football stadium to pay tribute to their fallen hero in Tennessee, I shopped and prepped for another tribute. How my heart ached for that other wife. I hoped she had as supportive a network around her as I had.

Tied up shopping for her children's clothes, Cyndi hadn't been on hand to provide advice at the salon. I was secretly relieved. Dan, Lord love him, patiently looked on while I pored over the style books. In the end, he'd counseled against a drastic color change--I was torn between blonde and deep burgundy brunette. The stylist sided with him on color, but agreed with me on a shorter, flirtier style. And as we waited for the funeral, my new hair remained hidden under my hat. Since it was a shock to me, I knew it would bring a whole lot of comments, and now wasn't the moment to reveal a *new me*. That would happen soon enough.

I'd never had a *Style* hairdo. Straight, parted in the middle, shoulder to mid-back in length. Period. My entire life. Boring. The color could be called ash brown if one were kind. Mouse brown if honest.

This cut was, well, as daring as the bobs of the twenties. Short, short, short layers in back, fluffed up high on my crown by product (mousse and some sort of wax) and the length angled down to just below my chin, making the most of my straight hair. My color had been enhanced to a warmer, more golden brown and highlighted with cleverly blended streaks of blonde. Good-bye boring librarian. Part of me wanted to throw off the hat, fluff up my styled hair and wow the crowd with my new look. The conservative, compliant side was terrified of how I'd be judged.

Even Dan, who'd said he liked me without any changes, was amazed by the transformation, if his wide eyes and open mouth were anything to go by. Cyndi just about flipped and told me it was cute, but it was *sooo* not the time for it. John gave me a quiet wink of approval and the kids told their mother to chill. I looked pretty, in their words. And that was that.

Me. Looking pretty. I never thought anything like it would ever happen.

We'd all rushed home to change and head for the viewing. I played bereaved, hiding behind my veil, letting Dad do the talking, and did my best to avoid looking at the open casket. The stainless steel military version with the flag imprinted on the inside of the lid. Dan had found it at an online discount casket house in Hayward. Overnight free delivery. Seventeen hundred dollars instead of six thousand. I'd really wanted the eight hundred forty-nine dollar casket, but with the military presence nearby, and Burt's parents...sigh. I bowed to a modicum of pressure.

I really must have been out of it, because I blinked when the hush fell over the church as I stepped into it for the actual funeral. The type of silence I was growing used to, the kind that fell when, I, the subject of discussion walked into a room. No time to look around more than to notice the church was full to bursting, I was gently pushed onto a hard pew bench. Dad to my left, Dan to my right. No cushions for us. More of the good hearty oak used to build the church a hundred years ago and polished by a thousand posteriors. When my grandfather Martin died, his insurance money had gone to the church to renovate and modernize. Ceiling fans and air conditioning, as well as a new furnace and some electrical updates. Maybe some of Burt's insurance, the policies he'd nearly dumped me from, could be used to buy the church upholstered cushions. Let his slut sit on that.

Bad thoughts. Bad, bad, bad thoughts. I needed to numb my brain to get through the day. If I didn't, I might stand up and give my own eulogy. A more honest version. The night before Dan had told me it wasn't a great idea. I accused him of stealing all my fun, when in reality he'd stolen my breath with a smoldering look.

The music started and Pastor took his spot in front of the altar.

The casket entered the church, wheeled forward by an honor guard of uniformed men. Thankfully the lid was closed and draped with a flag. The previous night had been bad enough. Easels holding large framed photographs of Burt, in winter blue and summer white dress uniforms, flanked the casket.

Why line caskets with satin and velvet?

Red, white, and blue flower arrangements flanked the photos, and from there the floral offerings from the world in general filled the altar, floor and tabletop, leaving little room for the pastors to move about.

The service flowed over and around me as I viewed it through the black haze of my veil and an extra dose of antihistamine to counteract the floral tributes and the grass at the cemetery. Just in case. But the veil, wow, what a fabulous invention. I'd never worn one before and the different view of the world mesmerized me. Dad pressed a handkerchief into my hand and I made a show of dabbing at my eyes under the gauzy drape, surprised to find tears on my cheeks. And here I'd thought I'd finished crying.

I stood when a hand under my elbow lifted me. I sat when an arm circled my waist and pulled me down. When it came time for communion, Dad pulled me to the front, to go first. I lifted the veil only far enough to sip from the cup. As I turned to go back to my pew, Burt's father clasped me in an anguished embrace. Both of Burt's parents had come from San Diego, arriving late the afternoon before. Much to my relief, since Burt's two brothers had come along--thankfully leaving their families behind-- they all had rooms at the local hotel and planned to leave in the morning.

They wouldn't be happy to learn most of Burt's things had already been disposed of. Thankfully, the crush of people coming up for communion forestalled any more outbursts from his family. We'd never been close and I didn't feel like starting.

I had no idea how long the service lasted, but finally, the men in uniform stood once more and wheeled the casket into the aisle. Dad escorted me behind it as they solemnly marched out of the church, carried the casket down the steps, and loaded it into the hearse. Our car was already parked behind the long black vehicle and Dan held the door for me to climb into the back, followed by Dad. No receiving line. Someone had changed the plan without telling me. Just as well. I didn't feel up to accepting false sympathy from people there for the show. I figured fifty or so out of the crowd who'd showed up really did wish to offer comfort. The rest were there for the sensationalism.

"Hand me that hanky, Chi-chi."

Automatically I held out the surprisingly damp square of linen. He replaced it with a dry one.

"You're holding up well, Rachel," Dan said from the front seat. The car was running and the AC blew on high.

"What's next?" I asked, even though I knew.

"Cemetery, then reception at the house." Dad lifted the veil and draped the leading edge on the hat brim. "You'll get more air this way."

"But--"

"The side windows are tinted. No one can see in."

Relief fizzled through me and I looked up to see Dan's eyes in the rear view mirror. "A few more hours, Rumple. You can do it."

"Am I really falling apart so bad?"

"You're doing great," he said. "Just keep it up for a few more hours and then the crowds will be gone. Okay?"

"Okay." I looked to the right, out the window beyond Dad. "Did a lot of people show up?"

"Yes, a good turn out," Dad said.

"Did they come for the show or out of true respect?" I wondered aloud. I didn't expect an answer.

"I'm guessing the church was split with both. Some people really did like and respect him."

"That's good, I suppose. I'd hate it if they only came to gloat."

"Very little gloating going on."

Did I see Dan and Dad exchange a look in the mirror? "Did she come?"

Neither man spoke, they knew who I meant. Julianna pain in the ass-- aka The PITA, as opposed to *puta*, but she was that too.

"By your sudden uncomfortable silence I'd have to guess she did."

"We don't know for sure, but there was one other veiled woman in the church. I would guess it was her," Dan finally answered. "Looks like we're ready to go. The motorcycle escort is in front of the hearse."

"He rates a full military honors funeral and a sheriff's escort?" I shook my head. "Amazing. All for a liar and a cheat."

"Easy, Chi-chi." Dad double checked my seatbelt and Dan eased forward, leading the parade behind the hearse.

Everything proceeded according to plan, except for the fact my ability to go along was fading fast. I wanted to rip off my hat and show the world my new look. I'd already made a statement with my blood red nails and skimpy-for-me dress. Of course the dress was black, but the appropriateness for a funeral ended there. The A-line, above-the-knee skirt gathered under the empire waist. Above that, two triangles of fabric covered my breasts, leaving a nice section of cleavage showing, and thick braids of fabric formed the straps. In the back, it wasn't low, but neither did it reach my nape. I showed a little skin. Again, no stockings, and I wore low heels. I could have ditched the hat, pulled off the pearls- -a fifteenth wedding anniversary gift, earrings and necklace--put on sparklies, heels and gone out to a party. I'd felt my mother-in-law staring at me all through the service. Along with Burt's brothers.

Fortunately, the drive to the cemetery wasn't long. I'd done as threatened and purchased a second plot, away from my mother's family section. The Martins of Bonchamps would have rather seen him lynched than buried in the hallowed ground they occupied. I perked up a bit at that thought. When the stone carver had asked me what I wanted on the marker I'd told him exactly what I wanted it to say.

Here lies Burton Earl Bruckmeister
Born August 12th, 1960
Married Rachel Winifred Dahlrumple June 17th, 1992
Died July 4th, 2009
May he rot in Hell

Dad crossed off the last line. Beside the fact Burt's family would object, we saved a few dollars. Too bad. I thought it was a fitting sentiment for all eternity.

And may God have mercy on my soul for that thought.

Chapter 15

The Fourth of July had many meanings for me. Always a treasured and savored holiday in our family, held sacred by a long military tradition on both sides, we relished the freedom fought for by our forefathers. The great-grandfather who'd built the house, Joseph Reginald Martin, fought in the Civil War. True, he'd been on the losing side, but he didn't let that stop him. He accepted the die cast, rounded up a herd of cattle and moved out West to start fresh. There were signs of his legacy everywhere. The house, the town, the ranch land. Even the cattle we raised had pedigrees going back to the longhorns he'd driven westward.

Samuel Joseph, his son, as the story goes, had been conceived on the Centennial. He too had fought for his country in the Spanish American War and returned home to build onto what his father had started.

His son, William Robert, fought in World War I. His son, Michael William, my grandfather, served in World War II. My mother, his only child, never served, but she married a man fresh out of the Vietnam jungles. His side of the family also had military men going back just as far, if not farther. Dad had once mentioned something about the Revolutionary War and the War of 1812, but the records had been lost in a fire shortly after his birth and we hadn't gotten around to retracing the lines.

So I'd been raised by honorable veterans of this country. I'd also envisioned I carried on the tradition by marrying a handsome Navy officer. Up until the previous weekend, I'd always felt pride in Burt's service. Hell, he too came from a military background, his father a retired Admiral, his two younger brothers still active career men. It had meant something.

But sitting at his graveside, my father, friends and neighbors surrounding me, I began to consider the Fourth of July my personal independence day. The day I'd found freedom from a man who knew nothing about honor or love. Maybe that day, sitting beside the casket hovering over the open hole, was the day I began to realize I could live for myself. An odd time to find my true self, to be sure, because I found myself staring across the flag-draped casket at my nemesis. A thousand different emotions hit me and near the top was probably the most petty of them all. I wanted to tear off the flag and burn it to ashes like Burt had done with the remains of our marriage.

He'd wanted to leave me for her? I couldn't see her well as, like me, she'd dressed for deep mourning. Her hat was smaller, but her veil was no less dark, and her suit looked hot under the relentless July sun, her nylons and gloves stifling. What did she hope to prove? That she suffered more than me? Her father stood nearby, avoiding my gaze--I recognized him from when Burt worked for him--but she sat between Burt's brothers, as if she knew them very well. Burt's parents looked uncomfortable, as well they should, but the brothers didn't appear at all uneasy about the mistress in their midst.

The few bites I'd had for brunch curdled in my stomach. She had some kind of nerve.

What little control I had on my emotions had almost burned out.

A bottle of water was pushed into my hand and I drank as directed. It was cold and refreshing in contrast to the heat of the day. Why were such events held when the sun was at its worst? The thermometer must've pegged out at a hundred in the shade of the trees dotting the grass of the cemetery. I greedily drank the water then handed the bottle back. Someone took it and patted my shoulder.

"Ignore her," Dan whispered in my ear.

"I can't. She's staring at me. All of them are staring at me."

"They always stare at the widow. It's normal."

"She shouldn't be here. What is she trying to prove? What does she want?"

"She doesn't have a leg to stand on."

Cyndi's hand came down on my shoulder at that point. "Shush. You're a lady, she's a tramp. Now act like it."

The words were barely loud enough to hear. I wished Cyndi had shouted them in her usual way. Fortunately, my angel appeared and silently demanded I lift her onto my lap. Mindy joined me under the veil and wrapped her arms around my neck. Other hands reached out to grasp my shoulders. John, Aggie and J.J. to the rescue. Dan's arm pressed against mine, the fine wool of his suit soft and warm. Dad on my other side. The little body in my arms and the people around me provided just the right amount of support. Dan pushed another white hanky into my hand but Mindy grabbed it and dabbed my cheeks.

"Don't be sad, Rachel, it's almost over. I saw lemonade at the house and I know that makes you feel better."

"Yes, it does."

"So does chocolate cake. I made one last night, just for you."

"Thank you." It was all I could choke out as she sponged up more tears.

"Good thing you didn't wear makeup today, you'd have coon eyes," she said matter-of-factly. When her uncle snorted, she smacked him. I couldn't help smiling. "As it is, you'll need Visine when this is over."

I wanted to ask how she knew about Visine, but apparently everyone had assembled because Pastor started speaking. Bless the man, he directed his comments to me and ignored the other side of the grave, making it clear there was only one legitimate widow present.

The flag was lifted and folded. There was a tense moment when the young sailor hesitated, clearly confused by the Admiral on one side. A cleared throat from Dan brought his attention around and the flag properly passed to me. Well, Mindy helped me take it and then held onto it for me. And here I'd had my rebuke all ready.

If he'd tried to present the flag to *her,* I'd have said, "Excuse me? I'm the widow. She's the whore who killed him. I don't think that rates her the flag."

Did I mention my rising crankiness over the situation?

Pastor handed me a small bouquet of three flowers. Roses, in red, white and blue, tied with ribbons of the same. Dan took the flag from my little angel. Mindy moved from my lap, and grasped my hand as I stood. I felt my head try to float off my shoulders. In a dream state, I reached out and dropped the flowers onto the casket as it began to sink into the hole while a bugler played *Taps*.

As Dan had mentioned earlier, I'd been holding it together fairly well. Until that point. However, I'd reached my limit, hit a wall. The tide had turned.

Personally, I suspected the bottle of water I'd been handed had come from my doctor. Between my usual allergy potions, his sedative, and the heat, a snowball had a better chance in Hell than I did of staying on my feet. I'd see his butt in court.

When I woke up.

Chapter 16

I recall little about that day. Every now and then a bird will sing or the wind rustle in the upper canopy of the trees, and I'll remember the casket suspended over the dark, deep hole. I'll see the flag I'd been handed and remember the white gloved hands folding and presenting it. A smart uniform will remind me of the pall bearers. The scent of fresh cut grass will bring back the sensation of floating amongst the grave stones.

What I remember most fondly about that day was waking up to Mindy sitting beside me on the bed, patting my cheek.

"The party's mostly over, Rachel. You need to come downstairs. Uncle Burt's daddy wants to talk to you."

"Oh?" I rubbed my eyes, hoping to clear them.

"I brought you lemonade. I had to save a glass. There's none left."

"Aw, sweetie. Thank you. Sure you don't want it?"

"I gots some. This is for you."

The only power on Earth who could move me right then was Mindy. For her, I sat up and took the glass. Cold and just the right amount of tart and sweet--sort of like the little fiend who crawled up beside me, the giggling one--it slid down my parched throat.

The giggler settled under my arm and hugged me. "You have bed head!"

"Great. After I drink the rest of this refreshing lemonade, I'll fix it up again. Why didn't you tell me this hairdo would take work, hmm?"

"You didn't ask me," she said archly. "But I like it. It makes you prettier."

"So you're saying I was pretty before?"

"Yes." Had to love her loyalty. "But you're prettier now. Uncle Dan thinks so too."

I coughed on the last swallow of lemonade. "Oh does he?"

"Yes, he liked you before, but he smiles when he looks at your new hair."

Couldn't slip a thing by the kids. They saw it all.

"Ahem."

Throat clearing of the manly sort came from the doorway. Delicious Uncle Deputy Dan leaned against the frame looking extra handsome with his disheveled hair and missing half his suit. He'd removed the coat and tie. He still wore the trousers and white shirt, but in that end-of-the-day relaxed way. The I'm-thinking-of-jumping-the-woman look.

"Glad to see you awake."

Hmm, did his thoughts mirror mine? His gaze definitely raked me from head to toe and back again. And he smiled. Mindy elbowed me to make sure I noticed that part.

I handed her the empty glass. "Take that downstairs, please."

Still giggling, she scooted off the bed and sauntered toward the door where Dan leaned over to tickle her, but she dodged him and ran down the stairs.

"She's right, you have bed head."

Any woman would try to pat her hair into place after a comment like that. "Thank you for carrying me upstairs. Again. Did I embarrass myself at the gravesite?"

Grogginess was leaving me faster than before. Did that mean the drug pushing doc had used a smaller dose? Or had he dosed me with a stimulant in the oh-so-innocent-looking-lemonade delivered by a sweet angel? The man needed a talking to, but I welcomed the wakefulness creeping into my head.

The devil-may-care grin on the decidedly delicious deputy kicked up on one side and kicked my heart into double time. "No, you gracefully fainted right into my arms and we made a hasty escape while muttering about heat and stress."

I'd been conspired against. "Ah. I seem to be fainting into your arms a lot lately. Especially considering before this past week I'd never once fainted in my lifetime." The legs didn't buckle when I stood, always a good sign. I stepped into the bathroom. "Thank you for carrying me out of the graveyard," I called through the door. The dress was fine, but the face and hair? Meh.

"A cold cloth should work."

"Thanks for the suggestion." I'd already figured that out. The tall man darkened the doorway to the bathroom and I spared him only a glance before closely assessing the damage the nap had done to my hair. A little flat on the back, but the front looked fine. My hairdresser had taught me how to fix it up. A little mousse, some fluffing, a spritz of spray, and I considered it passable. Especially for hair that had been stuck under a hat in the hot sun, then slept on.

Hair repaired, I reached for a washcloth and cooled my face. I wasn't nervous with Dan watching me, but I was a little excited. Waking up wasn't a problem with him nearby. The old hormones fairly danced for joy when he took the cloth from my hand and pressed it to the back of my neck.

"Oh, that feels good," I murmured. After being roasted by the sun, my skin soaked up the moisture of the cool cloth that took away the old sweat.

"Mmm-hmm," he rumbled. "For the record, I like carrying you around. One of these days I hope to do it when you're awake."

Right then and there, sweat popped out on my upper lip. I felt it.

Our eyes met in the mirror, my heart too raw to hide my feelings. I'd done my best to ignore the growing tension all week, but I could no longer deny it. The world had dwindled down to him, and me and that very intimate moment, which felt all too right.

"You're beautiful, Rachel."

He'd spoken so quietly I almost convinced myself it was my over-active imagination. I hadn't read one book this week. Not a single romance, mystery, or even a self-help on grief. Starved for a good story, the mind took over, right?

"Look at you. You're gorgeous," he said. "I wasn't sure I'd like a new hair style on you, but this one makes your eyes look bigger and it brings out the beautiful lines of your face. Almost fairy like. A pixie. An impossibly beautiful imp."

And when had he started hanging out in the fantasy section? But I liked his words, his thoughts. I liked how he touched me, one hand on my arm, the other pressing the warming cloth to my neck.

He thought I was beautiful? Gorgeous? I blinked and he broke from his trance enough to drop the wash cloth in the sink. And then he really touched me. Both hands on my arms, one dry, the other damp, he lightly rubbed, up and down. Very slowly. Nowhere near ready to think beyond the moment, I leaned back, ever so slightly and he was there, just as he had been all week, guarding my back, watching my six. Instead of my protector, he became my backrest, a place to relax. Breaking eye contact with the images in the mirror, my head dropped back to his shoulder.

When had the skinny kid grown into such a beautiful man? At close range I watched him through my lashes. He tried to hide it, but he was feeling the same nerves I was. The racing of his heartbeat gave him away. As did mine. I inhaled and drew in the scent of man. Cologne, well absorbed and heated, hit me like the rarest and most potent of aphrodisiacs. Warm, leathery, with too many notes to define, his scent filled my head and heat flooded my body. There had been teasing moments all week, but nothing as consuming as this. This was pure arousal settling deep and low in my body, where the heat coiled around my softening core. The equal and opposite reaction solidified behind me and I shifted against it.

The groan that rolled from his throat hit me like a super dose of pheromones. His hands slid down and off my arms to settle on my hips, pulling me back against him. It was slow seduction of the purest form and I wasn't sure I'd survive. Right there, a fraction of a millimeter from my lips, his clean shaven jaw hovered in conquest range. I'd been longing to kiss it, taste him, all week and I gave in to the temptation and brushed my lips against his warm skin. Sucking in air, he gripped my hips tighter, one hand sliding around to rest low on my abdomen. The pump was primed, the well ready. I wanted this more than I wanted air.

"Go on and kiss her," a young voice interrupted. "I know you've been wanting it, but honestly, just get it over with, wouldja? Mr. Dahlrumple wants her downstairs."

By the time Aggie finished delivering her message, we'd jerked apart, though her uncle stepped to the side away from her and leaned into the vanity. Fortunately for him, I was rooted by embarrassment and moved into dress smoothing mode. I knew the size of erection he wanted to hide. Aggie may have seen horses, but she was too young to get an eyeful of an adult human male.

Like we could fool her. She rolled her eyes and heaved a sigh. "Just don't make cow eyes at each other downstairs, okay? Come on, Rachel, they want you. The lawyer mumbled something about wills and such."

Great. The traditional post-funeral reading of the will. This was where I'd find out what David had dug up this week.

I fluffed my hair one last time, ignored my eyes, and followed Aggie out of my room and down the stairs. The horrific week was nearly over and I could kick all these people out of my house. At times I felt like I was on suicide watch. I just wanted to spend the weekend alone and then on Monday return to work and start making sense of my life again. The city accountant said I had plenty of hours, I could take another two weeks, but I didn't want more time off. Too much time alone.

Bare headed and bare footed, I stepped into the crowded library. My father-in-law, Rear Admiral Earl Theodore Bruckmeister, US Navy Retired, waited by the door.

"Rachel," he said gruffly and took my arm. Before I could back away he'd pulled me into a hug, much like the one at the church. He was a huggy man. Reminded me of a big old teddy bear. Not quite as tall as his sons, he was a bit broader in the chest. His wife, a tall slender blonde who'd once been a model, didn't do hugs so much, which could explain a few things. Either she was cold in general, or he hugged so much she figured adding her own would be overkill. When Earl released me, Catherine squeezed my hand. Thankfully she didn't do the air kiss thing either.

Dan arrived in time for the elder Bruckmeisters to step aside enough for me to see the tramp, aka Julianna whatshername, sitting on my settee, drinking tea from my china, looking for all the world like she owned my house. I had one word for her, her father, and her polished, beautiful Silicon Valley lawyer in his super expensive silk suit.

"Out."

This single word brought an immediate response from everyone present.

I pushed Dan away when he tried to step between me and her. "Out. I want you out of my house right now or the deputy here will have to arrest you for trespassing. You have thirty seconds."

"Now, Rachel," Dan said, physically restraining me with an arm around my waist. "I won't do that. They have business here and its legitimacy needs to be determined."

David and Dad were there as well. "Rachel," David beat Dad to the punch. "Dan is right, they're here to present a claim. We have to follow it through."

"Fine, but not here, not now. I want her and her posse out of my house and off our land. Make an appointment with a judge and we'll discuss it in chambers. I want them gone!" Straining at the hands and arms holding me, I wanted to grab her by the hair and haul her slutty butt out of my house.

"Easy, Rachel," Dad jumped in. "Let's do what we can out of court. Nothing will be decided here today. Let's just hear them out." He all but pleaded with me, his brown eyes anguished. No, nobody in this room recognized me right then, least of all me.

"I'm the injured party here! If she hadn't been fucking my husband he'd be here, alive. She's a husband-stealing home-wrecking toxic whore and I don't have to suffer her presence in my house. This is all her fault! I should be suing *her* for alienation of affection." Reasonable, no, probably not. Language I normally used? Most definitely not and it created several shocked stares and in-drawn hisses of air. How I honestly felt after a week of humiliation and pain? Absolutely. "And if she thinks she has a claim because of the bastard she *says* she's carrying I want DNA testing at the earliest possible date."

Julianna and her father both visibly flinched at my accusation. Well good, for all the times I'd heard her father speak out against extra marital affairs, served them right to be reminded that was exactly what his daughter had been involved in.

"She has signed documents, Rachel," David said.

"They're forgeries, they have to be. I want testing and analysis. I want court records showing notarized receipts of filing. She's already proved she's a liar and cheat by running around with a married man. If she weren't, she would have demanded he get divorced before sleeping with him." I managed to lean past the men blocking my way and glared into her eyes. "Don't you know if they marry the slut they leave their wives for, they'll sleep around on her too? Did you know he was still sleeping with me? He was cheating on you with his own wife, you dumb bitch."

The satisfaction of seeing that round of comments hit home made me feel better. Her face paled and her hand shook as she set down the tea cup and saucer. If she'd have broken it I would have maimed her. That was my great-grandmother's china and had no business being used for the reception. I'd take it up with whomever later.

"I don't have to listen to this abuse," she said.

"In my house, oh yes, you do. So either sit there and take it, or get the hell out and don't come back. Your lawyer can meet with my lawyer. I don't want you anywhere near this town. You don't belong here."

"Fine one you are to talk about sluts, you with your deputy toy boy there." She stood with the help of her father. Burt's youngest brother, Brad, stood on her other side.

"Unlike my husband, I've not slept with another person since the day I spoke my vows, up to and including today. The deputy is here because someone has been sending me threatening packages. Something you arranged, perhaps?"

Puzzlement crossed her face and I actually believed she didn't know what I was talking about. "Threatening packages?"

"Deputy, how many, total, have arrived over the past week?" I asked without looking away from my husband's lover. Killer. Only because she'd beat me to it. Details.

"Seven total, including one at the church today. It was mixed in with the arrangements on the altar. One of the church ladies had a severe reaction but was treated quickly and is resting comfortably at home."

I shot a glance at his grim face, then addressed the slut again.

"Interestingly enough, the first one arrived while you were doing the dirty with my husband Friday night and the second arrived the day after you'd killed him." Yeah, I was sticking to those words. If the toxicology and autopsy reports came back showing a heart condition and Burt had been using an unsafe amount of libido enhancements to get it up for her, then yes, I'd continue to call her a killer. I might not be able to make it stick in court, but I could make her life as miserable as mine.

"I didn't kill him!"

"The toxicology reports will make the determination," I said.

Her eyes widened in shock at that. "But the coroner said heart attack."

"I found the drugs and supplements. My doctor tells me they were a lethal combination if he had a heart condition. But since our family doctor wasn't consulted, we have to rely on the tests. And make no mistake, we saved a sample of his DNA. What week are you in?"

A black gloved hand covered her stomach. "Fourth."

"Good, six more and you can have the first DNA test. If that doesn't determine relationship, you can follow up with an amnio four weeks later." My gaze slid to her lawyer. "Make no mistake, tests are not optional."

He nodded. While his face was blank, there was a flicker of doubt in his eyes, one that gave me hope her claims were on very shaky ground.

"I won't submit to DNA tests until the child is born, if then." She challenged me, her dark blue eyes flashing.

"And your already weak claims won't stand up in court without them." David smoothly took control once more.

Dan pulled me back, making room for Julianna and her entourage to leave. Her lawyer lingered as David continued to speak. "I have your copies. We'll compare notes next week. Does Friday next work for you?"

The other lawyer nodded. "Noon. Your office here, or meet in Fresno?"

"Why should I give up the home field advantage?" David parried. "This case belongs in this county. My office in Hanford. Noon, Friday next."

With the enemy camp finally out of my house, awkward silence fell. The Bruckmeisters remained. I had no idea what side of the equation they belonged on. Brad, Burt's youngest brother, had known, that much was very clear. Had the others?

Earl and Catherine looked uncomfortable enough I gave them the benefit of the doubt. But Bruce? Not so clear. I was inclined to think not, but the three brothers had been reasonably close. If Brad knew, then middle brother Bruce most likely did as well.

"How much about this do you know, Brad?" No point in beating around the bush.

"I knew he planned to leave you." A careless shrug accompanied this statement.

"For how long?"

"A few months. He had his reasons, but what he told me doesn't match up with what I see now, or the Rachel we've all known for twenty years." The family blue eyes took in my new look, right down to my bare feet and red painted nails. "He never said you were looking so hot these days. New look since last weekend?"

I didn't miss the way his gaze flicked toward Dan, still standing very close to me. "Doesn't matter. Fact is you seem to have believed him."

Brad spread his hands, the expression on his face not quite making it to friendly. "From knowing you all these years, I had no reason to believe otherwise."

"We didn't know," Earl said. "I would have..."

"There was nothing you could do, Earl. If you'd been paying attention you'd have known he'd been sleeping around for years." I looked at Brad and pointedly aimed my gaze at his gold wedding band. I knew for a fact he'd done the same. "If you open your eyes, you'll notice little brother is just like big brother."

Bruce flinched. What did that mean? Did he know? Had he tried to talk both out of their tom cat ways? I'd never suspected him of messing around. Anyone could see he and his wife shared a close and loving marriage. Something I'd envied these past years.

"Brad?" The fury in Earl's voice made me step back a pace, right into Dan.

"She's lying," Brad said calmly. Much too calmly. And his parents knew it.

"We'll discuss this later." The ominous warning sent shivers of dread down my spine and I wasn't the focus. Brad wasn't too old for a reaming by the old man, and he surely needed one.

Brad answered by glaring at me. "You don't know when to shut up, do you? Keep your nose in your books, Rachel. You don't know squat about my life."

"And you know nothing of mine, other than the lies your brother told you. You're another one who doesn't need to be in my house."

"If it is your house," he sneered.

"It sure as hell wasn't Burt's. Actually, the house still legally belongs to my father. He hasn't passed the title to me yet."

That shut him up. For a minute. While his face blanched, then turned red. "What the hell?"

"Burt's name is not on any of the titles to the land, nor is mine," I told him. "Why, what did Burt tell you?"

"I own this land," Brad growled. "I bought it from Burt."

"When?" David and Dad asked at the same time.

"Last month. I gave him the down payment last month. He gave me the papers last week."

"Impossible." Again David and Dad spoke at the same time.

"Forgery," I repeated. "That's the only explanation. Same goes for whatsherface's supposed documents." I'd never claimed to be a saint. Therefore, with no small amount of satisfaction, I smirked back at my brother-in-law. "Your own brother swindled you. God, now I have to get the books audited. I wonder how much he's swindled me out of over the years?"

"You'll be hearing from my lawyer, but according to the paperwork I have, I own this house."

"Bullshit," my dad said. "Get out. Go through the courts, but there is no legal way you can own this house or any of the ranch. Burt had no hand in the running of it."

"I'll see you in court. You can count on it." Brad left the room and his remaining family stared at me with a variety of expressions from dismay to stone cold indifference.

"Please," I begged them, "please, I've had all I can take today. Obviously the will won't be settled at this time."

David, bless his little lawyer soul, firmly escorted them from the room while assuring them he'd keep in touch on the proceedings and they could feel free to return home at their leisure. I could really learn to love that man.

Behind me, Dan's cellphone started buzzing.

"Dispatch," he identified the number as I turned. "Weston." Whatever dispatch said had him frowning. "Location?" My heart stopped for a minute. "On my way. ETA fifteen. I'm in the 'Vette." With that he snapped the phone shut. "I have to go. All personnel needed."

"Sounds like war." My quip was weak, but I headed for the fireplace.

"Wait." Dan's voice stopped me. "I have a back-up." He went behind the desk to get his utility belt we'd hidden and locked in a drawer. He was concerned about Dad. How silly this whole thing about the safe was. Of course Dad had a right to know.

"Dad, lock the door, would you?"

He didn't question, but I did get a curious look when I swung open the hidden cabinet.

"I'll explain later," I promised. In less than thirty seconds, I had Dan's gun out. By the time he reached me, he had the belt in place and two seconds later his gun slipped into the holster as the cabinet snapped shut, hiding the safe once more.

He answered the question before I asked. "There's a gang war. Drugs. They need every hand, otherwise I wouldn't go."

The heart I'd thought already too numb to ever feel again clenched in icy fear.

"I have what I need in the car. Vest, jacket, more ammo. What I don't have, what I need right now, is a kiss." The apology I didn't need lurked deep in his beautiful eyes. "I don't have time to make it pretty, so I hope you'll forgive me."

We met in the middle, mouths already open. Hard, deep, fast, and completely breathtaking, he kissed me like it was the first time--which it was--and the last time--which it had better not be.

Before I caught my breath, his feet pounded down the front steps, his car roared to life, and the tires squealed down the street. I made it to the window in time to see the red and blues attached to the flipped down visor flashing as he rounded the corner in the dusk settling over our little corner of the world.

That kiss, that wonderful, wild kiss had been the most beautiful of my life. What had I been missing out on all these years?

Chapter 17

How did I remain standing, as I watched the tail lights disappear? My heart, my life as I'd known it, lay in ruins at my feet, but my legs stubbornly refused to buckle. Absolute and complete terror gripped my guts so hard I wanted to curl up and die. I'd never experienced this feeling before, not for anyone. Not even when Mom was diagnosed with cancer.

Dad answered the tapping on the library door. He and David spoke in low voices, before David collected his papers and briefcase, gently squeezed my shoulder and left.

A helluva day, as my grandfathers would have said while seeking out the nearest bottle of scotch. They had definitely agreed about good scotch, but tended to argue about everything else, all in the name of fun.

The distinctive clink of crystal against crystal barely touched my consciousness, until Dad handed me a glass of port.

"Come on, Chi-chi. I hear there's some food left. I think it's a good night for dinner and movie."

Dinner and a movie. Food and distraction. All right. Good plan. I might forget about Dan out there in the line of fire. Maybe. The confrontations I'd just engaged in were already buried. I could not deal with them right now.

At first I was surprised by Dad's choice of movie, and then again, I wasn't. Perfect. *On a Clear Day You Can See Forever*.

Picking at the remains of a tray of cheese and crackers Cyndi had assembled for us before she left for the night, we dined on appetizers, followed by some lasagna a kind soul had brought by the day before. Leftover raw vegetables served as our salad. The bottle of port traveled with us, the result of a great mind thinking ahead. Dad's great mind. Not mine. I went where directed, sat where indicated.

That movie...I loved the movie. Had seen it twenty, maybe thirty times over the years, possibly more. Mom started me early. It was one of the first VHS movies she bought, probably about two minutes after the

VHS movie market was created. I could almost quote the script word for word. Best of all, I loved watching and listening to Yves Montand play Dr. Marc Chabot, pronounced Sha-bow, like the college in Hayward. I could transport him forty years forward into my life, easily. As I'd heard other women say, I'd do him. In the movie, he stood the test of time. Much better than Daisy's oh-so-dated wardrobe. Seriously, at one point the lining of her coat matched her dress and the hats were something else again, not to mention the hairdos--and I thought mine took work. And those nails! I could never garden with those inch-long weapons, but hey, it worked for Daisy. Not to mention she had a platoon of wardrobe, hair, and makeup people looking after the details. And real gardeners.

What touched me this time, what wrenched my heart the most...sigh...I could really identify with the character of Daisy. Without the psychic talent. I was a competent gardener, but my plants didn't rush up from the ground for me, without a little organic plant food. I couldn't even predict when the phone would ring, and unless I'd seen the lost object, I couldn't find it, though that particular talent I'd love to have. For some reason Burt believed I could find anything he'd lost. No, where I felt a sisterhood with Daisy was the lack of character part. The go-along part.

The part where Daisy protested she had to leave but instantly caved when Marc pressed her. "Have another drink, Daisy." "No, no, I can't..." "A short one." "Okay."

She would have done anything for him. Anything at all. For the first time I could ever remember, the movie depressed me.

I sipped my wine, nibbled at the food Dad handed me, but essentially I wallowed in my spinelessness. I'd been the doormat my husband ground his boots into. I was left to brush off the filth of his life, and I felt dirty, used, and unappreciated. Pretty much how Daisy felt when she discovered Marc had been taping their sessions and she learned in another life she'd been Melinda.

Then came the scene where Marc put Daisy under hypnosis so he could talk to Melinda, to tell her goodbye. She lamented over her disloyal husband, Robert Tentrees, and how she should have known he would betray her.

Melinda: "He was too weak to be faithful. Why didn't I see that? Is love so blind?"

Marc: "No. But mistrust is so exhausting..."

God. Wasn't that the truth? I made Dad stop the movie right there and play the scene back twice to cement the words in my mind.

"That sums up my life with Burt," I whispered.

"Aw, Rachel, don't do this. The character flaw was in Burt, not you."

I wanted to believe, I really did. But what if I carried the flaw? One which drew me to men who couldn't stay faithful. Okay, okay, only one man had cheated on me. I didn't exactly have a track record of experience with men, especially long term. What's the old saying? *Don't let one bad apple spoil the whole bunch?*

Anyhow, music aside, I wasn't ready to believe the entire fault belonged to Burt. As much as I really, really wanted to.

"It takes two to make a marriage work or fail. I played a part in it, Dad. As much as I'd love to lay it all at Burt's feet, somehow I failed him. But how? Does it date back to the first time I suspected him of sleeping with someone else, and I buried it? Or was it before? Where did I fail? What did I do to drive him away? If I'd confronted him, insisted on counseling, could we have fixed it?"

Though he wanted to cure my heartache, Dad didn't have the answers. For the first time in my life, Daddy didn't have any words to guide me. Looking into his eyes, I saw the sorrow and pain he'd carried for years. I'd never seen him look old, but after the hellish week we'd been through, the weariness of living visibly weighed down his shoulders, dark shadows looked like bruises beneath his eyes where the skin sagged. Deep lines had been carved into his face over the years and I'd never noticed. Dark hair looked more gray, but nicely mixed with more at the temples giving him an attractive senior statesman presence. Life had brought on the changes. He'd been down this road before. He'd buried a spouse, and he'd added the weight of my loss to his and carried me through the week.

Daddy may not have had the answers, but he still had strong shoulders. However, he'd raised me to stand on my own two feet. I'd have to do it soon. I couldn't lean forever.

After patting my hand, he resumed the movie and while Daisy came to grips with her life, and thankfully dumped the nerd boyfriend, I thought about Dan. What did I really know about him? I'd spent years ignoring him and changing the topic when his name came up. John had once mentioned in passing Dan had been married very briefly. Lord, that had to have been ten years or more ago. I knew nothing about anything since. A short dating period with Cecile, which seemed to have ended amicably enough. No one--local--since. Dan, a player? Didn't fit what I'd learned of him over the course of the week.

Okay, I had to laugh to myself. When had it been about him that past week?

When had I asked him anything about himself? We'd talked about funeral arrangements, the kids, music, movies--we had similar taste in both. In books, we only matched on mysteries and biographies--he liked military figures and I generally chose influential women. On cars, he liked to show off the 'Vette and in college I'd had a sweet Mustang. We'd generally avoided discussing personal relationships, especially any topic having to do with our teens. Neither one of us wanted to talk about our history. Or maybe it hadn't been the right time. Fine. I'd been self-centered, but no more. I owed the man a little attention.

By the end of the movie, warmth and a tiny sense of calm had crept into my psyche once more. Then again, it might have been the wine. So when the doorbell rang, I waved Dad off.

"I've let a whole lot of people do everything for me this past week. Time to take control of my life again."

He eyed me dubiously, but didn't argue. Instead, he picked up our dishes and carried them to the kitchen.

Wine glass in hand, I tripped to the door and swung it open without once wondering who would call at this time of night. Hoping it was Dan, even though I hadn't heard a car on the drive, I swung the door open without peeping first.

Had I been involved with answering the door the previous week, I would have been more careful. Dan had said there'd been a delivery of the poisoned plants each day. I knew nothing of how most had been delivered or found. We'd already had the delivery for today, so it never occurred to me the sender was determined and clever.

I swung the door open, but no one stood outside the screen. An odd thump and a sinister rattle caught my attention a half second before danger struck. Literally. A truly pissed off rattlesnake bit quicker than lightning. Faster than the eye can track. Someone, whoever had rung my doorbell, had put a rattlesnake between the door and the screen. The moment I set it free, before I could react to the fact it was real and not a rubber toy, the snake coiled, lunged, and sank its fangs into my ankle.

Of course, I screamed. The crystal wine glass slipped from my hand and crashed to the hardwood floor, splintering needle-sharp shards into and around my bare feet while the snake disengaged and recoiled. I stumbled and fell backward onto my padded butt. Still bruised it.

The snake, probably confused by the shattered crystal, couldn't get back out the door, so he slithered past me and down the hall. Not a large one, it moved fast and slithered out of sight as Dad came running, cordless phone in hand. He was already dialing as he asked what happened.

"Rattlesnake," I gasped, trying frantically to remember snakebite first aid. *Keep calm* was in there somewhere. Right.

Dad still had his shoes on, so he had no problem crouching down to look at my ankle. "Shit," he said. "Looks like a young adult by the size of the bite. Stay still and as calm as possible," he advised.

Right. Calm. I'd already thought of that.

My phone had three numbers on speed dial. Burt's cellphone, Dad's house, and John's house. When 9-1-1 informed Dad the ambulances in our immediate area were engaged and were at least thirty minutes out, including Miguel who was on duty, he hung up and dialed John. He pulled out two of his remaining hankies and made soft bindings on either side of the bite. To keep the venom from spreading. That fact came to mind as he twirled the fabric before tying it around my ankle. Keeping the bite area low, way lower than my heart, was called for, so on my feet was the best place for me to be.

"You're doing good, Rache," Dad said. "I don't think you got the full venom, it isn't turning color or swelling just yet."

"Oh lucky me. It just hurts like hell."

"Sit still while I clear some of this glass."

True, I couldn't expect my father to lift me in his arms. Where was the deputy when I needed him?

Dad made short work with the broom, while I pulled splinters from my hands, then he fussed about my feet, picking shards out as best he could while John brought his SUV around. With the help of both men, I made it into the vehicle. Of course, we saw no sign of my attacker, who'd beat feet and most likely had already crossed the county line. Not hard to do in a small county.

"We'll get the rattler later," Dad said after dashing back to lock the door.

Doing my best not to panic, or cry from the pain, I barely kept from snarling. "Damn right we will. Call an exterminator as soon as you get buckled."

"I don't think they make house calls in the middle of the night."

"Like hell they don't." There was a damn rattlesnake in my house and I wasn't going back until it was caught and exterminated. No matter how good they were for keeping down rodents. What if the thing bit one of the kids?

John threw the car in gear and took off. Since he was with security at the Naval Air Station, he had blue lights in his SUV. While John drove and radioed the hospital we were coming, Dad kept an eye on me and put in a call to the Sheriff's Department. He didn't reach Dan, but he did leave a message about the snake.

We had two choices when seeking emergency room services. Fresno, most of an hour drive away, or the NAS hospital, which I was technically not yet eligible to use. Burt had deferred use of his base retirement benefits until age sixty. John didn't ask for an opinion and he didn't inquire about my dependent veteran benefits status. He told the base we were coming and to have the emergency room standing by. The base commander was welcome to poke his nose in and check things out if he so desired. End of story. Apparently John's rank and position were high enough he could throw out such orders. Didn't hurt that Burt and I had socialized with the base command staff from time to time. The admiral knew me and had attended Burt's funeral just hours before.

By the time we arrived, I felt ill, whether from panic or the venom, I couldn't guess. I barely remember being hauled out of the vehicle and dropped on a gurney as about that time I began feeling tingly and dizzy, and my ankle seemed to be on fire and swelling to gargantuan proportions. People wearing scrubs and gloves shouted at me. An oxygen mask covered my face and lights flashed past. I later figured out those were the fluorescents on the ceiling as they ran my gurney into the ER. I merely wanted to pass out, but decided I needed to concentrate on breathing. Asthmatic response, rather than a reaction to the venom, so they told me.

"Snake bite?" one man asked.

"Rattler," I gasped.

"How did you come in contact?"

The bed came to a stop. Arms moved back and forth over my face. Gloved hands grabbed me, turned my face, lifted my arms.

Dad's voice this time. "I'm not sure, I'm assuming when she opened the door it struck. Not sure how it got between the screen and the door."

"Do you know what kind? How big?" The doctor who seemed to be in charge shot out the questions, hardly waiting for a response. "Any idea how much venom she may have taken?

"Not a clue. I didn't see it. Apparently it's now hiding in the house. Rachel?"

I didn't get a chance to answer because I was too busy wincing as my feet were handled.

"What's with the cuts on her feet?"

"Crystal. Broken wine glass." Dad answered again. *Thank you, God.* "Check her hands, too."

More gloved hands reached for me and stretched out my arms.

"Glass in her feet?"

"Dropped the glass about the time I heard her scream. Probably a reaction to being bit."

"So what you're saying is, somehow, a rattlesnake got between a screen door and the front door. Possible it could crawl in there by itself?"

"Not a chance," Dad said as I shook my head. The oxygen mask made it hard to speak, so I was extra glad he was there. "The screen door is a security type. I installed it myself. Only the smallest ant could get past the seal. We've never had a snake up there."

The doctor lifted my eyelids one at a time and stared down at me. "Nod or shake your head. Was the snake big?"

I shook my head.

"Particularly small?"

I shook again. He asked enough questions until we narrowed it down to a young adult who may or may not have dumped his entire venom supply in me. The doctor didn't seem to think so based on swelling and discoloration around the bite. Shortly afterward, I was dosed with anti-venom through an IV.

I could feel them watching me, monitoring my vitals, keeping an eye on the bite site. They must have given me a painkiller as well, because everything started to get fuzzy and I wanted just to sleep.

"Who is she?" the doctor asked at one point.

"Rachel Bruckmeister. My daughter. Burt Bruckmeister's widow."

"Shit."

Yeah, that pretty much summed up my situation. Deep shit.

Chapter 18

Hospitals are strange places. In theory, sick people go there to heal from whatever injury or illness sent them there in the first place, but no one can get any rest in one.

I couldn't even blame it on the nurses and doctors. They were just doing their jobs, saving lives. For a while there I didn't want them to succeed. With mine, anyway. If I was going to spend the rest of my life dodging poison posies and viperous snakes in my house, then what was the point? Who hated me so much? Besides Julianna whatshername. At least I could understand, and match, her hatred. Well, Brad hadn't seemed too happy with me either, but I didn't think he'd resort to sneak attacks.

No, there was no rest to be found in the hospital. Between staff checking my vitals and keeping watch on the damage to my ankle, I dozed and wandered through a bizarre, borderline hallucinogenic dream world. At times I wasn't even sure if the nurses were really there or merely my imagination. I floated along, pretending I was Princess Jasmine looking for Aladdin and borrowing his magic carpet.

Yeah, I had some really weird dreams. Aladdin faded out and Dan showed up in scenes going back to my teen years. Mom was in some, Dad in others, each dream twisting and melding into others. One part of the dream involved the unfurling of a huge flag over a neighbor's house while the Star Spangled Banner piped out at full volume. Neighbors came out to salute and sing. And then I was drawn to a lake and a cabin on the shore. There was a very long dock and I crawled out of the water onto it. And then I was in the cabin looking through the kitchen window while a beat-up boat pulled up to the dock. Dan called out to me and I saw him working the controls through a cracked and broken windshield. He needed a towel, but was hidden from me by the deck railing. I handed him a towel and he got it wrapped around his waist just as a crowd of friends came up. Next, in the weird twisting way of dreams, I found myself on a motorcycle trying to drive it up a mountain on a snow-covered road. Someone was following me and I was losing ground on the ice. Me on a motorcycle, by myself, was odd enough, but on ice and snow? My goal was some dirty dive of a bar. Extremely unlike anything within my experience. I was there to meet someone, I had something important to tell them…and then it all faded.

I usually had very interesting dreams, but not quite so fractured or fraught with danger. I didn't like these much. In retrospect, the reality of the hourly checks probably blended with the dreams. The drugs they pumped into me most likely contributed.

I was pretty doped up and when I sank back into sleep, I dreamed of Dan touching me. I could feel his warm hand on my hip. Flesh touching flesh.

"Mmmm." I moaned and writhed, wanting that hand to travel a little further east. Instead it moved north to rest on my waist. The dream turned scorchingly erotic. The touch was soothing and hot at the same time. Even in my half sleep, I recognized the way my body readied itself, the softening inside, the melting feeling and the moisture gathering. "Yesss." I whimpered and shifted my hips closer to the hand touching me. With the stupid tube in my nose I couldn't smell anything, but my body remembered Dan's scent and my arousal spiked.

I drifted again, and dreamed of lying on a beach. A private, clothing-optional beach. Drunk on kisses and hot sun, my lover's hand rested on my lower abdomen, his pinky finger exploring the patch of curly hair I kept trimmed in the summer. The finger crept lower and I let my legs part. It took an eternity, but finally--finally!--that little finger, still bigger and stronger than my index finger, reached the part of me dying to be touched. The shock to my body was electric and I rose to it. Yes, he found my secret nubbin on the first try and used his finger, such a talented pinky, to stroke me. Primed and needy, I flexed my hips up to meet his finger and exploded.

The sheer shock of my orgasm rocked me and my eyes flew open. There, sitting beside my bed, his hand resting beside mine on top of the covers, was dark-eyed Dan.

Gasping for air and still horny as hell, I stared at him through half open eyes. I reached for his hand, only to find the one closest to him, the left one, was strapped to a board. Both hands were also wrapped in gauze, the result of the cuts made by my broken wine glass.

"Gaaaah!" My protest came out as a weak wheeze through a dry mouth and cracked lips. Ever so gently, he grabbed my wrist to keep me from flailing about.

"Did you…?" I wanted to know if I'd dreamed the orgasm.

"Easy, Rumple. Don't want to go disturbing your IVs or bandages." Leaning closer, he lightly ran his other hand over my hair, then lingered on my face. "Must have been some dream."

"Did you…?"

"Did I what? Did I…touch you?" Both brows rose in surprise as I nodded. "Hell no!" He sat back, taking his touch away. "I wouldn't take advantage like that, Rachel." His air of injured pride made me want to scream. I wanted him to touch me, dammit.

"Damn the IVs," I mumbled. My lips, face, hands…nothing on me seemed to want to move much, despite the fact most of the damage was below my knees. Okay, so my butt and back also hurt from falling. Apparently, I had some cuts higher up my legs from the shattered crystal. More bandaging covered those wounds. Once mostly awake, I felt the stinging, burning sensations all over my skin, stealing away the erotic dream. My lungs felt uncomfortable, each breath more difficult than it should have been, even with the oxygen tube across my face.

"Are you okay?" I managed to wheeze.

"Me? Sure, I'm fine. What about you?" The surprise on his face disappeared and his brow wrinkled. "Couldn't stay out of trouble for three hours, could you?"

"I did not invite the snake into my house." I let my eyes close again. "Is it gone? Did Dad call the exterminator?"

"The snake is gone. I found it and now it's dead."

A shudder went through me and Dan gently squeezed my wrist. So now I had to be on the lookout for poisonous reptiles as well as plants? If she'd wanted Burt, what did she gain by hurting me now he'd died? I hadn't killed him, so why was I under attack? John had tried asking those questions earlier, but I'd had no answer. I was also tired of talking about me. "How'd your call go?"

"Switching topics on me?"

Damn right I was. "You answered an emergency call, how'd it go?"

"Fine." He sighed. "We arrested a couple dozen kids for illegal possession of drugs and guns. No shots fired."

I breathed a very large sigh of relief. He sounded a little let down. I took it to mean he didn't get to beat the shit out of anybody. "What time is it?" My room was dark and the only windows I could see led to the hallway and the curtains on them were mostly closed, letting in little light from the hall.

"Five in the morning. I just got here and sent your dad home."

"I need to thank John..." Sleepiness crept up on me again.

"Don't worry about John. By the way, he and your dad are working out a system of surveillance cameras around the house. They've installed a few over the week, but they haven't had any luck yet. They'll catch this person."

"Okay." The sigh rattled and wheezed in my chest. "Just... do that...again."

"Do what again?"

"That touch..." I did my best to pull his hand toward my hips. "Touch me," I begged in a whisper.

"No, Rachel. I won't touch you until you're ready."

"I'm ready," I assured him. Wanting to see that sexy smile, the special one, I tried to open my eyes. "When do I get out of here?"

"If you're very good, today. If not, tomorrow."

"What does good mean? I can't do anything but lie here and sleep." Grumbling, I let my eyes slam shut again.

"Just sleep, Rachel."

"Not until you tell me who took off my panties."

"What?"

"Last week, when Doc first knocked me out. I woke up in a nightgown with no panties."

"Oh." Dan cleared his throat. "Since you weren't wearing any the night before, you know, when..." The chair squeaked when he shifted and I opened my eyes enough to see him looking embarrassed.

"What did you see that night?"

"I didn't look, I swear," he said quickly.

"I wasn't accusing you, in fact, I've been wondering..." The embarrassment spread to me.

"As soon as I laid you down on the chaise, I covered you with a blanket. I didn't cop a feel or look, but um, it was kind of hard not to notice." He cleared his throat again. "Anyhow, I figured you slept without, um, so, when it was my turn to look in on you, I, uh, slipped my hands up under the covers and just pulled them off. To make you more comfortable. I mean, I know some women get, ah, irritated by lack of, ah, air...down there...at night..."

God, I sure did love his voice. Even when he was embarrassed, it was deep and soothing. He had a range of tones and tempers that kept my ears peeled just waiting for the next words to come from him. What would he have sounded like with a Scottish burr? Oh, there, I felt the erotic rush again.

"It's okay, Dan. I'm not mad. In fact, I'm kind of...turned on."

"Oh no, not that again." He let out a deep groan. "I do not take advantage of unconscious women."

"I'm awake now." It was hard to purr with a throat raw from oxygen, but I did my best. "Please?" I begged. "It will help me sleep better."

"Not now. The point is to keep your heart rate down."

"My heart rate will also go up if I'm agitated."

Silence stretched out for a long moment then I heard his sigh. "Will it help if I hold you?"

"Yes." It would satisfy part of my need, and he was right, increased heart rate would be bad. I was only surprised no one had come to check after my orgasm.

In the dim room, Dan came around to the right side of the bed. Through careful maneuvering, he was able to climb in and pull me against his chest. My bitten ankle stayed low and we kept the cords and tubes from tangling.

Dan shifted. My IV moved enough I whimpered before I could bite it back.

"Easy, baby--"

I flinched at the endearment. Burt had used it, a lot. It had always made me cringe.

"Something hurt or...*Baby*?"

"No, no, no. No baby. Don't like it, never have."

"Okay, sweetheart. No more of the B word. Relax, I've got you. Comfortable?"

What a treat! I didn't have to explain. He got it the first time. "Um, mmm." I moaned. Single syllables seemed to be all I could handle as the warmth from his body seeped into me, lulling me as much as the steady thump of his heart.

The soft brush of his facial hair against my forehead reminded me I wanted to ask about the addition to his face.

"What's with the funky mustache?" I asked through a yawn. "Fu Manchu? Is that what it's called?"

"It's a horseshoe. I'll tell you about it later. Rest now. Maybe someday I'll show you what's special about my mustache."

"You mean mustache rides?"

"Sleep," he ordered, but I heard a trace of a groan in the single word.

Dan told me later, I was asleep with a smile on my face when a nurse came to check on me, soon followed by the admitting doctor. The fact that I sometimes talk in my sleep saved him from being tossed out of my room. Apparently I heard the doctor ask Dan what the hell he thought he was doing. Doc was gearing up to ream Dan for molesting his patient, but I spoke up.

"He's following orders."

"Whose orders?" the doctor had demanded.

"Mine."

And that was the end of the subject as I drifted deeper, smiling into my dreams, feeling safer in Dan's arms than I'd ever felt before.

Chapter 19

All my hopes of a weekend alone to adjust and get a fresh start, standing on my own two feet, failed to become reality.

Modern medicine couldn't heal hurts overnight. Where was Dr. McCoy when I needed him? Right, I was about four hundred years too soon for that technology. Shame.

I spent one night in the hospital, after arguing my doctor into letting me go home Saturday afternoon. Armed to the teeth with painkillers and orders to rest, Dad and John carefully tucked me into John's car and took me home, where Cyndi and the kids waited with cake and more lemonade. They plopped me down on my chaise with everything I could possibly want within reach. From lemonade and water to notebook, remote, phone, and a stack of the most recent romance releases, I only lacked a dishy deputy to hold me in his arms. Seemed he couldn't get excused from duty but had left a message with Aggie that he'd be by later.

Thankfully, the anti-venom had worked wonders. The wound, however, could take up to four weeks--*four weeks*--to disappear completely. My doctor, the comedian, also advised me to use care when opening doors as well as avoid the swimming pool, and amorous exertions for the time being. Dad's glare was potent enough to kill that line of discussion as he reminded the doctor I was newly widowed. The doctor may have shut his mouth on the topic, but I caught his glare, and fully understood his message. Spoilsport.

By the time dinner was cooked, served and cleaned up, I was visitored out. I loved my neighbors, and Cyndi could cook through any crisis her heart desired, but I was just plain worn out. Kicking them out without hurting their feelings was tough, so I did it the best way I knew how. I pretended to fall asleep on the sofa.

Only, pretense became reality and, when I woke next, it was to the sensation of bouncing along, accompanied by a dream of being carried on a sumptuous litter, cushioned by silk covered pillows, shaded from the hot, hot sun by yards and yards of fluttery silk curtains. Incense burners, held by servants keeping pace with my litter, smelled like leathery, earthy, manly cologne. The kind not found in any bottle.

"Don't forget my wine, boy," I imperiously demanded of one youth pacing beside my sedan. "The red."

When he turned to look at me, the voice coming from his mouth did not match the youthfulness of his sweet face. "Of course, my lady," he said with a deep, rumbling chuckle. The comfort of my ride was interrupted as I was thrown into the air.

The screech from my own throat woke me fully to find Dan easing through the door of my bedroom, and smiling down at me. My heart hitched at that.

"Good dream, Rumple?"

"Mmm-hmm." But the reality was better. Especially if he had a bottle of wine tucked under his arm and planned to crawl into bed with me.

"You can get back to it just as soon as you get ready for bed."

Someone had already pulled back the covers of white sheets. I really needed to do some shopping soon. I didn't mind white, as a rule, but I wanted more than plain sheets. It smacked too much of the sterile hospital, but at least they were clean and fresh with fabric softener.

Dan set me down in a sitting position on the padded chest at the foot of the bed. "Find your nightgown and get changed."

Dad was there, right behind Dan. "Everything is in your bathroom. The ointment, pills and your usual inhaler. Don't even think of going to sleep without using them all."

"Yes, sir." One did not argue with that voice. Was probably why he'd risen to the rank of Captain so fast back in his Vietnam days.

"We'll be downstairs. We're putting the final tweaks on the monitoring system."

That comment was more for Dan. The *we* and *downstairs* in particular.

"We'll show you all the bells and whistles tomorrow, but for now you need sleep."

"And will you be back to tuck me in, too?" Frustration, pure and simple, put the exasperation into my voice. Most unfairly on my part. Dad had done nothing but look out for me this past week or more. "Sorry." I immediately put on my most contrite face.

"No worries, Rache. You're tired of this whole mess. I understand."

"I'm glad you do, because I don't." Pushing to my feet, I moved to Dad and gave him a quick hug. "Thanks for your patience and your care." I looked over his shoulder to Dan. "You too. I don't know what I would have done or how I would have managed without you two taking care of me."

"All in a day's work, ma'am." Dan tipped an imaginary hat and gave me a wink. "Get some rest."

All in a day's work. I stuck my tongue out at the closing door. Still, I was groggy and forced myself into the bathroom to wash and medicate. But I broke the pain pill in half. Yes, I still stung and hurt, my joints ached from being bed bound, and my butt bruised after bouncing on the floor, but I was tired of being slug slow because of one form or another of sedative. Also, the dreams were just too strange. Okay, I'd liked the last one. That one could come back to haunt me all it wanted, as long as somewhere in there I got a massage from one hot deputy dressed in a loin cloth. The very thought made me shiver. If this kept up, I had the thought, I should try dabbling in some fiction myself.

Medicated to the eyeballs, I went in search of night apparel. Cyndi had sent a basic, loose, chambray dress to the hospital for me to wear home. I briefly mourned the loss of my second little black dress. That one I'd liked a lot and had contemplated keeping. Maybe I'd go back and buy it in the bronze color. Digging in my lingerie drawer, I only came up with frothy, see-through, not-meant-to-actually-sleep-in type gowns and nighties. Most of which Burt had bought for me for anniversaries or birthdays. Men should not be allowed to buy lingerie. Rarely did they pick out something flattering. There was nothing in the drawers I wanted to wear. And should I need to make a midnight snack run, with Dad in the house, and possibly Dan as well, nothing I had at hand was appropriate.

Automatically I moved to where I normally put Burt's t-shirts on the left side, and found the drawer empty. Of course, I'd thrown everything out. The sense of loss struck me as fast as the rattler had, and equally unexpected. Shaking, I backed up until my knees hit the blanket chest and I sat down. I hadn't saved anything of his. Not one t-shirt or dress shirt I'd purloined on a regular basis. I knew the rest of the drawers, as well as his side of the closet, were equally empty. I'd heard one shouldn't make drastic changes for at least a year after a spouse's death. Yes, Pastor had been yacking at me, offering grief counseling in small bites. He hadn't gotten to me fast enough on the *changes* part. Surgical strike had been my thought. Burt was dead, so like a dead limb on a tree, I cut him right out of my life. Only, I was finding it not so easy. Echoes remained, like a phantom limb, an amputated arm or leg. His side of the dresser stood as an empty, mute testimonial.

Never mind that this very same dresser had held the clothes of generations of other people. It dated as far back as my grandfather at least. Possibly his father. I tried to feel their spirits here, hoping it would make the dresser feel less empty. But alas, it was just a piece of furniture, fashioned from wood. And it felt vacant.

My life felt hollow and the remaining years stretched out ahead of me. I had no children of my own to fill my hours and demand my attention, forcing me to keep moving from day to day. I didn't know why I had to keep moving, only that I had to. The reason would come to me later if only I could stay the course. Maybe I wouldn't become Eleanor Rigby.

All out of tears, I stiffened my spine and forced myself to my feet. Somewhere, I had to have something I could wear to sleep in. Digging through the drawers resulted in camisoles and teddies being tossed aside as not suitable. Maybe when Dan and I got around to the seduction stage, maybe, but of course I'd want all new things by then. A pile started to grow. I'd already culled Burt's things, therefore I decided to also prune my things, those that were a part of him. I kept the lingerie I'd purchased for myself, but anything he'd bought, I added to the go-away pile. When I was finished, I'd finally found a cotton tank top and a pair of soft jersey shorts I could wear for sleeping. Add sleepwear to the shopping list. Bedding dropped to second place.

Wooziness began to set in, not that it had ever truly left me, but I made myself go to the bedroom door and call out, "Hellooo?"

Dan called up from the bottom of the staircase. "Yes?"

"I could use a couple more trash bags if we have any left."

"Why?"

"I found some more things for Good Will."

"Will two bags be enough?" Skepticism filled his voice.

"Two should do it."

"Be right there," he called back.

When he appeared at my door, two black bags in hand, he shook them at me. "You need to buy stock in Glad Bags. I think we've almost made it through a Costco sized box of these things."

I tried for a cheeky grin, but it came out weak. "We're far from done."

The good deputy's eyes widened when he took in the two piles of clothing I'd assembled on the floor. "What's all this? Burt was a cross dresser too?"

"Good one." I laughed. "No, these are things he bought for me. He had horrible taste in intimate apparel."

"I don't know about that…" Dan lifted a black lace baby doll nightie by its strap. One glance over his shoulder at the scowl on my face and he dropped it on top of the pile. "You're right. Horrible taste. Low class. Disgusting. There's nothing sexier than a thick flannel gown that goes from neck to wrist to the floor."

"Smart ass. If you would be so kind as to do me one more favor, would you please bag them up and send them to…to…I don't know. Would a women's shelter take them? Or wherever. I don't care. I just want them gone."

"No problem." The first bag easily snapped open and he bent to fill it. "So." He glanced over his shoulder, pointedly looking at my current ensemble. "Is that what you're wearing to bed?"

The tank top suddenly felt too thin, too tight. I didn't have to look to know my nipples tightened. "It's all I have for now. My one and only Victorian nightgown is in the hamper. I usually wear…wore one of Burt's…" the words trailed off and I gulped. I couldn't finish the statement.

"Ah." Silence held while Dan tied the first bag shut. "You know, Rachel, as much as you want the hurt to go away, it will take some time. You need to allow yourself to mourn. It isn't easy, but don't shut the feelings away."

He'd made a similar comment before and had promised to explain further. This of course piqued my interest and it seemed like a good time to dig a little deeper, what with my vow to show him some attention and all. "Is it true you were married?"

"You didn't know?" He looked surprised.

"I'd heard something…but I'm not one for gossip." Lamely, I spread my hands. Okay, I listened to gossip, but only John and Cyndi had ever spoken about Dan the years he was away.

"Even if you are dead center of it right now." He shook open the second bag and started on the second pile. Clothes that I'd never really liked, were past repair, no longer fit, or were far out of style. I seriously needed some new clothes. "The word has gone out about the attack last night, along with accounts of all the bouquets. Sympathy is running high for you right now. The snake was a really nasty trick."

"Oh?"

"Our beloved librarian has been the victim of the cruelest circumstances and someone dares to threaten her with deadly plants and reptiles?" He gasped in heartfelt dismay. A bit dramatic, but considering our town, it fit. I giggled a little. The pain pill, it made me goofy. No wonder I wanted to cut the dosage. "It doesn't help, or hurt, however you want to see it, that one of the church ladies was an unintentional victim as well."

"Oh dear." That was bad. It was one thing to go after me, but to get an innocent bystander? That pissed me off. "You were saying about your marriage?"

"Right. I married Janice right out of college, just as I joined the Navy. Dan and Jan." He winced. "It was just a little too precious from the start. Anyhow, I don't know why I married her. It seemed like the thing to do and anyone better was already married." He shot me a quick glance before bending back to his task. "So. We married in a quick ceremony out on Treasure Island and headed off on our Navy adventure. Things went pretty well the first year and a half. First stop, Hawaii."

"What happened?"

Dan cleared his throat and a wash of flush warmed his skin. "You happened."

Surprised stiffened my spine and I sat straight up. "Me? I never even met your wife. I hadn't spoken to you in years. Before or after."

Stuffing the last of the clothes in the bag, Dan straightened and concentrated on tying it closed. "True confessions time," he muttered then lifted his head and looked me in the eye. "I brought her home for Christmas. You and Burt were down for the holiday. I don't know if you remember that year, but it was unseasonably warm. You do know the kitchen window over there has a good view of your pool, right?" The house John and Cyndi now lived in had still belonged to his parents at the time.

"Right." I was trying to remember. There'd been so many Christmases in this house. Only once did Burt and I spend Christmas away. We'd gone to his parents' in San Diego early on. That had been such an unqualified disaster we'd never done it again.

"I woke early Christmas day, long before anyone else. John and Cyndi were still in Pensacola because she was pregnant. I was standing at the kitchen window watching the steam rise from the pool when you came downstairs, and started the coffee before heading out back for your morning swim."

"Since I did that every time we came to spend the weekend, this isn't sounding unique."

The pool was heated and kept open year round. My main form of exercise, I liked to roll out of bed and go straight for the pool, something I hadn't done all week and couldn't for the foreseeable future. Dad liked swimming, too. I really wanted to put up some shrubbery or fencing so

I could not bother with swim suits. Hadn't happened yet and I saved my skinny dipping for very late on very hot nights.

"Well, you came out, shrugged off your robe, wearing the skimpiest red swimsuit I'd ever seen. Kind of like that one poster of Farrah Fawcett, only hotter because it clung so tight it might as well have been called skin and not a swim suit."

Ah yes, with Farrah's recent death, her famous poster from the late seventies had made a comeback revival. Every man's wet dream. I also remembered the suit Dan spoke of. I rarely wore anything as bold as that red suit, but I'd been feeling Christmasy and it filled the bill. It had also been thin enough to make out certain features such as areolas and pubic hair. Back then I'd had the body to wear the daring suit, cut high at the leg, low in front and back. It was barely comfortable enough to swim laps in. Burt made me promise to never ever wear it to a public pool. He'd later made sure I never wore it again by playfully ripping it off my body. At least that episode of sex was pleasurably memorable.

"I remember the one," I said.

"Yeah, so do I." His grin was a rueful. "And Janice caught me drooling."

This was news to me, and I absolutely had to have every juicy detail. "And?"

"And she called me on it. Said I never drooled over her like that. I tried to avoid being cruel. I explained how long I'd known you, how you'd always ignored me as the pesky geek next door. How you were the crush of my youth." The boyishly sheepish look was downright adorable. Yes, I was pretty much a goner by then, and I grinned back at him like a maniac clown. He sighed and a touch of regret filled his face. "She didn't buy it. Seems I'd once called her Rachel by mistake. Maybe twice. It was twice too often. She tried holding it over my head, but that grew old very fast. By Valentine's, we'd separated and started divorce proceedings. With no kids, no assets, it was fast and clean."

"Not even two years? And she blamed me?"

He shrugged. "My fault. I never should have married her. It was comfortable for me, and I liked her, but I couldn't worship her the way she wanted, and deserved. Anyhow, my point being, even after so short a time, so little invested, it still took me time to get over the divorce. You've got years invested and the repercussions are just beginning. You can't process all this in just a few days or weeks. Give yourself permission to grieve. There are things you'll miss, like stealing a shirt to sleep in."

Just like a man to remember the original topic. I wanted to hear more about his marriage. Actually, I wanted to steal the t-shirt he wore right off his body. It was a plain dark blue tee, no logos or cute sayings, but it was big enough, he was big enough, the shirt would make a great night shirt for me.

"I suppose…" A yawn stole over me, ruining my covetous stare.

"And right now, you need to scoot your little butt into bed and get some sleep." Dan grabbed the bags and hauled them to the door. While he watched, I crawled from the blanket chest where I'd been sitting, up over the foot of the bed. Yeah, I thought I was being all sexy, until my knee caught on the covers and I fell face first into my pillow. Yup, real grace in action.

Dan laughed and tugged the sheet from under me as I tried to roll onto my back. When I made it, he lifted me with one arm and inserted a second pillow, to make sure my heart was higher than my ankle.

Disgusted, I flopped back onto my fresh pillow and blinked up at him as he pulled the sheet up over me. "So much for my role as Serena the Seductress."

His Adam's apple rose and fell under his heavy gulping action. "We'll get to that later. For now, sleep. Your guardians are on duty."

Another yawn claimed me, but I had a question. "You think my butt is little?"

When he didn't answer right away I opened one eye and found him staring at me in a way guaranteed to set the sheets on fire given a few more minutes. Slowly, his gaze shifted from my pelvis to my face. "Yeah, your butt is perfect. Just right for my hands."

I couldn't help smiling.

He let out a snort and turned for the door. "Go to sleep, Rumple." As far as goodnights go, it was rough and gruff. But I'd take it any night.

"G…night." I snuggled down into the bed and went in search of my last dream.

Chapter 20

Literary license here. July faded into August, which slid into September and the next thing I knew, October had arrived. The world lost icon news anchorman Walter Cronkite, Mrs. football player faded from the columns, Billy Mays's autopsy turned up cocaine in his system, Michael Jackson's doctor found himself accused of overdosing the star, and John Hughes, director of a bunch of eighties teen angst films, joined the obituary listings. My favorite film of his was *Pretty in Pink*, and not because of Molly Ringwald. Andrew McCarthy and Annie Potts made the movie worth watching. Okay, John Crier too, if I must admit it. Ted Kennedy and his sister, Eunice, Maria Shriver's mother, also passed on. The world lost some big names in a few short months.

During this time, all sorts of ups and downs occurred in my own drama, few of which bear repeating in detail as most led me to be a bit pissy and cranky. On the downside, the legal wrangling between my lawyer, Julianna's, Burt's and Brad's, was just too intricate to go into. In a nutshell, Brad's claims to the property were proven false. The money was real, two hundred thousand dollars had traded hands, but where the money now resided became a huge mystery. Searching for it had already cost close to five thousand dollars. I assured Brad once we found the money, and my lawyer was paid from those funds, he could have the rest back. Needless to say, we only spoke through our lawyers at that point.

The mystery of the safe deposit key remained. We'd checked all the bank branches within a twenty-mile radius. David's clerk continued to search farther out.

On the upside--score another point for me--Julianna's copy of the will also proved a forgery. Or at least Burt's signature on it was forged. A very good forgery, but not quite good enough. The notes were in his handwriting, but even Burt's lawyer had to admit he'd never seen the finished and signed document. If I'd wanted to be vindictive, I could have had her charged with the crime, but the expert seemed to think someone else had done the forgery for her, making her an accomplice, not the forgerer. Forger? All she had left was a claim for the child, if indeed it was Burt's. I had my doubts on that as the coroner had come back with the news that Burt *had* had a vasectomy at some time in the past, however, the vas deferens showed signs of reconnecting and, while extremely unlikely, it was possible one or two swimmers had made it from start to finish. One strong swimmer would be enough. The chances? Something along the lines of ten billion to one. However, it would only take one. I continued to demand DNA testing.

The search for Burt's--our--money continued. I discovered why he'd had me on such a tight financial leash. He'd been stashing money away in stocks, bonds, money markets…at least a dozen different accounts in addition to our joint checking and savings. Once probate cleared I'd be a rich woman indeed, independent of the ranch. For the time being, all I had access to was my stash of cash and my paycheck. The rent collected on the four rentals we owned was managed by my lawyer. The insurance companies were holding off pay-out, pending the findings of the investigations.

Yes, investigations. There was the little matter of the medications and the libido supplements. So Burt's medical records were under review looking for signs of foul play. Fortunately, I wasn't under suspicion and I'd turned over all of the medications I'd saved from his bathroom drawer. His floozy, however, was very much in the spotlight. The forged documents made her a person of interest. Bet it didn't sit so well with the morning sickness.

Enough of the legal details for now. Nothing exciting, just long, drawn out processes better left to the lawyers. The upshot? Money remained tight, my stash slowly dwindled and legal bills continued to mount with alarming speed. My lawyer would be able to comfortably retire when all was said and done. Probably with my retirement money.

Aside from the legal issues, there had been a few uplifting incidents to keep me from sliding into a perpetually cranky mood. Such as the night in August when Dan and I spread a blanket out back and watched the Perseid meteor shower. We came quite, quite close to making love there. We did make love, but didn't *go all the way*. We made love with hands and mouths, both on the blanket and in the steaming churning water of the outdoor spa. In its own way, the meteor show was as magical, if not as loud or bright, as a fireworks display. Each burning fragment died a quick death as chunks of space rock and ice created a bright spark upon entering the upper atmosphere. Several of which silently streaked across the sky in short lived display at the height of the first climax he brought me to. It wasn't enough, I wanted more. I wanted him. Badly. And yet he remained determined to hold back from the ultimate symbol of commitment until the moment was right, however he defined that elusive moment.

Nevertheless, life wasn't wholly defined by moments of yearning for a soul mate. Or one kind of soul mate. Other friends touched my life. One such being came from an unexpected quarter. I'd picked up a new admirer at the library.

Adam Makepeace, a shy, twelve-year-old seventh grader at the middle school, had been a friend from the time he'd been old enough to cross the street and come to the library by himself. But after Burt's death, when I returned to work, he made it a habit to bring me a bouquet of daisies once a week. As fall advanced, the bouquets grew smaller, but each Saturday he'd come into the library, with at least one daisy in hand.

Tow headed, he didn't look much like his mother except for his long lanky frame. His mother, Olivia H. Makepeace, preferred to simply go by the name Ohm. Yes, just like the yoga mantra. Her parents, she claimed, had been amongst the early flower children in the heyday of Haight Ashbury. According to her, she could remember her father lifting her up to slip flowers into gun barrels of the riot police lining Telegraph Avenue in Berkeley. From the way she dressed, it was easy to buy her story, right down to the ancient Birkenstocks she favored year round.

Where her son was a sun-bleached blond, she had dark blond hair, attractively streaked with gray, she wore in a waist length braid in keeping with her hippy look. A young looking forty-four, aside from the gray in her hair, she rented one of the two Main Street buildings we owned. Tucked in between the bakery and the herbalist, she lived above the shop, made jewelry, and displayed pottery and other art made by local artists. Lots of tie-dye stuff and peace symbols. She also carried crystals and other metaphysical items for sale. Artsy jewelry wasn't quite my thing, but every once in a while Burt had bought some pieces for me. One such item I often wore was a beaded bracelet in blues and greens that spiraled around my wrist. A blue glass heart rested over my pulse point, something Burt said was to remind me his heart beat in time to mine. I wore it because it was comfortable and I liked it, not because of the giver.

As summer passed and the semester settled in, Adam grew more comfortable asking questions about reference materials for school, or closer to his heart, the science fiction and fantasy books he liked best. Over the summer, I'd noticed he had a strong liking for Heinlein and I was able to use it to draw him out and steer him toward David Eddings' *Belgariad* series. Once he finished the second series, *The Malloreon*, I was set to hand him Dave Duncan's *A Man of His Word* series. From there I had high hopes of getting him to read *The Hobbit* and *The Lord of the Rings*. Tough to convince a kid who's seen the movies he needs to read the books, but I wasn't too worried. I had a good track record in that arena. After all, I had the fourth and fifth graders reading the Harry Potter series, start to finish, and the seventh movie was still in the works at the time. The teen and pre-teen girls were vying for the Twilight series to the point I had to dig out classics like Louisa May Alcott and Jane Austin to keep them in books between reservations. Deanna Taylor, a rough and tumble tomboy, even braved, and loved, *Anna Karenina* by Tolstoy. All huge successes in my book.

If there was a husband or father in the picture, neither Adam nor Ohm had ever said, and no one I knew had ever seen one around. Not unusual for our town. Letty Tisdale, the herbalist, and Sonja Neumeyer, manager of the Bonchamps Inn, were about the same age as Ohm and also had kids without sign of any man around on a steady basis. There were times I wondered if they'd met at an artificial insemination clinic. Their kids were similar in age, ranging from ten to thirteen. None of the kids looked alike or I would have suspected they'd all shared the same donor. But since Letty was a lovely shade of mocha and her twelve-year-old twin girls Ruby and Opal--what was it with people and old fashioned names in our town?--were two shades darker, the same sperm donor theory didn't work. Sonja had thirteen-year-old Samantha of the red hair and ten-year-old Matthew of the black hair. Sonja was blissfully strawberry blonde.

Like I did with most of the citizens of Bonchamps, when I saw the women on the street or in their establishments, I made a point to say hello at the very least, or stop for a short chat when I could. A few errands could take all afternoon unless I looked very rushed. One hint I might be moseying, and it could take two hours to visit three stores. All of them had moved to town within months of when Burt and I had moved back. They were close to me in age, but since I didn't have a child, I found little common ground with any of them. Until their children started coming to my library.

I had good relations with all the kids who came to the library, but Adam stood out. Something about his demeanor spoke of great loneliness and sadness. I had no idea what could inspire such feelings in one so young. All my life I'd been somewhat to one side, away from the crowd, to a certain extent because of the ranch and our perceived social position in town, and in part because I was a rather quiet child who sat on the edges and observed the people around me. Adults tended to become a bit unnerved at that. Still, while Adam seemed to be an observer as well, something else set him apart. Someday, I'd told myself over and over again, I'd figure it out, and I believed I was gaining ground.

The third week of October, two weeks before Halloween, I stood at the main desk working checkout on Saturday, about an hour from closing. The day was warm and each time the front door opened, golden sunshine spilled onto the polished hardwood floors.

The Fiona Butler Martin--great-grandmother on my mother's side-- Library building dated back to the mid 1920s, an elegant period in our town's history. Three floors above ground, one below, our carefully crafted shelves were stuffed with books. The town had been talking of building a newer, bigger library away from town center, but as the library committee reminded the council year after year, there was a lovely park between us and city hall. Instead of building law offices, we could use a third of the space to build an annex for the overflow and future expansion.

What I really wanted to do was build a state of the art building where we could store the older and more fragile historic books and periodicals. Stashed in the relatively climate controlled basement were magazines, newspapers, and books going back a hundred years and more. We had a veritable treasure trove of history in our hands growing closer to irreplaceable decay as each year passed. Volunteers scanned as fast as they could, but the work required patience and painstaking attention to detail. Not something all of my volunteers possessed. Some of them refused to learn how to use a computer. Hadn't had one during the Depression, still managed to live just fine without one. Drove the bank manager around the bend when he tried to sell them on online statements and bill pay.

Where was I? Oh yes, the third Saturday of October. The Halloween decorations were mostly up. I'd recruited some older teens to come in the previous week. Particularly the taller boys, who drew in the girls. The girls had the knowhow to make it attractive, the boys had the height to get it done. Worked for me.

Deputy Dan was off duty and hanging out at my desk, flirting with me and any female, from infant to senior, who entered the library. An attempt to tease me out of my funk. Bills had arrived in great profusion the day before and I was busy trying to figure out if I had enough money to pay them and eat too. Dad had never expected rent, but Burt and I had agreed to pay the taxes on that part of the property. Not cheap, and I did not want to go whining back to Dad about it. He'd already paid a significant number of my bills.

Working the checkout desk helped me forget my troubles, and the line had been steady all afternoon. My feet were as tired as the rest of me. Fortunately, the line petered out as everyone wanted to head home and get ready for Saturday night. Maybe I could lock up a few minutes early. The VFW doors would open in three hours for an all ages dance, sort of a social warm up to Halloween. Dan had it in his mind I'd be his dancing partner. My efforts to persuade him to stay in and watch a DVD were starting to make inroads when the door opened and Adam came in, a bunch of daisies in hand.

"Hey, there's Adam," I said as cheerfully as I could. Considering how Dan had been working to make me blush, it was a pretty cheery greeting, if a bit forced.

Adam looked from me to Dan and back again.

"How are you today? You're a bit later than usual. Everything okay?" I asked.

"Um, yeah. Just fine." Adam drew himself up, extending those long lanky bones, which had recently lengthened enough he now stood two inches taller than me. Not exactly a bragging point--most people stood taller than me. Which was why I loved the K through fourth graders. They were more my size.

"What are you looking for this week?" I asked.

"Finished *Guardians of the West*. What's book two again?" He slid the book across the counter. "Oh, here." He thrust the bundled daisies my direction.

"Thank you!" I held out the cleaned vase already complete with fresh water. "Just plop them right in, if you please." Memories of my poisoned gifts were still strong and I avoided touching plants without my gardening gloves on. Adam knew this and didn't think it odd. He untied and unwound the white ribbon wrapped around the stems and put the flowers, half a dozen today, in the water, careful to make sure the stems were seated between the clear glass marbles in the bottom. I'd discovered the marbles made wonderful weights and kept the vase from tipping over.

What I found interesting was how Dan subtly went into alert mode. After nearly four months of being near him as much as possible, I'd learned most of his body language. One moment he was loose and teasing, the next he was still smiling, but slightly tense, his gaze sharpened.

"Book two," I said to Adam, "is *King of the Murgos*. You'll find it on the shelf."

"Thanks, Miss Rachel." Adam skirted Dan and headed for the stairs.

"Miss Rachel?" Dan asked while his hand stopped mine reaching for the book.

"I've asked the kids to call me that. I don't like being called Mrs. Bruckmeister." A shudder of the not so pleasant kind rippled across my shoulders and I tried to pull my hand from Dan's.

"Got a plastic bag handy?"

"Why?"

"Check that book out to me. I need it for evidence."

I heard the words, but they didn't make sense. None whatsoever. "What?"

"Just do it, Rachel. I need to lift some prints from the book. I'll have it back to you in a couple days, I promise."

"Prints? You think Adam is my poisoned posy man?" I scoffed. "Really, he's a child. What could he have against me? He's a good kid, Dan."

"That very well may be. However, all the poisoned bouquets were tied with white ribbon identical to the ribbon that bunch was tied with and tied in the same manner." A thoughtful frown wrinkled his brow. "Damn, I wonder if I can get the ribbon from him?"

I wanted to laugh in his face, but as calm as his words were, they were chilling. "No. Can't be. It's a common way of tying up bridal bouquets. I can show you a dozen magazines demonstrating the style."

"Rachel," he said softly, his hand warm around my suddenly icy one. "I just want to be sure. You're most likely right, but this is the only lead we've had in months."

Short on rebuttals to his logic, I nodded. There hadn't been another attack since the night of the funeral. Community support for me had been amazing to say the least. I never knew so many people were aware of the details of my life, and with the house now fully covered by infrared cameras set to activate with motion detectors and heat signals in the human range, the deliveries had stopped cold. No fingerprints, no identifiable shoe prints, nothing. Anyone approaching me with plant material was closely scrutinized and community bulletins had gone out on how to find, identify and eradicate poison oak, poison sumac, poison ivy, ragweed and other toxic plants in addition to reminders about snakes and how to treat their bites.

In fact, anyone wanting to start a career in flora terrorism had a blueprint kindly provided by the Bonchamps city council. Fortunately, no one had taken up that line of work and I'd been left alone in the plant department, other than the daisies the kids brought me. Shastas remained on the *Highly Approved* list.

"All right, I'll find a bag. Hold on."

Lucky for Dan, I kept a few plastic grocery bags on hand for people who either forgot or couldn't afford the official library book bag. The staff had managed to sell close to five hundred of the new bags made from recycled materials. Weren't libraries about reusing resources? I thought about making him buy a bag just for the principle. After all, I'd designed the picture on it from clipart I had for doing the monthly library newsletter. Darn cute if I did say so myself. All proceeds went into buying more books and computers for the citizens of Bonchamps.

By the time I found a bag, Dan had the book in a careful hold and gently put it inside.

"Now what?"

"It goes to the lab for printing and comparison. We lifted a few partial prints from the first ribbon, but nothing that matches up with IAFIS."

"Aphids?" I knew what he was talking about, but I wanted to see if he knew what the acronym stood for. Tweaking him like that often provided much entertainment.

"The FBI's Integrated Automated Fingerprint Identification System, smarty." Ooh, that look said he was on to me. Darn. I was still trying to get him into me and having little success. Which was why he was pushing for a night out, as opposed to staying in. Part of the reason for my petulance.

Elbows braced on the counter to support me, I leaned toward him. "I love it when you spell out long acronyms, big boy."

"And that is precisely why we're going to the dance." The kiss to the tip of my nose in no way satisfied me at all.

"But I have a very special movie all picked out. One I've been told absolutely must be watched with a friend."

He raised a brow. I'd tried all sorts of chick flicks out on him with no success.

I leaned closer and dropped my voice. "It's a pirate movie with lots of eye liner on the actors."

"I've seen *Pirates of the Caribbean* and it's not a cuddling movie," he said dryly.

"You're close, but not quite on target... Add a few levels of maturity rating." Sheesh, could I get any more blatant?

While Dan choked, I considered our current circumstances.

Me, trying to seduce a younger man. Twenty years ago the situation had been completely reversed. Younger men, older men, all of them trying to get between the legs of any girl who would go out with them, even me.

A few misguided souls had considered plain, mousy me an easy mark. Ha! I'd proven them wrong.

Jim Santos had taught me a few things about what guys wanted from girls. I went to college wiser in many ways than my contemporaries, but still very naïve in others. Jim cared enough to teach me about condoms and being safe. Which reminded me, I'd heard he was back in town. Hadn't run into him as of yet. Maybe he'd be at the dance. Not that I was interested in him, but since Dan knew our past history, maybe…nah. I didn't play those games. Still, if Jim was at the VFW and if he did ask me to dance, I wouldn't say no.

"You planned to show a porno?" Dan gasped quietly, though his eyes immediately grew dark, his lids dropping to half mast. I wanted to do him right there.

Hmm, library fantasy time? How soon could I get the building emptied? Bad thought. Bad, Rachel. With a heavy sigh of heartfelt regret, I peevishly straightened and turned to the computer. "Nothing else is working on you." Now I'd thought about it, I felt quite grumpy over the situation. "Never mind, we'll go to the dance. If you don't want to play with me, I'm sure I can find someone else to dance with."

All right, all right, so I wasn't above a little game playing. I just loved seeing him choke on the words he wouldn't have spared me in private.

When it came to our relationship, groping wasn't the problem. We did plenty of groping and kissing and touching. But all action stopped when it came to Insert-Tab-A-into-Slot-B. Heavy petting under clothing. That's all he would allow and I'd been forced to buy new toys. Maybe I'd ditch him altogether in favor of my brand new Hitachi Magic Wand with attachments.

Before I could pull up the checkout information on the book, Dan vaulted over the counter and pulled me back against him. I loved it when he did those aggressive strength moves. Just to see those arm muscles bunching and rippling was worth needling him. Definitely a shiver factor of at least eight points involved. Maybe nine. Ten when he used those muscles to lift and carry me.

"You're playing with fire, Rumple."

"Yes, well, I'm on fire, so it only seems fair."

For an answer, he pushed his hips against me. My heart leapt and breath hitched, as instant desire flooded my entire being. I knew that protuberance I could feel through my proper cotton skirt and nylon slip, especially since I wore a comfortable cotton thong that day. All it would take, all he had to do, was lift my skirt and I'd be open to him.

Fortunately, or unfortunately, the sound of footsteps coming down the uncarpeted stairs gave us plenty of warning. Dan gave me a tingling smack on the rear, then pulled away and moved back to a corner where he could hide his erection. Wanting to smirk, I had a difficult time smoothing my face as Adam entered the lobby.

"Did you find it?" I asked.

Adam nodded and placed the next two books of the series on the desk.

"Reading that fast?"

Adam pulled his library card from his pocket and nodded. Back in shy mode. Probably because of Dan. I smiled and scanned the card and books, feeling a little sheepish myself. My behavior was not appropriate for public, especially in the library.

"Friday's an in-service day," Adam finally said with a small shrug.

"Ah yes." Not having kids, I didn't quite track school holidays as closely as others. Not that weekends meant a whole lot anymore. Since Burt's death, I'd chosen to work the weekends. Kids like Adam had parents who worked weekends, often leaving the kids no place to go if they wanted to be someplace other than their parents' shops. The library and the park beside it were better alternatives than video babysitters.

"Are you going to the VFW dance tonight?" I asked.

He merely shook his head.

"A handsome guy like you, you'd have plenty of girls to dance with."

Adam flushed but stuck his card back in his pocket and picked up the books.

"She's right, you know," Dan said. "How old are you now? Thirteen? Fourteen?"

"Twelve," Adam said.

"I was twelve when I started asking the prettiest girl in town to dance. She turned me down a few times."

"Oh? I thought I saw you dancing with Jane Beheymer more than once." I sniffed. She'd been at least five years older than Dan.

"Only because you wouldn't dance with me." He glanced at Adam and shook his head. "Older women are tricky. I asked someone even older to dance because I wanted to make Miss Rachel jealous."

Attention caught, Adam asked, "Did it work?"

"Eventually." Dan grinned at me. "She's going to the dance with me tonight."

"Maybe." I responded. "I'm looking for a partner who knows how to dance."

Adam looked at me, all big blue eyes and tousled blond hair. "I'll dance with you. If you go, I'll go."

"Then it's a date." I decided. Anything to help Adam break out of his shell a little. "I'll be there." And I'd wear something short, sexy and shocking. Could I get away with the red dress I'd bought while picking up end of season swim suits to replace the stock cleaned out on the Fourth of July?

"Always with the blonds," Dan sighed dramatically. "You guys get all the girls. Must be the beach boy look."

A smirk twitched at the corner of my lips. "That's just what you think." I turned to Adam. "Eight o'clock at the VFW. It's a date."

Chapter 21

The library closed at six, which meant I only had two hours to get ready and consume a bite of dinner. Less, figuring in stopping to pick up dinner and transit times back and forth. Dan of course, drove me home. My self-appointed escort. Not that I minded so much, but after a day on my feet, I really wanted to put them up...and up, and up. I had visions of Dan kneeling over me, my feet, bare, on his shoulders, also bare. That cemented my decision on what to wear. I'd just have to dress in such a way he wouldn't miss my message. It had been over four months since I'd had sexual intercourse with a live man and I had an itch toys couldn't scratch.

Since he'd come to the library already dressed for our date--creased blue jeans, white button down shirt, and boots--we were a cowboy town after all--we stopped to pick up take out from the deli counter at the grocery store. Not that there were many choices, but enough that we had a vegetable salad, macaroni salad, some sliced meat and cheese and an excellent focaccia. Throw in a bottle of zinfandel and we were set.

Enough weeks had passed without incident, Dad had moved back to his small bungalow in town. However, because he was still concerned, as was Dan, they both were able to log in and review the time stamped digital recordings from the surveillance cameras at any time from the comfort of their own homes. I could check as well, but I preferred to leave it to the experts. It was interesting to note the comings and goings of some of my neighbors. We all suspected Al Terpstra three houses down of having an affair, but none of us wanted to alert his wife, Melanie. Would I have appreciated it had anyone told me point blank about Burt? No, I wouldn't have. But I made a point of being extra nice to Melanie. She had little ones not old enough for school, so I invited them over to swim on Tuesday mornings when the weather was warm enough. For the foreseeable future, the weather was holding very nicely.

When Dan and I reached my house, we were alone. I waved at Cyndi through the windows and pulled the drapes. She smiled and waved even as she flipped me off. Dan glanced up from the kitchen island where he unpacked dinner.

"I'm tired of being on display," I said simply. There were a lot of curtains and blinds, so closing them took a few minutes. Finally, privacy ensured, I reached behind me and unfastened my skirt. At the sound of the zipper, Dan looked up from opening the sliced turkey. "Mind if I get a little more…comfortable?"

That Adam's apple of his bobbed, to my great satisfaction. "What was the movie you wanted to put on?"

My skirt hit the floor. "Movie? Oh right, the pirate one. You already said you don't want to watch it. I just need to get out of these clothes and then we can eat." The slip followed the skirt and I kicked off my flats. Turning so he could see the back side of my underwear, or rather, the lack of backside, I bent to pick up my clothes.

"Rachel," Dan growled from behind me a moment before he grabbed my waist. Had to give the man credit for silent movement. With one hand on my lower back, he held me bent over. "You're playing with fire, woman. What is it going to take to convince you, you're not ready for this?"

"I'm ready, dammit!" Blood rushing into my head made me a bit more emphatic.

"No, you aren't." His big hand landed on my exposed butt. It didn't hurt, but it did sting. "Be patient, Rumple."

In a jaw-dropping, over the top sexy, he-man move, Dan lifted and flipped me right side up and into his arms. One moment I was practically standing on my head, the next I was cradled in his arms.

"You've been restless and edgy since yesterday and you're trying to use sex to distract yourself."

"No, I want sex because I haven't had any and I'm horny!" Struggling didn't gain me much more than his arms tightening around me. Which would have been great had he intended to take me upstairs and ravish me properly. I wanted it so badly I would have sold my grandmother to get it, and he knew it, but he wasn't about to break his own precious rule. Whatever it was. He still hadn't explained it to me other than to say when the time was right, the time was right.

Ignoring me, as much as he could with me wiggling in his arms, Dan carried me upstairs. Hoping he was finally giving in, I looped my arms around his neck.

"Come on, we have time, we don't even have to go to the dance." Turning to the softer side of persuasion, I tried to beguile him into giving up his high-handed morals. If blowing in his ear and playing with the soft hair at his nape didn't work, I was prepared to shoot myself. Or him. I might even reduce myself to begging. "I don't have to be at work until one and you're off tomorrow."

"You have a date, remember? Don't you dare let that boy down." The reminder was made in as rough a growl I'd ever heard come from the deputy as he turned sideways and shouldered his way into my room.

My newly redecorated room. Gone was every navy blue accessory I'd ever used. In place were soft colors of sage, rose, periwinkle and lavender. Filmy drapes, silky swags on the four-poster, and the bedding made up with variations of the colors in soft, lazy waves and swirls that looked like a watercolor of a garden in the summer. Drifting with the fantasy gave the impression of standing in a riotous garden of iris, delphiniums, petunias, tulips, crocus and soft pink roses like the ones Dan had given me. The very ones still in the basket sitting near the doors to the widow's walk, lending a sweet fragrance to the air. Not one hard geometric line in the place other than the architectural details. All my room needed, all I wanted to add to my room, was the hot, hunky deputy holding me in his arms. This room had one purpose in mind. Seduction.

Dan hadn't seen my room in months, not since I'd recovered and my guardian force had moved back home. I watched his face as he took in the changes and my heart sank as his jaw tightened. I'd been seeing that look more and more as my libido started talking to me more and more.

"When we make love, it won't be a quickie, Rumple." He stopped by the bed, glared at me, then dropped me right onto the mattress, where I bounced. If he ground those molars any more, he'd have dust. "*When* we make love," he continued to growl, "it will take all night, most likely an entire weekend." His eyes smoldered with lust, but also a fair measure of anger. "But I'm betting on a full week." He walked to the door, his dress cowboy boots thumping on the hardwood floors. Hand on the door knob, he turned back. "Now get dressed. We leave in forty-five minutes."

"Fat lot of good it does me now!" I shouted and threw one of the smaller pillows his direction. The door thumped shut, the pillow bounced off it, and I rolled over and screamed my frustration into the bed.

I lay there for several minutes trying to catch my breath and bring my neediness under control. No luck. I was restless, itchy and aching. And if Dan wasn't going to give me what I needed, then it was time for him to suffer. Immensely.

Forty-five minutes later, I sauntered downstairs, freshly showered, hair dressed for maximum flirt, legs shaved, every inch of my skin lotioned to perfect smoothness and make up troweled on as only a cowgirl on the make could do. My earrings were big, flashy chandeliers sparkling with clear and ruby colored crystals, and my dress, what there was of it, swirled around my thighs. For warmth, as the nights had taken on a slight autumn chill, I had a webby black shawl of lace. My shoes had three-inch stiletto heels, as high as I thought I could stand for a few hours of dancing. And red. Scarlet red, like my dress. A little country ruffle, a lot sassy short skirt and clingy bodice with thin straps to hold the crossed panels in place as they formed a deep V, front and back, which pretended to cover me modestly. But as any man knew, one swipe and those straps would slide off my shoulders and down my arms. Wouldn't take much else for the rest of the dress to disappear. Beneath it, I wore a red lace thong and my sexiest perfume.

Dan looked up from the newspaper he'd been reading at the island counter. His eyes darkened but he said nothing as I strolled into the kitchen and silently proceeded to transfer items from my everyday handbag into a small black silk purse with a thin strap long enough to wear crosswise. I separated house and car keys from my heavy ring, pulled my license, credit card and what cash I had from my wallet, about fifty dollars in odd bills, and tucked it all in with the condom and lipstick I already had in the tiny bag.

Without saying a word, Dan watched it all. When I patted my purse into place and adjusted the shawl around my shoulders, he held out a napkin-wrapped sandwich made from a square of focaccia and the deli slices. "You can eat it on the way."

I took it from him. "Thank you." And headed for the back door.

"The car's out front," he said.

"I know." Hey, I'd read enough mystery novels to know one should never, ever, tell the opponent the plans. I made it out the door, and locked it, before he figured it out. By the time I slid into the driver's seat of my car, he'd made it out the door and stood on the back porch, hands on hips, glaring at me. Pushing my car to exercise its engine just a little, I made it to the end of the street before he made it to his own car. Someone had to lock up the house and Dan would never drive away with it unsecured.

And that, Deputy Dan, I thought, was how this game was going to be played.

Peevish enough to be reckless, I drove to the VFW and talked young Roy Hoskins into parking my car for me as all the best spots were taken and I didn't want to walk three blocks in my three-inch heels. Judging by how the twenty-two-year-old eyed my legs, he didn't want me to tire myself out too soon either.

I'd never, ever, been known for making an entrance. Not on my own. With Burt I'd made entrances, but usually as an accessory that never outshone the man. I'd glittered and smiled, but he'd been the star. Always.

If the Fourth of July had been my day of independence, then that night was my coming out. Letting the reckless mood carry me, I swayed up those steps, my flirty skirt swirling about my thighs. Just inside the door, I stopped and surveyed.

Conversation screeched to a halt and I was surveyed back by every eye in the joint. Of course people had seen my new hairdo soon after the funeral and had gasped in shock then, but they hadn't seen me in anything other than sober librarian garb, demure sundresses, or jeans and tees since. It was a fact, no one in town had ever seen me in scarlet, or in a dress with a hem four inches above my knees, or wearing heels over two inches high. The shawl slid down my shoulders to gather at my elbows. They looked. And stared. And whispered.

A few of the stares were hostile--from some of the women, married and single, in my age range--a greater number smiled with wicked glee. Edna had been telling me for weeks I needed to kick up my heels and set the town on fire, but this time, it was the men who sat up and took notice. Everything feminine in me purred with delight. If only Burt could see me now. *Take that, asshole.* And Dan. Asshole number two.

Before anyone else moved, Adam was there, dressed in clean black trousers and a pressed blue shirt that made his eyes look almost as blue as Burt's had been, hair combed and shoes polished. In fact, he looked so much like a younger version of Burt, my breath caught and I blinked. If I was seeing Burt in the face of a twelve-year-old boy, my situation was far more dire than I'd originally thought. Definitely, I'd been too long without sex. Well, I had a mission to end the dry spell and, wicked woman that I intended to become, I wasn't above using a boy to get my point across to a thirty-seven-year-old man. I took Adam's arm.

When Dan arrived, I'd claimed a chair between Mrs. Scarborough and Edna, who promised to watch my purse and shawl, not far from where my father chatted with his ranching buddies, and I was already dancing a two-step with Adam. Jim Santos stood on the edge of the dance floor, arms folded with a speculative twinkle in his eyes.

Twenty-four years after Jim and I'd had our short sweet week together, I once again noticed he didn't look bad at all. Without the cowboy hat this time, I could see his hair was still mostly black, but as he was a few years older than me, a few attractive silver strands touched his temples. Shorter than the men I was used to, Jim was still inches taller than me, lean in the hips and comfortable in his cowboy boots and creased black jeans. Complete with large, polished, silver buckle on his black leather belt.

Only Dan looked better. I could hear the whispers and see the heads bent together as tongues wagged and stories flew from group to group. But they weren't so preoccupied as to miss Dan's entrance and how he stopped to glower at me. Ruthlessly, I bent my full attention on Adam, who, with the heels I wore, matched me for height.

"Miss Rachel, you're the nicest grownup I've ever met," my young escort said.

"Thank you, Adam, I'm happy to hear it, but I must be truthful, I'm not nice at all." The night's earlier interaction with Dan had spotlighted me at my worst. *Perturbed and petty* described me fairly well, but I didn't feel like changing. Not at that moment. Not even telling myself I'd be ashamed later worked. The possibility I might have been PMSing had crossed my mind, and I half expected Dan to accuse me of such later. I'd already decided he'd die if he broached the subject, because any man who said it obviously had no right to breathe. Of course, I couldn't say any of this to Adam. It would have exploded his twelve-year-old brain. Ten years down the road he might understand, but not right then.

I enjoyed dancing with Adam. For his age, he was amazingly self-possessed and knew how to dance. A compliment to the same brought a pleased flush and a confession that his mother made him attend cotillion each spring.

The song was winding down and I saw both Jim and Dan starting our direction. "Take me over by Matthew. I'll dance with him next."

Adam raised a brow in a manner too old for his young face, looking even more like Burt. I needed to stay away from blond males if each one was going to remind me of my husband. "But what about the deputy?"

"I came by myself. I'll dance with who I want. Come get me for a waltz next, all right?" They usually played the first one at the end of the first set.

Bewildered, he nevertheless agreed and when the music ended, we stood near Sonja Neumeyer and her two kids, who were chatting with Letty Tisdale's twins. Ohm was there as well, talking with Sonja and Letty.

"Ohm, your son dances beautifully," I said.

She looked a bit startled. Her lashes fluttered and a hand flew to her throat, but she composed herself enough to say, "Thank you."

Because I was focused on the men working their way toward me, I didn't pay her any more mind and turned to the kids.

"Matthew?" The ten-year-old turned my way, his green eyes round. With his black hair he was going to be a lady killer in about five years. Six at the very most. Only an inch or two shorter than me, he was adorable now. "Would you be so kind as to honor me with the next dance?"

"Um…" He glanced nervously at his mother, who beamed, and Adam, who nodded. "Um, yeah, sure, Miss Rachel."

"Don't worry, I don't step on toes," I assured him and gently led him out to the dance floor where a few brave couples were attempting to Jitterbug. "Do you know anything about dancing?"

Swallowing nervously, he shook his head.

"No worries, we'll go gentle." Teaching boys to dance was nothing new. At the all-ages dances I tried to dance with a few of the teens, just as other adults made a point of dancing with the kids who were there. Little girls danced on their daddy's feet and moms tried to teach their sons to lead. Kids like Roy Hoskins had been my partners once upon a time. He was now popular among the teen girls, though he had his eye on Charlie Gibbs. Just a year older than him, she carefully ignored him, much to his amused dismay. I could see he was determined and silently cheered him on.

A few mis-starts, and laughs, later, Matthew and I settled into a rocking, swinging, sort of dance, loosely based on the Jitterbug, but without the fancy spins and twists. Adam danced nearby with Sonja's daughter, Samantha. I loved seeing that first blush of confidence bloom on a boy's face. By the end, we were a little breathless and laughing at the teens preening and posing for each other.

Before either Dan or Jim could get close, Roy claimed me for the next song. After him, the celebrated quarterback from the high school football team. I went from young man to teen to preteen, dancing with boys too young for either Dan or Jim to be cruel enough to cut in on. My father, however, had no such compunction and when the waltz at the end of the set came around, he cut in.

"Dad, I promised Adam."

"My apologies, Adam, but as father of the belle of the ball, I'm claiming this dance." He said it kindly and Adam bowed out.

"What's the game, Chi-chi?" he asked before we'd made the first turn.

Silently I sighed in relief. A man who really knew how to twirl a woman around the dance floor. My skirt flared out just the right amount and air swirled up my legs. In the hot room, on my sweaty flesh, it felt gloriously cool. For a second I caught the smoldering look in Dan's gaze and how it traveled down my body. He'd noticed my legs.

"Game?" I echoed Dad.

"I know when a woman's playing games. You're old enough to know exactly what you're doing." Under the brows drawn together, his eyes skewered me.

He also knew me. Score one for Dad. "Dan's being a pill."

"I figured that much out, but what is he doing?"

"It's more a matter of what he's not doing."

Did I really want to discuss sex and my itchy mood with my father? Did he really want to know? Dammit, I was thirty-nine and not nineteen. I didn't owe him any more of an explanation than I'd already given him.

Dad eyed me as if he could read every thought in my head. I'd confessed more crimes as a child under that stare than I cared to remember.

"Relax, Dad. Why do you think I'm sticking to the younger crowd? No chance of any molesting there."

He snorted. "You're messing with impressionable young minds."

"I am not behaving inappropriately with any of them." I wasn't. I kept them at arm's length and kept my expression and conversation friendly.

"I'll admit you've done more to get the kids dancing than anyone else."

I opened my mouth to reply, but he cut me off.

"But, you're being unnecessarily cruel to a man who has treated you with nothing but kindness and kid gloves."

"He's stubborn and domineering," I replied, even knowing Dad was right.

"Be that as it may, he's stuck by you through some rough times and will still be there when this whole thing is settled once and for all." He spun me around the edge near the band. Dan was twenty feet down in the direction Dad led me. "As long as you treat him with the respect he deserves for putting up with you."

"Putting up with me?" I gasped in outrage. "Putting up with me? When have I ever not been compliant and yielding to anyone around me? When have I ever put a toe out of line? I've been the good girl all my life and all I've gotten for it is men leading me on, cheating behind my back, pushing me here, there and wherever good girls are supposed to sit quietly and not complain."

As shocked as if I'd slapped him, Dad came to an abrupt halt. Ernie Cole bumped into him with an apology. "What are you talking about?"

"I'm talking about being a doormat for men. You all flatter me with shopping trips, dinner out, watching over, and petting me like I'm a fifty-seven Chevy, but do any of you actually care about what goes on inside of me?" I released Dad's hand and pointed to my heart. "Have any of you listened to what I say I need?" He opened his mouth to answer, but I rushed on. "No! You haven't. You know more about cars, horses and cows than you do your women. I'm a grown woman, Daddy, and I have needs. I'm tired of being patted on the head and told I don't know what I'm talking about."

Of course, by this time we had an audience, and being front and center, Dan tried to usher us toward the door. Refusing to be herded anywhere, I turned on him, and stabbed my finger into his chest. "And you! You're the worst patronizing he-man yet!" He wasn't, but did it really matter to me at that point?

Wisely, he kept his mouth shut, but unwisely he grasped my arm and continued to try and shepherd me toward the door.

Wrenching my arm from him, I turned and two steps--all right, two stomps--later, ran smack dab into Jim Santos.

"Care for a beer?" he asked, dark eyes glittering and sensual lips curved in amusement. The man had anticipated the break just being announced and held two ice cold bottles, dripping with condensation.

"Love one." I grabbed one Corona from him, stuffed the wedge of lime down into the bottle, tipped it up, and sucked the cold fizzy brew into my parched throat. It was the best thing I'd tasted so far that night.

The hard body against my back could only be one person. Jim's glare over my shoulder confirmed it.

"Back off, Deputy. The lady just agreed to spend the break with me." The tone was genial enough, but the sharp eyes and the words were not.

"She came with me," Dan said.

"I came by myself," I reminded him with an elbow to the ribs. "Jim, haven't seen you since the Fourth. How you been keeping yourself?" I took the arm he offered me and led him to the table where Edna and the ladies kept watch over my purse.

Dan wasn't thrilled with the power play, Dad sent me evil looks, Jim didn't like the fact I took refuge with some of the eldest of the town elders. J.J. got into the act and glared at Jim. I briefly flashed back to Dan's black eye and once more wondered what Jim had said that night to make J.J. mad. It must have been good because J.J. was, apparently, still mad, and Adam stared on thoroughly confused.

Edna patted my arm and smiled at Jim. "How are your parents?" she asked.

With a chuckle and grace, Jim relaxed in his chair. "Just fine, ma'am and how have you been keeping? You don't look a day older than when you were smacking my fingers in the library for talking too loud." He let out a playful yelp when Mrs. Scarborough whacked his arm with her cane from his other side.

I drank my beer, cooled down, and eased into the bantering, all the while trying to figure out how I was going to get myself out of there without a convoy of escorts following me home. Any chance of sneaking away for wild, uninhibited sex had evaporated like a puddle in the Sahara.

Chapter 22

Break over, the musicians started up again fifteen minutes later. In that time, I learned Jim was home between jobs to help his parents do some work on their house. He'd been living and working on the east side of the San Francisco Bay Area. Housing tracts had gone up like weeds the last twenty years and recently construction had slowly ground down to a near halt, giving him the time.

As the band began warming up, Jim finished the last of his beer, stood and extended a hand. "Dance with me?"

I sucked down the last swig of my own beer and let him help me to my feet. "Let me make a dash to the ladies room and I'd be happy to accept your invitation."

"I'll escort you." He held the empties in one hand and took my hand with his other. We left the twittering ladies--and I do mean talking face to face and not online, we did things the old fashioned way--and made our way through the crowd to the restrooms at the back. "Meet you back here," he said and I nodded.

Thankfully the rush was over, and I slid into a stall. A few minutes later I stood at the sink gently blotting my face with a cool, damp paper towel.

Cyndi found me there and, ignoring the stares of the few women still cycling through, she snapped, "Just what the hell do you think you're doing tonight?"

What I wanted to say, *Trying to get laid,* differed greatly from what actually came out of my mouth. "Leave me alone, Cyndi, I'm a big girl and if I screw up, then I'm the only one to blame for it."

"Screw up is right." She snorted and primped in the mirror. "Dan's been--"

"*--nothing but nice to me and stood by me all these months, providing emotional support and security.* I know the song and dance." I'd left my purse with Edna and didn't have my ruby red lipstick with me. Fortunately, it was the kind that would wear off sometime in the next decade. "Got some plain gloss I can borrow?"

Rolling her eyes, Cyndi dug in her purse. "You know I love you like a sister..."

"...and I you..."

"...so forgive me if I say you aren't acting at all like yourself lately."

Taking my time, I smoothed the gloss over my red lips, using the mirror to catalog the changes. More than just my hair and clothes--something inside me had changed. I didn't look meek or dull anymore. My eyes had a hard edged spark to them I didn't recognize. I didn't look like me, I didn't act like me, but most of all, I didn't feel like me. "You're right. I'm changing. I didn't like the old me, the doormat. I want to be more. I want to make my decisions about my life. If I don't learn to stand on my own two feet now, I might as well curl up and die." The question was, did I like the new me? I didn't know yet. I wasn't done changing.

"Aw, honey." The southern drawl was in full sugar force as Cyndi rubbed my arm. "I know this has been hard on you." The pity in her eyes overwhelmed me. I hated seeing pity in anyone's eyes.

"Did you know?" I interrupted the speech I'd been hearing in various forms from everyone in town for the last three months.

"Know?" Cyndi blinked her big blue eyes. "Know what?"

Not knowing who might be in the stalls, I leaned close and murmured as quietly as I could. "About Burt? About his cheating? And lying and... and...everything?"

"Honey." Cyndi's hand flopped as she tried to explain without saying anything, and another layer of ice adhered itself to the growing wall of it around my heart. Something must have showed in my face, because she rushed to explain. "Honey, I tried to tell you, but you didn't want to hear it. I prodded as gently as I could without sitting you down and spilling it straight out, but every time anyone tried to tell you, you changed the subject or left the room. It was going on right under your nose, and you didn't see a thing. I don't know how many times he hit on me."

Was there anything worse than being confronted with blindness in a public bathroom? "Fine, fine," I capitulated, and sagged against the counter. God, she was right. I'd seen him whispering in her ear. I'd seen him whispering in lots of female ears, and I'd seen the blushes and heard the giggles. The pain nearly knocked me to my knees right there. Thank heaven for the counter behind me. "You're right. I know you are."

"You're just upset about this DNA thing dragging out."

I covered my eyes with a shaking hand. "I just want it over. Not knowing is driving me crazy. What if it *is* Burt's? What if there are others? What if I spend the rest of my life with his bastards appearing on my doorstep? What's my obligation? How many could there be? Why don't *I* have any children?"

"Hush, honey." Cyndi hugged me lightly--didn't want to mess up her makeup or carefully fluffed hair. "It will all work out. Didn't the coroner say he'd been snipped? There can't be that many children out there."

"There shouldn't be *any*." Anger once more stiffened my spine. "The accountant we hired has found records of large amounts of cash withdrawn, one lump sum each month, the amount slowly decreasing each year as he works backward. It doesn't match with anything else and it doesn't account for any of the investments. What if it was child support? When will that child, or its mother, come to me demanding more? It's enough money that whoever it went to has to be noticing the lack of it by now."

Even though I'd been quiet, Cyndi flapped her hand and leaned close. "This is not the place to talk about it!" she hissed at me.

"Right, right. Of course you're right." Even with the constant background noise of music from the hall, flushing commodes and people washing their hands, conversations could still be overheard when you wanted it least. "Besides, I've got Jim Santos waiting for me." I handed back the gloss, fluffed the back of my hair, straightened my dress and smiled into the mirror. The smile looked cold and hard.

Cyndi pinched me as Ohm left a stall and moved to a sink nearby.

I was rubbing the spot when Ohm's gaze caught mine in the mirror. The look on her face led me to believe she had something to say, so I waited. Finally she nodded. "Those earrings look good on you," she said.

I remembered then Burt had bought them from her store. "You do nice work."

She shrugged, but the perusal she gave me felt odd. I didn't have time to figure it out because Jim took advantage of someone opening the door.

"Rachel? You still in there or did you sneak out through a window?"

Over the giggles, I called back, "On my way!" and ignored Cyndi's warning glare.

Jim grinned as I emerged. "Whoooeee! You sure are worth the wait, *querida*."

"Yeah, yeah." I took his arm. The first song was nearly over, but it segued right into the next one, a perfect two-step. Didn't have to live in Texas to know country and western dances and music. Jim spun me into his arms, pulled me close, much closer than my younger partners had dared to try, and expertly led the way.

"Good to dance with a man?" White teeth flashed from his wide grin.

"Although I love dancing with the boys, I do appreciate an experienced partner from time to time."

"And we have experience, do we not?" he murmured in my ear during a particularly close spin, one strong thigh pressed intimately between mine long enough to let me know just how much he wanted to resume relations.

Laughing, I pulled away to see his eyes. "I'm not much into discussing the good old days." Now I was there, in his arms, the appeal of going back in time had lessened. As I was different, Jim seemed like another man. Well that made sense, he'd been very young so very long ago. Younger than Roy was now.

His smile was charming, but his words seemed every bit as insincere as I expected them to be. "I've missed you. You didn't let me explain last summer. I came back for you later and found out you were married. It broke my heart."

Remembering Dad and his guns, I couldn't help my snicker. "I don't want to talk about it," I reminded him with a small smack on the shoulder.

"All right, let's talk about today. I know you work at the library."

"Yes. I'm in charge now."

"You're the one smacking fingers these days."

I laughed. "Not allowed, sadly."

"Political correctness is creating a spoiled generation."

"Not so much. The kids are good. They give me few problems beyond late returns."

"And how late does a book have to be before you punish the offender?"

Still shaken from the discussion in the ladies' room, I blinked at the subtle shift in conversation. I'd been expecting a proposition at one point, had even considered accepting, but something didn't feel quite right. I wasn't ready for this level of flirting. Not with Jim.

"So really," I tried to redirect the conversation, "you're home to help your parents? Adding on or just general fixing up?"

"Ah, Rachel, don't shy away. We were good together despite our inexperience. I want to show you how much better I am, how much better it can be between us."

The man refused to give up and I blushed. "Jim, I'm still raw…"

"From that bastard who cheated on you." He practically spat out the words and I gulped in the face of his anger. Sure, it seemed to be on my behalf, but why? What did he care? "Almost from your wedding day, from the rumors I've heard since July."

More rumors. I closed my eyes and my feet faltered. "Jim, don't. Don't do this."

Covering my stumble, he pulled me close against his body, using a spin as an excuse. "Ah, *querida*, I'm sorry." We danced in silence for few minutes, Jim's hand warm on my back, his body firm where we touched. Which was pretty much from chest to thigh. Gradually I relaxed into his warmth.

The song shifted, but we didn't react beyond adjusting to the tempo.

"I'm not that doormat anymore," I finally said.

"You never were a doormat."

I snorted. "Shows how little you've been home over the years."

"I stayed in touch and they kept me up to date."

"With the rumors. So. Tell me about you. Since we're on relationships, let's start with your first marriage. I want the details you skipped over last summer."

Jim laughed easily in my ear. "I get the point. Briefly, I married the first girl I met after I heard you were married."

I eyed him through narrowed lashes. This sounded too much like Dan's story.

"She looked like you but, alas," he sighed dramatically, "didn't have your steadfast and true heart. I caught her with the foreman of the company I worked for."

Remorse hit me like gut punch. "Ah, Jim, I'm sorry…"

"Sh-sh-sh," he crooned in my ear. "I got off easy. She married him and I didn't have to pay alimony. No kids, so no child support either. We didn't own shit, so she didn't get anything important from me."

"They always take something important."

"No seriousness, remember?"

"All right. What do you do for fun? Besides flirt with old flickers?"

"Flickers?" A dark brow lifted over amused eyes.

"I couldn't have been a flame, we were only friends for a few days."

He laughed and his hand slid lower down my back, almost to the top curve of my butt. "A flame indeed. I burned for you for a long time. I still have dreams of that first night…and the second…and then the afternoon under the weeping willow…"

My hand smacking his shoulder stopped the words, but he chuckled.

"If the truth be known," he said. "I still burn for you." And from the way his hips rubbed against mine, I could feel his, uh, candle flaring up.

"Yeah, well, that's just because there's no air between us at the moment. You just tell that thing to calm down. This here's a family dance and there are children present."

"We may have to dance all the way to the door and go outside for some air."

"Find something boring to talk about."

"Anything with you is exciting."

I rolled my eyes. "Be serious. Do you read?"

He put a straight look on his face. "As a matter of fact, I do. I confess I have a liking for mysteries and true crime stories."

"Really? Favorite authors?"

That conversation took us through another song and the candle, well, it finally died down.

"I need a break," I said. My feet throbbed from the unaccustomed heels.

"Would you like a beer?"

I fanned my face with my hand. "I'd adore some ice water."

The song ended and this time we eased apart.

"Go on and find Miss Edna. I'll bring the drinks. Think she'd like something?"

We glanced toward the table and saw her engaged in conversation with Dan.

"Buy him a beer and I'll pay you back," I said.

"Goes against the grain, but I'll take care of it and a soda for Edna."

I rested a hand on his arm. "Thanks."

He lifted my hand, kissed it, and turned toward the bar, leaving me to make my way to the table on the far side of the room. Jim almost beat me there because so many people stopped me. I declined six offers to dance and three gossip sessions.

When I reached the table, Dan stood and offered me the chair next to Edna. Jim arrived with three bottles of beer and four bottles of water in his hands. He plopped them all down on the table where three other ladies sat with Edna. All of them library aides ranging in age from sixty-five to eighty-three. Mrs. Scarborough was out on the dance floor with Mr. Nesbett, a spry youngster at age eighty-two, who gently swayed her in slow circles in the middle of the dance floor where everyone made sure they didn't get knocked into.

Jim grinned. "I've got one spare beer for the first lady to raise her hand."

I wasn't surprised when Edna beat everyone else to it. Jim handed her the beer and extended the third one to Dan, who took it with a small nod of thanks, but he didn't move away from me. I took one water bottle and Jim handed the others around. And the awkwardness descended. I was between Dan and Edna, who was between Jim and me. Dan had maneuvered that one well.

I sipped my water and tried to think of something to break the ice.

Enter Mindy. Couldn't have staged the timing better myself.

Wearing a dress of pure pink and white lacy confection, she wiggled between me and Dan and into my lap.

"Ugh, child, you're getting too big for me to hold," I told her.

"No way," she replied.

"Having fun?" Dan asked her.

"J.J.'s being a pill." Her little nose went right up into the air. "He won't dance with me."

I'd seen her brother's mutinous glare from the sidelines when Jim and I had danced past. Did I dare ask why he was hanging on to his mad? Jim hadn't even noticed, so may never have seen J.J.'s aborted launch at him that night.

"I saw you dancing with your daddy," Edna said. When I looked, her beer was half empty, the lime wedge floating like a little boat on the foam inside. She answered my raised eyebrow with one of her own, and Jim hid his snicker by sipping on his beer.

"I thought you were going to get her a soda," I stage whispered past Edna.

"They were out of regular Coke and she won't drink diet." He shrugged. "You could have claimed the beer first, you know."

"Hush up," Edna admonished us both and continued talking with Mindy.

Dan used the cover of their conversation to mutter in my ear, "What's with the sudden interest in Santos? And what's the deal with sneaking out the back door and driving yourself here?"

Oooh, he just had to remind me I was mad at him.

"What about dropping me on my bed and stomping away?" I muttered back through clenched teeth. His arm rested on the back of my chair and my skin quivered at the proximity. Actually quivered. I could feel the warmth of him and the starched sleeve of his shirt touched my back where the dress left skin exposed. The breath on which his words flowed into my ear sent coils of heat right down my insides to my core.

"It isn't time yet."

Could have fooled me. The way the man stared at my lips made me want to bite. Two inches. Just two inches away, from being kissed. I'd be damned if I kissed him first.

"I'm tired of hearing that. If you don't think the time is right, then go wander off somewhere until you think it is and if I'm not busy, I might be around to accommodate you. Then again..." I turned away from temptation, lifted my water bottle and shrugged. A glance toward Jim showed him watching very closely the interaction between me and Dan. Not that I could explain it.

"Don't trust him," Dan warned quietly, his breath caressing the side of my face.

"I don't have to trust him. I just want to get…" I glanced at Mindy who chose that moment to squirm on my lap. "I just want to relieve my…itch."

Mindy, bless her heart, looked up at me. "Does your back itch? I can scratch it."

The water sliding down my throat hit the wrong pipe and I choked as Dan started coughing. Napkins were thrust into our faces and Mindy jumped off my lap to race around behind my chair and start thumping me between the shoulder blades. As my coughing eased, I felt little fingernails scratching my back.

"There, Rachel, is that where you itch?" Poor Mindy, she sounded so worried.

"Yeah, honey, that's good. You got my itchy spot."

I was such a liar and every adult at that table knew it.

"Mindy, honey," I said. "It's getting late for us ladies who need our beauty sleep. Go ask your mama if I can take you home with me."

I didn't dare look at either Jim or Dan as I gathered my purse and my shawl. Edna crooked her finger and I leaned down so she could whisper in my ear. She only had one word for me, and it was the God's honest truth. No point in denying it.

"Coward."

Straightening, I looked her dead in the eye and answered her. "Yes, ma'am. Yes I am."

Chapter 23

The invite for one little girl to sleep over turned into a slumber party. Somehow I ended up with not only Mindy, but her brother, sister, Letty's twins, Sonja's two and Adam. Eight kids from six to thirteen. Three boys and five girls. Talk about chaperones. I felt like Maria with the von Trapp children, right down to the no-nookie-in-the-house part. If I really wanted sexual gratification, I'd have to lure a man out to the shadows under one of the weeping willows. I made Dan and Jim follow me home with the kids who didn't fit in my car. They also stopped by the homes of the town kids to gather sleeping bags, pajamas, a change of clothes and tooth brushes. Where was I going to put them all?

Dan was the brilliant one. He suggested the cleaned and stored-for-winter cushions from the poolside lounges. Probably because he'd been the one to clean and store them. That took care of four. The sofas and chaise took care of the rest. The twins were small enough they could share a sofa with heads on opposite ends, and Aggie said she'd share the chaise with Mindy. That left one long sofa for the three adults between rounds of making popcorn for the kids watching movies. Actually, the three hours the older kids lasted, I was the one in the kitchen popping popcorn as Jim and Dan took turns shuttling food and drinks to the living room media area, where the big flat screen was mounted over the fireplace. As the kids dropped off one by one, we draped spare blankets and afghans over them, until finally Adam, the last to drop, gave up the ghost and closed his eyes.

The three adults met in the kitchen under dimmed lights, where I opened the bottle of wine Dan and I had meant to drink with dinner. The kids had scarfed down those remains, too. I stared into a cabinet, considering my options for breakfast. Did I have enough oatmeal, or was I going to have to make pancakes?

"Eight kids," Jim muttered. "How the hell did that happen?"

I shrugged. "I sent Mindy to ask her mom if she could spend the night with me. Next thing I knew all of them were standing there waiting for me to invite them too."

"Sucker," Dan said and poured the zinfandel into three goblets, which were big enough he split the bottle three ways right from the start.

"Yeah, well..." I waved the accusation away. He was right. A lot of people were right all of a sudden. Did it mean I was wrong on so many things?

"Great way to get out of..." Dan glanced at Jim then shrugged.

"Get out of what?" I asked. "Don't play word games with me."

"Don't play head games with me," he shot back.

"Easy there," Jim cautioned. "Are you two sleeping together or not?"

"Not." Dan and I answered at the same time.

"Yet," Dan added. "Make no mistake, Santos, we're exclusive."

"Excuse me!" I hissed at him. Had the kids not been there, I would have shouted it, but I didn't want to wake them up. At one thirty in the morning, I was tired enough to sleep where I stood, but Dan and his attitude just kept needling me. "I am not your Kewpie doll to play with when you choose and sit quietly between play sessions. If you don't want to sleep with me, then back off."

He rounded on me then, using his body to back me up against the fridge. "I told you, you're not ready yet."

"Yeah, and how do you figure that? What makes you an authority on whether or not I'm ready for anything?"

"Rachel, I've come to know you, quite well, and you're still acting out of grief and shock. Example, tonight."

"What about tonight?"

"Everything from your little strip tease, to your tantrum, to dancing with everyone but me. You're not thinking things through, and Cyndi told me about your conversation in the restroom. Right where anyone could hear. It'll be all over town tomorrow."

Those green eyes with the amber streaks stared at me, the amber seeming to sparkle and glow from the intensity of his emotions.

"Back off, Weston." Jim was there at Dan's shoulder. "This isn't the time to freak her out."

"Oh, like there's a good time for that?" I glared at him and he gave me a half grin.

"No, I suppose not, but if there is a good time, now isn't it. You've got kids here."

Dan's gaze never left my face, but he did step back and reach for a wine glass. He handed me one and took another for himself. "Did you really have to speculate about the number of Burt's illegitimate children right there in the ladies' room?"

"I want to hear about the strip tease," Jim interrupted.

"Men." I groaned and dropped my head back against the fridge.

"Oh, come on," Jim lowered his voice. "I can think of at least one kid who fits the description of one of Burt's kids."

My eyes popped open and I straightened up, pinning Jim with the strictest glare I could manage at that time of the morning. "What? Who?"

He nodded toward the sleeping kids. "That blond boy, the older one. Adam? I may not hang around here much, but I was at the funeral and the kid looks just like Burt did at the same age."

"What?" I wasn't tracking. Burt didn't grow up here, how would Jim know what Burt looked like at age twelve?

"The pictures," he said slowly. "There were photos of Burt from swaddling to swaggering. There was one of him holding a fish, and he looked about the same as the kid in there."

"The pictures..." My eyes widened then. Literally and figuratively. "My God."

Dan was there, lifting the wine glass to my mouth. "Drink." He ordered and I obeyed, swallowing half the contents before he took it away from me.

"Oh. My. God." The world shifted and wiggled into a new alignment. Memories assaulted me...Burt bringing home a beaded necklace...while we lived in Los Gatos...

New jewelry artist, saw the shop at lunch, thought you'd like this.

Think, I told myself. *Adam is twelve.* I counted backward on my fingers. He would have been born in 1997. We'd been married five years, which meant we'd only been married four years when Burt had...

Weakened, my knees folded and I slid down the slick surface of the refrigerator door until I sat, knees bent, on the floor. Probably showing off my panties. If either man looked, they did it in such a way I didn't notice and I was hidden from the kids by the island. No, I was lost in memories of Burt bringing home jewelry made by Ohm.

Since you like that necklace, I bought you some earrings from the same artist.

Shift forward a few years. We'd moved back to Bonchamps. Our tenth anniversary, first in this house. Odd looking earrings to go with the diamond pendant on the platinum chain.

They're daffodils, Rachel, the symbol of the tenth anniversary. Like daisies for the fifth. Made by that hippy jewelry maker you like so much. The diamond is the symbol of forever, which is how long I'll love you.

He'd obviously looked up the gifts and flowers by anniversary. One time I was bored and had gone searching in the reference section. In the containers scattered around the garden were the plants he'd given me: carnation, lily of the valley, and hydrangea were among those from our first ten years. We'd dug them up from the beds at the Los Gatos house and potted them. Since moving here, we'd planted daffodils, tulips, peonies, chrysanthemum, and roses, and placed the planters around the beds and porches. I even still had the bird of paradise he'd given me for our ninth, and that had taken some doing. That sucker didn't like moving, not one bit.

I remembered the first time Burt and I'd stopped in Ohm's store, how she spoke to me but looked at him. The look so many women wore when they looked at him. As if she couldn't believe he was married to me and not her...

Rachel, this is Ohm. Her real name is Olivia, but she likes the sound of her initials better. She just moved to Bonchamps to be part of the downtown revival...

Pleased to meet you, Mrs. Bruckmeister. Your husband tells me you enjoy my jewelry.

I'd lied to her that day. I'd admired her shop and told her I thought she was talented. Her style of jewelry didn't match my taste very well, but I'd bitten my lip and praised her work and admired her little boy, who stared at me with huge blue eyes. How old had he been then? Five?

Blindly I reached for the earrings I still wore and slipped the wires from my ears. I'd never worn them before. I'd never had anything to wear them with. Ruby and clear crystals, and a watch. Traditional gifts for the fifteenth anniversary. I'd purchased him an expensive gold watch, and he'd given me these earrings I held in my hand. She'd made them to order, Burt's order, two years before.

"Rachel?" Dan and Jim both crouched in front of me. "Don't you own the building she's living in? The one with her shop?"

"Yes," I whispered. "She's two months behind on her rent."

"Because her extra income was suddenly cut off?" Jim asked gently.

"No, no, no." I held my hands over my ears. I didn't want to hear this. It couldn't be, he hadn't been so cruel as to bring his mistress to the town we lived in, had he? Had he bought the building specifically for her? Did he take money from our salaries to supplement her income? To feed Adam?

But what about Julianna? Where did she fit? Was he cheating on me with two women at once? No wonder he'd had so little energy for me the past year. Or had he broken it off with Ohm to spend more time with Julianna?

None of it made sense. If he divorced me, he'd have lost half of everything and he'd have to disclose every last detail to the courts. Everything we'd found in the search. And since the house, the ranch land, and the cattle were all in Dad's name, and worth much, much more than what Burt had stockpiled away, none of it would have counted in the divorce. He would have been better off waiting until Dad had passed the titles to me, and then filing for divorce. I would have owed him millions, which were all tied up in land and cows. Clutching my head, I tried to stop it from spinning. There was no logic here.

"Why?" I whispered. "Why?" I looked up at Dan, hoping he could explain it all, but he just shook his head. Jim too. Neither of them had the answers I needed.

"This is why you aren't ready, Rachel," Dan said softly. He shot a glance at Jim, who reluctantly nodded. "You're too vulnerable. You've got to process this, and I have a feeling you haven't seen it all yet. I think there's more to come. There are too many holes in the information we're digging up."

And the digging moved far too slowly. The accountant found more questions than answers, and John was putting his security expertise to work trying to break into the encrypted files on Burt's laptop. There had to be more clues somewhere, something that would give us the solutions to the gaping holes in the picture. There wasn't a word about Adam in the will and that made the least sense of all. Hadn't Burt planned for Adam's future at all? Could there be a hidden trust somewhere? I'd been through the safes and searched every corner of the house, to no avail. Unless Ohm had the paperwork? Holding my head, I squeezed hard enough to see stars, hoping to squeeze some useful memory out of it. It didn't work, so I eased up. A headache wouldn't do me one bit of good.

"And in the meantime, my husband's son is sleeping in my living room."

Dan nodded slowly. "At least everything seems to point to him, but remember, we don't have all the pieces just yet."

"Fuck." I said the word so quietly I wasn't even sure I'd said it out loud, but Jim's eyes widened a bit then twinkled with amusement. Still holding my head because it ached and my brains felt like swirling mush, I closed my eyes and prayed for darkness, as in unconsciousness.

"I'm glad you're amused, laughing boy," Dan said to Jim.

"Why is that?"

Dan slipped his arms under my legs and behind my back. "You're sleeping downstairs with the kids."

"What?"

I felt myself being lifted into the air and instinctively wrapped my arms around Dan's neck. I could seriously grow to like him carrying me. "I'm taking Rachel upstairs to her room. Someone has to supervise the kids. You just got elected."

"Wait a minute…" Jim protested.

"You get the extra couch. There's a blanket on the back."

Jim's expression turned challenging. "Where are you sleeping?"

"Uncle Dan?"

Mindy's sweet, sleepy voice snapped us all to attention and Dan turned, with me still in his arms.

"Mindy? You should be asleep, sweetie," I said and poked Dan to put me down.

"Why's Uncle Dan carrying you?"

"Rachel has a headache," he said quickly.

Eyes scrunched, Mindy stared up at us.

"Never mind, sweetie. Do you need to use the potty?" I asked.

She nodded. "Thirsty."

I prodded Dan again. "Take her upstairs, she can sleep with me."

Aggie's head popped up over the back of the chaise she'd been sharing with Mindy. "Me too?"

Out-maneuvered by the kids, I nodded and she untangled her long legs from the blanket.

"There's your bed, Uncle Dan." I pointed at the chaise, where we'd spent some lovely evenings making out and engaging in heavy petting. Ruthlessly, I quashed my itch. Maybe tomorrow night he'd give in. Probably not, but I could dream.

He grunted sourly while Jim chuckled.

"Come on." Dan lifted Mindy, while I put an arm around Aggie. We trudged up the stairs and got the children watered, emptied and tucked into my big bed. All I had to do was wash my face and change out of my flirty red dress. Maybe red wasn't my color, I decided. Sure, it got me noticed, but it was just a little too powerful, bringing about too much attention. I nudged Dan toward the door where he gave me a sweet kiss, just a brushing of lips. I ached anew with the need to sleep in his arms.

"I'm still here, sweetheart, and I'll still be here when you're ready."

"Yeah, yeah. You're all talk, Deputy." Too tired to put bite into my words, instead I smiled at him.

Lingering, he brushed a stray hair off my cheek. "Talk now, action later. Sometimes it's safer that way."

"I'm tired of safe."

"I'll take you out on the Harley tomorrow. Will that satisfy you for a bit?"

Yeah, it might work. I loved riding behind him on the Harley. It was like sitting on the world's biggest vibrator. I nodded.

"Sweet dreams. With that little wiggler," he nodded at Mindy, "you're going to need all the luck you can get."

I rolled my eyes and shoved him out the door, closing it quietly, but firmly, behind him.

It was surely the strangest overnight I'd ever had. Sadly, I suspected it was the high point of my week.

Chapter 24

"Bye now!" I waved, smiled and shut the door on the last and largest bunch of kids at ten thirty the next morning. Jim had stayed long enough for some pancakes but slipped away soon after, promising to stop by the library later to check out the new bestsellers. And probably to ask me out. Short on sleep, and fast getting short on good humor, I didn't take the time to wonder how I might answer him.

Ohm came to pick up the five town kids. She arrived dressed in one of the long black broomstick skirts and sweaters she'd taken to since July. We eyed each other carefully. I wore sweats and an oversized US NAVY tee, one of two Dan had given me shortly after my closet-culling episode. I remained civil, if not overly friendly, and let Dan play the part of the charming host. All the kids gave us tight hugs and said it was the best overnight ever, at which Ohm calmly raised a brow. The cacophony of them regaling her with the details of their night and how much popcorn they ate, and explaining how the men had snored on their sofas, kept us from getting too personal.

She thanked us and, with my new knowledge, I saw the signs of grief and bitterness etched in the lines on her face. The distance we'd always had between us now stretched into a chasm as wide as the Grand Canyon. Burt had always been the one to make things appear cordial, and eased the awkwardness which seemed ten times worse now. A twist of my own bitterness churned the coffee in my stomach. He really had thought I was stupid because he'd paraded his mistress--one of them--and his son right beneath my nose, and I'd never suspected.

But it wasn't her long term affair with Burt that truly ripped my guts out, it was Adam. Adam, the sweet, gentle soul, the sensitive boy who knew how to dance, who had his hand fisted around my heart. He should have been my son. Burt should have given him to me, not her.

Door shut, house empty but for Dan and myself, my smile dropped as I leaned my dizzy head back against the thick oak and swore. "Fuck."

"Not now," Dan said and pulled me into his arms.

I went gladly. Willingly.

"What do I do now?" I figured it was a rhetorical question.

"You talk to your lawyer, and then you talk to her."

My mind completely rebelled against such a logical suggestion. "No. No, no, no."

"And we get the fingerprints lifted from Adam's juice glass and book, and compare them to the prints found on the cards and boxes the arrangements came in."

Right. The poisoned posies. "Do you think she really did it?" The thought it might have been Adam was too ridiculous to consider. And what about the snake? No, I couldn't see either of them handling the rattlesnake…could they?

"I've been thinking about it all night. If she'd been having a, what, twelve, thirteen-year-long affair with Burt, and he'd just gotten a new raise, and he didn't want to share it in the form of more child support, it would be one way of her striking out. You were the weaker target."

Yeah, I knew how tough Burt could be when it came to prying an extra penny out of him. He'd told me the household budget would not increase in proportion to his raise. Didn't he know how expensive food and liquor were getting to be? The nice clothes he'd wanted kept pressed in the closet?

Dan and I stood in each other's arms for a long time. Comfort, like burning logs in the fireplace on a cold winter night, seeped into my soul. Dan's touch, like it had from the night before Burt's death, took the sting, the pain, the agony away.

"In the first note, she said he wanted to divorce me and marry her. If Burt was with Julianna, why would she make such a claim? There's still something missing. The chunk of cash could easily be child support for Adam, but why would she think he'd leave me for her after all this time?"

"Do you think she knew about Julianna?"

I leaned back to look up into his eyes. I could almost see the thoughts twisting and turning inside his head as he sorted puzzle pieces, trying to fit them into place.

"Could it be so simple as she only wanted to expose him to break us up? She had it good before Julianna, if there'd been no one else serious. I mean, there's no way we'll ever know how many women he slept with over the years, but if he provided steady support… Jim said last night he'd

heard rumors of Burt cheating on me practically from our wedding day."
Damn, just saying it out loud ripped a new hole in my heart.

Dan must have seen it in my eyes because he cupped my cheeks with
his hands, holding me, keeping my gaze on his. "Rachel, his behavior
wasn't your fault. There is nothing wrong with you. It was all him."

"That's not true!" I wrenched away, pushing at him to clear room
for me to get away, but he refused to budge. "I obviously didn't satisfy
him either because I'm too dull, too plain, or too stupid to be capable of
fulfilling his needs." Tears stung the back of my eyes, but they didn't
matter now. Dan had seen me cry rivers. I was tired of them, as he surely
must have been, but I couldn't stop.

"There's something deficient inside of me because I can't meet the
needs of anyone outside the damn library." I held my fisted hands against
Dan's immovable chest. "Need a book? Rachel's your girl, go ask her
where to find it. Need a man satisfied? Oh, well, you're out of luck
there. She couldn't keep her husband happy and she can't get the deputy
hanging around to sleep with her either. Something wrong with that girl."
I shook my head in imitation of the old men who sat on the park benches
shooting the breeze while feeding the pigeons. "Damn shame, too, she's a
nice girl. A bit plain, a little meek and mousy, not mouthy like my woman.
A man doesn't have to put in time worrying about her sneaking around.
She knows her place and sticks to it."

The angrier Dan looked, the more I mouthed off the thoughts and
overheard snatches of gossip I'd secretly kept to myself for years. "Oh
no, the little Bruckmeister gal, she don't cause her man any trouble. He
tells her to jump, and on the way up she's waiting for him to tell her how
high. No fire in that one. Nothing to keep a man up all night. Not like her
grandmother at all, now there was a helluva woman."

I finally managed to push Dan away and started pacing the foyer. "You
think I haven't heard them? Before Burt died, I was invisible in this town.
I was born here, but do any of them remember that? No! Burt was the
golden boy, and not even the circumstances of his death tarnished his
halo around here."

Turning back on Dan, I dropped my voice to imitate those bench
dwellers. "Died in the saddle, that one. Only way to go, one last glory
shot. Heard at one point he was juggling four fillies in addition to the little
woman, and not one of them knew about the other. Takes balls to do that.
Now my Betty Sue would have mine in the wringer if she ever caught a
whiff of something like that. Won't catch me sneaking off for piece of pie

on the side, no way. Not worth coming home to a shotgun aimed at my little soldier. She'd pull the trigger, too."

Taking advantage of my breath-break, Dan began to stalk me, his eyes burning with some emotion I couldn't name. "They're all fools and you're a fool if you believe them. You're a kind, generous loving woman who doesn't see the rotting cores in other people because you believe the best of everyone. You'd never dream of betraying someone you love, so you never thought someone you loved could betray you."

Backing down the hallway, I suddenly had the impression I'd pulled the tiger's tail one time too many. Not that I really cared, and I was angry enough to add a twist.

"How would you know?" Tired of running, I reversed my steps and got up in his face. He didn't move, but neither did I as I said my piece. "I've tried to give you my love and you throw it back in my face, telling me I'm not ready, like I'm some damn biscuit or bowl of bread dough set aside to rise. You don't want it? Me? Fine, then get the hell out of my house and my life. Men accuse women who act like you of being cock teases and make us feel dirty for trying to make something precious. Yet you do the same damn thing in reverse to me and it's supposed to be something holy and untouchable...until *you* say the time is right. Well I'm sick and tired of you making that decision for me. This is my body, my life, and if you can't stand it, then get the damn hell out of my--"

"This is something special between us, so don't you dare drag it down into the gutter," he growled right back at me.

"Well get me off the damned pedestal. I'm no goddess, I'm a woman who just, for once in her life, wants someone to carry her up the stairs like she's Scarlett O'Hara and screw her silly, just because I want it, not because you're in the mood, or not, as the case may be. I'm in the mood and I want my needs satisfied! If you're not the man to do it, then I'll find--"

Dan cut me off by pulling me to him and kissing me. Not tender and sweet, but rough, his lips mashing mine, his tongue plunging between my lips and shutting me up in a most effective manner. Did I acquiesce? Not immediately, oh no, not the new, more-demanding Rachel. I struggled and pushed back, taking my turn with my tongue in his mouth. We tangled, tasted, explored, nipped, bit, tugged, pulled and pushed. I wanted flesh, not wrinkled cotton under my fingers. I didn't stop to determine if his shirt had buttons or snaps. All I cared about was getting my hands on his skin. I gripped the two sides of his shirt where it came together and I yanked. Hard.

Little projectiles hit me and pinged against the floor around our feet. One may have hit the vase with the silk flowers.

"The shirt used to have buttons," Dan said against my lips, but his hands were down my sweat pants and discovering I wore not a stitch under them.

"Should have worn snaps." No mercy anywhere in my heart, I bit his lower lip and searched for his belt buckle.

"Blood thirsty woman," he mildly complained before wrapping his hands around my ass cheeks and pulling me tight against him. After another five minutes of counting my teeth with his very tasty tongue, he had my sweats pushed over my hips and lying in a heap around my ankles. "Kick 'em off," he ordered.

"Why?" I had his belt unbuckled and wondered if I could use it in place of handcuffs on him.

"I'm not making love to you on the hallway floor." His hands slid up under the loose t-shirt and cupped my breasts.

Oh God. Hallelujah. Singing every praise I could think of, I stepped out of those pants and leaped. He fulfilled my fantasy as he grasped my butt and lifted me higher so my legs wrapped around his waist.

"Upstairs, and make it fast," I threw out a growled order of my own.

Maybe the Navy didn't think he was strong enough to keep doing what he'd been doing when he got hit with a load of shrapnel, but the man hoofed it up the stairs as if I weighed no more than a sack of flour.

We made it to my bed and our remaining clothes flew to the far corners of the room. Grace, finesse and thoughts of going slow to savor our first time together evaporated with the explosive rise in heat. I lost count of the orgasms I had before he joined me. We only rested about five minutes before we started moving together again without ever parting. All I knew then and there, all I wanted, all I needed, was Dan touching me, loving me, melding with me heart and soul. In a searing flash that burned the old me to ashes, we reached ultimate bliss together once again. We held each other's gaze and we called out each others' name. And I knew, there'd never been such a life-changing moment in all the world.

* * * *

The phone rang, stirring me from post-post coital bliss. That would be after two rounds. One of which had included the long ago promised mustache ride, a wonderful treat that ranked very high on my list of favorite positions. Twice the afterglow, twice the satisfaction, twice the bone melting relaxation. But the phone and the clock destroyed a measure of my bliss. I was sooo late for work!

"Hello?" My heart might be thumping with agitation, but my voice hadn't caught up yet. I could have auditioned for a sexy role with the way I purred.

The chuckle coming from the phone sounded all too knowing. My second in command, a young man named Nevin Thirakul calmly asked, "I take it you're claiming a sick day?"

"No, no." I groaned. "I'm sorry I'm late, I…" First of all, what could I say? Second of all, I was the boss, so did I owe him an explanation? Since Sundays were slow, I didn't feel all that guilty about playing hooky, particularly since after Burt's death I'd taken Monday and Tuesday as my days off. Many of my employees had families with regular hours so I took the weekends to give them time at home with their loved ones. It also made the weekends pass faster and usually worked well with Dan's ever changing schedule.

Dan solved the problem for me, by grabbing the phone. Since he was still lying between my legs, he'd heard Nevin's question, which really wasn't a question but more a statement of fact. "She's not coming in today. Wednesday's looking iffy, too." He clicked off the phone and tossed it on the bedside table.

Dan rolled to his back, taking me with him. When we settled, with me sprawled across him like a cheap blanket, I buried my face against his neck. "I'll never be able to show my face again," I wailed. More like I made a weak effort at wailing. Completely pathetic and unconvincing, based on the rumble of amusement vibrating beneath me.

"That was a foregone conclusion when you stepped into the dance wearing a red dress. Nice dress, by the way."

"Thank you. But you didn't see my grand entrance."

"I heard about it."

I bet he had. In our little town, like all others I suppose, we did love our gossip, and I'd just shot to the top of the list for the second--or would that be third?--time this year.

"I didn't get to dance with you."

The bark of laughter from my man-mattress unsettled me a bit. Felt a bit like a shift along the San Andreas Fault.

"I tried, but I decided the under twenty-one crowd deserved one night of your attention. Won't happen again for a very, very long time. I figure you owe me all the dances for the next forty or fifty years. Sixty, if we age like Mrs. Scarborough."

Who could bristle at such a comment, especially when it came with a big hand lightly scratching erotic trails down one's spine? A good back scratch was almost as orgasmic as good sex. It gave me almost the same thrills and I wiggled in pleasure.

"What happened to 'I'm not ready for you'?"

"I think you proved me wrong." Those hands, both of them now, touched me in ways both soothing and stirring. "Mostly. You're still not ready for a full commitment, but I'll take what you're ready to give for now."

A prick of annoyance gave me the energy to lift my head and rest my chin on the hands I stacked on his chest. An interesting way to regard a person. "I think we've proven you're not completely an expert on me."

"Oh, I agree," he said, and tugged a second pillow under his head, the better to meet my stare. "But I do know you aren't ready to make a lifetime commitment just yet, and I'm cool with that. For now I'll take the next week."

"You were joking about Wednesday, right?"

"You have vacation time available, do you not?"

"Not. I used most of it up back in July." I didn't need to say the words, he knew the events all too well.

"You have time on the books, Rumple. I know you do. So do I. I'll call in later and tell them I'm taking the week off."

"Really? What are your plans?"

"Cheeky, you are. Feisty, cheeky and aggressive. I like it."

"Assertive. I'm not aggressive, I'm assertive and this time around I'm not accepting the patronizing act. Pat my head one more time and I'll bite you." To make sure he got the message, I bared my teeth and chomped them together.

Dan chuckled. "No, and I don't want you to. You were never truly meek, Rumple, but somehow the essence of you got buried. I don't want to see it happen again. I won't let it happen again."

"How about if you just swear to love me as I am and as I grow to be?" *And quit telling me how things are going to be.*

Those big hands proved how strong they were when they wrapped under my arms and he lifted me enough to pull me up his body until my face came even with his. "I can and I do."

Chapter 25

The next time we surfaced for food, water and a bath, not necessarily in that order, the shadows stretched to the east. Long shadows.

With Dan wrapped around me from the back, I stood at the fridge, door open, cataloging its contents. Not a difficult job. The locusts who'd come to stay the previous night had put a serious dent in my end-of-week supplies, Monday being my usual day to stock up on food and run errands.

"We need food, Rumple."

"Wow, I bet they let you play detective from time to time, don't they, Deputy?"

His hands released the very loose tie on my robe and delved inside. "I detect you want me again."

"Food first." Yeah, I really said that. The man had seriously worn me out.

"Where is it?"

"I have two eggs, one carton of yogurt, I think there might be a couple freezer-burned bagels at the back if you look under the frozen peas." There were other assorted items, each of which needed other ingredients to make a meal and most of those ingredients were missing.

"Lots of condiments."

Four different kinds of salad dressing, but no lettuce or fresh vegetables. Mayonnaise, ketchup and half a dozen varieties of mustard but no bread, cheese or sliced meat. Chutney and hoisen sauce, but nothing to pour them on. Salsa but no tortilla chips.

"This calls for drastic measures." Dan sighed in my ear. "Get dressed and we'll go get dinner, then swing by a grocery store to stock up. After that, I swear, we're not leaving this house until Thursday morning, or it burns down around us."

Knowing how nosy my neighbors were, I briefly considered moving this party to Dan's house. Which would never work since he lived in town and had more nosy neighbors than I did. Not to mention his house lacked a few amenities such as the large tub in my bathroom and the pool out back for midnight skinny dips. Hey, we were going for hedonistic rapture. No point in ignoring the venues right at our feet. The only better solution would be to find a hotel with room service. No. That thought didn't work at all. Reminded me too much of Burt, and I wanted to exorcise his memory as fully as possible. We'd park Dan's car in the garage.

"All right. But I ripped your shirt."

"No problem, I'll borrow back one of the t-shirts I gave you."

"Nearest grocery with late hours is Hanford. Or Fresno."

Teeth gently closed about one of my earlobes. "Even better yet. Less chance of running into someone we know. But, dinner first."

Growling from the vicinity of my stomach settled the issue, and thirty minutes later, we stepped onto my porch, where we found a plain box, the type used by the post office for flat rate shipments.

Dan turned back to the house to get a plastic bag, but I caught his arm. "Leave it."

"What?"

"Leave it. We know what it is, so let's get out of here. Call it in on the way."

The wheels turned in his head for a moment and then he nodded. "Fine, but I still want to bag it and put it out by the street."

As far as compromises went, it worked. I waited while he unlocked the door, deactivated the alarm and headed for the kitchen. While he did that, I looked at the box. It looked odd. The top was taped, but the bottom seemed to bulge a little, keeping it from sitting flat. Curiosity bit hard, but wary where anonymous boxes were concerned, I searched for a stick or something I could use to turn it over. I would have used my shoe, but I didn't want poison plant oil on anything I wasn't willing to throw away. At the end of the porch I had a planter with dead vines climbing an arrangement of small diameter bamboo poles. Perfect.

About three feet long, the bamboo was sturdy enough to lift and tip the box over. I heard Dan open the door behind me as something inside the unsecured flaps popped up and a mass of something dried and withered exploded into a smallish ball of flame.

Because of the fire danger to the old house, I used my stick to push the burning box off the porch and down onto the gravel drive. In my flash of panic, I breathed in a fair amount of the smoke, which also stung my eyes. Dan came from behind to pull me back and stomp out small embers along the way.

No, no, not a big explosion. The house didn't catch on fire. The box itself apparently had been holding down a spring that, when released, triggered a spark that lit a bundle of dried weeds inside on fire, producing a very fast, very bright flash of flame with a whole lot of smoke. By the time Dan pulled me back onto the porch, only wisps of smoke remained of the bundle, which was safely away from the house, but he got the fire extinguisher anyway. For good measure he gave the box a short shot of white chemicals while commanding me to grab his phone from his belt and hit speed dial one.

On the other hand, I had a lung trying to come out of my chest. A hangover from the summer ragweed, if the right allergen blew past me on a breeze, an asthma attack could come out of nowhere and I'd learned to keep a rescue inhaler close at hand. As I dug for it, we heard sirens screaming up the county road.

Dan set down the extinguisher, took my purse from me, and found the device. Before I could cough up the second lung, he had me back in the fresh air at the far end of the porch, doing his best to force the inhaler meds into my lungs by activating the sprayer mechanism in front of my mouth, hoping each inhale would include enough medicine to work. Fortunately, the fire department bounded up the steps with a bottle of oxygen and slapped a mask on me. Finally the combination worked enough I could catch my breath, but I had no strength and my eyes burned. Sheer exhaustion took over and when I could no longer keep my eyes open, the world went black.

* * * *

I woke but couldn't see, and was groggy enough I couldn't even be sure I had actually gained consciousness. Gradually the bleeping of monitors became clear and I had the sensation of scuba diving. The sound of air moving artificially in and out reminded me of a soft wash like waves on a beach. The sheets and blanket felt rough beneath the fingers I flexed. Hospital? Around me sounds seemed muffled, just like they'd been a few months earlier. Hospital, definitely.

Dammit! I wanted my dinner out with Dan. I wanted my three more days of making love. I'd earned them, I wanted them. Tears welled up in the eyes I couldn't seem to open, and I drew in enough air I started to cough. Very weakly, as my lungs burned, but I still managed to cough, which sent one monitor off and brought soft soled shoes hurrying into my room.

"There, she's awake now, just you relax, honey, my name's Judy and I'm your nurse. You probably don't remember, but you're at the hospital now." Warm hands touched my shoulders. "Easy, you've got tubes all over. Now you're awake we'll have the doctor come look at you and see if we can't get some of them out, don't try to talk, some of those tubes are down your throat and your eyes are covered, so just you rest now."

Okay, my eyes were covered. No need to panic.

Word of my waking spread fast. First a doctor, more nurses, respiratory therapists and lord knows who else passed through my room that night, as I was poked, prodded, had tubes switched out, removed and was generally put through a wringer. They called it a thorough examination with a few tests thrown in. By the time they allowed visitors, one at a time, I wanted nothing more than to sleep.

Blinded by the bandages over my eyes, I still recognized Dad by the sound of his walk, the grip of his hands around one of mine.

"Chi-chi, thank God." He raised my hand and kissed the back of it.

"Dad," I whispered.

"Don't talk, sweetie, don't talk. I know your throat is raw from the tubes, but you're going to be okay real soon. It was the smoke. More ragweed, but it was the poison oak again, and maybe more of the sprayed on oil from before, but the smoke carried the oils right into your eyes and lungs. Your skin might be a little raw too, but I imagine your lungs took the worst hit."

"How?"

"How did they do it? A clever set up…What?" Dad stopped when I shook his hand. "Oh, how did the emergency folks get to you so fast? I called them. I'd just checked the recordings and saw the box placed on the porch. I'm not sure who it was exactly, they kept their head down and came around from the side of the house. I'd already called the sheriff when you and Dan came out and I was dialing you…" He paused and cleared his throat. "I have to confess, I was spying. I stopped by the library and Nevin told me you'd, um, overslept and what Dan had said about you being tied up, er, busy for a few days…"

I squeezed his hand. "S'okay." Whispering didn't hurt too much.

"I'm glad Dan was there. I'm glad you and he…"

Squeezing his hand again was easier than answering. For both of us.

"Anyhow, I was watching as you used a stick to tip the box. Smart way to do it, but you shouldn't have done it at all. Scared me, Chi-chi. There were a couple times over the past year when I could have sworn someone meant to harm either you or me and then with Burt's death…Ow!"

Using all my insignificant might, I'd squeezed Dad's hand so hard he'd called out.

"What?" I demanded. What did he mean he'd thought someone meant to harm him? Obviously since Burt's death someone had meant me harm, but Dad too?

"Relax, Rachel, relax. I didn't mean to upset you, I was just saying there were a couple times I thought someone was following me, but it all stopped after Burt's death. Instead the attacks moved to you. I have a suspicion, but it's not proof. The sheriff's following up on some leads. Dan and I have been talking and we think we're right even though it doesn't make sense, especially since Burt's dead. Dan told me you think Ohm's boy--Adam is it?--is Burt's son. He looks like Burt, but again, it's not proof. Nevertheless, we have another clue I wanted to talk to you about this week. We found the location of the safe deposit box to go with the key from Burt's briefcase. We just need to take in the death certificate and we can clean it out. I'd hoped to do that later today, but…" He kissed my hand in response to the squeeze I put on his. "It can wait, we'll check on it once you're well."

In the background I felt the air shift as the door to my room opened. "Your time is up, Mr. Dahlrumple," said a kindly feminine voice.

"Oh, right." He kissed my hand again. "Can't kiss your cheek as you're covered in ointment. Love you, Chi-chi. Rest and don't worry."

His quiet footsteps left the room and faded down the hall, and the nurse came to my bedside.

"Looking good there, Miss Rachel. Your vitals are holding just fine and your oxygen saturation is coming up steadily." Her warm hand gently squeezed my wrist. "You just sleep now and next time you wake up I'll send in the hunk haunting the waiting room."

"How…long?" I whispered.

"You've been here just about twenty-four hours. From what I understand, it's been close to thirty hours since the attack." She tsked. "Poison oak smoke is no joke."

I smiled as best I could at her little rhyme.

"There now, you're laughing at my bad pun. You're gonna be just fine. Sleep now, delicious deputy later."

* * * *

Drifting in and out of sleep for another two days, I did make note my visitors altered between Dr. Sorrenson, Dad and Dan. It was dull, distressing and boring being captive in bed, but I slept amazingly well whenever a nurse told me to. Good drugs, and strange dreams, again. I didn't even try to remember them.

Shea McMaster

Finally, forty hours, more or less, after the little weed bomb--and it was a bomb filled with a few branches and leaves of half a dozen plants from the unfriendly plant list by the Asthma and Allergy Foundation of America--the doctor agreed to pull the bandages from my eyes. I could see. All things considered, even if my eyes had been permanently damaged, I was happy to be alive, but having my eyesight too was a bonus I wanted to celebrate. After swearing on a Bible--the doctor actually produced one--that I'd rest and not open unidentified boxes left on my porch ever again, he set me free.

In a scene all too familiar, the Westons were on hand to welcome me home. Dan assured me there were plenty of groceries in the house, a fact that pleased me greatly. Once more, I fell asleep on the chaise and the next morning when I woke, Dan's arms held me close, upstairs in my bed. Right where I wanted to be.

Except, he once more refused to make love to me.

"I thought we were past this," I rasped through a still raw throat.

"Not until you're better," he rasped right back. Though not as raw as mine, his voice had been affected by the smoke as well.

"What else are we going to do today?"

"We're not leaving the house. You need your rest." Spooning me, he pulled me tighter against his body, my rear tucked against his hips.

"Use that weapon on me, Deputy, and I promise I'll sleep a whole lot better."

"Breakfast first, I think."

Well, it wasn't a refusal. It gave me something to work with at least. "That's not what you said on Sunday."

"We had breakfast first on Sunday. It was lunch we skipped."

"And dinner was interrupted." I remembered Dad talking about the recording. "Do we know who did it yet?"

"We have an idea, but need proof."

"How will proof be obtained?"

"Your dad thinks the answer is in the safe deposit box."

My stomach chose just then to rumble. I hadn't had a decent meal since Sunday morning. My throat could only handle soft foods, and what the hospital served didn't exactly excite one's appetite. I couldn't dredge up one ounce of excitement about Dan's news. The safe deposit box would have to wait.

"Breakfast," Dan said.

Once we were downstairs, Cyndi saw us poking around in the kitchen and called to say she'd bring food over. Yes, she confessed to opening my curtains to keep watch over my house. Wonderful girl. She arrived bearing a basket containing freshly made custard and bowls of pudding and wiggly-jiggly gelatin. Hospital-like food, but better. The woman was destined for a career as a bed and breakfast owner. She whipped up scrambled eggs with fresh herbs while Dan made tea loaded with honey. They also made me drink clear juice. Apparently Cyndi had dug into her cookbooks and was going for maximum nutrition. She'd also done the grocery shopping and I was set for several days. What else could I do but hug her?

"So...?" She questioned me, complete with a perfectly plucked raised brow.

"So...what?" I returned to carefully eating my delicious eggs. No toast, but she'd also given us small bowls of Cream of Wheat swimming in butter and brown sugar. Health food only went so far when comfort obviously needed to be included too.

"What about you two?" This time she included Dan in the not so subtle prying.

"What about us?" Dan answered. I wondered how long he'd last under Cyndi's determined campaign to get the goods first.

"When will the wedding bells ring?"

"They won't," I said at the same time Dan replied, "At least a year after all the dust settles."

Shocked, I gaped at him, while the spoon paused halfway to my mouth, and Cream of Wheat dripped onto the eggs below. "I don't remember being asked."

"You didn't forget anything." A single finger pushed my mouth shut. "I'm not ready to ask yet, but by then, it will be only natural so the answer will logically be yes."

"You assume an awful lot, Deputy Dawg." Inside, my stomach and heart competed for which could do the most flips, but outside I did my best to resume eating as normally as possible. Complete with large splotch of hot cereal on my returned Navy t-shirt.

Of course, Cyndi loved the news and being the first one to hear it. While I finished my breakfast I had to listen to the plans already forming in her head. If she focused on future plans, she wouldn't hover over me. But I did put in my two cents.

"On the back lawn, late afternoon. Pool party afterward."

Silence held for a few minutes and then Cyndi nodded. "Perfect!"

Dan grinned. "Will you wear a bikini for the ceremony?"

"No, no, no, no, no," Cyndi wailed. "Sundress, big hat, lots of white flowers..."

"Daisies," I said. "I want daisies."

"Okay, daisies and those blue iris you have out front because without the iris the daisies will be too much white, especially if Dan wears his dress whites."

"No ice cream suit." He grimaced. "I'm retired and that means no uniforms."

"A white Hawaiian shirt will do." That decision earned me a relieved grin.

"And leis?"

"Only if we honeymoon in Hawaii."

"So, wedding next summer?" Cyndi leaped to find a pad of paper.

"Only if all this estate mess is wrapped up by then," Dan reminded her. "I want the legal wrangling behind us."

"June?"

"Not the seventeenth." I shuddered.

"Not the seventeenth, we'll leave the date undecided for now," Cyndi declared. "I'll consult the astrology charts and see if we can pick an auspicious day."

"What?" Dan and I spit out in unison. When had she gotten into astrology?

With her little southern belle wave, she dismissed us. "I need to practice for when Aggie and Mindy get married, so you two are my trial run."

"You do realize, everything may change in twelve to fifteen years, right?" I said it as gently as I could and still got a glare back.

"Hush up, y'all. I have work to do, so no running off to Reno or Vegas, y'hear?" She picked up her list and shoved it into the pocket of her jeans. "Leave the dishes in the sink, and I'll do them when I come back with dinner. What do you want? Spaghetti is soft, or Alfredo? I can cook up enough pasta to carry you for lunch for a couple days."

"Cyndi, there's little else I can do, I think we can manage meals." Okay, it was a token protest. Sleepy vibes shimmered through my brain and I wanted my nap. And--sigh--my meds to soothe my eyes and ease my lungs.

"Hmm, we'll reconsider it in a couple days. The library committee is itching to try out some new soup recipes on you, and I have to call them back this afternoon. Clam chowder? Corn chowder? Soft yeast rolls? Fruit salad with the pieces cut small should work." She pulled the paper out again and stopped at the counter to write things down. "Pasta salad but with soft cheese and only minced up veggies…think baby food," she muttered to herself.

"No, do not think baby food." Dan's protest, not mine, but he only beat me to it by a heartbeat. "Ice cream would be good."

"There's some in the there, also some premade milkshakes." The little southern hand waved toward the freezer. "All right you two, get your medicines, drink the teas, keep up with the water and juice, and I'll be back around five." She bent to kiss our cheeks, then whisked right out the back door.

Chapter 26

Recuperation was much nicer when the handsome hunk hovering over me was doing it in bed, too. I recovered faster due to the hours spent cuddling and gently making love. He wouldn't let me get wild. Okay, I didn't have the strength for it, but I refused to give up all sex.

On Friday, I finally had the strength to get dressed. Nagging and fidgeting got Dan to agree to drive me to the bank halfway between Bonchamps and Los Gatos, where Dad met us for lunch. Death certificate in hand, I was welcomed by the bank manager, who personally escorted us to the vault. The sign-in card indicated Burt had visited regularly, at least every other month, sometimes once a month, going back six years.

The room was, of course, little, so Dan waited outside while Dad helped me. He'd brought a satchel to carry the contents of the box, whatever they might be. Inside we found a thick folder, a large manila envelope and stacks of cash like I had stashed at home. He even had a cloth bag full of rolled coins including antique gold and silver, of the type a coin collector might have.

"Rachel, wait," Dad said when I would have opened the folder. "Not here. I called David and he's got time this afternoon."

The lawyer would, of course, be able to interpret what we couldn't. Reading might be a favorite activity, but legalese put me to sleep in three minutes flat. Since I had no need for the box, particularly at a location so far from home, I surrendered the only key I had and asked if there was another box or account in Burt's name. The search came up negative.

"Ryan," Dan addressed my father once we were outside. "Rachel's not strong enough yet. She probably shouldn't have come out today at all. For any reason." Of course, since he'd taken a crash course in toxic botany, he glared at every tree, shrub and bush around us as if one might burst into bloom or flame and create more poisoned air around me. Hell, he had list of *dangerous* plants to take to the city to petition for their removal. After

I threatened to burn it, he'd threatened to block up all my fireplaces. On the one hand it was sweet he'd taken it upon himself to become aware. On the other, frankly, it could be annoying too.

"Enough!" I protested and the two of them focused on me.

Dad shook his head. "He's right, Rachel, you're too pale."

I rolled my eyes and held out a hand. "I want to see them, Dad. You can take them to David and I can go home. After I read the papers."

He wasn't happy, but he also didn't argue. "Let's at least sit down in your car. You can look there and then I'll take the pertinent papers to David. You can take the rest home and put it in the big safe."

We all climbed into my car, which was parked next to Dad's in the bank's lot. Because he wanted me to go home and rest, Dad reluctantly handed the thickest file over the back of the seat. Inside I found financial paperwork clipped to the folder; ledger sheets on the left, monthly statements in chronological order on the right, the most recent dated June fifteenth of that year. The amount was a staggering two hundred thousand dollars and change.

Trust for Adam Burton Makepeace, Burton E. Bruckmeister, Trustee.

Damn.

Heart pounding, I flipped straight to the back of the folder to the first statement. The account had been opened soon after our move to Bonchamps in the amount of twenty thousand dollars. Not the money from Brad. That money could have only come from the sale of our house. Money he'd told me had been invested in the rentals we owned. The first of which was the building Ohm occupied.

Dan took the file from my nerveless fingers and passed it back to Dad. In return he accepted a large manila envelope stuffed with more papers and pulled them out.

"Looks like a codicil to his will," Dan said. "It's even notarized, and it's about Adam. The trust is to pay for college and in the event there's anything left after college, Adam gets control of the remains at age twenty-five. Or, at age eighteen in the event of Burt's early death."

For several moments, no one spoke, but we all had the same thought.

"Who assumes the position of Trustee in the event of Burt's death?" I asked.

Dan answered quietly. "You do."

My head snapped up. "What?"

"It plainly says, Rachel Dahlrumple Bruckmeister."

Lightheaded, I rested against the back of the seat. My God, had Burt's nerve, his sheer arrogance, known no boundaries? He'd never expected

Shea McMaster

to die so young. Had he been thinking of knocking off Dad, and then me, after Dad's estate was settled? A shiver of dread went down my spine. In that moment, every emotion I'd ever felt for Burt coalesced into a hate I felt with all my being. Forget the humiliation I'd been forced to endure. He'd put his illegitimate son's future in my hands for safekeeping?

"What's the date on the codicil?"

"Same as the start of the trust."

Well, he was thorough, if nothing else. "Where have the statements been going?"

Papers rustled in Dad's hands. "To her address. I wonder if the brokerage firm knows he's dead."

"So. According to California community property law, don't those assets have to be claimed by his estate? After all, it is money from our joint assets. Specifically, the house we sold in Los Gatos. And I bet later deposits can be traced back to our incomes."

Dad answered, as he had the most experience with estates. "Let David handle it. It's what he does best and what you pay him for."

"While you're at it, have him get an appraisal on the building. If those funds will pay for it or provide collateral, let her get a mortgage. I don't want to be her landlady."

"Easy, Rachel," Dan crooned, his hand reaching for mine. "One step at a time. First, let your dad take the papers to your lawyer. He's already working with the accountant. Let them see if this plugs at least one hole in the records, all right?"

What other choice did I have? Stomp into Ohm's store and demand she spill her guts and hand over whatever belongings of Burt's she had and the last few months' worth of statements? I wanted to rage and scream. Even though I knew he'd been a backstabbing cheater, each time another bit of proof came to light, the wound of his betrayal ripped open again. And despite my absolute conviction Adam was his child, a small part of me had denied it. The codicil and the trust statements stole from me the last tiny bit of possibility that it wasn't true. And Burt had had the nerve, the unmitigated gall, to name me Trustee for his son's trust? As if all that wasn't enough, the final nail came a minute later.

"There's documentation here," Dan said quietly. "Burt had three different paternity tests run. There is absolutely no doubt Adam is his." He flipped more papers. "Wait, a couple more pages …"

"Go on," I said. Would this never end? After these discoveries, how many more waited for me?

"One's from a sperm bank. It appears he left behind several frozen deposits. Dated... looks like the last one was about a year after Adam was born."

"1998?" I whispered.

"Yes."

"About the time we started seriously trying to get pregnant."

"Yes," Dan said quietly.

"Anything else?"

"Shortly after that, there's a copy of a medical record for a vasectomy."

"Oh. My. God."

Which realization was worse? He'd planned for a future child, but apparently not with me. He already had a son, one he'd claim as his heir if some future woman, some future wife or lover, didn't get pregnant from his stored sperm.

"Where's the place, where the..."

"Sperm?"

"...is stored?"

"The sperm bank is in Berkeley."

"Dad?"

"Yes, honey?"

"Find out from David if we can order the samples destroyed. I own them now."

A long silenced filled the car, laden with tension. Finally Dad agreed, and Dan's shoulders slumped with what I took to be relief. Had he feared I'd want Burt's child? Had I still been in love with Burt, I might have considered it, but Burt had killed my love with his actions. The last ash of my love drifted away with a breeze, like the leaves falling around us.

I reached for Dan, and he pulled me across the console between the seats until I half lay in his lap. Were it not for my elbow hitting the horn, the scene would have been perfect. Quickly shifting, he lifted, I twisted until the noise stopped and he kissed me, not in passion, but in comfort. I needed his arms around me. I needed him and his warmth and the magic ability he had to reduce the magnitude of troubles. The hurt, the pain of Burt's final knife in the back all receded in Dan's arms, his kiss a soothing salve began the healing I needed so badly. The desperation I'd begun to feel eased to a manageable level.

While this happened, I had the vague impression of Dad timing us on his watch.

At some predetermined length of time, he loudly cleared his throat. "Save it until you get home and stop smashing those papers."

Chuckling, Dan lifted me so Dad could pull the papers from his lap. "I'm not letting go, Ryan. Get the papers and run, because we're headed back to the house. Rachel's been upset enough for today and needs her nap."

"Yeah, yeah." Dad snapped the papers into shape again. "Just don't get pregnant this week, all right? Let's get through this mess first. Stress isn't good for a baby."

Stunned by Dad's words, I merely blinked at him over Dan's shoulder. Did he mean…? My senses already reeled from being knocked off center. To have this thrown at me at the same time, I was knocked back the other direction.

"Yes, sir. Thank you, sir." Dan spared one hand to shake Dad's.

"Yes, you two have my blessing, but again, I urge caution and a slow pace. We're a long way from done here." Rattling the papers for emphasis, he made sure I remembered the latest twist to the rapidly tangling plot.

"Yes, Dad." I kissed my fingertip and pressed it to his cheek. "Love you, Daddy."

His eyes brightened just before he turned away. "Love you too, Chi-chi." He climbed from the car and slammed to door shut.

"Guess we better make the engagement official."

My discombobulated brain still hadn't processed everything from the last half hour. I blinked at Dan. "What?" I needed a reboot to get my brain functions operating again.

"Rachel, your dad just gave us his blessing. Cyndi already gave us hers, and John has made it clear he expects you to be his only sister-in-law. Mom and Dad even called to tell me they were thrilled."

"John snitched?" I repeated tiny facts as they flared in my still-malfunctioning gray matter.

"Cyndi. Actually, it was Mindy, but Cyndi explained it to them. Point is, you're the one who hasn't said 'Yes' yet." Dan pulled me closer, settling me more comfortably in his lap so my back rested against the driver's door. Just like Sally Field sat in Burt Reynolds's lap in the first *Smoky and the Bandit* movie. A close second to the Harley ride I still wanted, nevertheless, a move I'd always wanted to try. I didn't dare ask Dan to drive home like that--his law and order side wouldn't allow it. The joy of the moment, the joy of being in Dan's arms, in public no less, held the darkness of our latest discovery at bay. I'd always been good at denial. If I didn't want to feel it, I pushed it away.

"I know you've just been through four months of hell, not to mention all the shocks today, and I don't really want to pressure you, but... What's your answer?"

He was so adorable. Usually very sure of himself and quite commanding, he hadn't looked so uncertain about anything since he'd reached puberty, a time when I'd loved tormenting him every chance I got. Once he'd grown taller than me, and stronger, I turned my efforts to ignoring him. Especially after the ill fated hide-n-seek game when he'd groped my breasts.

The brain synapses seemed to be firing again and I tried to push a little, force myself to see the past and look into the future. He'd been there for me, every step of the way since July. He'd made his claim clear when another man came around. But after months of also denying me the ultimate in connection, now, just a few days later, he wanted an answer to a marriage proposal? The brain short circuited again.

His hair was just long enough I could run my fingers through the strands at his nape. "Seems to me everyone has it figured out already. I think I know what I want to say, but damn, Dan, this day..."

One warm hand slipped under the sweater I wore with jeans. Under thick brown lashes, his eyes darkened to a stormy green, the bits of amber looking like dark bolts of lightning boring into me, looking deep into my soul, his gaze held me. Every cliché I'd ever read raced into my thoughts and sounded perfect to describe the experience. "I want to hear the word, Rumple. It doesn't count until you say the word... but I can wait. You've had some hard hits today, and a decision this momentous can wait until you can give it your full, undivided attention."

For a breathless moment, that one pretty much topped every single perfect moment I'd ever experienced. He knew what I was going to say, he just wasn't sure how I might say it. Everyone in Bonchamps knew the answer. But I loved the fact that he'd asked, almost begged, me to marry him. Burt had told me I was going to marry him. I was speechless enough I'd merely nodded and he'd accepted that in lieu of words. Dan, the man I loved, cared enough to ask, not order.

The arm behind my back, Dan's arm, tightened and pulled me toward him until my breasts touched his chest. The hand sneaking up my front side smoothly covered my left breast in such a way a casual passerby might mistake it for being not under my shirt.

"You can tell me later," he said against my lips. "Will five minutes be long enough?"

"You want an answer now? You maul me in the front seat of my very own car, in view of the entire town, and you think this is a romantic way to ask me the most important question of your life?"

When his forehead connected with mine, my third eye experienced a woo-woo moment, a very difficult-to-describe feeling. Sort of a tightening of the skin that made me want to rub my forehead. A very--oh, what to call it! Think Zen, yoga, Buddha, chakras--mystical feeling. A sort of zinging tingle ran through my body and I breathed in the scent of Dan. A little leather, a pinch of sage, sandalwood, very spiritual, a touch of lemon, and a bit of garlic from our lunch. This was Dan. In a crowd of men, I'd be able to find him with my eyes closed purely by his scent.

The feeling of mystical connection increased as he held me tighter to him. Not to mention, it kind of cut off my air, something I was very sensitive to at the time.

Whether it was lack of air, a deep spiritual connection, or angels on our shoulders, I had a moment of clarity, much like Babs as Daisy talking to Yves. I could almost see the distant future. Children with golden brown hair and hazel eyes, little replicas of Dan. Laughter and loving all lived in his eyes. I wanted that life. I wanted the love he promised me. I already knew he'd stand by me through the darkest times. I wanted to be with him through the happy times, too.

"Yes," I whispered, my throat too tight to speak louder. "Yes, I want to marry you."

I'd heard it said men most often convey their love for their mate through the physical, rather than speaking. The kiss he laid on me conveyed to me a message I could never mistake for anything but the pouring out of his heart, his very soul. The only way we could have connected more deeply was to get naked and do it the primitive way. Since the front seat of a car in a public parking lot was not the best place to participate in such an activity, we confined ourselves to exploring tonsils until neither of us could breathe. As my heart pounded in my chest, so I could feel his pounding in his.

"Home," I gasped.

There was just something about a man big enough and strong enough to lift and carry a woman I found extremely exhilarating. Dan had the strength, the ability, the pure male essence that made him my idea of a perfect, sexy, virile man. Without actually throwing me, he more or less flung me back into my seat, belted me in, belted himself in--safety first, always--then drove us back to the house in record time. Another deputy tried to pull us over, but Dan flashed his badge and the deputy saluted us with a round of the siren, then turned around and chased someone else. Dan did slow down once we reached my street--our street, because I was sure he'd be moving in with me over the coming weekend--and parked inside the garage, the door lowering before he'd killed the ignition.

"I can't wait, Rachel." The statement was a groan of suffering. "We'll never make it to the bedroom."

"Okay, where?"

Where, involved another fantasy. He bent me right over the hood of the car. Happy sigh. Yeah, it was that good. Then he laid me back on top of the hood. I vowed to wear skirts from then on to make impulsive activities like that much easier.

We needed sustenance afterward, which involved a few moments of straightening our clothes followed by a long, slow saunter into the house. Reclining with me on the chaise, he fed me slices of apple and strawberries and ate his portion from the artful display he made on my chest. Cyndi called over to suggest we take the snacking upstairs as the kids would be home from school very soon. I guessed she was jealous because I don't recall John coming home for a nooner very often. Not that I was ever home at noon, but I'd never heard the stories of him coming home for quickie.

Nevertheless, refreshed and fed, we moved upstairs, showered, and fell into bed where we promptly fell asleep. Or rather, I fell asleep. He later told me he'd spent the better part of three hours watching me sleep, holding me and listening to me breathe. Later, he said he woke me up once to suck on my inhaler. That improved the breathing part. All I knew or remembered was being warm and secure with the horrors of the day's discoveries held a bay. Dan's love was strong enough to protect me, body, heart and soul.

Chapter 27

Saturday morning, Dan and I reluctantly parted ways in the garage. We both needed to get back to work. After making me promise to spend the day at my desk, as much as possible, Dan tucked me into my car, then followed in his.

If things were quiet for him, he'd swing by with lunch. Once we reached town and I parked in my usual spot, he saluted, then drove on to his house. Something about needing a clean uniform. I'd had him tied up for so many days he had some clothes at my house, but only jeans and t-shirts. Tonight, we'd meet at his house and begin the official transfer of his belongings to mine, since he spent most of his time there anyway. Since we'd begun sleeping together, neither of us wanted to be apart. Besides, there was that semi-official engagement thing.

"Oh ho!" Nevin called out as I sashayed in. "Boss lady returns," he called to the librarians getting ready for the day. "Grab those dust rags and get these books back on their shelves. Vacation is over!" Chuckles and the smell of fresh coffee came from the office behind the checkout desk.

The next several minutes I spent assuring everyone I'd survived yet another mishap from my poisoned posy attacker. As usual, the rumor mill had been working overtime, and they'd expected me to be bandaged with half my hair burned off. They fussed, ushered me into the office and told me to stay put. Had Dan called ahead?

At ten, we opened the doors, and patrons started trickling in. I spent so much time waving at people leaning past Nevin that I finally pulled a long legged stool out of the corner and plopped it down at the checkout desk. All the easier for everyone to see I was just fine.

During story hour, traffic at the desk slowed, and I started processing returns while Nevin reviewed the overdue list.

"Interesting," he murmured.

"What's that?" I'd always like the rhythm of checking in returns. Almost rote and mechanical, it didn't overly tax the mind. The hard part was sorting the books onto the carts, but I loved the feel of a book, any book in my hands.

"Adam Makepeace has a late book here. Not like him at all."

"No, it isn't. What book?"

"It's a military book, which is odd for him. Navy SEALs."

Burt hadn't been a SEAL, but maybe he'd talked to Adam about them. I didn't know Adam well enough to know what he wanted to be when he grew up. "How late?"

"A month."

"Send the notice. He should be in today or tomorrow. I'll ask him about it."

"Sure you'll be in tomorrow?"

"I see you looking at me out of the corner of your eye. I fully intend to be here, barring any unforeseen circumstances." Another book thunked onto the book cart.

"So what's the story with you and the deputy of the year?"

"Deputy of the year?"

"That's what all the women call him. They're taking up a petition for the Sheriff's department to produce a calendar of half naked deputies. In addition to Deputy Weston, they would also like to see Deputies Martin, Sanchez, George, and Dean on this dream calendar." He accompanied the list with a snort.

"And what do you think?"

"First of all, I need to get a more masculine job." He shuddered for dramatic effect, but since he'd been raised smack dab in the middle of six sisters, I knew it was for show. He felt comfortable around women in a way few hetero men did. "If it gets Millie Carter in the mood to jump into bed with me, I'm all for it. Otherwise, I'd rather see the girl deputies in bikinis. Maybe they could do half women, half men?" He punched a button on the computer and overdue notices started printing. That was what I liked about Nevin, he could gossip and work at the same time. "You know, we should be able to do this by email. Would save tons of money on envelopes and postage."

"One step at a time, please, Nevin." I'd argued the point often enough and had already started gathering email addresses, but the fact was a good portion of our patrons were elderly and didn't own computers. Until every single person regularly used email, the old ways would march right along side by side with technology.

The phone rang, and since I was closest, I picked it up. "Fiona Butler Martin Public Library."

"I'm so glad you don't have one of those computer generated receptionist programs," Dan said. "That sure is a mouthful to say."

"Right now, me too. What can I do for you?"

"I'd rather you do me."

Just what I needed, flirting on the phone in the middle of the lobby. "Be nice."

"What do you want for lunch? Feel up to turkey on white?"

"Sure. You can even toss some bacon on that for me."

"Wouldn't you rather have a sausage?"

"Too messy to eat in the park. Not to mention you'd have to arrest me."

"As long as I get to use the cuffs in the setting of my choice, no worries."

A stack of books slammed down on the counter beside me. I jumped and looked up to see Nevin rolling his eyes. "Please, you're on a public phone in a public place."

"Jealous?"

"Get me a date with Joann who walks the downtown beat, and I'll forgive you two."

Dan laughed on the other end of the phone. "I'll see what I can do. She just broke up with her biker boyfriend."

I repeated the comment for Nevin, who backed away with his fingers crossed. "No way, if that's the kind of guy she likes, I'd be toast in two seconds. I want a sweet, gentle woman, one to worship my manly form and dream of geek gods."

"Chicken."

"You got it. I'm the ultimate beta hero. You can keep the alphas."

I flapped a hand in his direction and returned to the phone call. "What's the ETA on that, Deputy?"

"Fifteen. I'm already at the deli and next in line."

"Add some macaroni salad, please. I'll be ready."

"Eat in the park?"

"Ten-four."

That got a laugh. "See you in the park in fifteen."

"Roger."

"Over and out."

I could hear him laughing as the phone disconnected.

"Why are the newly mated so corny?" Nevin slapped down another stack of books next to me.

"You're just jealous."

"Got that right," he muttered. "How is it that you...never mind." He turned away to start sorting the books I'd placed on the carts.

"How is it that I, what?" I figured he was probably going to ask the question I'd been asking myself for months, years. "How is it I was married to the biggest player in the county and am now tight with the hunkiest deputy?"

Nevin snorted. "I know why Burt married you, but why did you marry him when you could've had--what is it those women call him again?-- Deputy Darling, all along?"

"Burt obviously married me because he knew I'd be so grateful a handsome man like him would even look at drab little me that I wouldn't question or complain too much. If at all." I muttered the last three words under my breath.

Nevin snorted in disgust. "Women." I was beginning to think, as the only male on the staff, that he'd been around the older women too much. "Listen to me, Rachel, and you listen good. Burt married you because you're beautiful, kind, sweet and easy to get along with. If you have a fault, it's that you're much too nice. I'll get drummed out of the Man Corps if they ever hear about what I'm going to say next, so don't make me repeat it. Ever. You gave him far too much space. A man needs a leash and you'd better tighten up the one you've got attached to your deputy."

I stared at my number two, mouth hanging open. "Thank...you...Dr. Nevin. Such wise advice."

"And don't you dare spare the whip, either. Lay down the law and make him stick to it, if you know what's good for you. Men secretly like that, you know. And of course, I'll deny it to the death if anyone tries to quote me."

"And that's my cue to leave for lunch."

Nevin stared at me, arms folded, shaking his head. "You're no pushover. Don't let a buff manly form and bedroom eyes turn you into mush."

Shaking my head, too, I grabbed my purse and trotted out to meet Dan at our favorite bench near the fountain.

The day was strange to say the least. My entire week had been strange. I tried to recall the brief flash of the future I'd had while cuddled in Dan's arms just the day before, and a measure of calm settled over me. Not that second thoughts crossed my mind, not at all, but revisiting the vision centered me. I had a goal for once. Get past the estate business, find closure to that part of my past, then move on and build a new life. Amazing how comforting those thoughts were.

I beat Dan to the park and found a sunny spot on one of the marble benches that had sat in the same spot for nearly a century. A bench my ancestors had probably sat on too many times to count. I belonged in this town. My roots were here. In this day of high mobility, I liked the feeling of staying put. My father had come to the area in high school, been my mother's sweetheart, attended college with her, then joined the Navy, was immediately sent to Vietnam, and returned to marry her. He'd chosen to stay and become part of the town. Most people had either forgotten he was an outsider or considered it a moot point. Even though he was now the sole owner of the ranch, it was still called by my mother's family name. The Martin place. Dad was a Martin as if he'd been born to the land, as I was. *That Rachel, she's the sole heir of the Martins.* Dan and our children, if at this late date we were blessed with one or two, would become part of the legacy. I nodded to myself. This was right.

I gazed around, taking in the things that hadn't changed in my lifetime. The fountain, the benches, the planters full of flowers. Though the trees weren't yet bare, leaves were changing colors and starting to fall. Walkers crunched by, waving and calling out. I wrapped my sweater about my body and nodded, but didn't encourage chit chat. The events of the previous day, though colored by my new relationship status, still hung with me, a ghostly image through the veil of numbness I'd erected.

From my vantage point, I could see small portions of Main Street. Mostly the backs of the buildings, but through the breaks made by streets and short alleys, I could see vehicles and people moving about. I'd never noticed before, but I could make out the bakery on the corner and one window of Ohm's shop next to it. The bakery had a deli counter, and I could see the line inside, but not Dan specifically. Because I was looking that direction, I saw Ohm's door open. The woman herself, still dressed in solid black, stepped out and took a moment to lock her door.

The following week business would pick up, but that week the town took a breath, gathering energy for Halloween, which fell on a Saturday. Storefronts were decorated and ready for the annual Trick or Treat parade that started at noon. From four to six, the party would be at the library, and after seven the school had a carnival. We kept the kids busy, recruiting the teens to help with set up, supervision, and generally making sure the under-twelve crowd had a fun and safe time. It had the added benefit of keeping most of the teens out of trouble. By the time the carnival ended, they were too tired to go out drinking and making mischief. For the most part. One or two always seemed to get in trouble, but we had fewer problems than some of the other communities.

While musing on the upcoming holiday, I didn't notice another person approaching from my blind side, not even to take note of the footsteps, until someone in a long camel-colored coat stopped in front of me.

At the sound of a feminine throat clearing I looked away from Ohm, who seemed headed my direction, and up at the woman standing in front of me. Julianna whatshername. Worthington. Blond and elegant, she stood with her hands in her coat pockets, a very chic maroon scarf around her neck, heeled boots on her feet under camel-colored wool trousers. A slight breeze blew a strand of her perfect golden hair across her face and she used a leather gloved hand to brush it back. Her coat couldn't quite hide the five-month baby bump she sported.

"Yes?" I said it as politely as I could, but honestly, the presence of this woman was just another burr under my saddle, as my grandfathers used to say. I sure missed them. They would have taken Burt out behind the woodshed a time or two, had they known of his activities.

"Your lawyer contacted mine this morning."

"And?"

"This child is a Bruckmeister. He's the heir to the entire Bruckmeister fortune, whatever it may be."

"The only way this child could be a Bruckmeister," I coldly informed her, "is if one of the other brothers fathered it. Burt had a vasectomy years ago. It's clearly documented. He got another woman pregnant and then got snipped so there'd be no more accidents."

"The child is Burt's," she insisted, although her face had paled.

"Then prove it. Why are you stalling on the DNA testing?" Did she know about the sperm bank? Had Burt made a withdrawal and used it to impregnate her?

"I don't have to prove it."

"You're delusional and need to spend more time with your therapist. Without a paternity test, you won't see a penny."

A hint of desperation entered her voice. "My child is entitled to a share of his father's estate!" The wild look in her eye had me somewhat concerned, but from the corner of my eye I could see Ohm hesitating on the far side of the square, Dan approaching behind her.

"Then provide proof. Your word isn't good enough. It's a simple test, so it doesn't make sense for you to refuse. If you're sure, then it will only prove your claim. No proof, no money."

"I won't put my child at risk with an Amniocentesis. Do you know how many times one causes a miscarriage?" The younger woman practically foamed at the mouth. She shouted the last sentence.

"Then we have a long waiting period." I spoke calmly, but there was no way in hell I'd settle out of court with her. Why should I pay for her mistake with another man?

"I need money for the baby." Hands clenched at her sides, her face turned red.

Briefly I flashed on the cash and coins we'd recovered from the safe deposit box the previous day. In fact, Burt's stash of cash alone had been close to twenty thousand dollars. I presumed he'd kept it for the same reason I'd started mine, for emergencies. Emergencies like mistresses with inconvenient children? Ha! No way would I offer her any of it. I had lawyer bills to pay.

"Not my problem. Get the amnio and if the test is conclusive we'll talk about a settlement. But until then, there's nothing I can, or will, do."

Thankfully, at this point I could hear Dan's approaching footsteps. Apparently Julianna did as well and stepped back. I silently breathed a sigh of relief and began to wonder if Julianna was responsible for the attacks on me after all.

She glanced over her shoulder and caught sight of Ohm. The change that came over her was incredible. From desperate and agitated, she morphed into icy cold, straightening to her full height, shoulders back and chin up. Clearly, she considered Ohm beneath her. I glanced at Ohm and saw a corresponding loathing as she stared back. There had to be fifteen years difference in age between the two women, with me pretty much in the middle. An odd triangle we made.

Dan skirted Ohm, approached and set the bag with our lunch on the bench beside me. "Ma'am?" He spoke to Julianna. He had to repeat himself before she turned her icy gaze on him, softening the moment she recognized the fact a handsome man in uniform had addressed her. Whether or not she recognized Dan, I wasn't absolutely sure. She perused him from hat to polished boots, lingering below his waist before looking up again to read his name tag.

"Deputy Weston." The breathy blond bombshell voice couldn't be more different from the screeching fishwife voice she'd just used on me.

"Is there something we can do to help you?" In full cop mode, Dan didn't react the way she'd expected. The pouting lower lip didn't work on him either. Without moving a muscle he seemed less friendly, more authoritarian.

"I...I..." she stammered, not so confident anymore.

"Unless you have a reason to speak with Mrs. Bruckmeister, I suggest you move along. Better yet, let your attorney do the talking, Miss Worthington."

Long lashes blinked over those blue eyes as she processed the information that he knew exactly who she was. And the fact he'd used my married title. The cold façade returned. "No, I've said what I came to say."

"Then I suggest you go home."

Nose in the air, Julianna turned on her heel, hesitating just long enough to skewer Ohm with a haughty glare. The venom in Ohm's return glower was enough to make me shiver. Had Burt ever been stupid enough to drag Julianna in front of Ohm? *The old mistress meets her replacement.* A wife was bad enough, but a newer, younger model had to be the ultimate slap in the face. Had Burt stopped seeing Ohm because of Julianna? What about Adam? Where did he fit into all of this? Had Burt been any kind of a father to the boy?

I remained on the cold bench, my stomach churning, as Dan stood guard beside me, watching Julianna stroll to her car, climb in and leave. One glance the other direction sent Ohm scurrying back to her store, leaving us relatively alone in the park.

"What was that all about?" Dan sat down and put his arms around me. Until then I hadn't realized I was trembling. "It's over, Rachel."

Where had my nerves of steel fled to? I'd held my own against Julianna, but now I shook like the leaves over my head.

"Are you cold, or having an adrenalin reaction?"

"Both?"

Dan cuddled me close, his warm lips on my forehead. I slipped my arms inside his lightweight uniform jacket, seeking his warmth for my icy hands. He waited until I stopped shaking, then asked for the high level report. *Just the facts, ma'am.* By the time I finished, his hand cradled my head against his shoulder.

"If she's so certain of the outcome, why is she fighting the DNA testing?" Dan mused out loud.

"And isn't that the two-hundred-thousand-dollar question?"

Chapter 28

As schedules permitted, we moved Dan into my house. In the interest of making him feel at home and not as if he were living in another man's house, we did a touch of redecorating. He had some paintings and prints which worked well with mine, so we swapped a few, rearranged some groupings and added his house plants to mine.

We didn't have many repeats, but what we had blended well. I allowed the Pac Man game to slide into a corner near the conservatory windows with the promise we could turn the old hay loft into a game room, complete with pool table. I even considered moving it to the top of the construction list, ahead of my cabana, if we included a bathroom.

However, I put my foot down on the recliner. I had to promise him a newer, better model with upholstery that matched my color scheme, but it was worth it. His recliner had seen better days. I didn't care how comfortable it was, the brown leather was cracked and holes had been patched with duct tape. I won my case by pointing out it wasn't big enough for us to cuddle in, so he gave way with a look of longing as he and John loaded it into the truck making a run to the dump. As long as it didn't ooze into my house, I didn't really care where it went.

Our days off matched that week, so we used them to clean his house. Not a hard job considering he'd only lived in it a little over a year, and hadn't been home much. By Wednesday night we had a For Rent sign in the window, which we celebrated with steaks, wine and a long night of making love.

The rest of the week we spent getting ready for Halloween by attaching dried cornstalks to poles stuck into bales of hay. Normally I would have put these decorations on the porch, but a part of me wondered if we were tempting fate with such flammables so close to the old wooden house. Neither Dan nor Dad felt there was much danger since we placed the decorations on the inside curve of the half circle drive near the street.

I didn't plan on being home Halloween night but, instead, Dan had permission for me to ride along in his cruiser after the library party. His patrol area encompassed the schools and the surrounding neighborhoods, keeping an eye out for mischief makers who might try to crash the school carnival or harass the trick or treaters.

I'd always looked forward to Halloween, watching the little ones in their costumes, dressing up, and eating treats. And I wasn't above stealing chocolate from the Weston kids. They knew this and planned for it.

Saturday morning came and, after our long, sensual, and very satisfying shower, I kissed Dan and pushed him out of the bathroom. He didn't go on duty until two, but I had to be at work by ten when the library opened.

When Dan worked on Saturday, he generally took the evening shift of four to midnight, allowing those deputies with kids to be at home in the evenings. Halloween, he had a twelve hour shift starting at two in the afternoon. I planned to ride along until I couldn't stay awake any longer and would have him run me home. Therefore, he would drive me to work. But first, I needed two hours to get dressed. For someone who normally showered and dressed in thirty minutes, my two-hour prediction left Dan confused. He had it easy for Halloween, since his uniform was his costume. Mine, well, I needed all two hours to dress and that was after a manicure and pedicure appointment the night before.

Promising coffee and a muffin with egg, Dan left me to do my thing. The deep purple polish on my toenails and artificially enhanced fingernails were only the beginning. Gathering the various parts for this costume had required the help of Aggie and her friends, starting with the color scheme. Purple, black and silver. Simple enough. Until one had to apply the comb-in temporary hair color. With crossed fingers, I set to work and only allowed the bedroom door to open far enough for the promised breakfast to be delivered. At ten to ten, when I carefully walked down the stairs, Dan waited for me. The keys he'd been tossing in the air fell to the floor in the general vicinity of his tongue. Yeah, he liked it.

Steampunk. That's what the girls called it. From the lace-up granny boots of black leather--surprisingly comfortable!--and black lace tights, to the layered skirt with leather straps and silver buckles pulling the front up to show my legs, and my black-and-deep-purple hair, I looked Goth and cool. My skirt was black, as was the waist cincher over an off-the-shoulder short, puffy sleeved, white blouse. I had boobs, and a waist that went with my hips. Hourglass defined. I wore fingerless black lace gloves, chunky silver bangles, dangly earrings with skulls, and a choker with a bat and dangling purple crystals. Pale mineral makeup gave me nearly white skin that made a perfect background for my heavily lined eyes. I drew the line at fake lashes because I had never been able to get them on right, but used several coats of blackest black mascara and shades of purple eye shadow. I also carried a small duffel bag with all my makeup so I could touch up during the day. Oh, I forgot the best part of all! Deep purple lipstick.

"Picture time," Dan mumbled. For once I agreed. I wanted a record of this costume because I didn't think I'd have the nerve to do it again. Then again, the way he looked at me…maybe I would.

We almost didn't make it out of the house, but I didn't let Dan touch me in any way which might smear my makeup. Two hours to get it all on had been a lot of work! In the end, he held my grandmother's black velvet opera cape for me and promised retribution. I liked his style of retribution and looked forward to it.

The day was hectic, as holidays tend to be. Not a big day for checking out books, but we had the wee ones coming in all day. Mostly babes in arms, dressed for maximum cuteness. I filled the data card on my camera and had to download it by two that afternoon. The teens began drifting in about three-thirty to help get the final pieces in place for the party. Mrs. Scarborough, who'd dealt with the youth of the sixties and seventies, once told me, "If you can impress the teens with your cool factor, well then, you've got it made." Advice I took to heart. They'd been expecting Alice in Wonderland or Little Bo-Peep, not the very antithesis of Mother Goose. To my face, they applauded my cool. Behind my back, well, if they laughed they were kind enough to be discreet.

Jim Santos came in when dropping off his teenaged nephew, who'd signed up to volunteer. Jim ended up staying and became my personal assistant and didn't leave my side until Dan swung early in his shift. I made Jim work for the privilege and Dan grinned when Susie Bettles dumped her Bloody Red punch on Jim's white polo shirt. Dan promised to be back for me no later than six-thirty and went off to continue his patrol with a grin on his face.

Because dusk had advanced to near dark and the school carnival would start soon, we had no trouble ushering the last of our guests out the door shortly before six. Two hours of partying with the kiddos had tired everyone out. It was fun to watch the teens get a taste of trying to keep up with the preschool and elementary crowd. I always figured it drove home the birth control argument, if not abstinence. One former teen mother agreed with me completely. C.C. Gibbs had been pregnant at sixteen, was seventeen when she delivered Charlie. She was happy she had Charlie, now twenty, but the early years had been tough. I remembered her as the girl who'd proven the dire warnings on why one had to be careful.

Nevin brought my purse and cloak from the office. "Get out of here. We'll clean up tomorrow."

I set the items on the checkout desk. "No, you go. Dan's coming for me. Until he gets here, I'll putter a little."

"If you insist. Can't say I didn't try."

"You made the effort. I'll put a gold star on your file. Go on." I gently, but firmly, kicked out the staff, making sure Mrs. Scarborough had a ride home. Tomorrow would be slow, which was ideal for cleaning up most of the debris. I intended to take care of just the stickiest messes before leaving for the night.

I loved being in the library by myself. After the chaos of the party, quiet descended like a thick blanket. In the normal course of the day, muffled conversations ruled the floors in keeping with the tradition of an atmosphere conducive to reading and study. At night, or early in the morning, true silence provided a measure of soul satisfaction. I could think, dream, or drift while doing small tasks. A little sorting here, a touch of organization there, or arranging a new display of the latest bestsellers.

There were times I almost felt as if I were communing with ghosts of the past. Certainly ghosts of my past. It was in those stacks, under the guidance of my grandmothers, I'd learned the Dewey Decimal system and the mysteries of the card catalog. Homework and pleasure reading had happened here and I treasured nearly every memory. All right, so the research for science class hadn't thrilled me much. Or math.

Mrs. Scarborough had tutored me in math all through fourth grade. Dad tried to teach me long division in second grade and ruined me for math ever more. That was one reason I'd allowed Burt to handle our finances. Thank God for computerized checkbook registers! My accountant showed an extreme amount of patience and each time we met, he double checked my efforts. Just the previous week he'd only winced once. I considered it progress. He figured I might be ready to do my own taxes in about fifteen or twenty years, contingent upon someone writing a program good enough to put him out of a job. Accountant humor didn't do much for me, either.

Hand on the lock, I'd just secured the door, when someone tried to pull it open. When that didn't work, a heavy knock fell on the other side of the three-inch oak panel. Oh well, so much for fifteen minutes of absorbing the peace and silence of the old building, I carefully pushed it open. There, on the threshold, stood an earnest-looking man. Wearing wire-rimmed glasses, and dressed in pressed khakis with a beautifully knit sweater over a collared shirt, he looked like a young professional in Friday casual. His appearance, about early to mid twenties I guessed, was neat and clean, but his light hair was ruffled as if he were the kind to run his fingers through it when distracted. He carried a worn leather satchel of the lawyer type in one hand.

"I'm looking for Mrs....um...Rachel Bruckmeister? I was told she might be here?" Blue eyes widened as he took in my costume.

No, I certainly didn't look like the average librarian. Not at the moment. "I'm Rachel, come in."

"Thank you."

Since he was a stranger--though he looked harmless enough, a bit on the thin side, I revised my guess and put him closer to twenty-five, maybe six--I left the door unlocked. Cute in a preppy way, he carried a fresh-out-of-college air about him, not yet hardened by his chosen profession. I waved him toward a reading table where I'd have a clear view of the door, and clear access if I needed it. I hated that my poisoned posy attacker had taught me to view strangers with such wariness, but the facts of our modern world demanded a woman alone needed to be careful.

Either my maneuvering was subtle, or my visitor was plainly on the up and up, because he didn't seem to notice. Instead, he plopped down in a chair and immediately began digging in his satchel. When I stepped back, putting distance between me and whatever was in the briefcase, he looked up in confusion.

"Maybe you'd better tell me what this is about. What's your name?" Okay, I was slow about that.

"My pardon. I'm sorry, I should have said from the beginning." He pulled a business card from the satchel and slid it across the table, much like one would offer scraps to a stray dog. "Erick Sunderland. Your husband invested some money in my venture, and I just found out about his...um, passing. My deepest condolences." Guileless eyes darkened for a moment and once more took in my appearance from head to toe. "I'm truly sorry for your loss."

"Thank you." I saw no point in saying more on that subject. "What sort of venture?"

"The exploration, development and production of alluvial gold from gravel deposits located in the South America."

"I see." Sounded interesting. My wariness eased and curiosity won over, letting me slowly move back toward the table where Erick now tapped together a small stack of paper and pushed aside the satchel.

No poison oak bouquets from there. I pulled out a chair and sat down across from him.

Because the library was already dim, I turned on the reading lamp. In the small pool of warm light, Erick looked a little older than the twenty-five I'd guessed. Maybe he was closer to thirty. Sandy hair looked sun-bleached, and faint lines fanned out from his eyes in his tanned face. Though his hands were clean, they looked rough, like they belonged to a man who wielded a pick and shovel.

"Burt was my major investor, and with the money he gave me in June, I was able to get in, get the permits and start work. We haven't hit a big deposit yet, but big enough I can return the money with interest. Ten percent return after four months. We're solid now and if you want the money back, I can cash you out or write up a new agreement, making you a major partner in the operation."

He tried to keep his eyes focused on mine, I had to give him credit for that, but they kept straying to my corset and what it did for my bustline. I didn't know what Burt had told him about me, if anything, but I clearly wasn't what he expected.

"Please forgive me for sounding ignorant, but the simple fact is I wasn't ever aware of this investment. How much are we talking about?"

Erick cleared his throat and played with the paperwork in his hands. "Two hundred thousand. That's what he gave me at the end of June."

I blinked. Brad's money? The amount and the timing were right. "I've been through Burt's paperwork, and I don't recall coming across anything that matches up with what you've told me."

The younger man blushed and looked down at the papers in his hand. "There wasn't any to begin with, but I have it now." He tapped the papers, a bit nervously, then reached out, extending them to me.

"Burt, do business without a contract?" My voice may have sounded mild, but inside I was wildly confused as I accepted the papers. Too unsteady to read them, I set them on the table.

"Ma'am, I know... Burt kept a lot of secrets. I'd always hoped he would change his mind." Erick sighed and leaned back in his chair, running both hands through his hair. In that moment he looked so very like... "I'd always hoped he'd introduce us. I'm his son. His first one."

The lump in my throat refused to go away with simple swallowing.

"But your name..."

"Not legitimate, no, you were his only wife. My mother, Sofia Sunderland, was a shore leave fling." Erick's mouth twisted just like Burt's had when he was unhappy. "However, when he came back on his next leave, Mom tracked him down and he took responsibility, provided support and stopped by for the occasional visit. Not quite a completely absent father, but not exactly hands-on, either."

"So you were how old when we married?"

"Twelve." Some dark emotion flashed in his eyes. How had his mother taken news of the wedding? And Erick, at just Adam's age?

Just twenty-two myself at the time we married, how would I have felt about a twelve-year-old stepson? "You remember that time?"

"Yes."

I heard the outer door quietly open and close, but thinking it was Dan, I didn't look that direction, and it was out of Erick's line of sight. He gave no indication of having heard the door. I couldn't look away from Erick, who looked so much like Burt as a young man. At nearly the age Burt had been when we met, looking at Erick was almost like looking into the past. He didn't have quite every feature of Burt's. But enough. He had enough that when he took off his glasses I nearly quit breathing.

"I understand I have a brother, who might live near here?"

"Um, yes, Burt has... had...another son--"

"My son!"

At the sound of Ohm's screech, Erick and I both jumped.

The older woman looked something like a banshee, her normally braided hair hanging loose and tangled about her shoulders. She wore the black she'd taken to since July, but instead of sad and grieving, she looked manic and psychotic. *Raving lunatic* came to mind. Drunk? Or smoking a little wacky tabacky?

"Adam is my son and you can't have him! I know about this other imposter, but Adam is Burt's son, his heir." She stopped short of me and pointed a long bony finger at Erick, who'd risen to his feet. "You have no business here. Leave us. Take your ill-gotten gains and go. I have enough trouble now that she controls Adam's birthright."

The trust. David had to have contacted her about it. Had that been what she'd wanted to talk about the previous week when Julianna had gotten to me first?

At a distinct disadvantage by sitting, I rose to my feet and tried to pretend I was once more the perfect hostess Burt demanded. My instinct was to scream back at Ohm for all she'd stolen from me, but I figured one crazy woman in the room was enough. Maybe if I acted calm, she would as well. "Erick, this is Ohm, one more of your father's mistresses. Ohm, this is Erick, Adam's half-brother."

"How do you know he's Burt's?" The finger moved with Erick, who casually strolled to my side of the table. Getting into a defensive position? "Burt insisted on three paternity tests from three different labs before he acknowledged Adam. How many tests did he require of you?"

"I've taken one," Erick said calmly. "But there's nothing for you to worry about, I'm not after any money."

Ohm rolled on, either not hearing Erick's words, or not believing them. "She won't give it to you. She has Adam's inheritance, and I should be the guardian of it. She sicced her lawyer on me. She has control of his trust and now she wants me to buy the building Burt bought for me! He bought the building to keep a roof over our heads. It's my building and she expects me to pay her for it? She expects me to pay rent? He bought it here so he could be with Adam, help raise his son, he said."

More likely to make sure a crazy woman didn't screw him up too much.

Once again I was struck by the realization of my own blindness. My gullibility. My misplaced trust in a man who'd had no respect for me, or apparently, any woman. It galled me to think I had anything in common with Ohm, or Julianna, or this Sophia woman. Yet we all had Burt in common. God, the offspring of Burt were crawling out of the woodwork. Were there only two? Or more? Was I expected to write checks to each and every one of them? Come to think of it, if I signed the building over to Ohm, would it get her out of my life?

Then I remembered the seed money to that account. Money I'd invested in my life by contributing to the down payment of the Las Gatos house. Money my parents and grandparents had given us as a wedding gift. Had it been taken solely from Burt's paycheck, I might have let it go. But this was my money we were talking about. Not to mention, I'd had to accept her jewelry as gifts for years. Enough. I'd done plenty for her.

"Ohm," Erick said calmly. "I'm so very pleased to meet you. I've heard about your boy. Is Adam here? Is he with you now?"

"Adam's at home. He's watching the store, handing out candy. I wanted time to set Rachel straight. It's almost impossible to catch her without her boyfriend hanging around." Her focus turned on me, and she raised her head to give the impression of looking down her nose while she sneered. "I'm not moving, I'm not paying rent, and I won't buy the building. It's mine. It's my home, my future. Adam's inheritance. Get your lawyer off my back and remove yourself from Adam's trust. I need those funds to finish raising him. If you were dead, those funds would come directly to me. You should have been the one who died. I was taking care of Burt, I was making his heart healthy."

I didn't dare look away from Ohm. I remembered Dan's suspicions based on Adam's ribbon around the daisies. "You were making Burt's heart healthy, how?"

"Until he started seeing that dirty little high and mighty gold digger," Ohm spat out the words, "I fed him healthy meals, nothing like the fat laden diet you served."

I had to raise my eyebrow at this. Burt had told me what he expected for meals, and if I didn't serve it his way, I paid for it with lectures, subtle and not-so-subtle verbal putdowns and silence. Over the years I'd learned to hate his punishments and found it easier to do as he wanted. I'd always had healthy options on hand and usually ended up eating them for my lunch the next day.

"I gave him vitamins and supplements. I made him teas and soups. He didn't understand the delicate balance and when he started seeing *her*," whom I assumed was Julianna, "he had no more time for us. *She* killed him. You set him up for it, but she delivered the final blow. The doctor told him Viagra was dangerous for him and yet, for *her*, he took them anyway."

"There's nothing sadder than a middle aged man who ignores the signs and keeps thinking he's in his twenties," I muttered. Erick must have heard me because he coughed. I wished I'd known him. I could have liked Erick as a kid, as I did Adam. It seemed odd to think I had a twenty-nine-year-old stepson, but I supposed it was better than one my own age.

"Ohm, what do you want from me?" I kept one eye on the door several feet beyond Ohm's back. Dan was due any minute now and, to tell the truth, we'd been teasing about having a quickie on one of the reading tables before continuing on his patrol. I had no idea how he'd choose to make his entrance.

"I want the deed to the building and Adam's account signed over to me." Did she think I'd give them to her? I couldn't promise her any such thing, but if I didn't, would she try to do something to stop me from leaving the library?

"Answer a question for me, Ohm, if you'd be so kind. What do you know about the gifts sent to my house?"

"The gifts?" For a moment her brow wrinkled, then it cleared. "You did get my messages!" The wrinkle reappeared. "But you ignored me."

"You didn't sign the cards. How was I supposed to know where to send a response?"

One hand raised to her forehead and she rubbed. "I…I thought you knew. I thought the first message was clear enough. Who else would Burt want to marry?"

"He married me, and he was sleeping with Julianna," I reminded her. In retrospect, defining the situation wasn't my most brilliant idea.

The reminder put the crazy glint back in her eyes. "It's all your fault! If you'd divorced him, he would have married me years ago and that new whore never would have had the chance to get her claws into him!" The shouted words echoed off the paneled walls.

This time I didn't remind her that Burt had never once asked me for a divorce. Behind her the library door swung open carefully and silently. Dan, at last, I prayed.

"You and your father." Ohm cursed us. "I tried to convince him to drive off the bridge and into the river when it was at flood stage, but he didn't take the hint."

"You tried to get him to drive off the bridge?"

Ohm waved my question away. "We had it all worked out. First your parents had to die, and your mother did oblige us by getting cancer. Your father foiled all my attempts to get him to die in an accident and got all protective. Your father needed to die so you'd inherit. After that, Burt could divorce you and he'd get half. It was me who figured out it would be better if you died and then he'd get it all."

By this time I could see Dan, fully inside, hand on the butt of his weapon, avidly listening to Ohm's confession. I carefully kept my gaze on her and followed Dan in my peripheral vision. I wanted so badly to run to him, but the hand Ohm wasn't flinging around was hidden in the folds of her skirt. For what reason? I desperately wanted to know. Did she have a gun, a knife, more powdered poisoned pollen to fling on me?

Moving slowly while Ohm ranted, Erick had positioned himself a step in front of me and one to the side. Should Ohm get violent, something I honestly didn't expect, he could get between us fast. I appreciated the thought.

"So you sent the bouquets, knowing full well I'm allergic?" If I kept her talking…

"I know there's no point in killing you now he's dead, but I thought you'd like the arrangements. Such a pretty combination, don't you think?"

"Sure, if you're Lucrezia Borgia."

"There you go, acting all superior, as if you're smarter than everyone else! Burt hated that about you, how smug you act. *Miss Rachel*." Ohm sneered. "Better than everyone else in Bonchamps just because one of her relatives named the town. Half the town is named for the Martins and now the Dahlrumple name is showing up everywhere. This should be Bruckmeisterville, and I should be the queen! Not little miss snotty you! I shouldn't have made the snake give up some of its venom. I should have let you get the full dose!"

She lunged for me, hands extended like claws.

Dan was still too far away, but Erick was right there and grabbed her by the wrists. Half a heartbeat later, Dan grabbed her shoulders.

"There, Ohm, just calm down now," Dan said quietly. "You don't really want to hurt Rachel anymore, now do you? You've already sent her to the hospital twice."

Erick glanced at me, brow raised exactly like Burt's and Adam's would have been.

"Poison oak, ragweed and other noxious weed arrangements. I'm allergic." When I shrugged, he frowned.

"What about the snake?"

"Young rattler that bit my ankle."

Erick's frown deepened, and Ohm shrank from it.

"I did it for us, Burt. So you could be with me. Adam needs a full time father." Ohm's pleading took on a pathetic tone as she mistook Erick for Burt. Easy enough to do, ignoring the age difference. My eyes met Dan's. She'd truly gone around the bend. Would her lawyer plead insanity? Might have a chance.

Dan took Ohm's arms one at a time as Erick released them, and snapped handcuffs on her. "I have to arrest you, Ohm. We have fingerprints and now I've heard your confession. Just be calm and the charges won't be major. You might even be able to keep Adam if you cooperate."

"No! You can't take Adam away!" She struggled then, and Dan's gaze briefly caught mine.

"You have the right to remain silent," Dan said, but his eyes spoke to me. He'd take Ohm in and come back, or he'd send someone to give me a ride home.

"I'll call Dad," I said.

Dan nodded and turned to escort Ohm out while reciting the Miranda rights. He'd have to do it again at the station because she was screaming and fighting to escape his grip on her upper arm. I'd have to give a statement. Weariness crashed into me then. How many statements had I made since Burt's death? And Adam, who would take care of Adam until this mess was straightened out? I supposed it would be up to me. My house had room, and he knew me enough to be somewhat comfortable. Maybe.

"Adam," I whispered as the door closed behind Dan and Ohm. "I need to get to Adam."

Erick jumped into motion. "I'll go with you. He's my brother. If he doesn't want to go with you, maybe he'll let me stay with him. I can be his guardian for a few days." In less than a minute, his papers were stuffed back into the satchel and he'd slid his glasses back on. "I still want to tell you about the mining operation."

"Fine. We can talk at my house. Do you have a car?"

"Yes, right outside." Erick turned out the desk light while I tossed the cape over my shoulders and grabbed my purse. He held the door and we stepped out to the top of the long staircase that went down from the entry porch to a landing half way down. The way the library was built, we had a daylight basement built at ground level, and dirt had been mounded around the sides to give the impression the library sat on a hill top. We had a wheelchair accessible ramp, added in the seventies, but the main entrance was a grand staircase of cement steps that met up with the sidewalk a full story below. Dan and Ohm stood on the landing midway down, Ohm yelling at a third person only a step away, who in the dark looked like Julianna, as I locked the door. It was the coat and the blonde hair. Just like when Julianna had confronted me in the park the previous week.

"Is she always like that?" Erick asked.

I looked at Ohm struggling against Dan's far superior strength as she tried to launch at the younger woman with curse-loaded shouts and rude names that lifted above the sounds of music, voices and traffic. I knew the feel of that hand wrapped around my bicep and wondered why she bothered to fight. Dan would win the physical struggle without breaking a sweat.

"No, she isn't." I recalled Erick's question. "She's a self-proclaimed pacifist. A child of the sixties, literally. Her parents were part of the movement in Berkeley and the Haight."

"Who's the woman she wants to rip to shreds?"

"Burt's latest mistress. The one he died on top of."

Erick winced. "I hate to admit I'm related to that man."

"I hate to admit I married him, and stayed married to him for seventeen years, so we're even."

We started down the steps and Erick placed a hand under my elbow. I looked up at him. Take off the glasses and I could imagine Burt on our first date, tall and strong.

"The shoes you're wearing look a little unwieldy and you're shaking. I hope you don't mind a little help on the stairs, unless you'd prefer the ramp?"

"No, no, this is fine. I appreciate it." I hadn't noticed my shaking until he mentioned it.

"Cold or reaction?"

I laughed. The same question Dan had asked the week before. "Both, I suppose. The second is far too common an issue lately."

Erick looked at me hoping for an explanation when a particularly loud pair of screeches tore our attention back to the landing below us.

Even as quickly as we turned our heads, Ohm tumbled down the stairs looking like a skinny witch rag doll. Dan leaped down after her, cursing the whole way, calling for an ambulance on his radio and knelt beside her crumpled form after it came to a stop, lying still in a heap of black cloth. Erick and I ran down the stairs and reached the bottom as Dan looked up, his hand on her neck searching for a pulse, pure horror shining from his widened eyes.

"The other...pushed away as Ohm lunged... She managed to pull away...off balance... I tried to hold..."

I dropped to my knees beside him and threw my arms around him. "I saw, I saw. You tried, you tried to keep her safe. It's not your fault."

Wrong thing to say. He stiffened in my arms, pushed away and rose to his feet, leaving me kneeling on the cold concrete. "It was my fault. I'm responsible for suspects in my custody."

"You're wrong, Deputy." Erick, who'd escorted Julianna down the steps, handed her over to Dan and gave me a hand up. "I saw it too. She fought you, she lunged for the other woman and pulled you off balance. Between the push and trying to correct, she twisted from your grip. People have a responsibility to be reasonable."

"Who are you?" Dan asked, his big hand holding the arm of Julianna, who stared down at Ohm, her mouth open and eyes wide.

"Erick Sunderland."

"What are you doing here?" Deputy on duty, Dan took in Erick's position beside me, hand now under my elbow, supporting my quaking body to keep me from falling back to the ground.

"I came to see Mrs. Bruckmeister about a business matter that involved her husband. I only recently found out about his death."

"What's it to you?"

"I'm his son."

"Where are you headed just now?"

"To go find my half-brother, who is going to need a responsible adult to look out for him...even more so now."

We all looked down at Ohm's still form and Julianna burst into sobs. Dan grimaced and let her sink down to sit on a step. "Don't go anywhere," he warned her.

I reached for my cellphone. "I'll ask Dad to pick up Adam and an overnight bag. Maybe he can take in both him and Erick."

Dan started to speak, but stopped when I held up a hand.

"For the night. I imagine child services have their hands full this evening. They can step in tomorrow."

We heard the ambulance siren approaching from one side and a cruiser from the other. "I need to deal with this," Dan said. "We'll talk, later. Call your dad, but hang here. All of you will need to make statements." From the chilling look he gave Julianna, I wondered if she would end up wearing the handcuffs.

As I hit the speed dial for Dad, I couldn't help but wonder, how did they treat pregnant women in jail?

Epilogue

I'm looking back a few years on all this and am amazed at how life turns out. When I have a moment to actually think outside my own life, I stop to wonder how the public figures who were so much a part of that summer are faring. Especially the wife of the football player. I can only hope she's found a happy ending that's eased her pain.

That Halloween night was long and horrible, but everything finally came together. Once Julianna started speaking, she wouldn't quit, and ended up with a mild sentence for forgery and narrowly avoided a manslaughter charge in the death of Ohm.

We also learned, after a court-ordered paternity test, that Burt wasn't the father of her child. The DNA was a close match, but not perfect. She finally pointed the finger at Bruce and a test confirmed it. He's now living on base in bachelor quarters and trying to support two families while his wife made off with most of his assets in the divorce. Brad, Burt's youngest brother, was ultimately pleased to hear what happened to his money and, less the amount to cover the legal expenses, has kept his money in Erick's operation. We're fixing a few strained relations there.

As for my happiness, well, it's pretty much secure, and the calm center of the chaos that whirls around me.

After wrangling with the authorities, Adam came to live with us and has been an absolute joy. Some awkwardness and grieving for his mother--and Burt, who had been somewhat of a father to him--made the first year a little rough. Having Erick around from time to time helped with the grief. In fact, Erick has made our house his home base when he's stateside.

Dan had his own issues to work through, but in the end he accepted he wasn't at fault for Ohm's death. We all adjusted to the changes, and Adam grew secure enough to become a regular teen, complete with attitude at times. Inside, I cheered to see him coming into his own and really accept us as parents.

We didn't adopt Adam because he wanted to keep his father's name and has a tenuous relationship with Burt's parents, whom he introduced to Erick. Adam's eighteen now and off to college in just a few weeks. He plans to join the Navy afterward, so he's looking toward an engineering degree.

The recruiters convinced Adam he has a good shot at becoming a pilot, and he's working hard for it. He chose MIT over the Academy, which confuses the hell out of both his grandfathers, and, thankfully, he's got the funds and the help of a few scholarships.

As mentioned earlier, Dan was exonerated in Ohm's fall and not even Adam holds it against him. In fact, the department keeps trying to promote him and he turns down anything but the pay raises.

Me, well, I got my cabana by the pool and Dan his game room over the garage. The cabana is really more of a small cottage, but it serves the original purpose and provides the bonus of a peaceful haven for overwhelmed adults from time to time. And it gets used as a retreat because I stay home with the brood for now.

Yes, brood. Five years and five kids later--two sets of twins, my mother is laughing, I just know it--I have five children under the age of five. Shoot me now! Seriously, I get a lot of help from Dad, who is in grandpa heaven, but it's still a lot of work. Good thing we can afford a weekly house cleaner, because when the kids nap, so do I. And when they're awake, no one gets any sleep. And since they rarely sleep at the same time... I have hopes of getting back to the library, if only for the peace and quiet for a few hours a day.

How did we end up this way? We started off easily enough. First we had a year to get used to Adam, with a side of Erick for two to four weeks at a time, and then I got pregnant. Ryan Martin Weston was born six months after our wedding on a hot summer night. June second, to be precise.

We decided to go for a Christmas wedding. Winter Solstice, actually, because Cyndi insisted it was the best day that season. I was three months pregnant and green with morning sickness, so December twenty-first versus December twenty-fourth or fifth, or thirty-first didn't matter much. The part I loved best was the honeymoon. After the first of the year, we spent two weeks on a nearly empty Pacific island. Dad kept Adam for us, so Dan and I truly escaped. When not making love in the warm ocean, Dan and I slept under shady palms. Heaven.

Ryan is his daddy's boy right down to the golden brown hair, hazel eyes and swagger. He loves to play cowboy, and my dad bought him a real Stetson for his fourth birthday. I can't get him to take it off unless we're swimming. Good thing he loves the pool or I wonder if I'd ever get him clean. He's also asked for a dolphin so he has an animal to ride cowboy style in the water. Thank you, Erick, for that suggestion.

Fourteen months after Ryan was born came another summer pregnancy, an all-summer pregnancy, and this time we had twins. Benjamin Jonathon, for Dan's father and brother, and Laura Elizabeth, for my grandmother and mother. I'm grateful for the fraternal part. I didn't think I could handle identical all that well. Twins were bad enough, but they sure do stick together. They're three now and their connection is a little eerie, but where one is, the other can be found, and since they live to run, at least I'm not running in two directions looking for them. They've forced us to fence in the back yard and the pool deck to keep them somewhat contained.

Ryan is hoping to teach Ben how to be a good Indian. I just hope he doesn't try to force Laura into the role of squaw. I still blame their father for the overdose of testosterone the boys seem to have. Then again, they'll need it when Laura grows up. She might have the traits of a tomboy now--a tomboy who likes ribbons and ruffles on her tree climbing clothes--but when she hits her teens, Daddy Dan will have his hands full. Right now he's laughing at his brother paying for the pageant circuit, but his day will come, as John ominously warns him.

And the other set of twins, no, not forgotten by any means, I just wanted to save them for last. Just six months old, they were kind enough to be winter babies. Late January. The swelling of my feet was much easier to handle, but with the toddlers around, I didn't get to put my feet up much. As soon as they were born pink and healthy, Dan got a vasectomy. Whew. I'm not sure where the twins came from, but here they stop. And these little bundles of joy, well, they're the apple of their daddy's eye. They look up at him with their wide, round eyes, and coo for him.

I know better. Once it's just me and them, I see the real devils inside. And they are identical, did I mention that? Bless their little hearts, they're identical right down to their little pink toes and the curly wisps of brown hair on their little bald heads. They try the innocent act on me, but I'm onto them, and so is Adam. In fact, Dan and Dad are the only ones fooled by the little actors.

Erick hasn't met them yet, but I'm betting he falls just as hard as Dan. He considers our kids his siblings and me his stepmom, since his mom died while he was in college. Great, I have a son ten years younger than me. At least he knows how to find gold and is helping to fund the college accounts for his brothers and sisters.

Yep. Sisters as in plural. Girls. You guessed it.

And to keep the illusion of innocence, Dan picked out their names. Daisy and Iris. Poor things, their clothes are decorated with the flowers they're named for so we can keep them straight--I keep the local machine embroidery shop busy--though we're starting to see some personality differences emerging. Even so, I'm very tempted to get them tattooed, just a little flower on each tush. Dan is vehemently opposed, but the first time they pull a switch on him I'm betting he votes for a tattoo on each of their upper arms. By then they'll be too old to do bum checks. For now, I paint Daisy's toenail white and Iris's purple. Makes it much easier to sort them out when they're wet from the bath.

As for Dan and me, well, we're still madly in love. He still works for the County Sheriff's Department and there's talk of him running for Sheriff when Mark wants to retire. Dan keeps saying no as he and John are starting up a security company. John's close to retiring from the Navy and needs something to do afterward or Cyndi will be chasing him with a frying pan. He's already getting a bit nosy about the running of the household and she wants to make sure he's well occupied and not hanging around with time on his hands to drive her crazy.

Dad has taken over managing the rentals for me. Dan's said he'll take over that part when Dad no longer wants to handle it. Since our town is attracting young families, we might section off another parcel and sell it to a developer.

I just watched *On a Clear Day You Can See Forever* last night. It's been a very long time since I saw it last and this time I was able to ignore Melinda's pain over the betrayal of Robert Tentrees. Instead, I was hooked by the hope at the end. Looking to the future. As Daisy--okay so there's still a teeny bit of the movie in my life, Daisy Winifred and Iris Melinda, to be exact--spun in her chair and told dishy Yves they'd be married in the year 2038 and it was beyond glorious, I smiled smugly. I'm still in this life and I've got my dishy deputy. This life with him is my reward for being a good girl for the first half. I'm encouraged to be bold and assertive, especially in bed. Five kids in five years, yeah, we like our lovemaking.

I'm sure once the kids are older we'll have more time and energy for it, but we do try to make it a priority. Sunday nights are sacred and the children are banished to their beds promptly at eight o'clock. At nine-thirty, when they're really asleep, we meet in the renovated cupola above our bedroom. By day it looks like a cozy reading nook, by night, a perfect little love nest for two.

When life gets overwhelming, I hum a few lines of the theme song from my favorite movie. If you haven't seen it, do. *On a Clear Day You*

Can See Forever. You'll find the meaning that works for you. It also gave me a great line.

My name is Rachel. Rachel Winifred Dahlrumple Weston.

Yeah, I like that sound of that. I wish you my best for a wonderful life, as I'm surely living my dream.

Meet the Author

The softer, sweeter side of Morgan O'Reilly, Shea McMaster lives for traditional romance.

Born in New Orleans, raised in California, Shea/Morgan got moved to Alaska in 1977, where she attended high school before running back to California for college. Alas, once back home she met and fell in love with her own forever true hero, a born and raised Alaska man. Since then she's had a love-hate relationship with America's largest state. With her one and only son half way through college, and mostly out of the house, Shea is fortunate to spend her days engaged in daydreaming and turning those dreams into romantic novels and novellas featuring damsels in distress rescued by their own brains and hunky heroes.

Shea's Website:
http://sheamcmaster.com
Reader email:
shea@sheamcmaster.com